Summer in the Scottish Highlands

The Scottish Highlands Series

Winter in the Scottish Highlands

The Secrets of the Glen

Return to the Lake House

The Boathouse by the Loch

Summer in the Scottish Highlands

Coming Home to Aviemore

AUTHOR'S NOTE

This series is best read sequentially to enjoy the story arc as it was intended.

Summer in the Scottish Highlands is the fifth book

Summer in the Scottish Highlands

The Scottish Highlands Series

Book V

ELISE DARCY

Penny Lane Press

ISBN 978-1-913147-37-2

"Your life does not get better by chance, it gets better by change."–*Jim Rohn*

1

'I still can't believe you're here,' said Jake, putting the kettle on.

Faye smiled. 'I can't believe it either.'

'I love it here!' Natty piped up.

'Well, you would say that,' commented Faye, turning in her chair and eyeing the resident dog – an Old English Sheepdog called Olive. Her daughter was sitting cross-legged on the kitchen floor, giving Olive a cuddle.

Faye turned back to Jake. 'Sorry she woke you up. I told her not to knock on your bedroom door so early, but she did it while I was using the bathroom. The problem is the interconnecting doors.'

Jake smiled. 'That's not a problem for me.' Gayle had kept the rooms free, and it was just the way he wanted them, the two attic bedrooms next door to each other. He wanted Faye and Natty close. And they had a floor of the house to themselves. But he had forgotten they were interconnecting rooms and that the door wasn't locked.

Natty laughed out loud. 'You silly dog!'

They both turned to look at Olive, who was licking her face.

'Natty, what did I say about keeping your voice down?' Faye

admonished her daughter. 'The house is still sleeping.'

'Oh, Mummy, what do you mean, the house is still sleeping?'

'We all arrived back here late last night after the party, so other people in the guesthouse are still fast asleep.'

'I don't remember coming back last night.'

'Well, no, you wouldn't, because you fell asleep in the car on the way back, and Jake had to carry you up to our room.'

'When will I see Evie again?' Natty asked.

'I'm sure it will be soon. Gayle said that Evie often comes to visit here.'

'But Evie said that she's going to work with her mum in a shop.'

Faye nodded. 'Yes, I remember her mum, Annie, mentioning she works part-time in Robyn's Interior Design, in Aviemore.' Faye turned to Jake. 'Do you think she'll change the name of her outlet, now she's found out she's not Robyn? It was all so strange, what you told me happened during that hypnotherapy session. Fancy spending all those months since the car accident on Christmas Day believing you were someone called Robyn Parker because you'd lost your memory, when in fact you were someone else entirely.'

Jake had made two cups of tea. He added some sugar and stood at the kitchen counter, stirring the tea. He didn't really want to start their first proper day together on holiday thinking about what had happened at the party; the three of them had only started their holiday the previous afternoon. He'd managed to arrange car hire, and a car had been waiting for them at the train station. He'd thought they might spend their first evening at Lark Lodge, sitting together and eating Gayle's delicious stew, but they'd been invited to Robyn and David's engagement and housewarming party.

He didn't know Robyn. He was aware that she ran an interior design outlet at Gillespie's General Store in Aviemore. Someone had hired her to redecorate The Lake House, his house, and the Rosses' holiday home, which incidentally backed on to Lark Lodge. It wasn't he who'd hired her, although it had crossed his mind to do so. He'd started to think about letting go of the house, selling up. After the accident on the ski slopes at Christmas, which had robbed him of his wife, Eleanor, he'd wondered who was ever going to use the house again.

It was a terrible thought that although she hadn't died, to him, she might as well have. She was in a residential home with staff providing the care that she would now need for the rest of her life, but Jake had yet to visit her after that fateful Christmas Day. As far as he was aware, none of the family had. That was terrible too.

He'd made a pact with Eleanor's brother, Marcus, that they would go together, as soon as he was well and had left the rehab clinic. When would that be? Marcus wasn't going to check into the clinic until Jake had returned to head up the Ross Corporation in his absence. It was a temporary arrangement while Marcus sorted out his substance abuse problem. But Jake hadn't told Marcus he'd returned to London, or that he'd organised a holiday with the woman he was falling in love with, Faye, hoping that in the course of the week away, he might discover if she had feelings for him, and perhaps, just perhaps, she might fall for him the way he had for her.

His thoughts drifted back to the previous day's invitation to Robyn and David's home, the boathouse on the loch, for a sit-down meal and a party afterwards. Who would have thought that inviting her stepmother, Judith, who had been travelling abroad for months, would set off a chain of events that would lead to another session with the hypnotherapist whom Robyn had been seeing? The session had led to a breakthrough regarding her missing memories and the revelation that she wasn't Robyn Parker at all, but a young woman called Bonnie Greene who had known Robyn, and Jake's wife, Eleanor, albeit briefly.

They'd met at Wilbur's Bookstore in Aviemore on Christmas Day when Bonnie had been running away from her boyfriend. She'd discovered a light on in the bookstore, and two women, Robyn and Eleanor. Jake had always wondered where his wife had gone on Christmas afternoon, before she'd met him and Marcus on the ski slopes for an afternoon ski post-Christmas dinner.

Robyn, the *real* Robyn, who had been working at Wilbur's Bookstore over Christmas, had told Bonnie she could stay the night with her in the little flat above the shop if she'd just do her a favour and take Eleanor to the ski slopes. She'd done just that, but on the way back she'd made a split-second decision not to return to the bookstore, but to skip town in Robyn's car. She'd collided with David, her now fiancé, whilst speeding along a snowy road in Robyn's car, and had lost her memory in the accident.

The question now was: what had happened to the real Robyn Parker? The shop was locked. Her things were gone. She appeared to have disappeared off the face of the planet that Christmas Day.

'Jake – are you all right? You've been standing there stirring that tea for a considerable time.'

'Huh?'

'The tea!'

Jake looked at the mugs. 'Oh, sorry. I was lost in thought.'

'Were you thinking about the party last night?'

'Yeah.' Jake took the two mugs of tea and placed them on the table, one in front of Faye, before taking a seat opposite her.

'Poor Judith. What a shock to get a party invitation, apparently from her stepdaughter, only to arrive back in England after months away to discover an imposter. They've hit it off, though, Judith and … it's Bonnie, her real name – isn't it?'

'Yes, I heard Bonnie wants to help Judith find her stepdaughter.'

'That's good, isn't it?'

'I guess.' Jake lifted his mug and took a sip of tea.

'Is something on your mind, Jake?'

Something was on his mind all right. He was thinking of Bonnie and the revelations in the hypnotherapy session which he'd attended with all her friends, who had been there for support. She'd met his wife, Eleanor, on Christmas Day, but he had a feeling there was something more. He looked at Faye. 'I just can't help but feel she's holding back.'

'Who?'

'Bonnie. I'm sure she was avoiding me at the party.'

Faye shook her head.

Jake raised his eyebrows. 'You don't agree?'

'Look, I think you're reading too much into things. She'd just got her memories back. She's bound to want to spend time with her friends.' She halted. 'Something just occurred to me. Why were *we* invited to the party? Was it because we were guests at Lark Lodge, and everyone else was going?'

'No, it wasn't that. I knew her fiancé, David. It was his idea to invite us.' He paused. 'I met him when I returned to Lark Lodge. He and Robyn – I mean Bonnie – were having some relationship issues, as I understand it. I overheard David and Gayle talking in the kitchen. It turns out he'd been staying at the guesthouse while Bonnie had been away in London. By the sound of things, she'd got a new interior design contract, but David wasn't happy. He was concerned she wasn't just going there for work.'

Faye looked at him quizzically. 'What do you mean?'

'I got the impression he thought there was more to her trips than her new commission.'

'Like what?'

'Perhaps he thought she was meeting up with someone from her past.'

'Well, all that's been cleared up now. Did you see them standing together on the balcony during the party? They are so in love, and they're having a baby together.'

Jake stared at Faye. Their eyes locked for a brief moment. Oh, how he wished with all his heart she was thinking of a future with him, just like he was.

Faye looked away. The spell was broken. She said, 'So, you said it was David who invited you, us, to the party?'

'Yeah, it was meant to be a surprise for Bonnie. We've never actually met. He thought she might want to meet one of the Rosses who owned the property she was working on – The Lake House.'

The strange thing was that when they had first arrived at the boathouse, he'd noticed she didn't seem exactly eager to meet him. All the other guests at the table had gathered round to greet him, but not her. That was before everything had kicked off, and she'd been taken down to the police station after Judith's revelation that the young woman calling herself Robyn was not, in fact, her stepdaughter. But even when they all returned that evening, and the party had got underway again, he was still convinced she had done her best to avoid him.

Faye interrupted his thoughts. 'I think the party was a bit much last night. I would have thought they'd reorganise it, considering what that young woman had gone through at the hypnotherapist session, finding out who she really was, getting her memories back.'

'She looked as though she was enjoying herself,' observed Jake.

'Yes, she was, but I bet this morning it's going to hit her, what she's gone through, being taken down to the police station and everything else. She probably thought all her friends had abandoned her, and that her life here, the one she'd been leading as Robyn Parker, was over. The relief she must have felt when she found out that wasn't the case …'

'I want to see her again.'

'I know. I'm sure you will.'

Jake was thinking that if he took Faye and Natty into Aviemore town centre that morning, he could stop by Gillespie's General Store and see if she was at work in her interior design outlet.

'But I can imagine she needs some time off work to get over what she's been through.'

Jake frowned. Faye was right. He doubted she'd be at work that day. The trouble was they were only there for a week. And it wasn't as if he could just turn up at the boathouse to see her. That would be intruding. He did know someone who could organise for him to see her, though. Gayle. Perhaps she'd arrange for Bonnie to visit her at Lark Lodge while they were there. Jake made a mental note to ask her. Or, better still, he could use The Lake House as an excuse to see her. She'd be working on the place after her time off. He'd just ask Gayle to contact Robyn – *Bonnie* – and let her know he wanted to meet at the house if she wouldn't mind. It occurred to him that she might want to discuss her interior design plans with him.

He perked up at the thought that he was sure one way or another he'd get to speak with her before they returned to London.

Jake finished his mug of tea. He looked across the table at Faye. 'Right, let's have some breakfast. Would you like something cooked, or there's toast and cereal if you prefer?'

'I'll just have some toast.' Faye put her mug of tea down. 'Do you think Gayle will mind us helping ourselves to breakfast before she rises? I thought the host usually prepared the breakfast.'

Jake put some bread in the toaster and put out a bowl of cereal for Natty for when she'd finished saying good morning to Olive, which he guessed was going to take a while. He smiled affectionately at Olive, even though he guessed that Faye would never hear the end of Natty asking for a dog now.

'Gayle doesn't mind at all. She likes her guests to treat the house as if it's their home.' He picked up both empty mugs and put them in the washing-up bowl.

'It's an unusual guesthouse,' commented Faye.

'It is that,' agreed Jake.

'I love it,' Natty said, clearly listening in to their conversation.

'You love the dog,' said Faye.

'Can I have a puppy – pleeeease!'

Faye rolled her eyes. 'I told you before, we haven't got time for a puppy.'

Jake looked at Olive and hoped Natty didn't spend the whole holiday badgering her mum for a dog.

2

'So, what are our plans for the first day of our holiday?' asked Faye.

Jake raised his eyebrows. *Plans?* Other than winning Faye's heart, he hadn't a clue. He'd spent the last week in London, avoiding Marcus's texts and enjoying the first week of the school summer holidays having days out with Faye and Natty to museums and London Zoo, and babysitting Natty so Faye could attend the last session of her course before she achieved the qualification she needed to apply for a headship. He hadn't had time to think about their holiday in Scotland other than hoping something didn't crop up which would mean they didn't end up going.

The toast popped up in the toaster. Jake put it on two plates and took them to the table. He sat buttering his toast, watching Faye do the same. She was looking at him expectantly.

'Well, I thought this morning we could go into Aviemore.'

'The little town that we arrived in by train yesterday?'

'Yes.'

'Oh good. Aviemore looks a lovely place. There are some nice shops I wanted to browse.'

Natty sat up the table, joining them for breakfast. 'Can I buy a toy for Olive?'

'I suppose so,' said Faye.

Natty poured some milk over her cereal and picked up her spoon. 'When we get a dog, I'm going to buy it lots of treats and toys.'

Jake looked sheepishly at Faye, who'd chosen to ignore the comment. He chose to ignore it too, and to avoid mentioning just yet his idea that he could buy Natty a puppy, but it would live at his house. He already had a plan. When they returned from Scotland, he had the rest of the school summer holidays to spend time with the puppy, house training, that sort of thing, before the school term started. He'd have to think about doggy day care when he returned to work, but the expense of owning a dog wouldn't be a problem for him because of the money he had tucked away from his very lucrative past career. Jake frowned when he remembered what could scupper that plan over the summer – his promise to Marcus to return to the Ross Corporation while he went into rehab.

He could so easily slip back into his old life from before the accident last Christmas, working as a corporate lawyer in the Ross Corporation. He was lucky, after he'd been orphaned, that he'd grown up in the care of the Rosses, one of the wealthiest families in the UK. He'd always felt he owed William Ross, the head of the Ross Corporation, a huge debt for taking him in as a young child after his parents had tragically died. He'd always felt he'd been destined to join the family firm, a multinational giant in construction, working his way up the corporate ladder along with Marcus – William Ross's son and Jake's best friend. Jake had never been adopted by William Ross, and when he had married William's daughter, Eleanor, they'd chosen to join their surnames, so he had officially become a Ross.

'What are you thinking?' Faye asked.

Jake didn't want to bring up his old life. He regretted promising Marcus he'd return to the corporation while he checked himself into rehab. But what choice did he have? The problem was that William Ross had lost interest in the business after what had happened to Eleanor. He spent most of his time on the golf course. Jake had left too, starting teacher training on the job, which was where he'd met Faye, his mentor in the school. That left Marcus in charge, on his own, working like no sane person could without some help of the chemical variety.

But things had changed. Jake hadn't been able to foresee that after he'd made that promise to Marcus an unexpected chain of events would lead him to a holiday in Scotland with the two people he cherished most in the world: the woman he was in love with and her young daughter.

He glanced at Natty. If it wasn't for Faye's daughter, they wouldn't be there, sitting at the table in Gayle's kitchen, in Lark Lodge, looking forward to spending the week together. On the last day of school, just over a week ago, Faye's nine-year-old daughter had done something completely out of character. Faye had dropped her off at breakfast club and watched her walk into the playground. But she had never arrived at the club. It had turned out that she'd had had it all planned. She was going to catch a National Express bus to Scotland to see Jake. Of course, they found her before she'd got very far. But finding out she was missing had meant Jake had cut short his trip to Scotland, returning to London to help with the search.

He still had unfinished business there. He didn't want to bring it up with Faye. This was meant to be a holiday. This was meant to be him looking to the future, not the past. Even so, he knew that in going there, he couldn't escape the past.

He didn't want to take time out of their holiday, but there were some things he needed to take care of. Jake finished eating his toast, and said, 'While you're doing some shopping, I just have a couple of things to do in Aviemore.'

'Anything I can help with?' Faye asked.

Jake shook his head. He wanted to visit Duncan Gillespie's general store. Faye was right: Bonnie probably would not be at work that day, or most likely next week. It would take time for her to process getting her memories back, and finding out that she wasn't who she'd thought she was. But it wasn't just Bonnie he wanted to see. He was thinking about what David's father, Duncan, had told him about what he'd heard; what a lot of local people thought they'd heard on Christmas Day – a gunshot up on the Cairngorm Mountain. It might have played a part in the avalanche that had buried them in the snow. But that wasn't all Duncan had told him. When the snow had thawed in spring, they'd found a body with, according to Duncan, a gunshot to the head. Suicide, they'd concluded. This had all been news to Jake.

They knew the date and time because the man's car had been traced. It had turned out that he'd parked his car in the car park and bought a ticket at a pay and display machine. Duncan had pondered why a man who was intent on taking his own life would buy a parking ticket. Jake supposed the poor man hadn't been thinking straight, and had bought the ticket just because that was the thing you did. Duncan hadn't known who the man was.

If Duncan had wondered why this revelation had caught Jake completely off-guard and appeared so important to him, to Jake's relief he didn't ask. Jake didn't want to go into the blame he'd placed on Marcus's shoulders over what had happened to Eleanor on that mountain on Christmas Day. Jake had been dug out of the snow first, before Eleanor. She'd been left too long, starved of oxygen. He'd always blamed Marcus for that, even though Marcus had insisted it wasn't him who'd dug Jake out. He'd maintained all along that there had been someone else up there with them. Jake hadn't believed him.

Jake hadn't been aware of anybody else on that mountain skiing off-piste, until Duncan had dropped his bombshell – not only had there been that poor soul who'd taken his own life, but someone else had been up there too. Whoever they were had dug Jake and Eleanor out of the snow and phoned mountain rescue, who'd sent a helicopter to winch them to safety.

It all made sense now, how mountain rescue had found them so quickly – something that, in the aftermath, Jake had never thought to question. He'd always assumed they'd been lucky and a rescue helicopter had happened to fly over and see them. Duncan had put that assumption to rest. Someone had made that call. But who? They had never come forward to take the credit for saving the Rosses. And that had meant that all along, Jake had presumed Marcus was lying when he'd said it wasn't him who had dug them out after the avalanche. But it was true that there had been an anonymous tip-off that there were three skiers off-piste who needed help.

Duncan knew this because his other son, Joe, was a local police officer, and although he hadn't been on duty that Christmas, word had got around about the tip-off leading to the rescue.

It meant Marcus had been telling the truth all along. Jake didn't just want to know the identity of the guy who'd fired the shot, and potentially caused that avalanche, but who else had been up there with them. And a peculiar thought had popped into his head – was the guy who saved them somehow connected to the poor guy who had lost his life up there? That was the reason he wanted to find out who the dead guy was. There was a possibility they were connected, and he might find the person who had saved them. Of course, it crossed his mind they could be one and the same person – the guy had done one last selfless act, saving their lives before taking his own. It would have been a possibility, but for one glaring fact – the dead man's mobile had been found in his car, apparently. There was no way he'd made that call.

Duncan had suggested Jake should talk to his son, David, who might know the identity of the body they'd found on the mountain through local town gossip – or perhaps Joe might have mentioned it to him. David had worked in his father's store since his ice hockey career had gone south, and Jake had an ulterior motive for going into Aviemore that morning – to see if by chance David was working that day. He wanted to find out who else had been near them on the mountain when the accident had happened.

Faye said, 'I know you have unfinished business here, Jake. If there's things you need to do …'

Jake stared at her. He didn't want to bring up the accident, and what Duncan had told him, and certainly not in front of Natty. This was meant to be a holiday. It occurred to Jake that perhaps he should seek his answers on a separate trip by himself. The problem was that when he returned from Scotland, he couldn't envisage when he'd be back. He had obligations. And then there would be something else, the thing he dreaded – finally going to see Eleanor after all these months.

Jake looked at Faye. 'Yes, it's true, I do have unfinished business.' He didn't want to lie.

'Is it about that photo?'

'Photo?'

'The one of the boy – Ralph. Remember, when we arrived yesterday, the first thing Gayle did was give you the photo that you'd left behind in your room here by accident.'

Jake remembered. He'd been in such a hurry to leave after that phone call from Faye telling him that Natty was missing that he'd left the photo behind – the one an old lady, Martha, had given him to try and trace her son. Jake guessed she'd given her son up as a baby, but that at some point, when he was a young child, he must have visited his mother, because the photo was taken at Cedar Grove, a grand stately home, now a hospice, where she lived in an apartment.

The young boy in the photo would be an adult now. Although Jake had promised Martha he'd find her son, whether he could or not was another matter. He realised he'd made a promise he might not be able to keep.

Jake did recall, when Gayle had handed him the photo, an awkward pause when it had appeared she had something she wanted to say. He was still wondering what had been on her mind – he had a feeling it was something to do with the photo.

Thinking of the trip to Cedar Grove reminded him of another discovery that had surprised both him and Marcus – Marcus especially – because it had proved that despite what he thought, Marcus did not have a complete handle on what was going on within the company. The Ross Corporation had bought a piece of land on the outskirts of Aviemore and was building something, according to the local gossip, courtesy of the receptionist who worked at Cedar Grove. Jake believed that had been the tipping point when Marcus had realised it really was time to check into rehab and get on top of his health.

Jake winced at the guilty feeling about prioritising being there, on holiday with Faye and Natty, over returning to the Ross Corporation. Jake really hoped that Marcus would make other arrangements at the company and just check himself into the clinic anyway.

The other thing he'd discovered was that Martha had a brother, also called Ralph, but that he'd gone by a different name for as long as Jake had known him, which was practically all his life – Aubrey Jones. He worked for the Ross Corporation, and was William Ross's right-hand man, but no one really knew what his job was at the Ross Corporation, apart from doing the jobs no one else wanted to do – like fire people, and escort them from the luxury apartment building where employees in London could choose to live. Perhaps he'd know where the younger Ralph was. But it was tricky. Did he know that his sister had had an illegitimate child and had given the child up for adoption? Jake had no clue. That was the reason he had not brought it up with Aubrey just yet.

Faye added, 'Of course, I don't mind if you want to visit Cedar Grove and see Martha again while you're here. I'm sure there are lots of things Natty and I can do together.'

Natty said, 'I want to play with Olive while Jake goes to see Martha.'

'I'm not sure I'll visit her this time,' Jake said. He felt a little guilty, but he had other priorities. 'I want to spend time with you guys.' It wasn't the idea that they went off and had a holiday on their own. He wanted them to spend the holiday all together. He just had a couple of places to visit first while they were shopping in Aviemore.

3

'Can I buy some ribbon?' Natty asked.

Faye threw her daughter a questioning look. 'What do you want ribbon for?'

Natty rolled her eyes as if she'd asked a stupid question.

Jake knew. 'You want to put some pretty ribbons in Olive's fur, like Evie showed you at the party.'

Natty nodded her head. 'Evie said they sell ribbon in Robyn's shop.'

'Did she?' Faye said. 'Are you sure?'

Jake sighed. He had intended to nip into Duncan's store on his own and speak to David if he was there. 'We'll go there together. I was going to visit the shop anyway. There's a little haberdashery in Robyn's side of the shop.' He paused, not sure if he should still be calling it Robyn's shop now everyone knew her real name. He turned to Natty. 'That's where you'll find things like ribbon, I expect.'

'Do you think Evie will be there?' Natty asked. 'Do you think we can take Olive? Then I can buy my ribbon and make her look pretty.'

'We can't take Olive out with us this morning, sweetheart.'

Natty threw her mother a grumpy expression. 'Why not?'

'Well, Nick will wonder where his dog is when he returns from his run.'

'But he let Olive stay here, with us, while he went running.'

'I know. That was very kind of him to do that, so you could play with Olive. But she's not our dog, so we'd have to ask his permission. And Nick isn't back to—'

Faye was about to say, *ask*, when she heard the front door open. They knew it was Nick before he opened the kitchen door because Olive had already scooted over to the kitchen door, waiting for him.

Nick opened the kitchen door to his excitable dog. 'Hey, there. I hope you've been good.'

Natty said, 'She's been so good, Nick. Can we take her out with us today?'

'Oh, er …' He looked from Faye to Jake.

Jake said, 'We're going into Aviemore. Natty wants to buy some ribbon.'

Nick smiled. 'I guess Olive is in for another makeover.'

Natty jumped up and went to give Nick a hug.

Jake imagined he was used to getting his dog back full of multicoloured ribbons tied in little bows in her fur. Gayle had mentioned that Olive was looked after by her or by Annie at the shop. She even had her favourite cushion, and enjoyed all the attention from the customers and Evie.

Nick said, 'If that's all right with you guys?'

Jake exchanged a glance with Faye, who nodded.

Nick said, 'If you've got other plans, I'm sure Annie won't mind you leaving Olive with her and Evie afterwards.'

Natty said, 'Is Evie going to be at the shop today?'

'I think so, yes. I heard that Robyn …' Nick hastily rephrased, 'I meant Bonnie … isn't returning to work just yet.'

No one was at all surprised.

'I think it's for the best,' Nick added, 'after … last night.'

Jake and Faye agreed.

'What about David?' Jake asked.

'Not sure, but I wouldn't be surprised if he doesn't hurry back to work either. I bet they want to spend some time together, especially after that announcement last night.'

Jake looked at Faye, wondering if she'd like more children. Not that he'd be so forward as to ask her. They weren't even in a relationship, not romantically, and yet it was something that had crossed his mind.

'Mind you, it's not like they're going to have the boathouse to themselves.'

'Why not?' Faye asked.

'It's Judith. She's declined Gayle's offer to stay at the guesthouse. She's staying on with Roby—' Nick shook his head. 'Bonnie. They're going to start the search for her missing stepdaughter. They also want to have some days out and see some of the tourist sites around here while they get to know one another better. I spoke with Judith at the party last night, and she said she didn't know whether they'd find her missing stepdaughter, or whether she even wanted to be found, but while she was here, rather than spend all her time on social media looking for any clues as to where she might be, she might as well get out and about, and see some of the amazing places to visit. Who knows, perhaps on her travels out and about she'll unearth something, or someone who knows Robyn.'

That's what Jake had in mind for Faye and Natty – to see some amazing places and make some wonderful memories. He wondered where Bonnie intended to take Judith, and whether he might be lucky enough to plan a day out where he might bump into them. Of course, that was highly unlikely. There was so much to see and do in the area, it was improbable they'd be in the same place on the same day. He'd just fall back on his original idea of trying to arrange through Gayle to meet Bonnie at The Lake House. Bonnie was taking time off work, but he hoped she'd make an exception for him, and meet him at The Lake House, as he was only there for that week.

'So, you think David might return to work at some point this week?'

Nick shrugged. 'Quite possibly. Alec, the student who helps out at the store part-time, is doing some extra work covering in the shop while Duncan is out doing deliveries at the moment, but I get the impression Bonnie wants to spend some time with Judith, just the two of them. They really hit it off, apparently. I think David is hoping that Joe will manage to track down Robyn.'

Jake nodded. 'Well, she can't have just disappeared into thin air.'

'Yeah, my sentiments exactly. She didn't return to university after the Christmas break. She must have had other plans.'

'I take it Judith doesn't have any idea what those plans might have been?' asked Faye.

'Not in the least. They didn't get on, apparently.'

Faye sighed. 'That's a shame.'

The room fell silent until Nick said, 'I'm going to shower. Nobody else up yet?'

Jake shook his head, no. There were no other guests staying at Lark Lodge; just Marty who, like Nick, lived in the guesthouse at the moment, along with Gayle and her mother, Doris.

'So, what are your plans for today?' Nick asked before heading towards the door. He smiled at Natty. 'Apart from making Olive look pretty.'

Jake had been planning to visit the Gillespie store, and speak to David, but there was no point now he knew neither he, nor his fiancée, would be there that day. 'We're going into town, so Faye and Natty can visit some of the shops in Aviemore while I ...' Jake felt a little embarrassed saying what he was going to do.

Nick stopped at the door, staring at him.

Faye and Natty were looking at him too.

'I'm going to visit the tourist information office,' he said sheepishly. For someone who holidayed there every year, at Christmas, and had spent his early childhood there, living at his parents' home, The Lake House, he really should have had some idea of what they could see and do in the area. But holidays at Christmas weren't like that. Apart from the Christmas Day ski in the afternoon, they stayed within the confines of The Lake House, rarely venturing out. In hindsight, that was a shame. But the wealthy Rosses – William, his wife, Grace, their children Marcus and Eleanor, along with Jake – were often recognised in the small town, so they ventured out less and less, and remained cocooned in The Lake House.

Nick said, 'You'll be spoilt for choice, I can tell you. There's a ton of things to see and do around here besides skiing.' The look on Nick's face said he wished he hadn't mentioned skiing in front of Jake.

'Can we go skiing, Mummy?'

'No! Absolutely not!' Jake exclaimed.

Faye raised her eyebrows at Jake.

Jake pursed his lips, realising he'd just put his foot in it.

Faye wasn't surprised by Jake's reaction, but if Natty wanted to try skiing, Faye didn't want what had happened to the Rosses to put her off encouraging her daughter to try something new. The look on Jake's face said he understood that. But Natty wouldn't be skiing this holiday. 'Sweetheart, it's the summer. We'd need to come back in the winter to go up in the mountains for the winter sports.'

'Actually, that's not true. You see—' Nick was stopped in his tracks by Jake throwing him a look across the room. Nick shut his mouth.

Natty ran over to Jake. 'Can we come back here in the winter? Can we spend Christmas here? I'd love to see the snow.'

The Ross family's last Christmas at The Lake House unfortunately came to Jake's mind, along with the thought that for the first time in years, the house would remain empty at Christmas. Or perhaps it wouldn't. He looked at Faye and Natty. If he followed through with his plans to sell the house after Bonnie finished redecorating, perhaps another family would be enjoying Christmas dinner and opening presents in the lounge in front of the open fire next Christmas.

Jake managed a smile.

Unfortunately, Natty took his expression as a yes and ran over, giving him a hug. 'Oh, you're the best.'

Jake glanced at Faye and caught her frowning, clearly annoyed either because he was making promises he might not be able to keep or because she didn't envisage another holiday together. Jake resolved to do his very best to make this a holiday to remember, hoping it would be the first of many together.

4

Jake left Faye and Natty browsing the gift shops in Aviemore and wandered across the road to the tourist information office. It was a strange feeling – although he had been born in Scotland, Jake realised he felt more like a tourist than a local. It was understandable. He'd spent more years living away, only touching base there at Christmas.

Jake made his way over to the reception desk and joined a queue of people. He overheard tourists at the front of the queue enquiring about holiday accommodation in the area. It was the first week of the school summer holidays, and unsurprisingly the tourist office was busy.

Jake waited patiently in the queue until it was his turn to speak with the friendly lady manning the desk. Jake needed some ideas of how to fill the week ahead. In the past, Jake had always spent Christmas in Aviemore with the Rosses. They skied and went for long bracing walks alongside the loch. His plans had never involved children – much to his regret.

He felt his mood change with thoughts of what might have been. He didn't want to dwell on the times Eleanor had returned from Harley Street with the same results and the ensuing disappointment – until the last time she'd returned, when he'd learned he was finally going to become a father.

'Can I help you?'

Jake stepped forward. 'I've just arrived in Aviemore and would like some ideas on where to take my family.'

My family? Jake stalled, thinking, *where did that come from?*

'Do you have children with you? If so, what are their ages?'

'Yes, a girl who is nine years old,' Jake replied.

'Well, you've come to the right place. There are loads of activities on offer for children during the school holidays. There's a visit to the Highland Wildlife Park, where she can see polar bears, red pandas, and my grandchildren's favourite – the Scottish wildcats. You could go to the nearby Insh Marshes nature reserve with trails to see birds and wildlife, or for the more adventurous there's an outdoor adventure park with treetop trails. I recommend a visit to the Cairngorm Reindeer Centre. It's not far from Aviemore. You can join a tour and feed the reindeer.'

Jake nodded. He'd heard of the Cairngorm Reindeer Centre.

'If she's into watersports, there's paddleboarding and kayaking at Loch Morlich beach, and nearby there are family-friendly forest trails to walk or cycle on. Of course, we're spoilt for choice when it comes to castles and history.'

Jake was well aware of that. He smiled.

'Now, something I particularly enjoy is taking the Cairngorm Mountain Railway to the summit of the mountain to enjoy the views and—'

'No!' Jake shook his head. He was not taking Natty or Faye anywhere near that mountain.

The friendly lady's smile slipped, Jake noticed. He hadn't meant to be rude. 'Um, I'll take the leaflets on the other things.'

'You can pick up free leaflets with more details of opening times and ticket prices in the racks by the door. There are leaflets covering all those things I mentioned.'

'All right, thanks.' Jake frowned wondering why he'd bothered to queue if it was just a matter of grabbing some leaflets. But the lady had been very informative, and had given him some really good ideas for how to spend the week.

'Some activities get booked up very quickly, especially during the summer, so I'd advise buying tickets online if you can.'

Jake thanked her for the advice.

'Do you need help with finding accommodation?'

'No – thank you,' replied Jake. 'We are staying at Lark Lodge.'

'That's a great choice – it's already getting quite a reputation.'

Jake wondered why, if it had quite a reputation, it wasn't fully booked.

'There are guests checking in tonight, and it's getting so booked up for the summer. Holidaymakers have been on the phone to us about holiday accommodation in Aviemore, and some walkers have turned up today, so we've made online bookings for them at Lark Lodge. You were lucky you managed to get a booking.'

Jake smiled. He didn't want to get into just how he'd managed to get the week-long booking. He'd already been staying at the guesthouse before the holidays started. Then he'd been unexpectedly called away when Natty went missing. Gayle had told Jake the room he'd booked would be kept available for him, hoping he would return to finish his stay. It hadn't exactly turned out that way.

Although Natty had been found safe and well, he'd waited a week to return – Faye had needed to attend the last session of her training course; she could now apply for positions as a headteacher. It had been worth the delay to be able to bring Faye and Natty with him. Gayle had organised the two interconnecting rooms in the converted attic in preparation for their stay.

Jake thanked the lady and made his way over to browse the leaflets. He recalled that he had arranged to meet up with Faye and Natty in an hour and glanced at his watch. He had been longer than he thought. He didn't have time to trawl through the row upon row of leaflets and find the ones on the sites and activities that the lady had suggested. He quickly cast his eye over them. The one with the picture of a large steam locomotive grabbed his attention. He picked it up and read the details. It was about the Strathspey Railway. Jake smiled. He felt sure Faye and Natty would love a trip on a steam train.

Jake quickly plucked a handful of assorted leaflets and made his way through the throng of people and strode outside. He glanced at the train leaflet, which gave directions to the train station. If he was very quick, he would have time to walk to the train station and pick up a timetable and to see if there was any availability to book a trip. As it was Saturday, he imagined there would be no spaces left for the weekend.

Jake arrived on Platform 3. The platform was heaving with ticket-holders waiting to board and excited children having photos taken beside the steam train waiting in the station. Every now and then, a burst of steam escaped from the top of the smoke-stack, enveloping the platform and exciting the children even more.

Jake stared at the steam train, thinking again that Natty and Faye would love it. He just hoped there were still some tickets available for after the weekend. He walked up to the older man who was organising a line of people and checking their tickets.

The man turned to Jake. 'Hello, can I help you? I'm George.' He pointed to the name tag on his lapel. 'I'm a volunteer at the station, helping people when they arrive for their journey of a lifetime.' George chuckled. 'Do you have a ticket?'

'No, not yet. I was wondering whether I could buy some tickets to take the train.'

'How many in your party?' George asked.

'Two adults and one child – nine years old,' Jake replied. He imagined there was a reduced rate for child fares.

'Now, you wait here while I go and check what's available – and could you keep an eye out for a little old lady on her own? It's the missus. She's meant to be meeting me here. Just don't tell her I called her a little old lady, or she'll have my guts for garters. Her name is Rose, by the way.'

Jake looked about him. There were plenty of older ladies, especially grannies with grandchildren, but no lady on her own, as far as he could tell.

George had only taken a few paces when he turned around and said, 'I'm afraid that as you can see, today's trip is very popular. They serve afternoon tea on the train as you travel through the beautiful countryside.'

He guessed George was giving him advance warning that it was most likely sold out that day.

'I'm sure it's sold out today. Can you give me your names in any case? I might have an idea.'

Jake told George their names. 'We're here in Aviemore for a week, if there are tickets for another day.'

Jake was slightly disappointed. It would have been perfect to have afternoon tea on the train that day. He could just imagine finger sandwiches, home-baked scones, and delicious cakes.

It was almost lunchtime. They'd planned to spend the morning in Aviemore, but earlier, when they'd just finished their toast, Gayle had appeared in the kitchen. They hadn't rushed out after all. Instead, Jake had enjoyed catching up with Gayle. Although they'd arrived the previous evening, the three of them had barely touched base with the guesthouse before they'd left to go to the party at the boathouse. That morning was the first real opportunity Gayle had had to get to know Faye.

Natty had been happy not going out immediately either. She'd enjoyed playing fetch with Olive in the garden while Jake and Faye had another cup of tea, and had ended up joining Gayle and her mother, Doris, for a second breakfast. Gayle had insisted on cooking them a fry-up. By this time, Nick had joined them too, having showered after his run, timing his appearance in the kitchen to coincide with a cooked breakfast. Jake didn't ask after Marty. It was Saturday morning, and the young man was probably still in bed.

Jake noticed the queue for the train getting much longer. He opened the leaflet and discovered the train timetables inside. The next one was due to leave in twenty minutes. Given that they'd had a large breakfast, late in the morning, afternoon tea on the train rather than lunch would be perfect. It would be cutting it fine if there were tickets available. Jake was just thinking he'd better contact Faye and tell her his whereabouts when he heard his phone ring. Taking it from his back pocket of his jeans, he glanced at the number. It was Faye.

'Jake, where are you? We've finished shopping.'

'I'm at the train station trying to buy some tickets for a trip on the steam train, but I imagine they're fully booked for today.'

'A steam train? I had no idea you could get a steam train from

Aviemore,' Faye replied.

Jake could just about hear her above the chatter of passengers on the platform waiting to board the train.

'Oh, the steam train leaves from Platform 3. That's where the ticket office is for the trips too. It's totally separate from the main line.'

'Sounds a wonderful idea. I hope you can get tickets.'

'Me too. They're checking to see if there's any availability as we speak, but it's doubtful. It's very busy.'

'I can hear a lot of people in the background. Shall I meet you at the train station anyway?'

'Yes, good idea.'

'We're on our way. We will be with you in a few minutes.'

Jake could hear Natty asking to speak to him, and Faye's reply, 'Natty, we're going to be there in a minute. You can speak to him in person.' He heard Faye sigh. 'See you soon, Jake.' She clicked off.

A moment later, Jake's phone rang. He answered it. 'Faye?'

'No, it's Natty on my new phone.'

Jake smiled. 'Hi, Natty.' He wondered if he'd imagined hearing Faye sigh again in the background.

'Did you find some ribbons for Olive in Mr Gillespie's store?'

'Oh, yes. I bought some pink, and red, and purple ones. Evie was there with her mummy. Her name is Annie.'

Jake nodded. 'I know.' He'd met Annie and her husband, Joe, at the party the previous night.

'We put some ribbons in Olive's hair while Mummy talked to Annie.'

Jake suddenly had a thought. He looked about him. There were no dogs on the station platform. He doubted they were allowed on this train. He'd forgotten all about Olive. Hadn't Nick said they could leave her with Annie in the shop? Olive was no stranger to doggy daycare at the interior design outlet in Mr Gillespie's General Store. She even had her own large cushion to laze about on, in between getting lots of fusses from customers, and Evie, by the sound of things.

Jake asked, 'Is Olive with you?'

'No.' Understandably, Natty sounded disappointed. 'Mummy said we had to leave her with Evie. It's not fair. I wanted to spend the day with her.'

'I know, but we might be getting a steam train, and dogs aren't allowed.'

'Can we pick her up on our way back?'

'I guess so.' He heard Faye in the background telling Natty to get off her phone. Jake smiled. He imagined Natty's new phone was going to be a bit of a novelty for some time yet. 'Natty, we will have to end the call now.'

'Why? I like talking to you on the phone.'

Jake thought, *no, you just like talking on your new phone.* He thought he spotted George heading his way through the throng of people on the platform. 'Natty, I have to go now and see if I can sort out the train tickets. See you soon.'

'Love you, Jake,' Natty replied.

Jake felt a lump in his throat, suddenly imagining a future without Faye and Natty in it. 'I love you too.' Jake ended the call and looked up. The older guy heading his way wasn't George after all. He'd been mistaken. Jake remained where he was, hoping George would find him and have good news regarding the train tickets. In the meantime, he glanced around the platform, keeping an eye out for Faye and Natty, and a lady on her own called Rose.

5

Jake heard a familiar voice exclaiming, 'There he is!' He turned around and saw that Natty was holding her mother's hand, pulling Faye forward. Natty let go.

'Natty!' Faye exclaimed. 'Don't run!'

Natty ignored her mother and ran down the platform, dodging people in her path. Faye was trying to keep up. Natty ran into Jake's arms and gave him a big hug as though they had been apart for weeks – not just an hour or so.

'Are we getting the train?' Natty asked, looking around wide-eyed at the queue of people waiting to board the train. Jake didn't want to disappoint Natty now she was there, but he had to explain that they probably would not be taking the train that day. Hopefully they might make the trip another day during the week.

Natty looked crestfallen, and Jake's heart lurched. He hated letting Faye and Natty down.

People were starting to board the train.

Jake looked around and spotted George hurrying along the platform accompanied by an older lady, around his age, whom Jake guessed was Rose. 'I found her,' George said as he stopped in front of Jake. 'And look!' He held out three tickets and beamed. 'You are in luck. I managed to get hold of three more tickets for the afternoon tea excursion that's boarding now.'

Rose gave George a sideways glance. 'Well, aren't you going to introduce us? I'd like to know who I'll be sharing our table with.'

'Oh, yes – of course.'

Jake frowned. 'I'm sorry, did you just say we're sharing a table?'

'Yes, it's the only way I could fit you in. You see, there's been a last-minute cancellation. You'll be seated with us. I bought tickets as a birthday present for my wife, and for a young couple, friends of ours, for their engagement present. The young lady in question had always wanted to go on this steam train. We knew we couldn't make it to her housewarming and engagement party last night, as we were away in Edinburgh. Arrived back this morning. So we'd booked this instead to meet up today. But … um …' George glanced at his wife. 'Something came up, which meant our friends couldn't make it, and the two places were free. I had a word with the catering staff and there was no problem fitting in your child too.'

Jake did not correct George when he said, *your child*, but he did say something else. 'Did you just say a housewarming and engagement party last night?'

'Yes.' George held out his hand, gesturing for them to follow.

'George! I thought you were going to introduce us?' said Rose, throwing her husband an impatient look. I'd like to at least know the names of the strangers I'll be sitting with.'

Jake exchanged a glance with Faye. He imagined they were both thinking the same thing – Rose was none too keen on having to sit with perfect strangers instead of her friends. Jake was considering changing his mind and booking tickets for another time when Natty piped up, 'This is going to be the best day ever!

I can't wait to get on the steam train.'

George chuckled and leaned over to speak to Natty. 'Well, young lady, you are in for a very special treat.'

When he stood up straight, he caught Rose looking his way, folding her arms and raising her eyebrows. George hadn't answered her question.

'Of course I'll introduce you. But first let's get aboard and find our seats. No time for idle chit-chat.'

Rose rolled her eyes. 'I hope you're not accusing me of idle chit-chat.'

'Me? Never!'

Rose looked at her husband for a long moment, clearly deciding whether he was being sarcastic or not.

Jake looked at Faye and thought of them growing old together and having these sorts of harmless little spats after so many years together.

They were in a queue outside one of the carriages. A young lady was checking their tickets.

George had all five tickets. He'd removed his high-viz jacket with the word *Volunteer* on the back.

It seemed a stupid question, but Jake said, 'Is this your first time on the steam train, George?'

'You will be surprised to know that yes, it is. I know I volunteer here, but I wanted to save it for a special occasion.'

'Your wife's birthday.' Jake looked ahead at Rose, who was boarding the train first, followed by Natty and Faye.

'Yes, eighty years young,' George said in a whisper. 'Where do the years go – eh?'

'You've been together a long time, I take it?'

'Oh, yes. We're still very much in love, even though we do have our little spats, as I'm sure you and your missus do. That's marriage for you.'

'Oh, she's not—'

The rest of Jake's reply was drowned out by the high-pitched sound of a whistle, followed by a rush of steam from the engine.

'All aboard!' someone shouted.

George stepped into the train, commenting, 'Feels strange being one of the passengers.'

Jake followed George on to the train and immediately spotted Faye and Natty about to take a seat at a table opposite Rose, who had sat down by the window. She still did not look overly happy about the unexpected guests who had joined their table.

Tables were arranged either side of the central aisle so that everyone had a view out of the large windows. The table arrangements looked similar to an old-fashioned dining car, with highbacked booths and comfortable cushioned benches. Jake took a seat on the bench next to Natty.

George sat down opposite Jake.

There was a moment's awkward silence at the table until Natty said, 'Mummy, can I sit next to the window?'

'Now, that is a good idea,' said George as Natty scooted over her mother's lap to sit in her spot by the window. 'You'll have the best view of the countryside on the journey. Who knows – you might be lucky to spot some wild animals.'

'Like bears and wolves?' Natty said excitedly, looking wide-eyed at George.

'Hmm. There are no wild bears or wolves in Scotland.'

Natty looked disappointed.

'You can visit the Highland Wildlife Park to see bears and wolves. But today, if you're lucky, you might spot a golden eagle or a red deer. There are our famous Highland cows too, and you never know, you might even see a red squirrel.'

'I've never seen a red squirrel – only grey ones in London.'

George nodded. 'I bet you see lots of cats in London, but here we have the Scottish wildcat.'

'Scottish wildcats,' repeated Natty, looking at him wide-eyed, before turning to look out the window. 'What do they look like?' she asked.

'Ah now, they do look like pet moggies, but they are quite large.'

'Have you seen one?' Natty asked, her nose glued to the window.

'No, but I've heard some can be twice as big as a pet cat.'

'So, they'd be easy to spot,' Faye said.

'Yes and no. There are only two or three hundred in the whole of Scotland, so you'd be very lucky to see one.'

Natty's shoulders sagged.

George noticed. 'But I'll tell you what you might spot – a mountain hare.'

Natty turned from the window. 'What do they look like?'

'They look like a rabbit but a lot larger, and they have very big ears.'

Faye smiled at George, and said, 'Thank you so much for letting us join you in your friends' absence.'

Jake got out his wallet to pay for the tickets. Although he didn't normally carry around a lot of cash, he had withdrawn some at the ATM for the holiday just in case.

George noticed. 'Put that away.'

Jake looked up. 'But—'

'We wouldn't have resold the tickets at such short notice anyway.'

That did not make sense to Jake. It was a popular trip, although he expected it had been advertised that they had sold out, in which case George was right – they hadn't had enough notice to sell them on.

Jake slowly put the cash back in his wallet. 'You said you'd booked these tickets for your friends to accompany you because you couldn't make their housewarming and engagement party?'

Jake caught George glancing at his wife before he answered. 'Yes, like I said, something came up which meant they couldn't make it.'

Jake caught Faye staring at George. Faye said, 'You're not talking about Robyn and David, by any chance?'

The expression on George's face gave him away immediately. 'By jove! You know them too?'

Jake nodded. 'We were invited to the party too.' Jake noticed that Faye had the foresight not to mention the name *Bonnie*. As Rose and George hadn't been at the party, it wasn't clear whether Bonnie and David had told them exactly what had taken place the previous night at the police station, and subsequently with the hypnotherapist. Jake had never met Bonnie before the party, so it really wasn't his place to tell Rose and George the incredible news about her getting her memories, and her real identity, back.

'You're friends of David and … Robyn too?' asked Rose.

George shot his wife a look.

The hesitation before she said the name *Robyn* suggested they knew her real name too. It sounded to Jake as though none of them wanted to bring up the name Bonnie and open that can of worms, just in case.

'Yes, she's working on my house.'

'Your house?'

'That's right. She's doing some redecorating.'

'She redecorated our house, and brought her interior design flair to the inside of our rather bland new-build house. That's how we first met her,' said Rose. She eyed them closely. 'I don't remember seeing any of you around and about in Aviemore.'

George butted in. 'Rose, I know Aviemore is a small community, but it's not that small.'

Jake didn't really want to mention that it was a holiday home. He didn't want to get off on the wrong foot with the local couple who might not take too kindly to that fact. 'I'm thinking of selling,' he said.

Faye turned to Jake. 'Oh, that is a shame.'

'Really?'

'Yes. Don't you want to keep The Lake House as a holiday home?'

Jake pursed his lips and gave Rose and George a sideways glance.

'The Lake House?' exclaimed Rose. She turned to her husband. 'You never introduced us, you know.'

'Oh, right. I didn't, did I?' He chuckled. 'This is Faye, Natty and Jake.'

'Jake?' repeated Rose. She reached for the tickets that George had left on the table.

'What are you doing?'

Rose looked through the tickets until she found Jake's. She looked up. 'This ticket says Jake Campbell-Ross.'

Jake nodded. 'That's me.'

'*The* Jake Campbell-Ross?' she blurted.

Jake heaved a sigh and smiled tightly. He would have much rather she hadn't seen the ticket, and they'd stuck to their first names only, but the mention of The Lake House had given him away.

Rose looked at him wide-eyed and became somewhat flustered – as Jake knew some people did when they found themselves unexpectedly in the presence of money or celebrity, or both. He had no real idea why it happened. Celebrities and the super-rich were no different than anybody else; just richer, perhaps luckier, with a skill at something that paid an extortionate amount of money, be it business, or the arts – more money than other jobs that were no less skilled or worthwhile or needed. It was unfair, but unfortunately just the way of things.

'Well I, er, had no idea ...' She turned to George. 'Why didn't you tell me?'

'Tell you what?'

She lowered her voice, and spoke through the side of her mouth even though everyone at the table could hear her. 'That we're in the presence of a Ross.'

Faye exchanged a knowing smile with Jake at Rose's reaction.

George looked at his wife, and shook his head. 'So, you mentioned that Robyn is redecorating your house?'

'Why are you all calling her Robyn when her real name is Bonnie?' Natty asked, totally oblivious to the clanger she'd just dropped.

At that moment, the steam whistle went off again, and the carriage jolted as the train began to move. The excitement in the carriage was palpable as the adventure began. Chatter arose in the cabin, along with excited children's voices – Natty's was one of them. 'The train is moving!'

Jake could hear squeals of delight as the train, billowing clouds of steam, gradually edged its way out of the station. People on the platform waved, and everyone seated on the train waved back. Jake relaxed, enjoying the rhythmic chugging of the engine as it set the stage for what George had theatrically described as a magical journey through the heart of the Cairngorms National Park.

6

A waitress appeared at their table and asked them if they would like tea or coffee with their afternoon tea. 'There's a selection of different teas and coffees on the menu.'

Everyone hastily picked up their menus with a silent agreement between the adults to ignore Natty's question about Bonnie.

Natty eyed the young woman before turning to her mum and whispering, 'Can I have juice?'

The young waitress heard Natty. 'Of course. We have cartons of orange juice and apple juice.'

Natty smiled shyly at her. 'Can I have apple juice, please?'

The young woman smiled and wrote it down on the little pad of paper she had in her hand. 'One apple juice.'

Jake and Faye both chose an americano coffee. George and Rose opted for English breakfast tea.

'I can smell smoke,' Natty said, wriggling her nose. 'I hope they haven't burnt our lunch – I'm starving!'

Everyone laughed, including Rose, who had suddenly warmed to her unexpected travel companions.

'What you can smell,' said George, 'is the smoke from the chimney.'

The waitress came over with a tray and set down a pot of strong black coffee between Jake and Faye, along with a jug of milk. There was a sugar bowl on the table already. She poured tea from a large stainless-steel teapot into two cups in front of George and Rose and gave them a small jug of milk too. She passed a carton of apple juice to Jake. 'We will be bringing the food shortly.'

They all thanked the waitress as Jake passed the carton to Natty. Natty pulled the straw off the side of the carton. Faye glanced at her. 'Be careful with that juice. Don't spill any on the nice tablecloth, will you?'

Natty shook her head.

'Shall I pour?' offered Jake, picking up the coffee pot.

Faye nodded. 'Yes please.'

The coffee pot was unexpectedly heavy, and the little cups and saucers smaller and daintier than he was used to. Jake overshot the cup spilling some coffee on the tablecloth. 'Oops.'

Natty frowned at Jake and tutted.

'Here, let me …' Rose quickly picked up a serviette and mopped up the coffee.

'Thank you, Rose.'

She smiled at him. 'Well, you're very welcome, Jake Campbell-Ross.'

Jake caught George rolling his eyes at Rose. He glanced at Faye and caught her expression too. She was biting her lip, trying very hard not to laugh. Poor Rose was still star-struck by Jake's presence.

The young lady appeared with two stands filled with sandwiches, cakes and scones. She set them down on the table. They started on the sandwiches. George picked up a finger sandwich and turned to his wife. 'Rose, are you enjoying your present?'

'Oh yes, George. It's simply wonderful. It's something I've always wanted to do. It was a lovely surprise when you told me this morning. I was so excited but then when David and Robyn …' she looked at Natty, 'I mean Bonnie, rang to say they couldn't make it, it sort of put a slight damper on the day.'

Then you found out George had invited three strangers to join you instead, thought Jake. He wasn't surprised she hadn't appeared happy about it – at first.

'But then George met you lovely people, wanting a ride on the train – and here you are. So now I'm more than happy.'

Once you found out who I am. Jake kept that thought to himself.

Rose was still smiling and staring at Jake intensely.

Jake felt a bit uncomfortable under her scrutiny. He got the feeling something was on her mind. Her eyes shifted to Faye and Natty.

George said, 'We've been looking forward to doing this for so long, haven't we, Rose?'

She nodded.

'We've just never got around to it until I surprised her with the tickets.'

Rose added, 'We were waiting to take the grandchildren. They're all grown up now,' she said sadly.

Jake got the impression that their extended family had probably moved away from the area for work, and rarely visited.

Rose looked at Natty, and smiled. 'Isn't this fun?'

'Oh, yes, so much fun,' said Natty with a mouthful of finger sandwich.

'Natty, please don't speak with your mouth full,' Faye admonished her.

'The food is lovely,' said Natty, ignoring her mother.

'I agree,' said Rose, smiling affectionately at Natty as she helped herself to another finger sandwich.

George told them what to expect from the journey as the train slowly picked up speed. 'It's not a long journey, but we have two stops on the way. One at Boat of Garten village while the train takes on water, then onto Broomhill Station for a twenty-minute stop whilst the engine is switched from one end to the other for our return journey. You can get out and stretch your legs if you wish, but don't wander too far if you do, because the train will certainly leave without you.'

'I don't want to get off the train,' said Natty.

Faye agreed. 'Me neither.'

There were murmurs of agreement from Rose, George and Jake.

As the train wound its way through the beautiful Highland scenery, the finger sandwiches soon disappeared, along with the scones, and for a short time all they could hear was the chink of cups and saucers, as everyone in the carriage had been served their afternoon tea and had settled down to eat the special treats and gaze in wonder at the scenery. George reeled off some fascinating stories about the railway's history.

Jake could tell he loved his role as a volunteer station master. 'So, how long have you been a volunteer at the station, George?' Jake asked as the train chugged along, bellowing out steam.

George was just about to answer when Rose cut into the conversation. 'We downsized, you see, out of a big old house into a new-build property. But we were the first people on the estate and had no neighbours. Not like in our old place. Then we met a lovely young lady who had just arrived in the area, called, um, calling herself Robyn, who suggested that George might like to volunteer at the station, and so he did and has never looked back – have you, dear?'

George looked adoringly at Rose and nodded.

'So, The Lake House is your holiday home?'

Jake wondered when Rose was going to come back round to that fact. There was something she wanted to know – he was sure of it. He nodded.

'I thought it was the Rosses' holiday home.'

'Jake's a Ross,' pipped up Natty. 'His name is Jake Campbell-Ross.'

'I know, dear,' Rose said smoothly.

Rose looked pointedly at Jake. I thought the house belonged to William Ross.'

Jake shook his head, thinking that was probably a common misconception. He said as much. 'It was my parents' house. I grew up there for a time before …' He glanced at Natty. The last thing he wanted to do was talk about dead parents.

'… before things changed.'

Rose eyed Natty. 'I understand.'

Jake imagined Rose did. It was common knowledge that he'd been taken in by William Ross as a young child after his parents – William's good friends – died in an accident. Although they couldn't live in The Lake House – William's business interests meant he, and the family, had to be mainly London-based – that didn't stop them all using it as a holiday home, especially at Christmastime.

'Jake was born here,' Natty volunteered. She had been listening in to the conversation whilst looking out of the window.

Faye turned to her daughter, 'Natty, it's not polite to butt into adult conversations.'

Natty turned from the window and threw her another a black look. 'But it's true.'

Rose looked at Faye. 'It's all right – really.'

It was obvious to Jake that Rose wanted Natty to continue. She was clearly intrigued and a little awe-struck by him. He could tell this was going to be the talk of the town, or at least of their social circle, once Rose returned home. He expected she would ring all her friends and tell them the news – she'd had afternoon tea on the steam train with none other than Jake Campbell-Ross, one of the heirs to the Ross fortune.

'How do you know that, anyway?' Faye asked Natty, looking at Jake. Clearly, the fact that Jake had been born in Scotland was news to her.

'Jake told me,' Natty replied, looking crossly at her mum.

'I see,' said Rose, giving Jake one of her inscrutable looks.

The uncomfortable silence was interrupted by the carriage suddenly slowing as the train pulled into the quaint Boat of Garten station. 'Wow – look at those beautiful hanging baskets,' Faye said as she pointed out of the window. Shall we get off and take some pictures, Natty?'

George reminded them that it was only a short pitstop there, but that they could get off at the next station.

It wasn't long before they arrived at Broomhill Station.

Faye repeated her question, 'Shall we get off the train, Natty?'

'Yes please! I want to take some photos on my phone.'

Jake looked at them both in surprise as he stood and got out of his seat so they could pass. *What happened to staying on the train?*

George turned to Rose. 'I suppose you've changed your mind and want to go too.'

'No, I'm quite happy staying here.'

Jake pursed his lips, throwing Rose a sideways glance. Somehow, that was exactly what he'd thought she'd say.

George said, 'Well, I think I'm going to join Faye and Natty and stretch my legs.'

Jake rolled his eyes. He had it on the tip of his tongue to say, *please don't go*. But that would have been weird.

'You go ahead, dear,' said Rose, smiling. 'I don't fancy going out. Besides, I'm sure Jake would be interested in some tips on how to spend his holiday – wouldn't you, Jake?'

Jake glanced at Rose and then at Faye, hoping she would help him out. But as they all squeezed out of their seats, leaving him to entertain Rose, he felt a sense of an impending interrogation coming his way. But then again, Jake felt he might learn a little bit more about Rose's friend, Robyn – or rather, Bonnie. Although he could just up and leave the train too, he sat back down opposite Rose, wondering what was on her mind – he was sure there was something. Whatever it was, he thought perhaps it was best said out of earshot of the others.

'I want to offer my condolences.' She paused, studying him intently.

Jake avoided her gaze. Eleanor wasn't dead, but he wasn't about to correct her on that score.

'But I am surprised to see a Ross back in Aviemore after …' she trailed off.

Jake slumped in his seat. 'After last Christmas.' He thought he might as well spit it out. She wouldn't. Rose was obviously trying to be diplomatic, although he was annoyed she had brought it up. He had a feeling this was going to be a long ten minutes. He hoped the others were quick taking their photos. He didn't want to be rude to Rose, but he also did not want to volunteer the reasons he was back in Scotland.

He looked out of the window at his primary reason for being there, and smiled at her. Faye. Unfortunately, Rose followed his gaze. 'She's very pretty.'

Jake pursed his lips and turned to face Rose. 'I know what you're thinking: it's not even been a year since I lost my wife in that skiing accident …' Nobody outside the family really knew if she was alive or dead. They'd kept the truth of her condition from the press, from everybody. Only immediate family, and now Faye, knew.

Rose surprised him by reaching out and placing a hand over his. 'Everyone deserves a second chance at love and happiness. Look at Robyn … Bonnie. There's a case in point. She's found her happy place, and happy person, at the boathouse, although I'm sure she's going to be a lot happier when she ties up loose ends and deals with that unfinished business.'

'What unfinished business?'

'You know, finding Robyn.'

Jake nodded. 'Yeah, of course.' He was thinking of his own unfinished business there in the Cairngorms.

Her eyes flickered out of the window to Faye. 'Sounds to me as though yours is with Faye, at The Lake House.'

Jake followed her gaze. 'Huh?' He'd lost the thread of the conversation.

'She's your happy place. They both are – Faye and Natty. You'd make a lovely family. Have you proposed? Are you engaged?'

Jake shook his head. 'I was hoping that coming here …'

Rose smiled. 'Well, you've certainly come to the right place. It's quite romantic, this part of Scotland, you know. I bet this was where your parents met.'

Jake nodded. It was.

'You know I can just imagine you all at The Lake House.'

'What do you mean?'

'If you don't mind me saying, and I really wouldn't be offended if you told me to shut up and keep my nose out of your personal affairs, but why sell The Lake House?'

Jake thought, *do I have to spell it out?* The place reminded him of Eleanor and what had happened at Christmas. Before he had a chance to be rude, and tell her to keep her nose out, she added, 'You're having the place redecorated. I can just imagine, after all these years, it could do with a remodel. I bet the place will look unrecognisable, in a good way, when Robyn … I mean Bonnie – goodness, the change of name is going to take some getting used to. But I digress. What I'm trying to say is, have you thought about starting a new life here, with Faye and Natty?'

Jake was already shaking his head.

'As Natty said, you were born here. If your parents had still been alive, you would have grown up here. Wouldn't it be rather fitting – coming home to Aviemore?'

Someone banged on the window, startling Jake.

Natty was at the window. 'Jake! Jake! Come outside. I want to take your photo on my phone,' she shouted. A moment later she was running up the train carriage, Faye following in her wake. They both grabbed his hands, and pulled him up.

'Come on!'

As Jake followed them down the carriage, he glanced over his shoulder at Rose. She sat there smiling knowingly.

Faye took his arm as soon as he stepped off the train. She whispered, 'I hope it wasn't a problem, me and Natty being here in Aviemore.'

He furrowed his brow. 'Why should it be?'

'You know, with your wife, um … word might get around that you're here with … well, with me.'

Jake caught Faye nodding at Rose, sitting in the train carriage window, staring at them.

She was right, tongues would wag. Not Rose's, though. She'd made her opinion clear – that Jake deserved to find happiness again. She just didn't realise his wife, Eleanor, was still very much alive. It would mean he'd have to divorce her – something he felt terribly guilty about. But the doctors had told him that there was no possibility of a future together as husband and wife. Even though Eleanor wouldn't understand, he knew he had to see her face to face and tell her himself.

'Come on, Jake – I want to take some photos!' exclaimed Natty, grabbing his arm.

Jake was rather enjoying standing on the platform with Faye's hand on his arm, leaning close. Even so, he smiled at Natty as she led him away to the front of the train to take a selfie of the three of them by the locomotive.

It wasn't long before he was back, with Faye and Natty in tow, boarding the train as the steam whistle blew for the return journey. George was already on board, taking his seat next to Rose.

'Are you all right?' Faye asked in his ear as they waited for Natty to take her seat by the window. 'You're awfully quiet.'

Jake cast his gaze over at Rose. Of course it had crossed his mind, a fairytale ending, coming home to Aviemore with Faye and Natty. But it was just that – wasn't it? A rather lovely dream. There were so many reasons why that wouldn't happen – Natty in her school, Faye in her job – not to mention his teaching post. And overshadowing all that was Eleanor.

7

'Did you all have a good time in Aviemore?' Gayle asked, stepping aside as her three guests trooped into the guesthouse, along with one Old English Sheepdog.

Gayle's gaze dropped to Olive, who had sat down by her feet. 'Oh … I thought you were dropping her off at the shop?'

Jake said, 'We did. Well, Faye and Natty dropped her off.'

'Ah, I can see that's where you've been.'

Everyone looked at the multicoloured ribbons in Olive's fur.

'I bought some ribbons,' said Natty. 'Evie was there with her mum, minding the shop, so Evie helped me put the ribbons in Olive's hair.'

'Fur,' corrected Faye.

'Fur,' Natty repeated.

'Well, she looks very pretty,' said Gayle.

'Yes, then we left her there for a bit, and collected her on the way back,' said Natty, patting Olive's head.

'What else did you all get up to?' Gayle asked as they walked down the hallway together.

'We went on a steam train!' said Natty.

'Really?'

'Oh, yes,' replied Natty. 'And we had afternoon tea with finger sandwiches, and cakes and scones. It was amazing.'

Faye put an arm around Natty's shoulder. 'And the scenery was stunning too,' Faye added.

Gayle smiled down at Natty. 'Did you see some deer, and a hare or two?'

Natty frowned. 'I wanted to see a red squirrel and a wildcat.'

'Well we've got all week, so you never know,' said Faye. 'But it really was a trip to remember – wasn't it, Natty?'

'Oh, yes.'

Jake smiled at the two of them as he followed them down the hallway. It was a perfect start to the holiday. He just hoped every day proved as successful and memorable as this one.

Natty took Olive's collar. 'Come on, let's play!' Natty told Olive to sit. 'Good girl!' She got out some more ribbons from her pocket and started to tie another one in Olive's fur. The dog didn't seem to mind. She loved the attention.

Gayle glanced at Olive, then turned her attention to Jake as they trooped into the kitchen. 'I didn't know you'd planned to do a train journey today.'

'I hadn't. It was pure fluke that after I visited the tourist information, while Natty and Faye were shopping in Aviemore, I turned up at the station to ask about the steam train, and they had two free tickets. They squeezed Natty in because she's a child.'

'Two free tickets.' Gayle looked at him in surprise. 'I'd say that's quite unheard of at such short notice. Must have been your lucky day.'

Jake exchanged a glance with Faye. 'Well, as it happens, two people cancelled.'

'It was Bonnie and David – wasn't it?' said Gayle.

Jake nodded. 'They were going with their friends, Rose and George. They couldn't make it to the party last night, so they'd bought tickets for Bonnie and David to join them on the steam train today.'

'I heard. I didn't realise Bonnie had cancelled, although I'm not surprised after all she went through yesterday.'

'No, me neither.'

'You saw Rose and George then?'

'Actually, it was George I asked about some tickets. He was volunteering at the station before his trip on the steam train with Rose, and he sorted out the tickets. We sat with them.'

'They're such a lovely couple,' said Faye. 'At first I didn't think Rose was too keen on us joining them.'

'Yeah,' Jake agreed. 'I didn't blame her. George did kind of spring it on her, strangers joining their table for the trip.'

Faye said, 'I was worried about Natty. How Rose would feel about having a child at the table too.'

'Oh, Rose and George would have loved to take their grandchildren when they were young, but it wasn't to be.'

Faye nodded. 'Yes, Rose mentioned that.'

'I bet Rose and George enjoyed having a little one join them,' said Gayle. 'And not to mention a Ross too.' Gayle smiled knowingly at Jake.

Jake returned her smile. 'Yes, Rose was rather surprised when she found out who I was.'

'And a bit awe-struck to meet a Ross,' added Faye.

'Just a bit?' Jake joked.

'I'll bet,' said Gaye. 'One thing I will say about your family, Jake – William Ross was always so generous, donating to worthy causes in the community, especially at Christmas, but it would have been lovely to see the Ross family out and about, and meet them … you.'

Jake knew what she was getting at. 'Yes, we did keep ourselves to ourselves when we holidayed here. In hindsight, it's something I regret.'

'You're making up for that now. And to think, if Robyn, I mean Bonnie, hadn't started redecorating The Lake House, I expect you would have returned there instead.'

Jake looked at Gayle. That wasn't strictly true. She'd only brought in painting materials, and wallpaper, leaving them in the rooms she was about to start work on. The house was big enough to have still stayed there himself with Natty and Faye, avoiding the rooms that had been prepped for redecoration. But he still didn't want to stay there.

Something Rose had said about The Lake House came to mind. *I can just imagine, after all these years, it could do with a remodel. I bet the place will look unrecognisable, in a good way.* But would it erase the ghosts from his past – the memories? He doubted it. *So make new ones there.* Jake raised his eyebrows at that thought, along with Rose's final comment on the matter – *have you thought about starting a new life here, with Faye and Natty?*

'I'm glad we're staying here,' said Faye.

'Me too!' shouted Natty from the hallway, clearly listening in on the adults' conversation.

Jake had met some lovely people while staying at the guesthouse – Marty, Nick, David, and of course Gayle and her mum, Doris. He felt part of a little community there – a family of sorts. Jake realised it was what he needed. He smiled at Faye as he said as much to Gayle. 'I wouldn't change a thing. It's great staying at your guesthouse.'

'Shame you can't, you know, stay on,' commented Gayle as she flicked the kettle on. Jake and Faye took a seat at the kitchen table.

Jake looked about him. 'Here, like your two permanent lodgers?' He thought it a strange question.

'No, I meant in Aviemore.'

'Ah.' Jake glanced at Faye. 'My life is in London.'

Gayle's gaze shifted to Faye. 'I understand. Shame, though. The Lake House standing empty. Would make a lovely family home.'

There was an awkward silence. Jake saw Gayle raising an eyebrow knowingly. He knew she meant well. She was thinking it would make a lovely home for him, Faye and Natty. He imagined she would like her new friends to become her new neighbours, which they would if they moved into The Lake House, which backed on to her property. But he couldn't possibly ask Faye and Natty to drop their lives in London to move there, with him, even if he wanted to. Besides, he and Faye, they weren't a couple – yet. He was working on it though. He knew she felt something for him that was more than friendship. But could she trust opening her heart to another man? And did she want a new daddy for Natty? Those were the questions he hoped might be answered over the course of the holiday.

8

Natty walked into the kitchen with Olive and asked, 'What's The Lake House?'

Jake looked at her in surprise. She clearly hadn't been listening to some of the adult conversation on the train when the subject of The Lake House had been raised. She had probably been too busy staring out of the train window, trying to spot a wildcat.

'It's Jake's house, here in Scotland,' said Gayle matter-of-factly.

Natty had sat down at the table, Olive by her side. She stopped what she was doing – tying her last ribbon in Olive's hair – and looked at Jake. 'Can we stay in your house, Jake?'

Jake came over all flustered. He hadn't anticipated the subject of The Lake House cropping up again, although he should have. After all, the place backed on to Gayle's, and the rooftop of his house through the trees could be seen from the window of the attic bedrooms. Not that he had any intention of pointing that out to Faye or Natty.

Fortunately for Jake, Faye stepped in. 'But you like staying at the guesthouse, and besides, it would mean you'd have to leave Olive.'

Natty suddenly flung her little arms around the dog's neck. 'I don't want to leave Olive – ever!'

Jake turned to Faye and mouthed *thank you.* He'd already had this conversation with Faye, when she'd mentioned them staying at The Lake House for their holiday.

'Can we see your house?' Natty asked.

Jake didn't know what to say. He'd hardly ever said no to anything Natty had asked of him. What reason would he give?

Gayle looked at Jake, clearly sensing he was having a problem answering that question. She changed the subject. 'Would you like to join me for dinner this evening?' she asked them all.

'I thought the guesthouse was bed-and-breakfast?' said Faye.

'Jake booked bed-and-breakfast, but I do evening meals on request.' Gayle smiled. 'And I'm requesting that you guys join me.'

'Oh, we'd love to join you,' said Faye, not catching Jake trying to imperceptibly shake his head and catch her attention so that she did not accept the invitation. Faye had yet to find out that Gayle was not a good cook. At all. Luckily for him, he'd managed an intervention on Gayle's stew the last time he was there, before he'd had to eat it, but who knew what she'd cook up that evening.

'Yes please,' said Natty. 'Can we have dinner in your kitchen? I like your big kitchen with the huge table, and the Aga.'

Jake turned to Natty. 'Do you?' He knew of somewhere else with a huge kitchen, and an Aga – his very own house – The Lake House.

'Oh, yes. It's a *proper* kitchen.'

Faye put her hands on her hips and frowned across the table at Natty. 'So, isn't the kitchen at home good enough anymore?'

Jake looked from mother to daughter and smiled as Natty put her hands on her hips, mimicking Faye. Her chin up, Natty said, 'There is nothing wrong with our kitchen.'

'Well, good. I'm pleased to hear it.'

'But it is small.'

Jake's mouth curled into a smile as Natty got the last word in.

Faye shook her head and turned to Jake. 'You didn't have other plans for this evening, did you?'

Jake had it on the tip of his tongue to lie, but he couldn't. Gayle looked eager for them to join her, and despite her terrible cooking, Jake didn't want to let her down. He said, 'Not at all. An evening meal here sounds … great.'

'Fantastic!' Gayle beamed. 'Three more for Scottish meat pies and vegetables it is then.'

'Sounds amazing,' said Faye.

Jake gave her a sideways glance, thinking that it might sound good, but what it would taste like was a whole other matter.

Gayle was getting out some mugs to make tea when she turned from the counter. 'Oh, I'm assuming no one is vegetarian, because I can try my hand at a vegetarian pie if—'

'Natty and I are not vegetarians,' said Faye. 'You're not either, are you Jake?'

He shook his head. 'The meat pie is fine by me.'

'I have to warn you that I've just started to experiment with the pie crust and haven't quite perfected the recipe yet.'

I bet, thought Jake, not at all surprised that Gayle was almost pre-warning them that things might not go quite to plan in the baking department.

'I'm going to start preparing the meal.' Gayle continued. 'I'll try to have it ready around six, if that's not too early for you all.'

'That's perfect,' said Jake. 'Will there be other guests joining us?' He recalled the helpful lady in the tourist information mentioning that the guesthouse was fully booked from that night.

He thought there must be other guests arriving.

'No. My other guests have arrived today, but they've booked evening meals in a restaurant in Aviemore.'

Lucky them, thought Jake, wondering if they somehow knew in advance about Gayle's cooking or simply didn't realise an evening meal at the guesthouse was an option.

'Can I play with Olive in the garden before dinner?' Natty asked, looking at Gayle and then at Faye. 'It's still light out.'

Gayle said, 'It's going to be light for quite some time into the evening. It's the summer, remember? After dinner, we could take our pudding outside and have it at the garden table on the patio if you like.'

Natty grinned. 'I've never done that before. We haven't got a garden at home. Mummy, can we sit outside with our pudding?'

'If you're sure that's okay, Gayle.'

'Of course – why wouldn't it be? My guests have the run of the grounds, as well as the house. And talking of going out in the garden, I have just the thing Olive enjoys playing with outside.'

Everyone watched Gayle walk out of the kitchen. They could see her through the open doorway as she opened the cupboard in the hall. Inside was an assortment of coats, boots and umbrellas. Olive was watching too. She suddenly scooted after Gayle, squeezing around Gayle's legs, her nose sniffing around the inside of the cupboard.

'Here we are,' said Gayle as she leaned inside and pulled out an old, rather chewed, frisbee. She returned to the kitchen with Olive scampering after her, getting excited. Gayle passed it to Natty.

Olive sat at Natty's feet, looking up at her, tail wagging furiously, ready for a game.

Gayle said, 'Now, just make sure you don't throw the frisbee too high as it might disappear over the hedge into a neighbour's garden, and then Olive might disappear after it. And we don't want that – do we?'

Jake, Faye and Natty shook their heads. Jake imagined that Gayle didn't want to be the one to tell Nick that her new guests had lost his dog.

'I think I'll go out in the garden with Natty and Olive,' Faye said. 'The grounds look lovely, and it would be nice to stretch my legs for a while after the train ride.'

Jake imagined that wouldn't be all she was doing. Jake had an idea that Faye was going to keep an eye on Olive.

'Right, I'm going to prepare the dinner.'

Jake stared at Gayle, wide-eyed. Oh, how he wished he'd remembered to book a table at a restaurant. It had been his intention, but he'd got wrapped up in the train journey and had forgotten.

Jake followed Faye, Natty and Olive out into the hall.

Faye turned to Jake, 'Do you want to join us in the garden?'

'Yes, come and play with us,' Natty said, taking his hand.

Jake would have like nothing better, but there was something else he needed to do first if they were going to have a decent meal this evening. 'I'll come out soon, I promise. There's just something I need to do first.'

Faye raised her eyebrows.

He turned to her, keeping his voice down so Natty didn't hear, otherwise she might repeat it. Natty was busy checking Olive's ribbons were still in place after Olive had scratched her ear with her hind paw.

'Look, Gayle isn't exactly a whizz in the kitchen.'

'Huh?'

Jake didn't know how to say this diplomatically, so he just came out with it and said, 'Her cooking isn't very um … nice.'

'But her fry-up was lovely.'

'Yes, I agree, but then it's all downhill from there, I'm afraid.'

'Oh, dear.'

'So, I'm going to offer to help in the kitchen.'

'Help?'

'Yes, I did it once before when she wasn't looking. I heard she now makes the most amazing stew. New recipe.'

'She must have seen what you did to her stew.'

'She must have caught me putting her condiments back in the cupboard, but was too polite to call me out on it at the time.'

'Oh, how funny.'

'You wouldn't think so if you'd tasted the original stew.'

'Ah, that doesn't sound good.'

'It didn't taste good either,' said Jake in all seriousness.

They both turned at the sound of Gayle in the kitchen, getting out pots and pans.

'I think you'd better go and see what's happening.'

'I think so too.'

Natty skipped past them to the front door, carrying the frisbee, Olive hot on her heels.

'Natty, wait for me!' said Faye, as Natty and Olive left the house.

Jake caught Faye's hand. 'I'll come out as soon as I'm sure there's something edible in the oven.'

Faye grinned. 'That sounds so mean.'

'I know. But like her stew, Gayle will be on cloud nine when she finds out her pie has turned out much better than she expected.'

Jake should have let go of Faye's hand, but he didn't want to. Then again, Faye wasn't exactly letting go of his either. He was just about to draw her closer, when Natty shouted out, 'Mummy – how do I throw a frisbee?'

Faye rolled her eyes, and Jake had to let her go, reluctantly.

Jake wandered into the kitchen.

Gayle turned around, an apron tied around her waist, the words, *World's Best Cook*, emblazoned across it. Jake did a double-take, and bit his tongue, avoiding a sarcastic comment – or laughing out loud. He wondered if someone who knew Gayle well had bought her that apron.

'Ah, Jake. I thought you'd be in the garden with Faye.'

Jake looked at the ingredients that were sitting on the kitchen counter along with a large dish. 'Gayle, can I ask you a big favour?'

'Anything, Jake. What are friends for?'

Surprisingly, Jake suddenly felt a lump in his throat. He was going to miss this place when he had to return to London. If he lived in The Lake House, they'd be neighbours.

Jake dismissed that thought. If he wanted to be with Faye and Natty, that was never going to happen.

'Look, it's been a long, long time since I cooked with someone …' Jake knew this was going to seem a strange request, but it was the truth.

'You and Eleanor?'

'Oh, no – not us. It was William and me.'

'William Ross?' she said in surprise.

Jake didn't really want to get into how all that had started – when he'd first lost his parents. He'd been a withdrawn little boy, but it was William who'd coaxed him out of his shell, encouraging him to join him baking. It had become something they'd always done together, especially at Christmas when they'd all meet at The Lake House. But sadly, he hadn't seen William in months, not since the accident, and he knew those days of gathering in the kitchen at Christmas to cook the Christmas dinner together were over.

'Jake?' Gayle touched his arm.

'Oh, sorry. Lost in thought there.' Jake tried to make light of it.

'Did you just say William Ross likes to cook?'

Jake caught her expression. She looked very surprised indeed. Jake guessed it wasn't because William was a guy, but because he was a Ross, and she imagined he had far more important things to do with his time than cooking.

Jake wanted to say, *yes, he cooked, and even took the rubbish out on occasion.* 'You'd have liked William.' Sadly, Jake doubted she would ever have the chance to meet him. 'He's a very down-to-earth guy.'

'I heard. That's what my father told me.'

'Oh, yes, I forgot your late father met him once.'

'Not in the most auspicious of circumstances.'

Jake remembered. It was over Christmas one year, and William had thought he was having a heart attack. It had turned out to be indigestion.

Jake was about to tell Gayle that if she met him on the street, she'd have no idea he was the head of a global business empire – he was that down to earth.

'So, what is William Ross's favourite dish?'

'He loves a roast dinner, most especially Christmas dinner. But he also loves to bake.' Jake doubted he still did. He seemed to have lost interest in everything – apart from golf – since the accident.

'Cakes and pies?'

'Pies especially.'

'I don't suppose you remember one of his recipes, by any chance?'

Jake grinned. 'Oh, yes. Would you like me to show you?'

'But you're my guest, and I'm meant to be cooking the dinner …' She trailed off before asking, 'Would you mind?'

'No, no, not at all. Have you got another apron, by any chance?'

Gayle grinned. 'I do.' She opened the pantry door. Hanging on the back were several. 'Here we are.' She held it up. It said, *World's Second-Best Cook*.

Jake smiled. 'That'll do.' He tied it around his waist and clapped his hands together in anticipation of the task ahead. This was just what he needed. He found baking very therapeutic, and even more so when he had someone to share the task with.

Gayle reached up to a shelf above the cooker and took down a well-thumbed recipe book which was years old. 'Mother used this for all our meals when we were children, and I must say, she was a marvellous cook – unlike her youngest daughter.' Gayle looked at Jake, waiting for him to agree, but he just smiled. 'Who says? Your stew was amazing.'

Gayle eyed him for a long moment. 'Still, I'm looking forward to learning one of William Ross's pie recipes this evening instead.'

Jake watched her put the recipe book back on the shelf, and happened to glance out of the kitchen window into the front garden. He saw Natty and Faye throwing a frisbee, and Olive in between them, running to try and catch it. They were both laughing, having a tremendous time. Jake smiled.

Gayle glanced out of the window too. 'I bet with her teaching career, and that headship course you said she was doing, Faye doesn't get a lot of time to spend just having fun with her daughter.'

Jake hadn't really thought about that until now. He was so

wrapped up in thoughts of winning Faye's heart this holiday that he hadn't spared a thought for Faye's relationship with Natty. They needed time together too.

'I'll be right back,' said Gayle.

'Where are you going?' Jake asked. He was looking forward to cooking with her.

'Oh, don't worry, I won't be long. I wouldn't miss learning one of William Ross's recipes for the world. I'm just going to let them know they can play in the back garden. The lawn is bigger, so they'll all have a lot more room to throw the frisbee.'

Jake watched Gayle nip out into the front garden. He waved at Faye and Natty, and craned his neck watching as they walked around the side of the house, until he could see them no longer.

Jake nodded to himself. This whole day, the first day of their holiday, had gone so, so much better than he could ever have envisaged. As he collected the ingredients to make the pie, he thought that now the day was going to end on the right note too, with a fabulous home-baked pie.

Faye's father Patrick had given him some simple advice about this holiday with his daughter – *don't screw it up*. As far as Jake was concerned, day one was in the bag, and with his help, not even Gayle's cooking could spoil such a perfect day. So why did he have a sinking feeling in the pit of his stomach?

'Right, where were we?' Gayle asked, rolling up her sleeves.

Jake was staring out of the window, wishing Natty, Faye and Olive hadn't gone into the back garden where he couldn't see them. He turned to Faye. 'Is the fencing secure at the back? Olive won't get out – will she?'

'Oh, don't worry. Rest assured, she's better off in the back garden than the front.'

'Oh, yes – of course.' Gayle's driveway was open to the road if the gates were left open. They were closed, but then again, she might still have guests arriving.

It wasn't the dog he was worried about. But he couldn't put his finger on what exactly was bothering him.

9

Faye and Natty walked around the gravel pathway which led to the back of the house. 'Wow – this is lovely!' exclaimed Faye as she stopped to admire the large, beautifully tended lawn and array of summer borders. She'd had no idea that the back garden was even bigger than the front. She wondered where Gayle found the time to keep her garden so beautiful when she had a guesthouse to run.

Faye cast her gaze down at Olive, who was sitting on the lawn by her feet, looking up at the frisbee in her hand. Faye looked at the frisbee too. 'I think we need to be careful where we throw this.' Faye had a thought. 'Perhaps we should go back to the front garden.'

'No, Mummy, I like this garden. It's bigger.'

'Well, as long as we keep the games on the lawn. I don't want Olive diving into the flower borders.'

Natty knelt down in front of Olive and wagged a finger in front of her nose. 'Now, you heard Mummy. No trampling the flower borders.'

Faye sighed, wishing Natty hadn't used the word *trample.*

Olive licked Natty's finger.

Natty giggled. 'Hey, that tickled!' She looked up at her mum.

'Can we play the same game? Piggy in the middle?'

'Yes, I think that's a good idea. If we keep well clear of the borders, more towards the middle of the lawn, and throw the frisbee between us, then Olive can try and catch it like before.'

'Can I be piggy in the middle?'

'No, I don't think so. If I throw it to Olive, I'm a bit concerned she might miss it and go chasing it into the flower borders.'

Natty frowned. 'All right.'

They took their places, Faye reminding Natty, 'The frisbee, and Olive, mustn't stray past the lawn, all right?'

'Yes.'

'Right, I'm going to throw the frisbee!'

Olive flopped down on the grass between them.

'I don't think Olive wants to play anymore,' Natty said frowning at her playmate.

Faye said, 'I think she does. Just watch!' Faye held up the frisbee high in the air.

Olive stood up and looked from Faye to Natty.

'There, you see,' Faye called out as she tossed the frisbee into the air, in Natty's direction.

Natty reached up at as the frisbee came flying toward her but Olive got their first, jumping up on her hindlegs and nabbing the bright orange plastic frisbee in her jaws.

Faye called Olive.

Olive didn't seem inclined to give up her prize. Flopping down on the grass in the middle of the lawn, she dropped the frisbee.

Natty shouted, 'Olive! Come here!'

Olive put a paw on the frisbee as if to say, *no, it's mine.*

'Don't you want to play fetch?' Faye asked, walking towards Olive. She slowed as she neared the dog. Faye wasn't used to being around dogs. Would Olive give up her prize, or would she start growling? It was the first time Olive had caught the frisbee.

'Good dog,' said Faye, in a soothing voice. 'There's a good girl.'

Olive nudged the frisbee toward Faye.

Faye grinned. 'You want to play again?'

Olive stood up and barked, looking from the frisbee to Faye.

She picked up the frisbee and walked backwards, making sure she stopped before she reached the flower borders, then reached up and hurled the frisbee into the air, in Natty's direction.

A breeze caught the frisbee and sent it gliding high up in the air, straight past Olive, who jumped up, trying to catch it, then past Natty, who did the same with no luck. It flew onward over the high hedge into the property backing onto Lark Lodge.

'Oh, Mummy! You've lost the frisbee!'

'Well at least it didn't land on the flower borders,' said Faye, relieved.

'It probably landed on someone else's,' Natty pointed out. She looked about her. 'Where's Olive?'

They both turned in a full circle. Olive was nowhere to be seen.

'Olive!' Faye yelled, thinking, *oh god, I've lost Nick's dog too.*

A dog barked.

'Olive?' Faye exchanged a glance with Natty.

Natty pointed. 'I think she's in there.'

They both ran up to the dense hedging separating Gayle's garden from the one behind. 'There must be a gap somewhere,' said Faye. 'She's a big dog, so it must be obvious where she got through. You go that way, Natty and I will look over here.'

Natty walked along the hedge calling out 'Olive! Olive – where are you?' Suddenly she stopped. 'Mummy, I found the gap – come and see.'

Faye went over to where Natty was standing, and frowned. 'Oh, no.'

'See the flower border,' said Natty.

'Yes, of course I see it,' said Faye tightly. The flowers had been trampled where Olive had escaped Gayle's garden through a gap in the hedging beyond the flower border.

'I bet Olive already knew about this escape route,' Faye said a little suspiciously, wondering at the possibility that Olive had been allowed out in the back garden, on her own, and had taken herself off on a little adventure in the neighbouring garden.

Faye frowned at the gap. 'Oh, god. I hope Olive isn't digging up a neighbour's garden.' She frowned. 'I don't think I can crawl through that gap.'

Natty stepped forward. 'I can.'

'No!' Faye went to grab her arm, but Natty was too fast. She'd stepped on the already-trampled flowers, hunkered down, and crawled through the gap. The last thing Faye saw was the soles of her shoes before they disappeared.

Faye squatted down. 'Natty – are you there?'

'Yes, Mummy.'

'Come back this instant.'

'But I want to find Olive.' There was a pause.

'Natty?'

'Oh, wow!'

'What do you see?'

'The garden is ginormous.'

'Bigger than Gayle's?'

'Definitely.'

'And the house too. It's ginormous. I'm going to find Olive.'

'No, Natty – come back this instant!' Faye paused. 'Natty?'

This time there was no answer.

'Natty!' She'd lost the frisbee, and Olive, and now Natty! Faye remembered to breath, telling herself, *nobody is lost.* Natty isn't lost like before when she bunked off school, and got it into her head that she was catching a National Express bus to see Jake in Scotland. No, she was just in a neighbour's garden. Just the other side of this hedge. Trespassing!

Faye had no idea who the neighbour was. She had the impulse to return to the house and tell Gayle and Jake what had happened.

'Mummy.'

Her eyes went wide. 'Natty – is that you?' Faye winced. What a stupid question.

'Yes, it's me.'

Faye didn't know whether to laugh or cry at her equally absurd reply. She was just so relieved to hear her voice. 'Have you found Olive?' Faye shouted through the hedge.

'No, but I think someone else is in the garden.'

Great, thought Faye. If a big Old English Sheepdog probably destroying their borders wasn't bad enough, they were going to come across a child trespassing too. She didn't stop to ask whether they'd spotted her. 'Come straight back, Natty – right now!'

She held her breath. 'Natty?'

This time there was no reply.

Faye looked back at the house and thought of fetching Jake. No, there wasn't time. All she had to do was get in that garden.

Faye got on her hands and knees, deciding that she'd just have to buy Gayle some new plants, and somehow managed to get through the gap, coming out the other side with twigs and leaves in her hair, scratches on her face, and soil all over her light fawn chinos, which she imagined no amount of washes would get rid of. She stood up and brushed her hair out of eyes. She imagined her normally straight blonde bob looked as though she'd just backcombed it.

She put her hand to her face to shield the sun and called out, 'Natty?' She stood looking around the beautifully manicured grounds. The gardens were so peaceful, so tranquil. Natty had been right – the garden was ginormous. Faye drew in a breath when she caught sight of the house. 'Wow! What a beautiful house.' Although it appeared a bit rundown, and could do with a lick of paint and some exterior repairs – one of the exterior window shutters was hanging off its hinges – it was a stunning piece of Scottish architecture, and she could just imagine what it had looked like in its heyday.

10

Faye thought she heard her daughter's voice. She looked about her and saw Natty, Olive, and a young man with red hair who looked to be in his twenties walking across the lawn towards her.

Faye slapped a friendly smile on her face, hoping she wasn't going to get a mouthful from the owner about being an irresponsible dog owner. Olive bounded over with the frisbee in her jaws, her tail wagging furiously, obviously excited, as though she hadn't seen her for weeks.

Natty ran over and stopped in front of her mum, looking at her wide-eyed.

'Oh, sweetheart, when I didn't hear your voice, I wondered where you were.'

'Mum, you look really messy.'

'Well, that's not surprising. I just crawled through that hedge.'

'Why did you do that?' asked the young man, shaking his head but smiling all the same.

Faye suddenly felt embarrassed. Natty was fine. Olive had been found and didn't appear to have trampled any of Gayle's neighbour's flower borders. The young man seemed pleasant and clearly had not had words with Natty about trespassing. In fact, he knelt down and gave Olive a fuss.

'Mum, this is Marty.'

Faye wondered how someone so young could own such a wonderful property. *Maybe he won the lottery,* thought Faye*, or comes from a wealthy background.*

'Hi,' said Marty.

Faye thought he looked familiar. 'You were at the party last night.'

'That's right.'

The conversation stalled. If he was a good friend of Bonnie's, he probably didn't want to talk about her or the party in case he betrayed any confidences. Faye looked down at the dog, about to apologise.

'You're staying at the guesthouse,' commented Marty.

'That's right. This is my daughter, Natty.'

'We've already met.'

'Oh, of course you have.' Faye was feeling flustered. She knew why. It was very silly of her, but she imagined this was how some people felt coming face to face with very rich people – the way Rose had felt meeting Jake. Faye cursed herself for being one of those people, feeling a little intimidated under his gaze.

Faye cast her eyes down at Olive. 'I guess she can be quite the escape artist when she wants to be. It was my fault, though. I threw the frisbee too hard and it sailed over into the garden. 'Sorry about that,' Faye added. 'I hope she hasn't dug up any of your wonderful borders.'

'Not as far as I can see,' commented Marty.

'Mummy, Olive was really good, wasn't she, Marty?' Natty was looking imploringly at Marty, hoping Olive was not in big trouble.

Marty knelt again and stroked Olive's head. He got a big

sloppy doggy kiss as a reward. 'Olive, how many times have I told you not to do that,' said Marty, wiping his face.

'Oh, so you know Olive?' Faye sighed. Of course he did. The dog probably kept getting into his garden.

As if he'd read her mind, Marty said, 'You'll have to show me where she got through the gap in the hedge. Then I might be able to block it off.'

Faye and Natty led him over to the hedge. 'It's definitely somewhere along here,' Faye said. Unfortunately, the hedging all looked the same to Faye. 'At least I know it's along here where Lark Lodge backs on to your property.'

Marty gave Faye a quizzical look, and asked Natty, 'You mentioned the steam train. Did you have a nice time?'

Natty nodded her head, great big gestures indicating she'd had the best time.

Faye added, 'We had afternoon tea on the train after Natty and I had an hour or so exploring Aviemore.'

'We sat with Rose and George,' Natty chimed in. 'It was Rose's birthday. It was fantastic – but I'm starving.'

Faye suddenly remembered that Gayle was preparing the evening meal. 'Look, it's so nice of you to catch Olive for us. She belongs to one of the guests at Lark Lodge and it would have been awful if she'd got out onto the road and disappeared.'

'No worries on that score,' Marty chimed in. 'She won't wander far. In fact the only other place she ventures is into this garden. And seeing as I'm here most days, I guess she knows where to find me.'

Faye was just so glad he was being a good sport about Olive. She imagined that some people with a beautiful garden such as this would not take too kindly at all to a boisterous dog like Olive getting into their garden.

'So, we need to make our way back to Lark Lodge, and not by way of the hedge again. Can you show us the way?'

'I'll do more than that,' said Marty, rolling his shirt sleeves down. 'I'll accompany you.'

'Is it far?' Natty asked. 'My legs are tired.'

'I know a short cut,' whispered Marty. 'But it must be kept a secret.'

'A secret!' Natty's eyes went wide. 'Is it a secret door?'

Faye rolled her eyes. Natty's favourite reading book was *The Lion, the Witch, and the Wardrobe.* It had been Faye's favourite story when she was a child too.

'Well, I guess. It's a secret garden gate to a lane that leads between the houses and out to Gayle's road. And I have the key!'

Natty jumped up and down, getting excited. Olive joined in, barking. Faye just sighed. She didn't care how she got back to Gayle's, as long as she didn't have to go back through that hedge.

'It's a lot quicker than walking all the way down the drive and along the road to the next street.'

'You don't have to accompany us all the way back to Lark Lodge,' said Faye as they walked along the lawn.

'I think I should,' Marty replied.' 'It's nearly dinner time, so I need to wash up anyway because Gayle likes us to be prompt when she's cooking.'

Faye looked at him in surprise. She didn't realise that Gayle's neighbour was joining them for dinner.

'I must say, you all are very neighbourly, having dinner together. We live in London and barely know our neighbours.'

'Well, that's what comes from living in such close proximity to one another.'

Faye raised her eyebrows. She would not exactly call the two big houses, especially this grand house, and extensive grounds, living in close proximity to one another. Rather, the small two-bed maisonette in the old house where she and Natty lived, which had been converted into three flats, was what she would call close proximity.

As they crossed the lawn to the far corner, Natty and Olive following, Faye took in the back of the house again. 'You have a beautiful home. And the gardens are amazing too.'

Marty halted. 'Excuse me?'

Faye turned around to look at the young man. 'Your house. It's lovely.'

'Oh, you mean *this* house?' Marty laughed.

'Yes, this house. What else would I be talking about?' She paused. 'What's so funny?'

'I think you've mistaken me for someone else.'

'I have?'

'Yes – the owner!'

'Oh, right. So, just to clarify – you don't live here?'

'Nope. I can see we've had crossed wires. I'm here most days, I'm just not the owner.'

'Then who are you?'

Marty held up the garden fork he was carrying. 'I'm the gardener.'

'Oh.' She had noticed the garden fork. 'I thought you were just keen on gardening.'

'I am – in other people's gardens, for which I get paid. Although I think I will rather enjoy doing my own garden when I move in.'

'Oh, you're buying a house?'

'Yes, thanks to Jake Campbell-Ross. He's helping me out buying my home.'

'Oh, really?' Faye couldn't hide her surprise. Marty must be a good friend of his. 'That's so kind of him.'

'Very. In the meantime, I am staying with my good friend, Gayle, whilst waiting for my new house to be built.'

Faye shook her head, and laughed out loud. 'Oh, now I get it. When I said you are all very neighbourly, having dinner together, I thought you were actual neighbours.'

'Oh, I see how that must have been a bit confusing when I mentioned living in such close proximity to one another – I meant that I am in a bedroom just across the hall from Gayle, not in the house that backs on to hers.'

Faye laughed, wiping the tears from her eyes. 'How silly of me. I didn't see you at breakfast this morning.'

'Nah, I got up late.'

'We must have left already when you came down to breakfast.' Faye glanced at Olive. It all made sense now, why Marty wasn't fazed by the large Old English Sheepdog appearing in the garden – he lived with Olive.

'You're Faye, aren't you? I heard that Jake was returning to Lark Lodge and bringing a … friend with him.'

Faye caught the pause before he said *friend*. Yes, we're booked into two rooms. We've got the bedrooms on the top floor.'

'I heard you met when he started teacher training in London.'

'That's right,' Faye said warily. She did not want to get into a conversation about her personal relationship with Jake. She changed the subject. Looking over at the house, she asked, 'So who owns this beautiful house?'

She turned back to Marty when he didn't answer. She noticed

he was looking at her quizzically. 'What is it?'

'It's none of my business but …'

'But what?'

'I'd have thought Jake would have told you.'

'Told me what?' Faye was getting a bit tired of the game of twenty questions.

'Well, there's a nice view of this house from the attic bedrooms.'

Faye shrugged. She hadn't really taken much notice of the views from the bedroom window.

'Didn't Jake tell you about this house?'

'No.' Faye was thinking, *why should he?* It was just a gorgeous house that backed on to Gayle's gorgeous, albeit smaller, guesthouse.

Marty said, 'I guess I assumed he'd have mentioned The Lake House. I know he's not staying at his house because it's being redecorated but—'

'Oh, I knew he has a holiday home in Aviemore. I did think we would be staying there, but like you said, it's being redecorated, and besides, the house has a history, what with his wife, you know. I get the feeling he would rather not stay there with me … us.' Faye frowned, wishing she hadn't said all that.

'*Stay here*, you mean.'

'Here – I don't understand?'

'This *here* is The Lake House.' He swung his arms wide indicating the grounds of the lovely home.

Faye gaped at Marty, then at The Lake House. 'You have got to be kidding me.'

11

'I thought it was odd that you assumed I lived here. We weren't introduced at the party, were we?'

Faye shook her head. 'I'm not surprised, though. There was a lot going on.'

Marty agreed. 'Wasn't there? It just goes to show that you never know where life will take you.'

Faye agreed with that remark. But she wasn't just thinking about Bonnie. She certainly hadn't expected to find herself in Scotland, with Jake Campbell-Ross, a man she was falling in love with, and especially hadn't expected to be in the grounds of his Scottish home. She cast her gaze towards The Lake House. 'The house is amazing, isn't it? It's a wonder he wouldn't want to come back and live here,' said Faye.

'Who says he wouldn't?' remarked Marty.

Faye swiftly tore her eyes away from the house and settled her gaze on Marty. 'Did he say something?' She'd been afraid that Jake would return to his old life. Not there, though. That hadn't crossed her mind.

'Mummy, Jake's coming back to London with us – isn't he?'

Faye turned to her daughter and saw her bottom lip quiver.

She knelt down in front of her. 'Of course he is. That was just silly adult talk. Jake has a job in London, remember? And a house.' Although Faye was aware he was only renting in London. He hadn't really put down any roots. But there was one root in London, a very entrenched one – The Ross Corporation. That was what she was really afraid of; that if he stepped back into his old life, covering for Marcus while he was in rehab, he might get sucked back into that life – for good. And leave them behind.

Faye willed herself not to think about that. But it was one of the reasons she'd accepted his invitation to spend a week's holiday with him in Scotland – to delay his temporary move back to the Ross Corporation. She had noticed before they left that Jake had not been answering his phone or his text messages. She guessed they were from Marcus. She hoped Marcus just went to the rehab clinic anyway before Jake got back. Then he wouldn't have to return to the corporation – ever. She was afraid of losing him.

She wanted to spend this holiday with him more than anything, even though deep down she was still afraid of letting someone into her and Natty's life in case he bailed and broke Natty's heart – and hers. She was still undecided whether she could risk it. *But I'm here – aren't I?*

Olive ran up to them both.

Natty knelt down. 'Hey – no more kisses,' she said, after Olive had licked her cheek. Natty wiped her face and gave Olive a hug, giggling when Olive rolled over for a belly rub.

Faye knelt down and gave Olive a belly rub too. She stood up, looking at her daughter, wavering at her decision to accompany Jake on holiday. She'd been thinking of herself, not Natty. She'd forgotten her golden rule – Natty comes first. She'd kept all the dates she'd had at a distance, all the casual flings, not bringing a single man home to meet her daughter. She wasn't looking for a relationship. But unbeknown to her, she'd started a relationship, albeit a platonic one, with a man whom she'd inadvertently let into Natty's life, and into both their hearts.

What am I going to do? Her head said she should take Natty home right now and end the friendship with Jake in case something went wrong. Her heart said differently.

Faye looked at Marty. 'We'd better get back.'

'Do you want to see inside The Lake House?' asked Marty. 'I have a key. It might be your only chance before Robyn … I mean Bonnie … works her magic and totally transforms the place.'

Faye shook her head. When they had been on their way to Scotland, she'd assumed they would be staying at The Lake House, but now she was pleased they weren't. She didn't want the ghosts from Jake's past – meaning Eleanor Ross – muddying the waters. He was still married. She imagined it was hard enough for him to be there, in Aviemore, with her. She didn't think this house would help either of them.

'I want to go back to Gayle's house,' said Natty, 'and see Jake.'

'Me too.' Faye looked at Marty. 'Let's head back. Gayle will be wondering where we've got to. If we're not careful, I imagine she'll send out a search party.'

'Yeah, like what happened with Jake when he got that phone call and—' He stopped abruptly.

Faye looked at Marty. 'What was that?'

Marty dropped his gaze, and lowered his voice, although Natty was now out of earshot, running around the lawn with Olive. 'Sorry, I shouldn't have brought it up.'

'Brought what up?'

'When you phoned the guesthouse, hysterical-like, asking for

Jake. He was here in the garden when you phoned, but his mobile phone was on silent. He was, um … busy doing something. Gayle sent me to fetch him.'

'Oh, yes. I see.' Faye dropped her gaze, embarrassed.

Marty touched her arm. 'Don't be embarrassed. I understand Natty went missing. I'm glad everything worked out.'

But had it? Suddenly Faye thought of Bonnie. Everything had worked out for her. She was living in the boathouse with the man she loved and had a baby on the way. She'd had a rough time of it, by the sound of things, and Faye didn't begrudge her happiness, but it did serve to remind her that her situation was quite different, and more complicated. She had a child. And Jake was still married. What if Eleanor got better? It played on her mind, even though he'd said there was no chance of that.

She looked at the house – his late parents' family home and the Rosses' holiday home. It was much grander than she had imagined. In fact, it was nothing like she'd imagined. Unfortunately, the house brought it home to her how different their backgrounds were. Why should that matter? But still, it was another thing that was playing on her mind, another reason why, if their relationship became more than platonic, it might not last. He was used to this. This house, and a life a world away from teaching in an inner-city school. He said he loved his job, his new life in London. But she glanced at the house and thought how there would always be the spectre of his old life, the one he was accustomed to – perhaps more in tune with than he thought – calling him back.

Oh, how she wished she hadn't thrown that blasted frisbee too high and ended up there. She tore her eyes away from the house and said to Marty. 'Where's that garden gate?' She wanted out, and she'd crawl back through the hedge if she had to.

'Just over here,' said Marty. He stopped.

'What is it?' Faye asked.

'Where are Natty and Olive?'

Faye had thought they were just behind her, playing on the lawn. She turned a full three hundred and sixty degrees. There was no sign of them. 'What the hell …?' Faye yelled, 'Natty!'

Natty didn't answer, but Olive did. They both heard the dog bark. Marty took Faye's hand. 'Don't worry. I know where they are.' He led Faye across the lawn towards the house, then took a sudden left turn towards a six-foot-high hedge, heading through a gap that led into a small, hidden garden.

Natty was standing on stepping stones in the middle of a flower bed when Faye and Marty walked in. She pointed. 'Look, Mummy. I found some gravestones.'

Faye creased her brow and followed her outstretched arm to where she was pointing.

'And one of them is broken. The white one.'

Faye turned to Marty, wide-eyed. 'Are they pet gravestones?'

Marty shook his head and whispered, 'No.'

Oh, my god. There are people buried in the garden? she thought. *Aren't there laws against that?*

'This is a memorial garden for Jake's parents.'

'I see.' Faye liked that it was called a memorial garden, and thought that explained why this small, intimate garden was secluded, hidden almost from the main grounds by high hedging.

Natty skipped over and took her hand. 'Why is the white one broken?'

Faye looked at Marty.

He in turn glanced at Natty.

Faye said, 'Natty, why don't you take this …' Faye had picked up the frisbee from the lawn where Olive had dropped it. 'And go play with Olive for a moment.'

'All right.'

Faye watched her skip out of the memorial garden with Olive before she turned to the memorial stones. She shivered. It was all rather odd, their being there. No wonder Natty had stopped in surprise when she'd run in there. It was the last thing she'd expected to see. Faye felt the same. She turned to Marty, expecting the explanation she'd assumed he was about to give – out of earshot of Natty.

Marty looked at her. 'Now, I'm not in the habit of talking about my friends behind their backs …'

Especially not your friend who is also your employer, thought Faye. 'But …' Faye prompted.

'I take it from your reaction that Jake hasn't mentioned any of this …' Marty signalled the memorial stones.

Faye shook her head, thinking, *why would he?* He didn't talk about his past life with Eleanor, or The Lake House. She wandered along the six stepping stones in between the flowers, drawing closer to the memorials, to take a closer look. She thought she saw the word *Elea*, on one broken slab, and *nor*, on the other.

'I was going to clear that up,' Marty said.

Faye had seen the wheelbarrow close by, containing some fragments. It looked as though Marty had been in the process of doing just that when he was interrupted by Natty and Olive appearing in the garden.

'Someone put up a memorial stone for Eleanor – Jake's wife?' Faye said in surprise. She was about to turn and throw Marty a questioning look when she caught sight of something else. 'What's this?' she said picking up a sledgehammer.

Marty heard her. 'That's what was used to break it up.'

'That must have been hard work.'

Marty drew closer. 'Oh, that wasn't me. It was already in pieces. I was just, you know, finishing the job.'

Faye looked at the sledgehammer, and then turned her attention to Marty. 'I'm sorry, have I missed something?'

'How do you mean?'

'The memorial stone for Eleanor …' Faye didn't get it. Eleanor Campbell-Ross wasn't dead. Then again, from what little Jake had confided in her about Eleanor's condition, it was an awful thing to think, but perhaps she might as well be. She could just imagine, in a fit of anger and despair, and grief, that he'd had this erected. Then, realising what a terrible thing it was to do, he'd destroyed it – or tried to.

'I think he was having some sort of breakdown,' confided Marty. 'I asked him if he wanted me to try and fix it. I'm not a stone mason, but I thought I could ask around town. Perhaps Mr Gillespie knew someone. But he was adamant it had to go.'

'Of course it had to go. She isn't—' Faye stopped abruptly.

'She isn't – *what*?'

Then it dawned on her. No one knew, outside the family. They'd kept Eleanor's condition, even whether she was alive or dead, a closely guarded secret. The presumption was that she'd died. And that's the way the family, the way Jake, had left it.

Faye shook her head. He'd confided in her, and it wasn't her secret to tell. 'Nothing … nothing.'

'But it is – something, isn't it?' remarked Marty, looking at the gravestone.

'Really, it isn't.'

'You know something, don't you?'

Faye dropped the sledgehammer. 'Now, where is that daughter of mine?' said Faye, swiftly changing the subject as she marched out of the little memorial garden, thinking of that blasted frisbee.

'Mummy! Come and play.'

Faye marched over and took her hand. 'No, the game is over.'

'Why?'

'We've got to get back to Gayle's for dinner, remember? You said a moment ago you wanted to go back to Gayle's and see Jake. You want to do that – right?'

Natty kicked a tuft of grass. 'I suppose.'

'Good.' Faye glanced over her shoulder. Marty was following. 'Marty, can you lead the way please?' She wished she knew where the shortcut was so that she could just take Natty and Olive back herself.

'This way,' Marty said.

They walked in silence through the gate and down a narrow lane between houses. It led into Gayle's street. Faye was relieved they'd walked in silence. Marty had not asked any awkward questions about Eleanor. She did not want to put her foot in it.

Marty seemed to sense that the subject was closed. 'So, I expect Gayle will be wondering where you were. I think perhaps best not mention Olive getting through the hedge into the garden. Don't want to get Nick's dog into trouble.'

Faye got the idea that Marty was good friends with Nick and didn't want him to leave because of his naughty dog.

Marty added, 'Olive has become a big part of the family at the guesthouse. She is so gentle and friendly. You can't help falling in love with her.'

'My lips are sealed,' said Faye.

'So are mine,' said Natty, making a show of zipping her lips together. She didn't want Olive to leave the guesthouse either. 'Besides, it wasn't really Olive's fault, it was yours, Mummy, because you threw the frisbee too high.' Natty had the frisbee in her hand. She held it up.

'Yes, I'll own up, of course. I just hope I haven't spoiled dinner.'

Marty quipped, 'I think Gayle can manage that all on her own.'

'What was that?' Faye asked.

Marty sighed. 'Ah, you didn't eat at the guesthouse last night. I'm afraid that unless Gayle is cooking stew, you'd better be prepared to sneak in a takeaway later.'

Faye stared at him. Jake had forewarned her. 'Sounds bad.'

'Yeah, I'm afraid so.'

'What's bad?' Natty asked. She'd been busy playing around with the frisbee behind her back, taunting Olive. Now the dog had it in her jaws playing a game of tug-of-war with Natty. Natty let go of the frisbee and looked at her mum.

Faye was not in the habit of lying to her daughter. 'Apparently, Gayle's cooking.'

Natty frowned. 'Can I have fish fingers instead, then?'

'We'll have to see if Gayle has any in her freezer. I think I might join you,' Faye joked.

'Count me in,' said Marty. He was not joking.

Faye said, 'Gayle is cooking a pie, apparently. Sounds as though she's going to a lot of trouble.'

They both knew they'd be duty-bound to eat it. Faye just hoped that Jake had managed to help bake the pie, otherwise who knew what they were in for.

As they approached the front door, Natty said, 'Does Jake know the white stone was broken?'

Faye came to an abrupt halt at the front door. She rolled her eyes. She should have known that Natty wouldn't let it go.

Marty said, 'I think Jake was having some sort of break—'

'In!' Faye quickly said. She turned to Natty. 'Someone broke in and damaged it. Now it's beyond repair and needs removing.' Faye inwardly groaned. So much for not lying to her daughter. She glared at Marty, who clearly didn't spend much time around children. She'd rather he didn't go saying things about Jake having a breakdown in front of a nine-year-old. Even though she wouldn't understand what that meant, she would ask, and most likely ask Jake.

'Right – Marty?'

He looked at her quizzically.

She reiterated, 'It must have been a break-in – right?'

He looked from Faye and Natty. 'Okay, I get it.'

Faye turned to Natty once more. 'Now look, it's not nice when that sort of thing happens.' Faye was thinking of Jake's breakdown, but as far as Natty was concerned they were talking about the break-*in*. 'I'm sure Jake won't want to talk about it or have you ask him more questions. So, can we agree to keep this between us – our secret?' That was another thing Faye hated – secrets. But sometimes you just had to keep them for the greater good.

Natty nodded. 'Yes, Mummy.'

Faye turned around and eyed Marty.

He nodded too.

Faye said, 'Good. Now that's settled, are we ready for that pie?'

'I want fish fingers!' Natty said.

'So, do I,' Marty murmured. They all trooped into the house and were surprised by a rather lovely smell of home-baked pie wafting from the kitchen.

Natty turned to her mum. 'Can I have the pie instead?'

12

'So, how long are you staying at Gayle's?' Marty asked as Faye opened the front door.

'For a week.'

'Something smells nice,' said Nick, walking down the stairs towards them, a look of surprise on his face. 'I think I might take up Gayle's invitation to dinner after all.'

Marty said, 'Yeah, I was thinking the same thing.'

'Can I have pie too?' Natty asked again.

'Hey, guys,' said Nick, looking from Faye to Natty as Olive jumped up at him for a fuss. 'How was your day?'

Faye nodded. 'Oh, yes. We went into Aviemore and took a trip on the steam train.'

'It was fun,' said Natty. 'I liked the finger sandwiches, and the little scones.'

Faye smiled. 'Yes, we had afternoon tea on the train too.'

'Sounds amazing.' Nick looked at his dog.

'Oh, Olive didn't come on the train too,' said Faye. 'We left her with Annie and Evie at the shop in town, and collected her on the way home. Hope that was okay.'

'Of course.' Nick petted his dog. 'I hope you've been a good dog for the new guests today, Olive.'

Everyone fell silent, even Natty.

Busy giving his dog a fuss, Nick looked up. 'What?'

'Mummy threw a frisbee too high and it went into Jake's garden.'

'The Lake House?' said Nick.

Marty nodded.

'Anyway we got the frisbee back, thanks to Marty.' Faye deciding she'd much rather not elaborate on exactly what had happened. They'd all agreed they didn't want to get Nick's sweet dog Olive into trouble.

Nick stared at Faye. 'You've got a little twig in your hair.'

'Oh, have I?' She patted her hair, found the twig, and felt her face grow hot with embarrassment. She'd forgotten how she must look, with her hair a mess and her chinos muddy at the knees.

'What happened to you?' Jake said in surprise, walking out of the kitchen and catching sight of Faye. 'I thought I heard the front door.' He was wiping up a dish with a dishcloth.

Faye sighed. 'It's windy out there,' she said lamely.

Jake cast his gaze down at her chinos.

'I, um … slipped over playing frisbee. You know what? I'm just going upstairs to freshen up before dinner.' She rushed up the stairs.

Jake smiled after her. 'All right. There's a real treat waiting for you. I think Gayle's pie is going to turn out rather delicious.'

Marty and Nick exchanged a glance. Nick whispered, 'Do you mean *your* pie?'

Jake held a finger to his lips in a shushing motion.

Natty eyed the adults and frowned. 'Are we keeping another secret?'

Jake turned to Natty. '*Another* secret?'

Natty looked up at Jake sheepishly before grabbing Olive's collar. 'Come on, let's go in the kitchen.'

'So, what are your plans for tomorrow?' Nick asked Jake as he, Jake and Marty followed Natty into the kitchen.

'I visited the tourist information today, and the lady made some good suggestions. I picked up some leaflets, but I haven't decided yet.'

'Do you like cycling?' Nick asked.

'Actually, I do. I cycle into work and back, helps me clear my head either end of the day.'

'I've got a bike,' said Natty, 'but I left it at home.'

Nick grinned. 'You know, that's not a problem. You can hire bikes.'

Natty brightened as they all walked into the kitchen.

Gayle shut the oven door after checking the pie. She turned around, still wearing her apron.

'If your pie tastes half as good as it smells, Gayle, I think you've lived up to …' Nick pointed at the apron ... '*World's Best Cook*.'

'Oh, I wouldn't say that.' Gayle smiled all the same, looking rather chuffed with herself. 'Of course, Jake did give me a hand.'

Nick exchanged a knowing glance with Jake but didn't let on that he knew who had really baked the pie.

'What were you saying about cycling?' Gayle asked, taking off her apron and hanging it up behind the pantry door with the apron Jake had already taken off.

'There's some great cycle routes around the lochs,' said Nick.

'What about the Green Loch?' said Gayle.

Nick eyed her. 'The Green Loch?'

'You know, the loch in Glenmore Forest Park. I'm sure you've taken a run there.'

'Oh, yes. I drove to that one, though. It's not far from Loch Morlich, about a fifteen-minute drive from Aviemore.'

Gayle turned to Natty. 'Legend has it fairies live there.'

'Fairies?' Natty looked wide-eyed at Gayle.

She smiled. 'Yes.'

'I'd like to go there.'

Nick turned to Jake as they both took a seat at the kitchen table, along with Marty. 'Have you done much cycling in this area?'

'Nah, we used to spend most of Christmas at The Lake House.'

'I like The Lake House,' commented Natty, kneeling in front of Olive, rearranging the ribbons that were all askew after her dash through the privet fence.

Faye had just walked into the kitchen, and heard Natty too. She stopped abruptly and looked at Jake.

Jake's smile dropped. 'What did you just say, Natty?'

'I like your house, and your garden. It's much bigger than Gayle's house and garden.' Natty looked over at Gayle. 'I like your house too – lots and lots.'

Gayle smiled knowingly. 'Would that have anything to do with Olive being here by any chance?'

Natty replied, 'Maybe.'

Jake looked from Natty to Faye. 'What were you doing at The Lake House? You didn't mention that.'

Faye thought, *that isn't all we haven't mentioned*. She stared at Natty, hoping she didn't bring up the memorial garden, or the white memorial stone, or the lie she'd spun about Jake's break-in. That business with erecting a memorial stone for his not-dead wife definitely sounded like some sort of breakdown, as Marty had said.

She threw him a sideways glance. Marty avoided her gaze and said, 'Gayle, do you need some help dishing up the pie?'

Faye frowned. He was clearly keeping out of it.

'Mummy threw the frisbee too high, and it went over the hedge into your garden. We went to fetch it.'

Jake's face softened. 'Oh, I see. Easily done.'

'Yeah, and Marty found the frisbee,' continued Natty. 'He told us it's your house.'

Faye glared at her daughter. *Please, please do not mention—*

'Jake, can I go and play frisbee in your garden with Olive? I love it there.'

Faye exhaled in relief, thinking, *oh, thank god, she can keep a secret.*

'I promise I won't go in the hidden garden with the gravestones.' Natty whirled around and looked at her mum, her lips forming into a great big *O*.

Faye's shoulders sagged.

Nick and Gayle said in unison, 'Gravestones?' turning to Jake.

Marty said, 'I told them they're memorial stones, for your parents and—' he halted, his eyes locked with Jake's.

'And the broken one,' said Natty thinking she was being helpful, when she wasn't.

There was a moment's silence. Everyone in the room, apart from Natty, sensed that the conversation had moved on to a subject that had touched a nerve.

'Well, if I don't dish up the pie,' said Gayle in the awkward silence, 'it's going to spoil.' She bent down by the oven and got out the pie while Nick asked Faye and Jake, 'So, are you going on a bike ride tomorrow to the Green Loch?'

Faye, who hadn't ridden a bike for years, and probably would have preferred an amble around the lake, was so relieved by the change of subject that she exclaimed, 'Oh, yes! It will be such fun!' a little too jovially.

Jake gave her a sideways glance. She imagined he'd recalled that she didn't actually care much for his mode of transport back and forward to work.

Nick grinned. 'You'll have a great time.'

Faye slapped a smile on her face, hoping she remembered how to ride a bike and not fall off. She did not fancy having another embarrassing episode like the one that day, returning to the guesthouse looking and feeling a right mess. She had changed out of her dirty chinos. She decided that the next day, she was going to wear a pair of dark blue jeans, just in case.

13

Jake pulled the car to a stop in the car park beside the bike hire hub in Glenmore Forest and smiled when he saw the long row of bikes for hire. He hadn't booked anything in advance, hoping there were suitable bikes available for two adults and a child. Although Natty was very keen to ride a bike, and so was he, he knew there were plenty of walking trails in the forest if it didn't work out. They'd woken up to blue skies and sunshine, so Jake didn't hang around on the internet trying to pre-book. They were all keen to leave the house and get the most out of the day exploring the forest and loch.

Apparently Glenmore Forest Park was a really good choice for cycling routes, although Nick had mentioned that you could cycle from Aviemore along the Old Logging Way, a six-mile gentle trail that was traffic-free and would take them all the way to Glenmore. He'd suggested the idea to Faye. He could have organised having hire bikes delivered to the guesthouse. But although she'd appeared enthusiastic the previous evening about going cycling, she was honest enough to admit that she might find it a struggle cycling six miles to Glenmore before they'd even started riding the forest trails.

'I'm going to choose a bike!' said Natty excitedly as she opened the car door.

Faye said, 'Wait for us, Natty. Remember, you're in a car park!'

Natty waited by the car for Jake and her mum before walking over to the bike hire.

'I want this one!' Natty exclaimed, choosing a bright red mountain bike.

Jake and Faye chose a mountain bike each too. While one of the employees adjusted the height of the seat for Faye, Jake went into the shop to pay. He walked out carrying three helmets and a map of cycle routes in the forest.

'So, I've booked the bikes out for half a day.'

'But I wanted to spend the whole day here,' said Natty.

Jake smiled. 'And we will. There's plenty of time for some rides in the forest.' When he'd paid for the bikes and had been given the map, they'd suggested The Lodge Trail, and the lower section of the Ryvoan Trail from the visitor centre, which were easy cycle routes through the forest, suitable for everyone.

'Then in the afternoon we can have a picnic by the loch.'

Faye said, 'It was really thoughtful of Gayle to pack us a picnic.'

The picnic basket, along with a picnic blanket and foldaway chairs, was in the boot of the car. 'Yes, it was so kind of Gayle to make us up some lunch.' Jake slipped his helmet on. Faye was just buckling the strap of Natty's under her chin.

Jake stood by his bike and glanced over at the visitor centre. He imagined there was more information there about the forest, lochs, and family activities. Gayle had mentioned there was a café on site, but she had been right when she'd said they'd be lucky to find a table. With the number of cars in the car park already, he imagined it would be very busy come lunch time. He turned to

Faye. 'I think Gayle was right when she said the café would be busy for lunch.'

Faye put on her helmet. 'I prefer a picnic. Didn't Nick mention there was a beach where we could sit with our lunch?'

'Yes, across the road from the visitor centre is Loch Morlich beach and the start of the cycling trails.'

Faye had put on her cycle hat but was having trouble adjusting the strap to clip the buckle. 'What am I doing wrong?' she asked, sounding frustrated.

Jake looked at her, hoping the cycle ride wasn't going to turn out to be a bad idea. He and Natty were looking forward to it, but he got the impression Faye was looking forward to getting it over with. He hoped that wasn't really the case, but the look on her face suggested otherwise.

'I'm bored. When are we going?' Natty asked, sitting astride her bike, feet on the floor, moving the bike back and forward underneath her.

'Natty, will you just give me a minute!' Faye sounded irritated. 'Oh, these blasted straps. I can't seem to …'

Jake stepped in front of her. 'Here – let me help you with that.'

Faye let go of the straps as Jake first adjusted the helmet on her head. 'I think you had it too far back. It needs to sit on your head like so.'

'It keeps wobbling.'

'Ah, that's the problem.' Jake took the hat off her head and made an adjustment. 'There, it should fit better now.' He put it on her head. 'How's that?'

'It feels tight.'

'Yeah, it's meant to be snug.' Jake made one more adjustment and put it back on her head. 'Better?'

'Yes, not loose but not too tight either.'

'Oh, come on!' Natty exclaimed.

Jake took the straps and did up the small plastic buckle under her chin to secure the hat.

'I feel like I'm five years old,' complained Faye as he did so.

Jake smiled. 'There, we're all set.'

'Thank god!'

They both turned to Natty, Jake finding her comment rather funny. Her mother, on the other hand, did not. 'We'll have none of that lip, young lady. Otherwise there will be no bike ride.'

'But all I said was—'

Faye shot her a warning look.

Natty sat down on her saddle and fiddled with the handlebars.

Jake slung his backpack, which contained some water bottles, snacks, and the cycling trail maps, on his back and sat astride his bike, watching Faye gingerly sit on the saddle. 'You two go ahead,' he said. 'I'll follow.'

Natty had just set off when she stopped abruptly. Jake stopped too. 'Everything all right?'

'Can I have my own water and snacks? I want to put them in my backpack.'

Jake glanced back at Faye, waiting for her to catch up. The bike wobbled as she tried to change gear. Jake took a deep breath, hoping the bike ride didn't start with her falling off. To his relief, she changed gear and caught up with them across the car park. She braked abruptly. 'Ooh. Going to take some getting used to.' She looked from Natty to Jake. 'Why have we stopped?'

'Is it okay if Natty has her water in snacks in her backpack?'

'Of course.'

A moment later, Natty not only had water and a snack bar, but a compass and binoculars as well that Nick had lent Jake the previous evening.

Faye looked at Jake and raised an eyebrow. 'Looks like someone is prepared for an adventure.'

They reached the road and walked their bikes to the other side, where the cycling trails began.

'Best we all stick together on the paths,' Faye said to Natty as they got back on their bikes.

'Don't worry, Mummy. We won't leave you behind.'

Faye mumbled something Jake didn't quite catch. He imagined when she'd said sticking together, she had been picturing just Natty riding off too far ahead.

As they set off through the pine trees, following the cycling trail, the forest appeared ethereal in the low-lying mist. Jake slipped the route map into the map holder on his handlebars. He checked the time, as they needed to be back by lunchtime. The bikes were booked out to other people for the afternoon. Jake was looking forward to the surprise he had in store for Natty in the afternoon – courtesy of Marty's recommendation that morning.

The early morning sun started filtering through the tops of the trees as they slowly cycled along the gravel path. Jake was in the lead, Natty followed, and Faye brought up the rear. Every now and then, Jake cast a glance behind him, checking he wasn't cycling too fast. It wasn't Natty he was worried about leaving behind.

'It's just as well we've got mountain bikes with thick tyres,' Faye shouted out. 'Even so, I think I'm going to have a sore behind by the time we get back.'

Natty laughed out loud, finding the comment very funny. Jake just nodded. He'd forgotten about that issue for someone who hadn't cycled for years, although Faye had chosen a bike with a large, padded saddle which would hopefully prove comfortable for the duration of the cycle ride.

A moment later, Natty appeared by his side as the path widened. 'Oh, I thought we'd stay in formation, you know, one behind the other.' Jake wasn't sure if they'd meet other cyclists coming from the other direction, but if they did, there would be room to pass without stopping.

'But the path is wide here, and I want to cycle next to you.'

Jake glanced back at Faye. She didn't seem to mind; her attention was drawn to the lush forest scenery.

'Well, all right. But if we see any cyclists up ahead, do you think you could quickly drop back behind me to let them pass?'

'Yes.'

'Great.' Jake smiled at Natty cycling beside him. She said, 'We could race!'

Jake shook his head, reminding her what she'd said not five minutes ago to Faye: *Don't worry, Mummy. We won't leave you behind.*

Natty frowned. 'Oh, yes. I forgot.'

Jake lowered his voice. 'I don't think Mummy has ridden a bike for years, so I think we will have to keep it slow, so she can keep up.' He glanced behind him once more, to find Faye had got into a rhythm. She was smiling, clearly enjoying herself. She caught Jake looking her way. 'This is wonderful. I'm so glad we did this after all.'

After all. Jake smiled and nodded, relieved she was finally enjoying herself. He had noticed she'd been very quiet on the way to the forest. 'Me too!' he shouted back.

'This is such fun!' Natty exclaimed. 'Can we stop for a snack soon?'

Faye heard that. 'We've hardly started. Let's not stop just yet.'

Jake agreed. 'I think we'll come across some nice views, and even a bench along the trail where we can stop for a break.'

'Sounds great!' Faye said.

They kept to the well-defined cycle path, and the landscape of scented forest pines continued.

'Look at the mountain!' said Natty, taking her hand off the handlebars and pointing.

'Wow!' Jake looked up at the majestic views of the Cairngorm Mountain over the treetops. 'What an amazing backdrop.'

'What was that?' Faye called out.

Jake glanced over his shoulder and repeated what he'd just said, raising his voice so she could hear him.

'This bike ride is just amazing!' Faye replied.

Jake was beyond pleased that everyone was having an exceptionally good time. He felt confident that the second day of their holiday together was going to turn out just fine, in spite of his initial misgivings about the bike ride idea.

14

They continued through the forest, the silence only interrupted by their bicycle tyres crunching softly on the gravel path. Jake kept his eye on the map as they reached a fork in the path. 'Natty, we're going to turn here.' He put his arm out to indicate they were turning right on to another track.

'Hey!' Faye shouted, 'are we having a driving lesson?'

Jake heard Natty giggling, and he smiled. The air was cool but filled with the fresh scent of pine trees, which stretched high above, casting long shadows over the trail.

'I think we'll have to cycle one behind the other now,' said Jake realising that the trail was slightly narrower there, with more twists and turns, which meant it wasn't really advisable to cycle in pairs just in case someone on a bike whizzed round a bend from the other direction.

Natty started pedalling eagerly ahead. 'Can I take the lead?' Natty asked even though she was already ahead of Jake.

Jake glanced at the trail map. The obvious route continued now until a loch, so Natty could easily take the lead and they wouldn't get lost. Even so, Jake glanced over his shoulder at Faye to check that was okay. He didn't want to make the mistake this holiday of stepping on Faye's toes when it came to her daughter. As much as he would have loved to be, he was not Natty's dad. Right now, he was a family friend who did not want to mess things up with Faye.

'Is it okay if she takes the lead?' Jake called over his shoulder.

'She already has!' Faye called out, but there was no sarcasm in her voice. 'Don't go too fast, please, Natty.'

'Don't worry, I won't!' she called back.

On a straight stretch, Jake dropped back to cycle next to Faye, Natty in front of them. 'Are you enjoying it?' Jake asked, even though he could tell she was.

'Oh, the scenery is amazing. And this is *so* much better than walking. We're seeing so much more of the forest.'

'Yes, and it won't be long to the loch where we can stop for a break, before heading back.'

'Sounds like a plan.'

Jake grinned as they cycled on together in silence, Jake keeping an eye out for any bends in the trail and oncoming cyclists in case he needed to quickly change position.

Faye seemed to read his mind. 'If we see anyone, I'll slow down, and you can go in front of me behind Natty.'

'Sounds like a plan,' Jake said, repeating what Faye had said a moment ago.

They exchanged a smile, their eyes lingering on one another. He thought about how, if he wasn't riding a bike, and they didn't have cycle helmets on that would clash, he could just lean in and kiss her. He suddenly wished they weren't on bikes, but walking together instead – a romantic walk through the pine forest. Then, maybe …

Jake thought of arriving at the loch. Perhaps a little walk there.

Would they hold hands, perhaps kiss?

That lovely thought was interrupted by Natty shouting out, 'There's someone on a bike!'

Faye slowed down, and Jake sped up to get in between Faye and Natty. They all stayed in a line on the right as several cyclists, teenagers in mud-splattered cycling gear, whizzed past them at speed. By the state of their clothing and their bikes they'd clearly been mountain-biking proper and had just come down to join the easy meandering family-friendly forest trail. Jake glanced over his shoulder and saw the four young men disappear off the trail into the forest.

'Well done, Natty, for spotting them!' Jake called out.

'I heard them first.'

'Well, you make an excellent cycle trail leader. Keep it up.'

'I will.'

Jake rejoined Faye, cycling beside her, and saw her smiling at him. He wondered why. 'What?'

She nodded in Natty's direction. 'It's great, you've given her some responsibility. It's great for me too. I find it …' she paused. 'Being an only parent, raising her on my own, I know I find it hard to let her go, be her own person. That does sound silly, I suppose. It's not like she's a teenager yet. She's only nine, but I sometimes wonder when I'll ever let her spread her wings a little. Obviously, though, when she skipped school and scared the life out of me by trying to get to Scotland, that was just a step too far.'

'Sorry about that.' Jake still felt he was to blame. After all, it had been him she was trying to find.

'No, don't apologise. I want to say thank you for this. It's the little things, like today, building her confidence – and mine, that I can give her a little independence and responsibility. And that's all because of you, Jake.'

Jake didn't know what to say. *Does that mean I'd make a good dad?* That was what he wanted to say. But of course, how could he? The first thing he needed to know was whether their relationship could go to the next level. Did Faye think he'd make a good partner, a good husband? He presumed she did, otherwise why would she be there? Deep down, Jake was aware that wasn't really the issue. Was she ready for that sort of commitment? That was the question. He suspected that was what she was there to find out.

They rode on in silence, passing dense clusters of ferns and wildflowers, their vibrant colours brightening the woodland. Jake thought he'd spotted something in the forest. He had told Natty that if they were lucky, they might see a red squirrel darting through the branches or catch a glimpse of a deer through the trees.

Jake was beginning to feel quite warm, with the mid-morning sunshine filtering through the dense pine trees either side of the trail. Although he cycled to work and back every day, this was different. The route, which was on a gentle incline, needed more effort than the tarmacked roads in London. The mountain bikes were also quite heavy, the wide off-road tyres slowing their progress on the gravel bike trail. He glanced at Faye, whom he noticed had dropped back a little. He imagined she was starting to find it an effort too. The only one who wasn't was up ahead, the distance between Natty and the two of them growing bigger.

Faye noticed too. 'Natty!' she called out breathlessly. 'Please slow down a bit, darling, and let us catch up.'

Natty braked and came to a halt at the side of the trail, waiting for them.

Jake cycled at Faye's pace for the hundred yards to Natty. Faye came to a halt behind her. 'Oh, thank you, Natty. Mummy is getting a bit tired.'

'I'm not!'

'I gathered that,' Faye replied as she turned to Jake. 'Is it far now – the loch?'

Jake handed her a bottle of water and shook his head. 'We're nearly there.' He'd chosen the route to Loch an Eilein, originally intending to stop for a picnic and a walk around the loch afterwards, but the lovely picnic hamper that Gayle had packed was too big to carry with them. And besides that, they only had the bikes for half a day, which meant that even if he'd taken all the packed lunch out of the hamper and packed it in his backpack, there would not be time for a leisurely lunch. It was better this way, to do the cycle ride with a pitstop at the loch, and then return the bikes, leaving them free for the rest of the day to enjoy a leisurely lunch at Loch Morlich beach, and then pop into the visitor centre.

Faye put the cap back on the water bottle and handed it to Jake. 'Right, let's set off,' she said. 'The sooner we get to the loch …' she trailed off, avoiding Jake's gaze.

Jake eyed her. He imagined what she was thinking – *the sooner we can get back and ditch the bikes.*

'Let's go!' said Natty.

They set off again, Jake beside Natty. He didn't want her sailing past the sign for the loch.

Natty spotted the sign first. 'Race you to that sign!' Natty shouted as she pumped the pedals, moving ahead of him at a speed.

Faye shouted out, 'Be careful – not too fast!'

Jake noticed Natty was now mastering her gears as he caught up with her. She was waiting by the sign. 'Can I be the leader on the way back?' Natty asked when Jake came to a halt beside her.

He smiled. 'I don't see why not. We're returning the route we came. Do you think you can remember the way?'

She nodded.

Even if she didn't, Jake would still let her stay up front, keeping an eye on the route himself.

They both stood by the sign, astride their bikes, holding on to the handlebars, waiting patiently for Faye to join them. 'Is it much further?' Faye asked when she stopped by the sign too. 'My arse needs a rest from this saddle.'

'Mum, you just said a naughty word!' Natty remonstrated, giving her mum a stern look.

'Oh, I um, meant bottom.'

With a wisp of a smile, Jake pretended to look at his map, not wanting to be caught laughing at Faye being told off by a nine-year-old.

Natty said, 'You don't need to look at the map. The sign points down there.'

Jake folded the map away before they set off.

15

As they neared Loch an Eilein, the landscape opened up to reveal the serene waters of the loch, its surface glimmering in the sunshine. The ancient ruins of a small castle on the island in the middle of the loch stood enveloped in a sense of timelessness and mystery. Faye spotted some picnic benches along the edge of the loch. They cycled over and stopped beside the nearest one. Faye propped her bike up against a tree nearby and stood taking in the peaceful view of the loch. 'It's so beautiful,' she said in a hushed voice, almost afraid to interrupt the tranquillity. She turned to Jake, who was smiling. Natty's eyes were wide with wonder. In the distance, the haunting cry of a curlew echoed, a reminder of the untouched beauty of the Scottish Highlands. The combination of the forest, the loch, and the wildlife made the ride feel like a magical adventure, one Jake hoped Natty, and Faye, would treasure for years to come.

Faye said, 'I wish we'd brought the picnic after all.'

Jake placed his bike next to Faye's. 'I know, but there wouldn't have been time. We can have a snack here before we set off.'

Faye nodded. 'Good idea.'

Jake took the rucksack off his back to find a banana and a

cereal bar. Natty rummaged in her backpack and found her own snacks. A group of ducks paddled lazily across the water, leaving gentle ripples in their wake. 'Before I have my snack, I'm going to feed the ducks,' Natty shouted excitedly as she ran toward the water's edge with a brown paper bag in her hand.

Faye and Jake followed her to the water's edge. 'What has she got in her hand? Faye asked, turning to Jake.

'Nick said he often cycles to the loch,' Jake replied. 'It's one of his favourite spots. And he always brings some bird seed. So this morning he filled up a bag ready for Natty to bring with her.' He kept an eye on Natty as she stood on one of the small boulders lining the shore.

'That's so thoughtful of him. I'm really enjoying staying at the guesthouse, Jake. Meeting Gayle and her mum, and Nick and Marty – it feels like a little family, doesn't it?'

Jake nodded in agreement. 'And don't forget Olive.'

'How could I? Natty is banging on enough about getting a dog.'

Jake pursed his lips, hoping that didn't spoil Faye's holiday, or her stay at the guesthouse. He changed the subject. 'It's going to be a bit different from this evening, because it won't just be us, Gayle, Doris, Marty and Nick.' Jake purposely didn't mention Olive again.

'Oh, that's right. There are more guests arriving.'

'Yes.' Jake hoped the new arrivals were a nice bunch and didn't spoil their holiday. Gayle's guesthouse wasn't that big. He pictured late-night revellers who came back at all hours, talking loudly, and were disrespectful to the other guests, who needed their sleep. It wouldn't work. There was an alternative if that were to happen. Jake's thoughts turned to The Lake House as they stood in silence, watching Natty's progress as she followed the ducks along the shore, pausing to throw small handfuls of seed in the water. The silence was broken by the quacking of the ducks vying for the food.

'Don't go too far!' Faye shouted, looking anxiously at her daughter.

'Calm down, Faye – she hasn't gone that far,' Jake blurted, instantly regretting that remark.

'What do you mean, *calm down*?'

Jake sighed. He was about to apologise for that thoughtless comment, but Faye was already reminding him why he should not have made it.

'You have no idea what gut-wrenching fear I experienced thinking I had lost Natty for good when she went missing.'

Jake stared at her. Actually, he did have an idea. Of course he did. He loved Natty like he imagined he would his own child. But he kept his mouth shut while Faye admonished him for his remark.

'You are not a parent. You have no clue the hellish time you go through when you discover your child is missing.'

She was right: he wasn't a parent. And Faye had every right to be angry at him for forgetting just what she'd been through a little over a week ago.

Jake mumbled an apology, feeling embarrassed. He cast his gaze over at the wooden picnic tables set back from the shore behind them and thought it best he went to sit over there and give Faye some space. He hoped she forgave him for that comment. He was about to do just that, sit with the bikes by the picnic table alone, thinking Faye would prefer some time with Natty, when she caught his arm. 'Where are you going?'

He pointed. 'I'm going to sit over there.'

'Stay – please.'

'But I thought, after what I just said—'

'I'm sorry, Jake.'

He looked at her in surprise. 'I'm the one who needs to apologise.'

Faye cocked her head to one side. 'You're talking about Natty playing truant to try and find you.'

Of course he was. It was his fault what Faye went through when Natty went missing. He said as much. 'So, there's nothing for you to apologise for.'

Faye exhaled loudly. 'Oh, but there is.' She turned to look at him. 'For starters, I know how much Natty means to you.'

Jake eyed her, thinking, *but do you know how much* you *mean to me?*

'And what you mean to Natty. You're like a father to her. She asks me all the time if you can be her daddy.'

Jake swallowed, trying to keep his emotions in check.

'I shouldn't have said what I said about you not understanding because you're not a parent. That was really thoughtless of me. I hope you can forgive me.'

Jake looked away when he guessed Faye wasn't just referring to his relationship with Natty, but another child – his child – whom he'd lost when a pregnant Eleanor had been injured so badly. He'd told Faye about the fact that he'd just found out he was going to be a father, and then that terrible Christmas had robbed him of both his wife and his unborn child.

'I hope you can forgive me, Jake.'

Suddenly, without thinking, he put his arms around Faye, drawing her close.

She didn't resist. Instead, she melted into his embrace. She stared up at him, and their lips moved closer. All the while, Jake was thinking, *this can't be real, only the second day of our holiday – our first kiss.* He'd just closed his eyes, anticipating her soft, rosy-red lips on his, when he heard a child scream, and then a splash.

Jake's eyes shot open.

Faye was already running along the edge of the loch. 'Where's Natty?' he yelled. He couldn't see her.

Catching up with Faye, he saw she was holding a brown paper bag in her hands. 'Oh god!'

Jake looked at the rock, which was more like a stepping stone, which Natty had been standing on just a moment ago. There were several more which led towards the water.

'She fell in!'

Without thinking, they both dived into the water and came up for air almost simultaneously, gasping. 'I can't see her!'

'I can't see anything down there!' Jake yelled back. He could feel his heart beating in his chest in abject fear. He stared at Faye, who was shivering. She was as white as a sheet.

They were staring at each other as they both took another deep breath, about to go under the freezing water again. Then they heard a familiar voice. 'What are you doing?'

They both looked towards the shore to see Natty standing there with the water lapping at her feet. She was completely dry and eating a bag of crisps, looking at them quizzically.

'Natty!' they both cried with relief.

She said, 'I didn't think we were swimming in the loch.'

'We weren't swimming! We thought you'd fallen in.'

Natty munched on another crisp and screwed up her nose, frowning. 'How would I fall in the loch from the stones?'

'But we heard a scream, and then a splash.'

Natty sighed and shook her head. 'A duck came right up and pecked my ankle. I screamed, and ran up the beach with it charging after me. I threw my bottle of water at it. The bottle must have landed in the water.' She looked at them. 'Didn't you see me running to the picnic bench?'

Faye and Jake exchanged a glance. They'd been too busy nearly kissing. When they'd heard her scream, they'd looked straight to the water's edge. She was gone. If they'd only looked the other way they would have seen her standing by her bike, looking for a packet of crisps in her bike basket.

They clambered out of the loch, shivering with cold and feeling very, very silly.

'You're very wet,' said Natty, stating the obvious as she continued to stand there, eating her crisps, staring at them.

'And very cold!' said Faye.

Jake put her arm around her, and pulled her close. Not that it did any good; he was just as wet and cold as she was.

Faye suddenly started to laugh. 'Don't we make a such a silly pair.'

Jake's lips curled into a smile. 'That we do.'

Faye added, 'At least there's nobody else about.'

That gave Jake an idea. 'Come on.' They walked to the bikes and the rucksack Jake had left on the ground by his bike. He got out two three-quarter length lightweight rain macs. 'Here.'

'What's this for?'

'We can get out of our wet clothes.'

Natty said, 'You could hang your clothes over the bikes to dry.'

Jake shook his head. 'Unfortunately, that won't work.'

'Why not?'

'They're dripping wet, Natty,' replied Faye.

'Look, if we cycle back wearing the rain macs, I know it's not ideal, but I wouldn't be surprised if the visitor centre sells hiking gear. I'm sure we'll pick up a change of clothes.'

Faye frowned. 'Only if you go in there and buy some.'

Jake smiled. 'All right. You could hide in the toilets.'

'Good.'

Natty finished her crisps and shook her head at them, tutting. She commented, 'What were you thinking?' sounding like a parent, not a child. 'Shall we go, then?'

The rain macs were large enough to slip on over their wet clothes so they could change out of their clothes with some dignity and privacy. Jake thanked his lucky stars that along with the picnic, Gayle had insisted he pack the rain macs she'd found in the understairs cupboard.

'I hope I'm not going to be too hot,' said Faye as she rolled up the sleeves and sat on her bike.

Jake got on this bike too. 'Let's put it this way – at least we're not freezing cold.'

As they set off on the trail back to the car park, Jake heard Faye comment, 'I hope we don't meet anyone on the way back.' He looked down at his bright yellow rain mac and thought exactly the same. He said to her, 'Well, at least yours isn't yellow!'

'Seriously, Jake? You think I feel any better because mine is blue? I just want to get back.'

'Me too.' He glanced at Natty up ahead, leading the way, and looked at Faye.

She said, 'What is it?'

Jake spoke his mind. 'This must be what being a parent feels like, abject terror one minute, and the most unbelievable relief the next.'

'Welcome to my world.'

Jake smiled. 'But I wouldn't change it for a thing.'

She shot him a look. 'Diving into a freezing loch for nothing?'

'No, not that – being here with you and Natty.'

Their eyes locked for a moment, until Natty shouted out, 'There's some people on bikes.'

Jake heard Faye groan. 'And to think I chose to wear jeans for this trip just in case I fell off the bike and got my trousers muddy. I didn't think I'd need to bring along a whole change of clothes!'

Jake glanced at her once more, cycling along wearing nothing but a very long raincoat. He tried to think of an amusing quip to lighten the atmosphere, but thought better of it when he caught her expression.

'The last thing I expected was an icy dip in a loch, and to return with soaking wet clothes!'

Jake sighed. Before they'd arrived at the loch, Faye had been enjoying the cycling trail, and he'd been thinking that this was going to turn out to be another successful day. Now he wished Nick had never suggested hiring bikes, and he'd never agreed to it. As they made their way back to the car park, he hoped they could salvage something of the afternoon.

16

'This is the best picnic ever,' said Natty.

Jake just felt relieved that after they'd arrived back at the car park, and handed back the bikes, he'd visited the shop in the visitor centre and discovered they did sell clothes. Faye had stayed behind, hiding in the car. There hadn't been a lot of choice – black and grey walking trousers, t-shirts, shirts, and fleeces – but at least they had a dry set of clothes each. Jake had changed in the toilets and returned to the car with Faye's new set of clothes.

They didn't sell underwear, but Jake had managed to dry theirs under the hand dryer in the toilets, ignoring the strange looks from other guys using the facilities as he dried Faye's bra.

Faye had changed in the car, somehow managing to dress under the rain mac.

As he and Natty stood outside the car, holding the picnic basket, waiting for Faye to finish changing, he thought that perhaps in the future, when he and Faye had grown old together, they'd look back on this outing and laugh about it. Oh, how he hoped that would all happen.

Faye opened the car door and got out. 'What do you think?' She did a twirl.

The black trousers and grey t-shirt suited her. He grinned.

'I couldn't have chosen better myself. I really like the clothes, Jake.'

'Me too.'

Jake had also bought her a fleece that zipped up in case it got a bit chilly by the loch where they were planning to have their picnic.

Jake had asked for directions to the Green Loch when he was purchasing the clothes, trying to avoid the stares of other customers at his bright yellow rain mac. Jake had said, in a loud voice to the shop assistant, 'I fell off my bike into a load of mud.' It was a lie, but he wasn't about to tell anyone about their impromptu swim in the loch.

The Green Loch – or, to use its proper name, An Lochan Uaine – was just a short walk from the visitor centre, along a forestry pathway adjacent to the road. It was surrounded by Caledonian pinewoods, with the backdrop of the mountain Sgòr Gaoith.

As they walked, Jake repeated what the shop assistant had told him. Locals called it the Green Loch because of its deep turquoise colour, which apparently was the result of a combination of the green algae in the water and the pine trees surrounding the lake reflected in the water.

Of course, there was the local folklore about the fairies, which the shop assistant had also shared with Jake and Natty. As they walked to the loch, Natty told her mum that the reason the loch was green was because fairies washed their clothes in it. 'The lady said I should wear something green for the fairies.'

Faye looked at Jake. He shrugged, 'Yeah, she said some local people wore green out of respect for the fairies when visiting.'

Natty wanted to wear something green. There hadn't been much in the shop, but the young lady had helpfully found a dark green baseball cap with the words *The Green Loch* emblazoned on the cap. Natty had worn it since leaving the shop.

Faye smiled. 'Ah, I wondered why you'd bought that when Natty already had a sunhat.'

It wasn't long before they arrived at the loch. It was stunning – the description and photos Jake and Natty had seen in the visitor centre were amazing, but even they couldn't do it justice. It was wonderful to actually see it, especially on such a beautifully calm summer's afternoon.

'Oh, my god, Jake,' exclaimed Faye. 'This is just beautiful. I'm so glad we came here today.'

Jake was so relieved that the day would be salvaged after all. The cold dip in the lake, their wet clothes, and the uncomfortable return journey on the bikes had all but been forgotten.

They found a spot on the shore of the loch, spread out the tartan picnic blanket, and unpacked the basket. 'Oh, it was just so kind of Gayle to pack us all this food,' said Faye.

Jake was just as surprised as Faye when they discovered not just finger sandwiches, but sausage rolls, scotch eggs, vol au vents, and small slices of quiche. There was a bowl of salad, fresh fruit, and a selection of little cakes and scones with jam and a pot of butter.

'It's like afternoon tea on the train,' observed Natty.

Faye grinned. 'So it is.'

'There's a lot of food,' Natty added.

Faye said, 'Well that's just as well, because after that bike ride I'm starving.'

'So am I,' agreed Jake, passing them each a plastic plate and matching cutlery from the picnic hamper. He glanced at Faye. The mention of the bike ride didn't seem to have dampened her mood.

'And don't forget your swim in the loch, Mummy.'

'How could I forget?' Faye commented. She started to laugh. 'What a silly pair we are – aren't we?'

'Yes, Mummy, you are.'

Faye threw a smile in Jake's direction.

Jake joined in the laughter, relieved that all this – the picnic lunch, the magnificent setting on the shore of the loch, and Faye's new, dry clothes – which she'd insisted she'd pay him back for – would make up for what had happened at the last loch they'd visited.

Faye said, 'This time, we are keeping you firmly in our sights.'

'Oh, yes.' Jake thought that the last thing either of them wanted was a repeat. In fact, Jake was not only going to keep Natty firmly in his sights, but he was going to accompany her near the water, hold her hand tightly, and not turn his back ever again.

Jake inwardly sighed. So much for that earlier conversation with Faye about Natty spreading her wings, when Faye had thanked him for suggesting that Natty could cycle ahead, leading them on the ride, giving her some independence and responsibility. Faye had said that sometimes she wondered when she'd ever let Natty spread her wings a little. Jake was quickly changing his mind about letting her go too.

When Natty stood up, a sandwich still in her hand, and took a step forward, Jake immediately said, 'Wait! Where are you going?'

'I just wanted to go to the water's edge.'

'Hold on!' Jake hastily got up.

Faye grabbed Jake's hand. 'Let's all finish lunch.' She turned to Natty. 'Together.'

Natty reluctantly sat down.

'There'll be plenty of time to explore once we've finished eating. And besides, we don't get down from the table at home until we've finished eating.'

'But this is a picnic, Mummy. We're not sitting at a table.'

Jake looked at Faye. She did have a point.

'Yes, but the same principle applies. And it's nice to all sit together.'

They finished eating lunch, staring at the spectacular loch. They didn't have it to themselves, and didn't expect to; it was one of the main draws of visiting Glenmore Forest Park. They were the only ones having a picnic, though. Jake imagined other people had had lunch at the visitor centre. It had been busy when he'd nipped in there to buy some clothes. The food looked very nice, the service was quick, and the little café was brightly lit and welcoming. But even so, on a glorious day such as this, he couldn't think of anything nicer than being outside in the spectacular scenery.

He glanced at Natty. As she couldn't walk down to the water's edge yet, she'd done the next best thing – actually, Jake thought it was better. She had a pork pie in one hand and the pair of binoculars in the other, and she was looking through the binoculars at the loch. 'The water looks *so* green.'

'Yes, remember what the lady in the shop said about the green algae in the water, and the reflection of the tall pines around the shore?'

Natty looked up at Jake and frowned. 'Gayle said it's the home of the fairies.' Natty went on to explain. 'Like the lady in the shop, Gayle said it's a green colour because this is where they do their washing.'

'Oh, and when did Gayle tell you that story?' Faye said as she joined them at the edge of the loch. 'Last night when she knocked on our door to say goodnight. You were in the bathroom. I told her we were going on a bike ride, and she said our journey took us to a magical loch. And here we are. But I haven't seen any fairies yet.' Natty looked through the binoculars again and pouted.

Jake and Faye exchanged a knowing glance. Now they knew why she couldn't wait to get down to the water's edge.

Faye said, 'Why don't we save the cakes and scones until later?'

Natty jumped to her feet. 'Does that mean we can go for a walk now?'

Faye looked at Jake. 'If that's all right with you.'

'Of course it is.' Jake quickly finished his finger sandwich while Faye packed away the plates. They left the hamper on the picnic blanket and walked together down to the loch.

'Maybe we'll spot a red squirrel in the trees,' said Faye.

Natty took hold of Faye's hand and then Jake's so that she was walking in the middle. 'I want to find the fairies.' She let go of their hands and skipped ahead, following the shoreline.

She was barely a few feet ahead when Jake yelled, 'Don't go too far!'

'I won't.'

Faye turned to him. 'Are you okay?'

Jake wouldn't take his eyes off Natty. 'I'd prefer it if she'd hold hands.'

'So would I, but what about letting her spread her wings?'

'Sod that!' Jake replied, shaking his head furiously. 'I'm not taking my eyes off her.'

The next thing he heard was Faye laughing. He did glance at Faye for a millisecond. 'What's so funny?'

'You. I seem to recall you almost admonishing me when I yelled at her *don't go too far* at the last loch, telling me to calm down.'

'Well, I shouldn't have.'

Faye took his hand.

As much as he wanted to take her in his arms and kiss her, properly this time, unless they were positioned where he could still keep an eye on Natty, he wouldn't dream of it. Well, he decided he *would* dream of it, but that was all.

17

Together they followed Natty, still looking for fairies doing their washing in the loch, as they enjoyed the views and each other's company.

Natty glanced back at her mum and Jake and beamed. She put the binoculars away in the little canvas shoulder bag and took out her new mobile phone.

Jake and Faye paused mid-stride, realising she was taking a photo of the two of them. Jake put an arm around Faye's shoulder, feeling Faye's arm around his waist. This was just what he'd hoped for – a walk around the Green Loch, hand in hand.

Natty finished taking photos, of them and of the loch, and got out her binoculars again. She was just turning full-circle as she looked through them when she suddenly stopped, aiming her binoculars at the pine tree forest behind them.

She ran over to them, and put her fingers to her lips to warn Jake and Faye to remain silent. She whispered, 'There's a red squirrel!'

They crept silently up to the trees where she pointed to a red squirrel hanging upside down from a bird feeder. She got out her mobile phone very quietly, slowly aimed her camera and then clicked. The squirrel, startled by the sound, flew up the tree, jumping from branch to branch. It stopped momentarily, looking down on Faye, Jake and Natty, and then disappeared.

'Why don't we see red squirrels in London?' Natty asked, looking up at Faye.

'I'm afraid I don't really know, sweetheart. I imagine Grandad would know the answer to that question. You know he's always loved wildlife and the countryside.'

Jake knew that Faye's dad, Patrick, was Irish, although she hadn't talked about him much, because they'd been estranged up until recently. When Jake had first met him, during his search for Natty, Patrick's strong Irish accent had been unmistakable. 'Did he grow up in rural Ireland?' Jake asked conversationally.

'Yeah – in Dingle, County Kerry. It's a small town, but quite rural. You know, I thought he might return there when he retired from the police. I often wonder why he didn't.'

Jake grinned. 'Oh, I know why.' His eyes shifted to Natty. He didn't mean to make Faye feel guilty over stopping Patrick seeing his grandchild, but the look on her face said she did anyway.

Jake turned to Natty. 'Unfortunately, it's very rare to spot a red squirrel in London, Natty,' he said, noticing Faye had gone quiet. He imagined she was thinking about her father. 'I believe the numbers started declining around the 1920s and now they are close to extinction in the UK – that's why we mainly see grey squirrels in the parks or sometimes in our gardens if there are trees around.'

'What does *extinction* mean?' Natty asked.

Faye looked at Jake and smiled a knowing smile when he didn't reply.

Jake caught her smile and imagined just what she was thinking

– you did volunteer to answer the first question, and you should know my daughter by now.

'Well, you know dinosaurs …'

They returned along the loch, heading back to where they'd left the picnic blanket and basket. A couple were shouting at their dog, who had run over to the blanket and was sniffing around the basket. Fortunately, they'd shut the basket and fastened it with the leather clasp so that not even a clever dog could get inside.

The couple picked up their small dog and told him off, even though it was perfectly understandable. The food in Gayle's picnic hamper smelled delicious.

The three of them sat down on the picnic blanket. Jake had an idea. He assumed they'd sit for a while longer and eat some of the cakes and scones. 'After we've finished lunch,' he said, 'why don't we revisit the visitor centre on the way back to the car?'

Faye said, 'That's a good idea. I'd like to look at the gift shop.'

'Me too,' said Natty.

Jake looked at Natty. 'What about picking up a pocket-book on Scottish wildlife?' He was sure he'd seen one in the shop.

'Jake, can you buy me a book about the fairies? Maybe they'll have pictures of them in case I don't get to see one.'

'Of course. I'll buy you anything you want.' The moment he said that, he realised his gaffe. He looked sheepishly at Faye. Either she hadn't heard him, being too busy organising the scones and cakes on the plates, or she had chosen to ignore it. Either way, Jake silently cursed himself for saying it without thinking.

He'd got into trouble with her before when she'd discovered he'd been buying Natty anything she wanted. He'd been spoiling her rotten – and he had the money to do so. Faye couldn't compete with that. But he suspected that wasn't really the problem. Jake was being irresponsible. You didn't give a child anything they wanted even if you could afford it. There had to be boundaries.

Jake quickly backtracked. 'What I meant, Natty, was that I'll buy you any *book* that takes your fancy.' That wasn't what he'd meant, obviously, but it would take time to get out of the habit of giving her what she wanted without a second thought.

He caught Faye looking his way and nodding approvingly. He guessed she had been listening after all.

In no time at all, they picnic hamper was almost empty. Jake looked inside and found the last pork pie. He held it up. 'Anyone want this?'

Faye and Natty shook their heads. As Jake ate the last of the picnic, Faye packed up the plates and the plastic cups. Natty had had some juice. Gayle had packed a couple of bottles of something fizzy and non-alcoholic for them both. They were soon making their way back to the visitor centre, and not long after that they were back in the car, with Natty enjoying more than just a book from the gift shop. Of course, Jake had asked Faye's permission before buying her anything else. She'd wanted a small cuddly red squirrel.

He'd also bought her a notepad and some colouring pencils. She'd checked the set had a green pencil. As Jake backed out of the parking space, he glanced over his shoulder and saw Natty drawing something in green. It was the green loch. 'Are you going to draw a fairy doing their washing in the loch?' Jake asked.

'Yes.'

Jake exchanged a smile with Faye before they set off.

Faye said, 'It's been a wonderful day, Jake.'

'Oh, the day isn't over yet,' he replied with a grin.

She looked quizzically at Jake as he turned out of the car park on to the forest road, but not in the direction of Aviemore. 'Where are we going?'

'You'll see.'

As they drove through Glenmore village, Jake said, 'Everyone look out for a parking bay along this road with a sign saying—'

'Look, over there!' Natty exclaimed pointing at the brown sign up ahead that said *Reindeer Centre*. 'Are we going to see some reindeers? I just love reindeers. But it's not Christmas. Will it be open?'

'Oh, yes.' Jake pulled over and parked behind a line of cars in a small parking bay on the opposite side of the road. He rummaged in his jacket pocket and handed Faye the leaflet about the reindeer herd. He gave one to Natty too.

Jake switched off the car engine. 'So, there's the reindeer centre and shop up there.' Jake pointed to a grassy bank on the other side of the road. A short tarmac drive led up to the reindeer centre with a gift shop housed in a wooden cabin. 'There are reindeers we can see here in pens. But I thought it would be even more special to see them up there.' He turned in his seat and pointed in the direction of the mountain ahead. 'But first I need to collect the tickets. I'll be back in a minute.'

Faye put the leaflet down. 'Aren't we coming too?'

'We can look in the gift shop afterwards,' said Jake. 'Once I've got the tickets I'll come back to the car as it's a short drive further along the road where we meet our guide in a small car park. They take small groups up into the mountain.'

'We're climbing a mountain to see the reindeers?' Natty asked.

Jake caught Faye looking worried. 'No, not exactly. We'll be going up on the mountain to see them, but the route is suitable for everyone. So don't worry, we won't be doing any mountain climbing, if that's what you're thinking.'

'Oh.' Natty sounded disappointed. Her mum, on the other hand, said, 'Oh, thank god,' breathing a sigh of relief. She turned to Jake. She held up the leaflet. 'When did you manage to arrange this?'

When I was in the tourist information office before we got the steam train yesterday.' Jake replied. He'd gone online the previous night to book the tickets. Spaces were limited, so he'd been lucky to get some. 'I packed our coats in the car this morning, and Gayle had some hats, gloves and scarves which are in a bag in the boot. We may need them because although it's summer, I imagine there's going to be quite a wind when we get to the reindeer.'

Faye said, 'I did wonder why you insisted on bringing our coats on such a beautiful day.'

Jake hadn't wanted to let on what he had planned for the afternoon when they'd set off that morning for the loch. He'd wanted to keep the afternoon treat of seeing the reindeer as a surprise.

'Right, let's go.' Jake started the engine, and within five minutes they were parked in a car park at the side of the road. Several cars were already there, with people milling around, chatting and waiting for the tour to start.

Natty and Faye were already out of the car, getting their coats on. He could see the guides. There were two – a young man and a woman. They were carrying small sacks, which Jake imagined was the food they would be given to feed the reindeer.

Jake sat in the car, lost in thought. He hadn't realised where the reindeer centre was until he'd booked the tickets. It was on the road to the Cairngorm Mountain ski resort. Where they were parked now was but a short distance. If they'd continued along that road, it would have ended at a huge car park below the ski resort. He hadn't driven along this road since Christmas Day. Unfortunately, that day – when he'd discovered that Eleanor, dressed in her skiing outfit, had decided to join them for their Christmas Day ski after saying she wouldn't – came straight back to mind. How could it not?

'Jake?' Faye peered into the car through the open door. She'd obviously been about to shut the car door when she'd noticed Jake still seated in the car. 'Everything all right?'

'Oh, yeah. Sure.' At least they weren't going anywhere near the ski resort. The gentle mountain walk was on the other side of the road, leading off in the other direction.

They joined the rest of the group, and after introductions from the guides, and some safety information, they set off on the thirty-minute walk to find the reindeer. Natty joined a group of other excited children doing the tour, and Jake could hear her telling them all about the fairy loch.

'I hope it's not too far,' Faye spoke quietly. 'Only that bike saddle has really made my bum rather sore.'

Jake noticed she was whispering so that no one else heard. It was something he hadn't thought of – how they'd get on doing a hike after a morning of riding bikes.

'Don't get me wrong – I'm so pleased you managed to book tickets. This is quite something, isn't it? Going to see reindeer in the wild.'

They followed the line of people making their way along a well-trodden track. The guide had brought food for the reindeer, which they would share out when they reached the herd. The track rose gently, crossing a long wooden footbridge, and soon they came to a gate and a plateau on the mountainside.

Natty spotted the reindeer on the brow of a hill. The reindeer slowly came down, making their way towards the group, who stood in a circle, awaiting their arrival. There were more reindeer than Jake had anticipated.

'They must know there's food for them.'

Jake agreed. 'They know the drill,' he quipped, speaking loudly against the wind.

Faye put her hat on and wrapped her scarf around her. 'So glad you brought these, it's so chilly up here.'

Jake nodded.

'They're beautiful, and so docile,' Faye said, watching the herd.

Natty sidled up to Jake and held his hand. 'They're very big, and some of them have got huge antlers,' Natty said, looking up at Jake with a slightly worried look on her face.

Standing in a semi-circle, the guides handed out bags of feed. *Oohs* and *ahhs* could be heard as the children held out tentative hands with food.

Natty got out her mobile phone to take photos. Faye took photos of Natty and Jake feeding the reindeer.

Soon her confidence returned, and she mingled with the other children, asking the guide questions.

Faye stood transfixed. 'The scenery is amazing, Jake,' she said, turning around to take in the views. 'I love the snow-capped mountain backdrop – don't you?'

Jake glanced up at the mountain behind them and frowned.

'What a lovely finish to the day,' continued Faye, staring at Natty, who was feeding a young reindeer.

She turned to him. 'You deserve a break from cooking this evening.'

Jake sighed. 'Well, unless Gayle is cooking stew, it would have to be takeaway, and I think Gayle might be a bit offended and disappointed if we don't join her for dinner. Besides, I've already promised Gayle we'll try out a recipe in her mother's old cookery book together this evening. It's the least I can do after that amazing picnic she prepared for us.'

'That's true – not to mention these hats, scarves and gloves she found for this trip.'

Natty ran over to them. 'I've run out of reindeer food.'

Jake noticed the guides walking back towards the gate. It was time to leave.

'It's been such fun, hasn't it?' said Faye, taking Natty's hand as they walked ahead, following the guide.

Jake stood for a moment, looking up at the snow-capped mountain.

'Jake – you coming?'

He turned in their direction. Faye and Natty had let the rest of the tour group pass to wait for him. He strode over to join them.

'What's the matter?'

'Unfinished business,' he mumbled. He tried to lighten the mood. 'Come on, we'd better get back before Gayle takes it upon herself to cook dinner – then we really will be in trouble.'

18

Jake sat on the sofa in the lounge and placed all the leaflets he'd collected from the tourist information centre in front of him on the coffee table. He spread them out.

Faye wandered in with two mugs of tea. 'Where's Natty?' she asked, noticing Jake sitting on his own.

'Gayle said she had a book that Natty might be interested in, so they've popped into the library to find it.'

Faye looked at her watch. 'I didn't realise they'd gone out. Wouldn't it be too early for the library to be open? We've only just finished breakfast.' She placed the two mugs on the table and lowered herself into the easy chair beside the fireplace.

'Still a bit saddle-sore?' Jake grinned. Faye threw a cushion at him, which just missed his steaming mug of tea. 'They haven't gone into Aviemore. Gayle has her own library here.'

'A house with its own library! Now that is something,' Faye replied, raising an eyebrow.

'It's not that sort of library. It used to be Faye's father's study, but she's turned it into a bit of a wellness room, full of calming scented candles and bookshelves full of self-help books.'

Faye laughed. 'What would Natty need a self-help book for?'

Jake laughed too. 'No she wasn't finding her one of those. I heard her saying to Natty that there are some books that her nieces and nephews left behind from when they visited when they were younger.'

'That would be great if she could find something to read. She's already read that little pocket-book on Scottish wildlife.'

'She has?' said Jake in surprise.

'Yes, cover to cover. She loved it, but I think she could do with a story book. Silly me – I forgot the reading books we picked up from the trip to Foyles before the holiday. I thought of visiting Wilbur's Bookstore in Aviemore.'

Jake wasn't sure he wanted to. It was where Bonnie had bumped into Robyn and Eleanor on Christmas Day, the last place Eleanor was … well … Eleanor, before the ski accident took her away.

Faye was still talking while Jake's thoughts were consumed by memories of his wife. He hadn't been listening, and just caught the tail end.

'… and I promised Natty we would visit. It would be nice if she found a book or two to keep her going before then.'

Jake nodded, realising she was still talking about the bookstore in town.

'She really loves reading, which I try to encourage as much as possible.'

Jake smiled. 'You can take the teacher out of the classroom, but you can't take the classroom out of the teacher,' he said with a chuckle.

'Mmm … well, you're a fine one to talk – giving Natty a history lesson yesterday about how the reindeer herd came to be in the Cairngorms.'

All Jake could do was smile ruefully. It was so true. Oh, how he loved his new job. He changed the subject. 'Where would you like to go today?' he asked, pointing to the leaflets adorning the coffee table.

Faye came and sat beside him on the sofa. At first, Jake hadn't been that impressed with the small, old and springy sofa in the lounge. Now he loved it very, very much because it was so small, which meant Faye had to sit close.

Sipping her tea, she took a cursory glance at all the choices. 'I think we need a month's holiday, not just a week, to even touch the surface of this lot,' Faye said, picking up a leaflet and opening it. 'Failing that, we'd have to move here,' she quipped.

Jake nearly spluttered in his tea. 'Seriously?'

Faye slapped in arm playfully. 'You're funny.'

Jake hadn't meant it as a joke.

'Yes, please! Can we stay for a whole month, Jake?' Natty said, bouncing into the room and flopping down on the easy chair beside the sofa. As usual, Olive wasn't far behind. She sat by Natty's chair, her head on Natty's lap, sad brown eyes looking up at her, waiting patiently for the next pet, or playtime, or some food.

'I don't have to be back at school until September,' said Natty, petting Olive on the head.

Faye said, 'The thing is, Natty, I doubt Gayle will have vacancies here at the guesthouse.'

'That's all right.'

'It is?' Faye didn't understand.

'We can go and live in Jake's house.'

Jake stared at Natty. It was a consideration. Faye and Natty didn't have to be back in London for any reason, and neither did he, if he reneged on his promise to Marcus. But would The Lake

House be a good idea?

'You know that I'd love you to stay as long as you like here,' Gayle said. She had wandered into the room and overheard the conversation.

'You've still got vacancies for the following three weeks?' Jake asked eagerly, although he was sure the lady in the tourist information office had said otherwise.

Gayle slowly shook her head from side to side. 'I was going to say that whilst I'd love you to stay, no, I haven't got the vacancies, I'm afraid. I suppose I could cancel some bookings.'

Faye said, 'No, don't do that. Besides, we were just joking around.'

Jake wished they weren't.

Faye said, 'You've got the reputation of your guesthouse to think of. It hasn't been open long, so you need to give it time for word to get around, in a positive way.'

Gayle nodded. 'I know.'

Jake grinned. 'Actually, it already has.'

'How do you mean?' Gayle said, wandering over to the sofa opposite Jake and plonking herself down in the squishy cushions.

Natty came and sat beside her. Gayle gave her a cuddle while they listened to Jake.

'I was in the visitor centre, and they already had your guesthouse on their system – and noticed it was fully booked. People were making enquiries about it on the phone too. Looks like your website is working.'

Gayle smiled. 'Wonderful!'

Jake noticed that Natty had a book in her hands. 'Did you manage to find a book to read in Gayle's library, Natty?'

'Oh, yes. There are lots of books, so I won't run out of things to read, especially if we're staying on for a month,' Natty said, looking imploringly at Jake.

Faye said, 'But didn't you just hear what Gayle said. There's no vacancies.'

'I know. But Jake's house is only through the gap in the hedge.'

Faye frowned. 'Natty, I don't think we will be staying on after the week,' she said.

'Why not?' Natty shot back.

Jake was thinking the same thing.

'What about seeing Grandpa over the summer holidays? He was looking forward to taking you out on some day trips.'

'That's all right,' said Natty, sounding as though she had it all figured out, 'Grandpa can come here. Your house is very big, Jake.'

'Hold up your book and let me see what you found,' said Faye, noticeably changing the subject.

Natty held up the book so Faye could read the title. '*The Treasure of the Loch Ness Monster*. That sounds interesting. In fact …' Faye rummaged around the leaflets on the coffee table and picked up just what she was looking for. 'I think we've solved the problem of what to do today.' Faye handed the leaflet to Jake.

He grinned. 'Hands up all those who'd like to go in search of the Loch Ness Monster?' Jake said.

'Now who sounds as though they're still in the classroom?'

Jake joked, 'You can take the teacher out of the classroom …'

Faye laughed, snatching the leaflet back to read the details.

Natty looked at Jake and her mum and rolled her eyes. 'They can be really silly sometimes,' she said, turning to Gayle with a serious face.

Gayle smiled. 'Right, I'm off to check my website for any new bookings,' she said. 'I'll leave you all to plan your next adventure!'

She wandered out of the door, heading towards the library, which now also doubled as her office.

❖

'Whoa! Where's the fire?' Gayle said, walking out of the kitchen with a picnic hamper in her hands and catching Natty charging down the stairs.

Natty stood waiting impatiently at the front door for Jake and her mum. She'd already rushed upstairs to clean her teeth and gather her coat and backpack. 'I'll just be a minute!' Faye had called to her daughter from the bathroom. Natty knew what that meant. Another five or ten minutes at least before they would be ready to leave. Her mum always forgot something at the last minute, so this time Natty decided she would make sure her mum had no excuse to dilly-dally. 'I've got your coat and bag, mum, and I think Jake is waiting in the hall.'

Natty had decided that a little white lie would surely be okay, as Jake was bound to appear before her mum anyway. And Jake had said that they would have to get a move on as he had booked an early slot at the Loch Ness Centre and then a boat trip on Loch Ness itself, where Natty was hoping to get a glimpse of the monster. She knelt down and gave Olive a hug. 'Sorry, Olive, but you can't come with us.'

Gayle put the hamper down beside Natty. 'Now just in case you're all a little bit peckish before your boat trip this afternoon, I've prepared another picnic lunch and some nice cherry cake that one of Marty's clients gave him for doing their garden.'

'He gets paid in cake?' Natty looked at her.

'That's quite a novel idea,' Jake said, joining them at the door.

'Yes, apparently it's an arrangement he's had for quite a while with some of his older clients – the ones he retained when he took over his father's gardening business. And we do rather like some of the goodies he brings home from time to time,' Gayle added.

Jake looked down at the picnic hamper and smiled his appreciation. 'You do know that if you keep spoiling us like this, we won't want to leave?' he quipped, picking up the hamper.

'Who's not leaving?' Faye said, making her way down the stairs.

'Never mind, mum – we'll tell you on the way,' Natty said, opening the front door and almost pushing her mum outside. Natty turned and gave Gayle a big hug. 'Will Olive be here when I get back?' she whispered to Gayle.

'I'll be sure not to let her out in the garden. We wouldn't want another trip through the hedge to The Lake House.'

Natty shrugged. 'I don't mind.'

Faye took her hand. 'Well, I do. Come on, let's go find Nessie.'

❖

They had just finished the Loch Ness experience, which was great fun. 'I was so impressed how they brought to life the history and stories of the area using animation and videos in the museum,' Faye said, opening the passenger door and climbing in beside Jake. 'I have to admit I was a bit sceptical at first, but the presentation really exceeded my expectations.'

'I liked how we could vote whether the monster exists or not at the end of the experience,' Jake added.

'What did you vote for, Jake? Natty chimed in as she clipped her seat belt on in the back seat. Natty didn't give him a chance to answer. 'I voted that Nessie is real, and maybe we might spot it today,' Natty continued as she picked up the guidebook and flicked though the pictures.

'Right, who wants to stop for a picnic before the boat trip? Hands up to vote,' Faye said, turning to Natty, who was still fiddling with her seat belt and trying to open her guidebook at the same time.

Natty dropped the book and both hands shot up. 'Good!' Jake said approvingly, taking count of the hands in the air. 'We'll stop at Dochgarroch village first and find a picnic place and then make our way to the boat, which is only about five minutes away.' He turned the engine on and slowly made his way out of the car park.

Jake led the way along the gangplank and onto the boat. There were already families ahead of them, and some were already seated, waiting for the journey to start. 'Can we sit on the top deck?' Natty asked as she waited for her turn to board.

'Yes that's a great idea,' Faye replied. 'Gayle said we'll get a good view of Urquhart Castle as the boat turns.'

Jake led them to some seats on the port side of the boat, which he hoped would give them unobstructed views of the shoreline as they approached the castle.

The boat gently pulled away from Dochgarroch Lock, gliding along the calm waters of the Caledonian Canal before merging into the mysterious Loch Ness. The crew entertained them with stories about the area and the Loch Ness Monster. Jake looked around at the faces of the children. They were mesmerised by what they were hearing. It was times like this that he knew why he had chosen to become a teacher. Faye was looking about her at the children too. She and Jake exchanged a knowing smile. She said, 'It's all worthwhile, isn't it? When you see how children are inspired by the world around them.'

Surrounded by the expansive dark water of the loch and the rolling hills of the Scottish Highlands, Faye noticed how fresh and crisp the air was. As the boat cruised deeper into the loch, the ruins of Urquhart Castle came into view, perched dramatically on the rocky shore. Natty turned and watched other children making their way to the back of the boat with their parents. 'Can we go and take some photos from the back of the boat?' Natty asked her mum.

Although the water was calm, Faye preferred to remain seated inside. 'Why don't you go with Jake, Natty?'

Jake stood and held onto Natty's hand. They made their way down the aisle. The perspex doors slid open to allow them on to the deck outside.

'Would you like a photo taken together?' one of the crew asked as they stood admiring the views.

'Oh, yes please!' Natty said. 'But I need my mum to be in the photo too.'

'Aye, you go get your mum – I'm not going anywhere,' the chap said.

'Mum, mum, come quick, we are having our photo taken!' Natty shouted as she stepped through the perspex doors again.

Faye glanced over her shoulder at the sound of Natty's voice. Standing, she made her way to the stern of the boat, holding on to the back of the seats as she went along. 'I haven't found my sea legs yet, Natty,' she said as the joined Natty outside.

'What's sea legs?' Natty asked as she stood between Jake and Faye, waiting for the photo to be taken.

'As Natty swayed on the deck, the crew member grinned and said, 'Don't worry – sea legs aren't real legs! It just means getting used to the boat rocking. If you see a pair of legs floating by, instead of Nessie, well, you'd better let us know.'

Natty giggled at the joke while the photo was taken.

'Here,' the crew member handed Natty back her phone.

'Thank you,' Natty said, taking the phone as she stood confidently on the deck. 'Do you want to go back inside?' Natty asked her mum. 'I don't think you have found your sea legs yet.' She had noticed that her mum was holding tightly onto Jake.

'I'll look after your mum while you take some more photos.' Jake used it as an excuse to put an arm around Faye's waist, holding her steady. She didn't object. She moved closer, tilting her head towards him even though the water was calmer now. They stood at the back of the boat, ignoring the spray and enjoying the stunning views of the loch.

As they made the return journey, Natty stood on the deck beside Jake, clutching her binoculars tightly, scanning the rippling surface for any sign of the legendary Nessie. The chilly wind whipped through her hair, but she barely noticed; she was too focused on the dark, mysterious depths below. Every shadow, every wave made her heart race with the thrill of possibly being the first on the boat to spot the elusive creature.

Arriving back at the start, they began to disembark. The skipper came to say goodbye as they left the boat. 'Did you enjoy your trip?' he asked Natty as she was about to walk down the gangplank.

'It was amazing,' Natty replied, 'but I didn't see Nessie.'

'Well, you're not always lucky the first time round,' the skipper replied, winking at Faye and Jake, 'which means,' he said, pausing, 'you'll have to come again.'

'Yes, I will!' Natty replied as she said her goodbyes. 'We're going to stay in Scotland for a month!' she added.

Faye rolled her eyes at Natty.

'I'd like to live in Scotland,' Natty said to herself, loud enough for her mother and Jake to hear.

'But I thought you liked the city,' Faye said in surprise.

'Sometimes. I like the museums, and the zoo.'

'And school. And your friends.'

Jake frowned when he realised that Faye was trying to convince her otherwise. It had pleased him no end that Natty loved Scotland.

'But I like it here more.'

So do I, a little voice in Jake's head said.

19

Natty followed Gayle into her study the following morning.

'So, you're visiting a castle today,' said Gayle, turning to Natty as she wandered over to the bookshelves. Olive was out on a morning run with Nick, so Natty was missing her playmate. Gayle knew that wasn't the only reason she had left the kitchen as soon as she'd eaten her breakfast cereal. It had been the same on Sunday and Monday morning too.

New guests had arrived on Saturday evening but were choosing to eat out at a restaurant in Aviemore in the evenings. However, since Sunday the kitchen had been full at breakfast time, with all her guests sitting around her large kitchen table in front of the Aga. While Gayle cooked a hearty breakfast, they all chatted amiably, enjoying getting to know one another – everyone apart from Natty.

Gayle had noticed she wasn't her usual exuberant, chatty self at breakfast, and quickly realised why. Natty was the only child, and she was just nine, so she was quite shy in front of all the new faces and felt rather left out of the adult conversations. Sometimes one of the new guests tried to include her, asking questions about her school, and her favourite subjects – that sort of thing. But then it put Natty in the spotlight, and Gayle imagined it made her feel even more uncomfortable. She'd seen her squirming in her seat, avoiding their gaze as she answered their questions. Olive had been in the kitchen the last couple of mornings, and the distraction had helped Natty settle down to breakfast with all the unfamiliar faces. However, with no Olive that morning, Natty had gulped down her breakfast cereal and had asked to be excused to go and play.

Gayle had excused herself as soon as she'd dished up the cooked breakfasts and had found Natty standing in the hallway outside the kitchen door, looking at a loss as to what to do with herself. Her new mobile phone didn't even have internet – Natty had explained to Gayle that she had something called a brick phone, a bog-standard old-style phone that could receive and take calls and texts and could take photos. Gayle realised she must be scrolling through her photos, obviously waiting for her mum and Jake to finish breakfast.

Faye had mentioned they were visiting a castle that day. Gayle had an idea she might have some old tourist leaflets, and even a booklet or two from years earlier in the study, so she'd asked Natty to come in too so they could see what she had.

'I think it's called Braemar Castle,' Natty replied, standing next to Gayle as she put on her reading glasses and grabbed a pile of leaflets off the shelf. 'Okay, let's see if we have anything here about that castle – shall we?'

Natty nodded.

Gayle had more leaflets and booklets than she'd realised once she started go through some drawers of her father's old desk too. Her parents had never got rid of anything, so she wasn't surprised.

'Why don't we both look?' Gayle suggested, spreading them all out on the desk. 'Let's see what we can find.' She sat down in the office chair while Natty stood beside her and took a pile of leaflets too. It wasn't long before Natty shouted excitedly, 'Is this about the castle?'

Gayle looked at the booklet in her hand, which was a small guidebook to the castle. It was several years old and dog-eared, but she recognised it. 'My nieces and nephews often visited the castles in the area when they came to stay with their grandparents here, who took them out on day trips,' she explained.

'Who are their grandparents?' Natty asked.

'Ah, that was my dad, who has sadly passed. He was a local doctor, and this used to be his study. And of course, you know my mum, Doris.'

Natty grinned. 'I like Doris. She's funny.'

Gayle reserved comment and just smiled. Unfortunately, her mum had dementia, so to a young child some of the things she said or did must have appeared funny, certainly peculiar, although sadly it wasn't intentional on her mother's part on either score.

'My grandad, Patrick, is funny. And he speaks with a funny accent.'

'He does?'

'Yes, he's Irish.'

Gayle laughed. 'I guessed.'

'You did?'

'His name. It's a very Irish name.'

'Have you been to Ireland, Natty?'

She shook her head.

'Would you like to visit, see where your grandad came from?'

Natty shrugged. 'I like Scotland.'

Gayle grinned. 'Well now, there we are both in agreement.'

Gayle returned her attention to the booklet. 'This might be a bit outdated, but at least you can flick through the photos inside and read a little bit about the castle on the journey there.'

Gayle caught her frowning. 'You don't have to take the booklet if you don't want to.'

'I want to. It's just … can I read it now?'

Gayle didn't understand. 'Of course, you can read it any time you like.'

'Good because I think Mum and Jake are going to be ages having breakfast.'

At that moment, laughter erupted in the kitchen.

Natty pulled a face. 'See what I mean?'

Gayle tried extremely hard to keep a straight face. 'Look, why don't I go and make you some toast and jam, and you can sit in here, in the cosy chair over there, and read about the castle while they all finish breakfast.'

Gayle was taken aback when Natty suddenly threw her arms around her and gave her a hug. 'I love you, Gayle.'

Gayle hugged her back, a tear in her eye as she said, 'I love you, too.' Gayle had never had children – not through choice; it was just the way the cards had fallen in her life. She hadn't been particularly close to her nieces and nephews when they were growing up, and that wasn't through choice either. Her two brothers – one a lawyer, the other a renowned surgeon – led busy lives a world away from Gayle's former life as a nurse before she'd moved back to the home she'd grown up in to care for her parents.

Her sister's life was a world away too – she owned her own estate agency firm, selling high-end property. Of course, their differing lifestyles shouldn't have stopped them having a close relationship, and Gayle seeing her nieces and nephews, but Gayle knew the reason that her three elder siblings were closer. Gayle had been the baby of the family, the child her parents had not expected to have later in life when their other children were already teenagers. Gayle had really grown up as an only child – like Natty. Technically, Gayle wasn't, but she might as well have been. Before she was even Natty's age, her siblings had all flown the nest, off to university and onward to start their careers.

Seeing Natty sitting at breakfast, looking uncomfortable and out of her depth with all the adults around the table, had brought to mind Gayle's own childhood, sitting for breakfast at that very table when her three older siblings had returned from university.

When they were home, the family dynamic had changed considerably. She hadn't realised it at the time, but when she was older it had dawned on her that before she'd come along, they'd been a family of five, who'd had memories and experiences together as a family that Gayle had never had and would never be part of. And it didn't seem to Gayle that they'd gone out of their way to include her. She could understand that now. As teenagers, and young adults, her older siblings had been into their educations, and careers, and making plans for their future. They hadn't had time for the baby of the family. In fact, she wondered if they might have even been resentful of her.

Natty ran over and got comfortable in the easy chair positioned by the bookshelves, where there was a reading lamp and scented candles. Gayle watched Natty cast her gaze around the room approvingly before she opened the book. 'I like this room. It's cosy and … quiet.'

Gayle smiled. 'I like it too, for the same reason.' Although she liked the quiet, the room was available for her guests too. Apart from her and her mother's bedrooms, along with their private bathroom, she wanted her guests to have the run of the place so that they felt at home. A home away from home. She hoped it set her guesthouse apart from the competition. It wasn't just a bed-and-breakfast that people were turning up to, with an impersonal bedroom and a breakfast room with tables and chairs set up so that guests wouldn't talk to one another. Gayle had wanted people to feel they were staying in a home away from home, and to feel part of the Lark Lodge guesthouse family.

'I won't be a moment, Natty, and then I'll go and make you some toast and jam.'

'Okay. Thank you.'

Gayle sat looking through the leaflets and booklets to see if she could find anything else Faye and Jake might be interested to see during the remainder of their stay. Unfortunately, it was Tuesday already, and their week at Lark Lodge was flying by far too quickly. She gazed at Natty for a moment, thinking how quickly Natty and Faye and Jake had become part of the fabric of her little guesthouse, of her life.

She didn't want to think about the end of the week, and them departing back to London. *Why do they have to go back?* she thought as she continued sorting through the leaflets. Jake had an amazing house right there. There was a lovely primary school in Aviemore, and she was sure Faye and Jake would eventually find teaching posts. It wasn't as though Jake didn't have the money for them to live off for a bit while they looked for jobs. And the best part was that Jake's house backed on to hers. They were already good friends, but even better, they could be neighbours too.

Gayle sighed as she started to put the leaflets back in the drawer. One caught her attention – it was all about ice-skating and the snow disco. She turned to Natty, about to ask if she'd ever been ice-skating, but she was immersed in the castle guide, so she didn't disturb her. Gayle stared at her, still thinking how wonderful it would be if they could stay in Scotland. It was a lovely dream, but a dream, nonetheless. Jake wouldn't return to The Lake House. How could he, with the ghost of his relationship with Eleanor in that house? Gayle thought he'd never return to live there. Besides, their lives were back in London. But she'd miss them.

'Penny for your thoughts?'

Gayle shifted her gaze from Natty and smiled at Nick. He'd popped his head around the door, beads of sweat on his forehead. He was still jogging on the spot after his morning run and checking his watch.

Gayle breathed a sigh. 'I was just thinking I'll miss Natty, and Faye and Jake, when they return to London at the weekend.'

Natty immediately lowered the booklet. 'We're staying here for a month.'

Gayle's eyebrows shot up. 'You are?' When had they decided that? She'd overheard a conversation the previous morning between Jake and Faye along those lines, but when she'd told them she'd have loved them to stay on but there were no vacancies, she was sure Faye had said they were just joking around.

Her heart lurched in her chest when she thought she could have reserved those two rooms for them for a whole month if only she'd known sooner. 'Oh, Natty, I'm afraid I've got no vacancies. There are other people booked to stay in the attic rooms next week.'

'That's all right,' Natty said nonchalantly. 'We can stay at Jake's house.'

'The Lake House? Really?' Gayle's eyebrows shot up again. That had been decided too? She happened to glance at Nick, who was still standing in the doorway, looking as surprised as she was.

She expected he was wondering the same thing – what had changed Jake's mind about staying at The Lake House?

'Is that what they said?'

Natty pursed her lips, and said in a small voice, 'Yes.'

Gayle stared at her. Had Natty misconstrued an adult conversation? It was possible, although she seemed so sure that it was the plan.

Olive nudged past Nick's legs and ran straight up to Natty.

'Hey, your breath smells of bacon!'

Nick frowned. 'I wondered why she darted into the kitchen. You've been begging at the table, haven't you?' He looked apologetically at Gayle.

Luckily for Gayle, her new guests loved Olive too and were not fazed at all by the exuberant Old English Sheepdog, barely out of puppyhood. They were all taken in by her sad brown eyes routine or her trick of rolling over for a belly rub to suss out who were her friends and to garner some treats.

'Can I have my toast and jam now, please?' Natty asked.

20

Jake and Faye were waiting in the car for Natty.

'Natty!' Faye called out, sounding exasperated. She lowered her voice and commented, 'How long does it take to say goodbye to a dog?'

Jake shrugged as he looked past Faye, out of the car window. Natty was giving Olive a hug and not letting go.

'Well, that wouldn't be a problem if it was our dog, because we'd all go out together. After all, pets are part of the family.'

Jake winced the moment he'd said that, wishing he'd just kept his thoughts to himself. Faye did not want a dog. She probably didn't want a family either, not that sort of family, not with a stand-in dad at any rate. Jake rubbed his forehead. It was Tuesday, halfway through their week's holiday already, and the romantic week away he was daydreaming about had remained just that – a daydream.

Each evening since they'd arrived, once Natty was in bed sound asleep, they'd joined Gayle and her mother, Doris along with Nick and Marty in the lounge. They'd chatted, played board games, watched TV and just hung out together. Marty had a girlfriend, Dee, so one evening she'd joined them when she stayed over. Two of the new guests had wandered into the lounge too after their evening meal out. It reminded him of the Christmases in The Lake House, when the Rosses would enjoy spending time together – which, with their hectic corporate lifestyles, was a rarity.

It was a delightful atmosphere at Lark Lodge, and they all got on well, but Jake was beginning to see a huge downside to staying at the guesthouse, which he should have anticipated – he never had any time alone with Faye. If they'd rented a little cottage …

Jake sighed heavily. It was too late for that now. He heard Natty's parting words to Olive. 'I'm sorry you can't come with us to the castle. But don't worry, Olive, I'll be back later, and then we can play in the garden.' Natty looked toward the car.

Faye sighed. 'She still doesn't get it – does she?'

Jake knew what she was on about. He'd seen the look Natty had just thrown her mother. Faye had already made it clear to Natty at the breakfast table that taking Olive with them that day just would not work. Olive couldn't go with them on a tour of the castle, and it wasn't fair to leave her on her own for long periods cooped up in the car, not to mention being dangerous. Although it wasn't exactly going to be a hot summer's day, the sun was out, and even with the windows wound down a little, it could quickly get too hot for a dog left in the car unsupervised.

Faye and Jake waved at Gayle, who was standing on the doorstep holding onto Olive's collar. Olive was trying to wriggle out of her grasp.

'Well, that conversation wasn't awkward at all,' commented Faye, eyeing her daughter as she approached the car.

Jake frowned. 'Look, I shouldn't have mentioned getting a dog …' And us being a family either, thought Jake miserably.

'Oh, I'm not talking about the dog. I wouldn't be surprised if we do end up getting one.'

Did she just say, *we*? Was that just a figure of speech or worse, was she just referring to her and Natty? He stopped himself from querying the comment, preferring to believe that she meant the three of them. Instead, he said, 'Then what are you talking about?'

'That conversation with Gayle before we left.'

'Oh – *that*.'

Natty opened the car door and got in the back seat. She put her backpack down beside her and opened the booklet about the castle. Jake noticed that Natty was ignoring her mum, obviously still cross with her about Olive.

Faye turned in her seat. 'Why did you tell Gayle we're staying on another three weeks, and that we're moving into The Lake House? I thought I made it clear there are things we've planned to do in London next week.'

Jake pursed his lips. Unfortunately, those plans didn't involve him. He knew why that was; Faye was aware he still had that blasted promise to Marcus to keep – stepping back into a suit and into his old role in the Ross Corporation, covering for Marcus while he went into rehab.

Jake had been checking his phone. There had been no more texts or calls from Marcus since their arrival in Scotland. Marcus hadn't left any messages – he didn't have to. Jake knew what he wanted to ask: where was he, and when was he coming back? Marcus had obviously got the message that wherever Jake was, he was avoiding his calls. Jake knew what Marcus would think – that he'd changed his mind about that promise to return to the fold, albeit for a short time.

Jake hadn't changed his mind. He'd still do it. But he'd changed his mind about doing it straight away. He'd been secretly hoping he'd get a message from Marcus to say he'd checked into rehab anyway, which would absolve Jake completely of his promise to return to the Ross Corporation. He felt guilty about thinking like that. What he was dreading, as a consequence, was getting a message from Lydia, Marcus's fiancée, telling him something had happened – like last time, when Marcus had gone missing and had turned up at Jake's house after he'd been mugged.

Natty's question cut across those unwelcome thoughts. 'What things?' Natty asked.

Jake had lost the train of the conversation. He turned to look at Natty. She was sitting with the dog-eared guidebook in front of her face.

'I thought we went over this too?' Faye said. 'Grandpa is looking forward to seeing you.'

Natty slowly lowered her book. 'And I thought I told you that Grandpa could come here and see me.'

'Don't be rude, Natty.'

'*You're* being rude.'

Jake slowly turned in his seat, wishing he was anywhere but there. This was getting awkward. He imagined they did have words at home, but they never rowed in front of him. And to think this was all because they were there in Scotland. And Natty had seen his house. Now he was beginning to think this holiday was a bad idea altogether. He'd thought, hoped, that the holiday would bring them closer. He'd never for one second thought that taking them there would be anything other than a positive experience. Now he really hoped it didn't just prove to Faye that she couldn't let another man into the inner circle to be a permanent part of their lives, their little family.

Jake stole a quick glance as Faye shook her head, folded her arms, and turned in her seat.

'You're very quiet. Aren't you going to say anything?' Faye asked.

Jake kept his eyes on the driveway as he put the car into gear. He shook his head. She was in a bad mood. He'd known her long enough to be aware when not to answer her question in case he instigated something far worse. If he wasn't careful, Faye might, on the spur of the moment, decide the holiday was over, go and pack their bags, and leave. That would be a bit extreme, when they had but a few days left, but she was under no obligation to stay.

And to think that a moment ago I was only worried about getting some alone-time with Faye in Lark Lodge. Now, he was really worried she'd bail and go home.

'Are we …' meaning *you*, 'still up for a visit to a Scottish castle today?' he asked tentatively.

Faye turned to him. 'Of course – why wouldn't I be?'

'Oh, er … right. I thought …' he glanced over his shoulder. Natty had put her headphones on and was listening to something on her iPad.

'Oh, I have this all the time. We're both strong-willed. She's just a lot more well-behaved when you're around.'

'Really?'

'Oh yes.'

'I don't understand …' Jake said, although he was incredibly happy to hear that.

'I do. You spend time with her, Jake. You're such a calming influence. With my job, and having the sole responsibility of raising her, I obviously get stressed, and I'm not always … well, present, you know. Always got things on my mind. Then sometimes the least little thing descends into an argument because

I haven't got the time to spend talking to her or working out what's going on with her. And it's hard. I've got nobody to share my worries and anxieties with.'

Jake looked at her, and blurted, 'You can share them with me – always.'

Faye smiled. 'I know. But you're not my—'

Jake looked at her. Was she going to say *partner, husband*?

'But I could be. I want to be.' He dropped his gaze, wishing he hadn't said that. He'd played his hand, told her how he felt about her, and now his stomach was churning at the thought of what she was going to say next, or worse, do. Would she call the holiday off? But surely, she knew this wasn't just a holiday with a friend. He wanted something more. She did too – he was sure of it. She just had to get out of her comfort zone and let him into her life, their lives – permanently. Commitment – that was Faye's problem. Not to her job, or her daughter, but to relationships.

He inwardly squirmed. He'd avoided just this sort of scenario. He knew she felt the same way about him. After all, they had nearly kissed when they'd stopped at the loch in Glenmore Forest during their bike ride. But he didn't just want a casual fling with Faye like the other relationships she'd been in that had gone no further.

'Will you have dinner with me?'

Jake's eyes went wide. He had not expected that question, and certainly not now. Was she seriously asking him out on a date?

'Gayle said she'd babysit so we could go out and have a meal together in Aviemore this evening.'

Jake swallowed. She *was* asking him out on a date.

'Don't get me wrong. I love the guesthouse, and spending evenings with Gayle, Doris, Marty and Nick, and some of the other guests, but I was hoping we could spend some time together

– just you and me …' She trailed off.

Jake stared at her. He couldn't believe his ears. He silently cursed himself for not having had the guts to ask her himself. He knew why that was. He was still afraid she'd back off, retreat back to her life as soon as they returned to London, back to those casual flings, refusing to commit to a relationship.

Faye dropped her eyes from his gaze. 'Look, we don't have to if you don't—'

Without thinking, Jake reached over and gently lifted her chin. 'Of course I want to go out with you! I'll book a restaurant when we get back.'

Faye put a hand on Jake's arm and smiled. His hand crept to her cheek as she moved closer. He leaned in. Jake's heart was thumping in his chest in anticipation of their first kiss. He couldn't believe this was really happening. They were going out on a date – a proper date, and they were about to—

'I'm bored! When are we going?'

Jake's shoulders sagged as he dropped his hand from Faye's face. Completely caught up in the moment, they'd both forgotten they weren't alone. They did exchange a smile when Faye nodded her head, indicating Natty in the back, and whispered, 'I don't think this was the right moment.'

'The right moment for what?' Natty asked in the back seat.

Jake replied to Faye, 'I agree.' They both ignored Natty's question.

Natty unclipped her seatbelt and sat forward in her seat. 'Were you going to smoochy-smoochy?' Natty asked.

Jake looked at Faye, and grinned. Her daughter didn't miss a thing.

Faye turned in her seat. 'Never you mind. Now get that seat

belt back on. We're going now.'

Natty eyed them for a moment longer.

'Natty.'

Natty sat back, clipped in her seatbelt, and picked up the castle guidebook. 'I want to see the dungeon.'

Jake felt relieved when Natty changed the subject. He didn't know what she might have come out with next after the *smoochy-smoochy* comment. He switched on the car engine. 'Well, I'm sure Braemar Castle has a dungeon – most castles do.'

'Okay.'

Jake exchanged a smile with Faye. 'Right, let's go.' He was just putting the car into gear when Natty said, 'Are you getting married? I want you and Mummy to get married because then you can be my daddy.'

Jake stole a glance at Faye. She turned in her seat, staring at her daughter. He knew her golden rule – she'd had relationships in the past, but she never brought men home or introduced them to her daughter for fear the relationship could break down, and Natty would have formed an attachment she'd lose. Faye did not want that for her daughter – father-figures flitting in and out of her life – even though by the sound of things, it was Faye who broke up her relationships if things were getting too serious.

But Natty had already formed an attachment to Jake during the many months he'd been her babysitter. The thing that Faye had tried to avoid had happened right under her nose. Of course, Faye and Jake hadn't been in a relationship; she could have suspended babysitting duties and just removed him from their lives at any time. But once they started dating, Natty's expectations, not to mention his own, regarding where it would lead – to marriage, and the wonderful idea of his being Natty's dad – were obvious. He just hadn't expected Natty to come right out and say it. The timing couldn't have been worse, just when they were planning their first date.

He closed his eyes, wondering if date night was off. He'd rather know now if that was the case. He wouldn't know how to get through the rest of the holiday if that was the end of the chance to start a romantic relationship with Faye. He gulped down a breath and said, 'Shall we cancel our date?'

'You're going on a date?' Natty asked.

'We're having dinner together this evening, just the two of us,' said Faye.

Jake thought, *did I just hear her right?* 'The meal is still on, then? I can still book a table at a restaurant?'

Faye turned to him and smiled. 'Of course it is – why wouldn't it be?'

'Because Natty just said—'

Faye put a finger to his lips. 'It's all right.'

Jake took her hand and kissed her palm.

'Smoochy-smoochy,' said Natty, giggling.

Faye looked over her shoulder at her daughter. 'So, Gayle has agreed to babysit. Are you okay with that, Natty, staying at Lark Lodge this evening while we go out?'

'Oh, yes. I love it there. I can play with Olive, and sit in Gayle's library in her comfy chair, and read a book. Then I can play board games with Gayle, Doris, Marty and Nick. I like monopoly.'

'Sounds as though someone already has the evening all planned,' said Jake as they set off.

Natty said, 'Do you think Evie could come for a sleepover?'

'I don't think there will be time to organise that for this evening – perhaps another time.'

'When, though?'

'Well, I do want to visit Aviemore again and look in the souvenir shop. Perhaps Evie will be there in Robyn's outlet, and we can ask her mum. How about that?'

'All right.'

Jake glanced at Faye. It seemed peculiar, still calling it by that name. He said, 'By the sounds of things, Bonnie won't be returning to work this week, so I expect you'll see Evie and her mum when you visit next.'

Faye nodded. She asked him, 'Have you been to Braemar Castle before?'

'I'm not sure. I think so. I would have been quite young. I don't remember much.'

'What do you remember?'

Jake drove through Aviemore, passing the long stretch of shops either side of the road until he passed the train station and approached the roundabout that led out of town.

'When I was looking up the castle opening times yesterday evening, and the directions to get there, I did have a vague memory.' He remembered a long drive through stunning mountain scenery until they had eventually arrived at a turreted castle.

Faye said, 'Such a shame that you obviously wouldn't remember the route your parents took from Aviemore.'

Jake glanced her way and grinned.

Faye knitted her brows. 'Don't tell me you *do* remember.'

'Nah, of course not. I was too young.' Jake had done a journey planner online too and had discovered there were two routes to the castle from Aviemore.

Jake thought they might as well make the most of the journey and enjoy some amazing scenery on the way. That was the reason he'd chosen not to take the A9 via Pitlochry, the main road and the most direct route. They were in Scotland. It was summer, and the weather was fantastic, with sunshine forecast for most of the day. Jake had decided to make the most of the drive and take the very scenic route through the national park – especially as he was quite sure that, even though he hadn't known it at the time, it was the road he'd been taken on as a child. It would take longer. He estimated it would add at least another half an hour or even forty-five minutes, depending on whether they stopped to take photos, but they had all day.

So far, they had stayed quite local, visiting the nearby lochs and forests and venturing into Aviemore. That day, Jake wanted to take Faye and Natty on a scenic drive and see the wild beauty of the national park, as well as the castle.

21

As he drove through Aviemore and approached the small roundabout leading out of the town, Jake ignored the SatNav directing him towards Pitlochry.

Faye looked at Jake. 'I think you missed the exit for Pitlochry.'

'Nah, we're not going in that direction.'

'But the SatNav—'

'It will soon re-route,' Jake said, grinning.

Faye must have caught his expression. 'What are you up to?'

'We're taking the Old Military Road instead.'

'The what?'

'Don't worry, it's perfectly fine to drive. It's the scenic route through the mountains.'

'The mountains? Is it safe?'

'Oh, perfectly. The road is well maintained, and it takes you right through the national park to lush valleys, and past rivers and lochs, and there's even an upland plateau where the road traverses an almost lunar landscape.'

'It sounds as though the drive is going to be spectacular. Is that the route you took when you were a child – do you think?'

Jake hoped this was the journey that had stayed with him from many years ago. 'We might catch a glimpse of Balmoral.'

'What's Balmoral?' Natty asked, listening in on the conversation.

'The Royal Family's Scottish residence, sweetheart,' replied Faye. 'It's called Balmoral Castle.'

'Can we go there too?'

'Not today, sweetheart.'

'Tomorrow?'

Jake looked at Faye. When he had been researching which castle to visit, Balmoral had popped up in the search results. 'I think it's mainly the grounds that the public can visit. I thought Natty would like to go to a proper castle where we can go inside and explore.'

'I still want to visit Balmoral.'

Faye rolled her eyes. 'We haven't got time today, and there aren't that many days left of our holiday, so I don't think we'll be driving over this way again.'

Jake didn't want to think about the end of their holiday. Instead, his thoughts turned to their date that evening, and where he should book an evening meal.

Faye was still talking to Natty. 'We can always plan to visit next time we're in Scotland.'

Jake turned his head to look at Faye. *Did she just say next time we're in Scotland?*

'But we can still go this time. We've got another three weeks.'

'Natty, we talked about this. We can't stay another three weeks. Gayle hasn't got vacancies, and I imagine things are pretty booked up round here as it's the school summer holidays.'

'But what about Jake's house?'

Jake continued driving, looking straight ahead and pursing his lips. Like Natty, he didn't want to return to London either – not at the end of the week, at any rate.

'Look, Natty. I think Jake is having his house redecorated.'

'The *whole* house?' asked Natty.

Out of the corner of his eye, Jake saw Faye turn in her seat to face him. She'd seen the house. Who could resist a holiday in a Scottish mansion, complete with gables and turrets and pretty shutters on the windows? But Jake was still undecided. Not about extending the holiday. He'd do that in a heartbeat. But he knew it would be ridiculously hard to find vacancies around Aviemore. The Lake House would be the only option, but he had his misgivings – how would it affect him, staying there with the little family he'd fallen in love with? How could he not think of the events of last Christmas if he stayed in that house? Could he still enjoy his time with Faye and Natty there? Unfortunately, the very fact that he was undecided answered his question.

Even so, he couldn't lie to Natty, even if that meant a day of pester-power to get them to both relent to staying on into August. He'd just have to do his best to find other accommodation. He was about to tell Natty that the whole house wasn't being redecorated – in fact, that week, with Bonnie off work, the house wasn't being decorated at all – when Faye said, 'Yes, the whole house is being redecorated. Now, put on your headphones and listen to one of your audiobooks.'

Jake glanced at Natty in the rear-view mirror as she put on her headphones and scrolled through the iPad. He waited until she found a book and he was sure she was listening to that and not to what he was about to stay next. He glanced at Faye. 'Why did you say that?'

'I don't understand … she likes listening to her audiobooks.'

Jake shook his head. 'No, I meant about …' he lowered his voice even further, 'The Lake House. It isn't being decorated all at once. In fact, right now, Bonnie isn't there doing anything at all.'

'Yeah – I guessed that.'

'Then why—'

Faye whispered, 'I know your house has a history, and you don't want to revisit your past.'

Jake didn't want to revisit his past full stop. He looked away, embarrassed, when he remembered what Natty had said about the broken memorial stone she'd discovered in the grounds of his house. He wondered what conversation had ensued between Faye and Marty after that discovery – that Jake had lost his marbles for a time, convincing himself that Eleanor was dead, his subconscious protecting him from the truth of her condition.

Jake breathed a heavy sigh. He did want to know what Marty had said. 'Look, about that memorial stone Natty mentioned—'

'It's okay, Jake. You don't have to explain. That's all in the past now.'

So Marty *had* said that he must have had some sort of breakdown. That breakdown was in the past, but Eleanor wasn't. The visit with Marcus to see her was waiting for him when he returned to London. Jake still wanted to avoid it, and the thought of returning to his old life at the Ross Corporation while Marcus checked into rehab. The thought of staying on in Scotland for three more weeks – hell, the entire school summer holiday – seemed very, very enticing. And Natty was right: why couldn't Patrick come and join them for a holiday? There was still the issue of where they would stay, but he'd just have to cross that bridge if Faye agreed.

Jake was about to mention it to Faye when Natty shouted out,

'Are we nearly there yet?'

Nowhere near, thought Jake. 'We've got a little while yet.'

'Can we play I Spy?' Natty asked.

As Jake, Faye and Natty travelled along the winding road from Aviemore to Braemar Castle, the rugged beauty of the Scottish Highlands unfolded before them. The road cut through vast stretches of heather-clad moorland. Tall, craggy peaks loomed in the distance; their tops covered with patches of snow even though it was the middle of summer. They passed shimmering lochs nestled between the hills, and dense pine forests.

Natty shouted out, 'I spy with my little eye something beginning with d!'

Jake had just spotted a deer darting between the trees before it disappeared. He guessed that's what she'd seen too, although he didn't let on. Natty enjoyed keeping them guessing. It made Jake wonder if years ago, he himself, younger than Natty was now, had sat in the back of a car with his parents, driving along this very road, playing I Spy. He smiled at the thought that all these years later, he was back travelling this road with—

'What is it?' Faye asked, placing a gentle hand on his arm again.

Jake took his eyes off the road for a second, realising she must have caught him frowning. He managed a smile. 'It's nothing. Just concentrating on the road ahead.' That was a lie. The road ahead didn't need an awful lot of concentration. He'd been thinking about being back there, all grown up, with his own family – with Faye and Natty, hoping things worked out that evening with the romantic meal. Hoping it would be the start of something wonderful.

It occurred to him that when he thought of family, he always thought of them. He knew that Eleanor, the woman he'd married, along with his unborn child, was gone, but he never imagined what his life would have looked like with them if the accident hadn't happened last Christmas. *You're just protecting yourself from going down that rabbit hole,* Jake told himself, although he knew there was more to it than that; it was the guilt about knowing that if the accident hadn't happened, he wouldn't have met the love of his life. It felt as though he and Faye were meant to be together.

'Are you sure everything's okay?' Faye asked. 'We can change our plans if this trip is bringing back painful memories of your parents.'

'Not at all.' Jake smiled reassuringly. He wasn't about to tell Faye what had been on his mind. 'It's a fantastic drive, isn't it?' he commented, glancing her way once more. He could tell by the look on her face that she wasn't convinced by his reply. But thankfully she let it drop.

Natty's voice from the back provided a welcome distraction. 'Are we still playing I Spy?' she asked.

'Yes!' Faye exclaimed. 'And I know what it is. Look!' Faye pointed at another deer.

The sky was wide and open, with clouds high in the sky casting shadows across the valleys in the distance, creating a dramatic and ever-changing view. 'I'm so glad you chose this route to Braemar,' said Faye.

'Mum, the mountains look like cakes covered in icing sugar,' Natty said, turning around admiring the views out of the rear window of the car.

The I Spy game petered out. Natty put her headphones back on to listen to a story. Faye asked for the guidebook and flicked through the pages for a bit while Jake drove. Then she cast it aside to look out of the window. They drove on, Faye oohing and aahing over the scenery, exchanging a smile, here and there, with Jake.

Jake looked at the SatNav. 'Not long now.'

22

As the car approached Braemar Castle through the quaint village, the freshly restored fortress came into view. Surrounded by manicured lawns and backed by the rolling hills, the castle looked both imposing and inviting.

'Wow! Is that the castle? Natty said excitedly. 'It looks different to the photos in the brochure.' She looked at the picture again on the front cover.

'I think it has had a lot of restoration work done recently and was closed for a time, so we're really lucky that it's open for us to visit today,' Jake said, pulling the car into a space in the car park.

'It looks like the Disneyland Palace we visited with Grandad, doesn't it, Mum?' Natty said, gathering up her summer jacket and backpack.

Jake was about to get out of the car. 'You took Natty to Disneyland?'

Faye paused before she got out of the car too. 'Yeah – in Paris. Natty has got a long memory. She must have been three.'

Jake imagined a trip like that would stay in Natty's memory no matter how old she'd been. He hoped this trip, in fact her whole first holiday in Scotland, would be something that stayed with her, and she looked back on it fondly in years to come.

'We went with Yousaf and Patrick before ... well, before things went wrong.'

They both got out of the car. Faye said to her daughter, 'This is nothing like Disneyland. This is a *real* castle.'

'I've never been to a real castle before.'

Jake smiled when he heard that comment – her first trip to a castle. He was so glad he'd chosen one of the best ones in the Highlands.

'Brilliant! Come on, you two slow coaches – let's explore the castle!' Natty said, climbing out of the car and hopping impatiently from one foot to the other as Jake and Faye gathered their coats and bags together.

They started walking towards the entrance. Natty suddenly stopped. 'I forgot the guidebook.'

'That might be a little outdated now, Natty. Let's buy a new one and then you can keep it as a souvenir of your holiday.'

Jake and Faye paused to marvel at the towering stone fortress, its turrets and battlements standing proudly against the backdrop of the rugged Cairngorms.

'It was well worth the drive here, wasn't it?' Faye commented.

'Oh, yes. The photos in the guidebook don't quite do it justice, do they?'

Faye readily agreed.

Natty had been running ahead. She stopped and ran back with her phone to hand. 'I want to take a photo of you.'

'All right,' said Faye. 'Do you want to take the photo here?'

Natty nodded. She ran behind them. 'Turn around. I want a photo of you and Jake with the castle.'

Faye and Jake stood awkwardly together. It was a silly thought, but Jake wasn't quite sure of the etiquette, standing with Faye, for the photo. They were going out on a date tonight. Did that mean they were officially dating? For a second time, they had nearly kissed. Even so, he was undecided. Should he put an arm around her shoulder, like last time, or hold her hand, or wait to see how things panned out this evening?

'Closer, closer,' Natty said, waving a hand at them. Jake caught her looking at a family – a couple and two children. The chap was standing with an arm around the woman he was with, presumably his wife or partner, as he took a selfie of his family using an extendable stick. Jake hadn't thought to buy one of those so that he could take photos of the three of them together.

Natty shouted, 'Jake, put your arm around Mummy.'

Jake was only too happy to comply. However, he did look at Faye first. 'Is it all right if I—'

'You know it is,' said Faye.

Jake put a gentle arm around her shoulders, stepping closer and giving her a hug. He suddenly felt Faye's arm behind him, circling his waist.

'Say cheese!'

'Cheese!' Faye and Jake replied.

'Excuse me,' the young man who'd just taken a selfie had walked over. 'Would you like a photo of the family?'

The family. Is that what they looked like – a family? Jake grinned at the young man, who would probably be quite surprised that the couple he was photographing hadn't even kissed and were going on their first date that evening.

Jake got out his phone and handed it over. He got back in position, with his arm around Faye's shoulders, noticing that she hadn't corrected the young man regarding that comment about *the family* either. Natty stood in front of Jake. He rested an affectionate hand on her shoulder.

The guy took the photo and handed Jake his phone. He'd just thanked the young man and watched him stride back to his family when someone called out, 'Would you like a picture of the three of you together?'

An older gentleman with a volunteer name badge pinned to his shirt walked towards them.

Jake and Faye exchanged a glance, thinking the same thing – the volunteer had just missed the young man taking a photo for them. Jake was about to tell him this, when Faye said, 'Yes, please. Here – take my phone.'

'But Mummy—'

'Shush! Mummy wants a photo on her phone too.'

Jake grinned at Faye. They stayed in position. The older guy took a lot longer to take the photo. Natty started to fidget.

'There – all done,' he said finally. 'I took several. Hope that's okay.'

Faye took her phone and looked at the photos. 'Oh, they're perfect – thank you.'

Jake glanced at the photos. The first one was the same as the one on his phone – Jake and Faye together, Natty in front. In the next one, a fidgety Natty had moved to stand between them, holding hands with her mum and Jake. The final one had Natty pulling a silly face.

'Have you just arrived?' the man asked Faye as she smiled at the photos.

'Yes, we haven't been in the castle yet.'

'I'm sure you and your family are going to enjoy touring the castle.'

There was that word again – *family*. Jake looked at Faye. Once again, she did not correct the use of the word.

'My name is Angus, and I'm a volunteer at the castle three days a week. So, if you ask for Angus once you've bought your tickets, you can join my tour of some of the main rooms if you wish. It starts just after ten when the castle opens and lasts around forty-five minutes. We meet by the spiral staircase in the great hall. You can't miss it. Let me show you to the ticket office.'

When he'd said *you can't miss it*, had he meant the spiral staircase or the tour? Jake wasn't sure.

'It's so kind of you to let us know. We'd love to join the tour,' Faye replied as they followed Angus to the castle entrance.

'Oh, and in case you didn't know, the castle doesn't have a restaurant, so if you need a bite to eat afterwards, there are some really nice cafés in the village,' Angus continued. 'I usually make my way into the village after I've finished my morning here for a cuppa and a teacake. If you're around later, you might find me in a little café opposite the gallery.'

'Now that sounds like a plan,' Jake replied. He just hoped they found a table in one of the busy cafés for lunch. That day, Jake had declined Gayle's exceedingly kind offer to make them up another picnic hamper. He'd thought that there would be a café on site near the castle, but hadn't checked. 'I'd like a chance to see the village while we're here.'

23

After a very entertaining and informative tour led by Angus, who was patient and didn't pressure the small group of visitors on the tour into moving on to the next room, despite almost everyone lingering to take some photos of the many fascinating items of furniture, art and kitchenware, they reached the castle's historic rooms. Angus regaled them with stories of Jacobite rebellions, which captivated Natty's imagination. Angus suggested that to keep things fun for Natty, they might like to join a family-friendly treasure hunt, following clues around the castle grounds. Natty loved exploring the hidden corners of the castle's walled garden and stopped to take photos.

'I'm going to keep a journal of my holiday in Scotland,' Natty said to Faye and Jake, who were following her along one of the nearby woodland trails with the sun warming their faces.

'That's a great idea,' Jake said. 'You could collect some wild-flowers from our walk and press them for your journal as a keep-sake.'

Natty came to a halt. She turned around and looked at Jake. 'What does *that* mean?'

Jake said, 'Pressed flowers?'

Natty nodded.

Faye turned to Jake. 'I'm afraid we just don't get around to doing things like that – hobbies and arts and crafts together, although I'd love to.'

Jake could hear the disappointment in her voice. He understood. She was too busy with work and her headship course. He knew all too well, because of the increasing amount of time he'd been spending looking after Natty at the weekends while she did coursework and caught up on the never-ending paperwork from her school. It didn't sound to him as though she'd had a proper holiday with Natty for years, let alone spent time together doing things other than work and homework.

Jake had an idea. 'Let's all collect some wildflowers, and we can press them this evening.'

'But I don't know how,' said Natty.

Jake smiled down at her. 'It's easy. All we need is some heavy books – thick books with lots of pages ...'

'Gayle has lots of big books,' said Natty, slipping her hand in Jake's as they walked together.

'Great. And we need some absorbent paper. I'm sure I saw some in Gaye's kitchen drawer. Then you fold the paper, put the flowers inside, and then put the sheet in the pages of a thick book, and leave them to press flat as they dry. Then you have some nice dried flowers to put in your journal.'

'How do you know all this?' asked Faye.

Jake paused for a moment. 'You know, it's all coming back to me.'

'What is?'

'My childhood in Scotland.'

'Is that when you were living in The Lake House before ...'

Faye trailed off, glancing at Natty.

Jake knew what she meant – before his parents died and his life changed forever. He nodded. 'Yes, my childhood was vastly different here. Later, London was private schools, and chauffeurs, and jetting off to foreign climes in the holidays, and visiting museums, art galleries, and London theatres, and all the cultural things Grace, William Ross's wife, loves to do. Don't get me wrong, I did love London, and all those things too, but—'

'But …?' Faye prompted.

'My childhood here was …' Jake was trying to put into words how he felt. 'Slow.'

'Slow?' Faye creased her brow. 'I don't really understand.'

Jake hoped in time she would, but one week wasn't enough to understand. He tried to explain. 'We were always busy in London. When we weren't in school, or doing extra-curricular activities, then there were all the cultural things to do in London, not to mention jetting off to other countries. There was never time just to … well … do nothing.'

The look on Faye's face said she still didn't get it.

'What I mean is, here, after school, and at the weekends, we'd just do what took our fancy. Dad was away a lot on tour with the RAF, so it was just Mum and me, and when he returned on leave, it was just the same; we'd wake up and just do what took our fancy – simple stuff, like some baking or crabbing, or going on a bear hunt …'

Faye smiled.

'Like the book!' Natty asked.

'That's right!' Although the book had been written years after he was born, it summed up his early years living in Scotland.

'It was a simple life. We'd do things like go and pick berries and make a wild berry pie. It's been years since I thought about that.' Jake cast his gaze down at Natty. Being there with Natty and Faye, doing simple things like riding bikes through the forest, and having a picnic by the loch had, for the first time in decades, brought back memories of the wonderful childhood he'd had with his parents there – memories he'd suppressed.

He'd never wanted to revisit his early childhood because of the emotions – hurt, anger, grief – that he'd never really confronted. He'd been afraid to open the lid on it all. But with Faye and Natty there, all he felt was grateful that even though that life with his parents had been short, the time he'd had with them had been quite wonderful. Rather than trying to suppress his memories, he knew he should treasure them. His parents still lived on in his memories – and in his house.

In that moment, he realised he could never sell his childhood home.

'Is that how you know about pressing flowers – because you did that with your mother?'

'Actually, it was my father.' Jake remembered now. His father had been away a lot, but when he had returned on leave, they'd had the most wonderful time. His father had been a man of contradictions – his career was in the military, and yet his passion couldn't have been more different – horticulture. He had been great friends with Marty's father, the gardener who'd worked in the grounds of The Lake House back then. He'd often join the gardener. It made Jake wonder whether, in another life, his father might have been a gardener instead.

Jake knew that his paternal grandfather had been in the military, and his great-grandfather too, and he had heard talk of being sent to boarding school when he was eight, like his father had been, although he suspected that it would never have happened. He did recall asking his mother once what boarding school was. He didn't remember her reply verbatim, but she'd basically told him it was nothing to worry about because he was staying right there in Aviemore and remaining in his local primary school. How wrong she'd been, Jake thought sadly.

He perked up when he thought of those trips he'd gone on with his father, just the two of them, when his father was home from leave. Jake had loved those trips. Because he saw his mum every day, it had obviously been decided that every time his father returned, Jake would spend time with him, just the two of them. And he remembered what was so special about those trips.

'You know, sometimes we'd go camping.'

'On a campsite?' Faye asked.

Jake shook his head. 'Uh-uh. Wild camping.'

'You mean like in the middle of a forest or by a loch?' The look on Faye's face said that was the last thing she'd want to do.

'Weren't you scared?' Natty asked. 'Sleeping in a tent in the middle of a forest – what if a bear had come and eaten you up?'

Jake laughed. 'There aren't any bears in Scotland – unless you count the ones in zoos. Highland Wildlife Park near Aviemore has polar bears.' The zoo was up there on Jake's list of things to do, but unless they really did intend to stay on for three weeks, or even longer, until the end of August, he really didn't see how he'd fit it all in.

'How come?'

'How come – what?' Jake asked Natty. He'd rather lost the thread of the conversation.

'How come you can only see bears in the zoo?'

'They became extinct, sweetheart,' said Faye.

Jake nodded. 'That's right. There used to be a lot of brown bears roaming Scotland – for thousands of years, actually.' Now it was all coming back to him, the conversations he'd had with his dad during their camping trips. Of course, he must have asked if there would be any bears. He remembered being very afraid as a child, like Natty, that one would come for him in the night and gobble him up.

'Where did they all go?' Natty asked.

'They may have been hunted and killed, perhaps for their skins, thousands of years ago, as people tended to wear bear skins in the winter.'

Natty grimaced. 'That's horrible.'

'Yes, but I will tell you a nicer story that my father told me about a special bear called Hercules.' Jake couldn't help but be amazed as the memories of his childhood came flooding back. He did briefly get out his phone and google to check he wasn't imagining the conversation with his father. Sure enough, there were several articles about the famous bear.

'Hercules …?'

Every now and then, as they were chatting, they all paused to pick some wildflowers. Soon, they were each carrying a small bunch.

'Yes, I forgot all about Hercules. You know, for a brief time there was a grizzly bear in the wild in Scotland.'

Faye looked at him sharply. 'What?'

'He wasn't a danger to the public, or, as it happens, any animal. He didn't like raw meat, so he wouldn't feed on the wildlife. Lost almost half his body weight.'

'I don't get it,' said Faye. 'I thought bears liked raw meat. What on earth was the zoo feeding him?'

'Ah, he didn't escape from a zoo. He escaped while he was filming a Kleenex television advert.'

Natty and Faye had paused to pick some more flowers. They both stopped what they were doing and turned to look at Jake. Faye burst out laughing. 'You had me there for a minute. What really happened, Jake? How did he escape from the zoo?'

'No, he was honestly filming a TV commercial for toilet roll.'

Natty said matter-of-factly, 'I like the Andrex puppy.'

Faye just stood there gaping at Jake. 'You're being serious.'

'Yep, and it gets stranger still. He didn't live at a zoo. The Highland Wildlife Park didn't have room for another bear cub, so they sold him for fifty quid to a retired wrestling champion.'

'No way!' Faye exclaimed. 'Is that even legal?'

'Well, it must have been back then. We're talking about the seventies, when people could have all manner of weird and wonderful pets.'

'But a bear …'

'I know, right? A big grizzly bear. Hercules lived with the guy and his wife and children in Perthshire for twenty-five years until he died. He was completely tame and loved ice cream.'

Natty laughed. 'He loved ice cream?'

Jake smiled. 'Apparently so. After his escape in the wild, he became quite the hit around the world – the news got around about the huge tame grizzly bear who'd much rather sit down with a roast dinner that eat the wildlife.'

'Like Paddington Bear,' said Natty, 'who lives with Mr and Mrs Brown.'

'But Paddington Bear is a fictional bear, sweetheart.'

Natty frowned at her mother and shook her head vehemently no. 'Paddington bear is real. He lives at 32 Windsor Gardens with

Mr and Mrs Brown, and their children Jonathan and Judy.'

'And don't forget the housekeeper, Mrs Bird.'

Faye rolled her eyes at Jake. 'Really?'

'Yes, that's her name.' He grinned at Faye, knowing what she was really getting at – his encouraging Natty to believe.

Jake had taken Natty to see the most recent Paddington Bear movie, just the two of them, one Saturday afternoon when he'd been babysitting. Faye had been busy with her coursework for the headship. He wished she'd been able to come with them.

'I wish I'd seen the movie,' remarked Faye. She changed the subject. 'Hercules really ate roast dinners?'

Jake shrugged. 'Who knows. Quite possibly. The one thing everyone knew about the bear was that he only liked cooked food.'

'How did they find Hercules when he was lost?' Natty asked. 'Did the man and woman go and find him like Mr and Mrs Brown went to find Paddington Bear when he was lost in Peru?'

'Paddington was lost in Peru?' Faye asked.

'Mummy, you should have come to the cinema with us.'

'Ah, it wasn't quite so adventurous as the movie,' Jake replied to Natty's question. 'Someone spotted him swimming in a loch, and he was reunited with his family. I imagine everyone in the local area knew about his escape into the wild and were on the lookout. I mean, a six-hundred-pound bear isn't exactly something you'd miss.'

'No, I imagine not,' Faye said, looking at him wide-eyed. 'A bear who loved ice cream. How do you know all this?' Faye asked.

'We started to talk about wild camping, and Natty asked about bears, and then I remembered.'

'You remembered Hercules?'

'Yes. You see, my father and I once went camping in a place

called North Uist, an Outer Hebridean Island.'

'Wow, you've got a good memory. Not sure what this has to do with the bear, though.'

'Oh, my memory isn't that good. I wouldn't have remembered the name of the island or where exactly it was. I do remember travelling for quite some time in the car, and then – unusually – taking a ferry to an island, where we camped. Apart from the ferry ride, why I remember that camping trip, in particular, was that my father told me the story of the bear who escaped and had an adventure on that island. So, I've just googled on my phone to check it out.'

'Ah, I wondered why you were on your phone a moment ago.'

'Yes, you know the bear is buried in the place where he had his adventure in the wild. There's a statue memorial to Hercules at Langass Woodland where you can learn more about the bear.'

'That would make an interesting day out,' commented Faye.

'Yes, it certainly would. It's just a very long drive, and a ferry boat ride, so I expect we won't be able to get around to it this time.' Jake was disappointed about that. He would have loved to show Natty the statue.

'That's not a problem, Jake. It will just serve as an excuse to come back here, to this part of the word, and have another holiday.'

Jake's heart leapt at the prospect that they were already thinking of their next holiday, the three of them together. He'd be returning to his favourite place in the world, with his favourite people.

'We'll just have to make it for longer than a week next time.'

Jake came crashing down to earth. All that talk of staying on for longer, perhaps another three weeks, or even until the end of the school summer holidays, had been just that – talk. Although he had to acknowledge it really was Natty who was pestering to stay on longer.

Natty had run ahead to collect some more flowers, and had been out of earshot, otherwise Jake knew that her pestering about staying at The Lake House would have resumed. She returned to show them what she'd picked.

'They're wonderful,' commented Faye. 'You know, we're going to have far more flowers than we need for your journal. I think I'd like to write a journal for this holiday too – then we can press some of these flowers for my journal. It will make a lovely keepsake of our first holiday together.'

Jake had a lump in his throat at what she'd just said, as though their future together was all mapped out and assured. *Don't screw it up*. Patrick's words came back to haunt him again. He couldn't possibly see how that could happen. This holiday was exceeding all his expectations, and tonight he had their first date to look forward to.

Jake looked at Faye and suddenly felt absurdly nervous. He knew why – so far, their relationship had revolved around Natty. What would happen when it was just the two of them, all evening, sitting over dinner? They'd sat and chatted often enough before when Natty was in bed. But this was different. It was a proper date.

'Sounds as though he had quite an adventure,' said Faye, cutting across his thoughts.

For a moment, Jake had lost the gist of the conversation. Then he realised they were still talking about the bear. They resumed the walking trail, looking for more wildflowers. 'Imagine, though, if you were out on a walk, and suddenly came across a huge grizzly bear.'

'I don't want to go camping,' said Natty.

'I second that,' Faye added.

Jake was disappointed to hear that. He hadn't camped for years and years, not since early childhood, and the wonderful memories made him yearn to do it again. But it wouldn't be the same if he couldn't share the experience with them. He sighed, realising that even just one night under canvas in the Scottish Highlands with them wasn't going to happen. Although he did have the most bizarre idea. He smiled ruefully. Perhaps camping wasn't off the table after all.

'What are you grinning about?' Faye asked.

'Oh, nothing.'

'It *is* something.'

'I'm just thinking about our plans for the rest of the holiday.'

'Why don't we just think about today – we've still got to find somewhere nice for lunch in Braemar village. When we drove through on the way to the castle, I thought it was just what I imagined a Highland village should look like. Traditional stone houses and a river running past the village. It's picture-postcard perfect. I'm looking forward to having some lunch in one of the little cafés.'

Jake nodded, preoccupied.

'You're still thinking about what to plan for the rest of the holiday.'

Jake nodded. 'Sorry.' He smiled, nonetheless.

'Well, as long as it's not camping …' Faye trailed off.

Jake carried on smiling, ignoring Faye's comment, lost in his own little world of holiday planning as they walked into Braemar village for lunch. If he could pull it off, his plan would mean a night to remember.

24

As Natty skipped ahead, Faye put her hand on Jake's arm and drew him closer. They were walking back to the car park after lunch in Braemar village. Natty was carrying two small paper bags from the castle gift shop, where they'd stopped briefly before heading back to the car. One bag contained the brand-new castle guidebook and a little gift for Gayle; the other she'd been given for her flowers. They'd explained to the young man serving in the gift shop that she'd collected some wildflowers for her holiday journals, which they had yet to buy.

'Did I ever tell you that you're the kindest, most thoughtful man I have ever met?'

Jake halted, surprised by the sudden compliment. He didn't know what to say. Instead, he planted a kiss on the back of her hand.

Jake saw Natty stop in the courtyard and turn around just at the right moment, catching Jake and her mum standing close together, her mum's arm entwined with his – and that impromptu kiss.

Natty ran over and took Jake's hand as they crossed the car park to the car. 'I can't wait to tell Gayle all about my adventure in the castle. This is the best day ever!'

Jake thought he'd heard her say that the previous day was her best day ever – or had that been the day before that? It didn't matter. *It's been the best day ever for me too, the best week so far,* thought Jake as he smiled at the little girl who together with her mother had captured his heart.

'Will we have time to stop in Aviemore on the way back, to buy a couple of journals?' Faye asked as she got in the car beside Jake.

He checked his watch. They'd arrived at the castle mid-morning, and after a couple of hours of visiting the castle and wandering the grounds, they'd spent an hour having lunch. It was now two in the afternoon. 'If we make it back to Aviemore by four, that will give you an hour or so before the shops shut.'

'Can we go to Mr Gillespie's store?' Natty asked. 'I want to see if Evie is there and tell her about the castle.'

Faye glanced over her shoulder at Natty. 'I'm not sure if they sell journals there.'

Jake said, 'You could try one of the gift shops in Aviemore, or Wilbur's Bookstore.'

'Wilbur's Bookstore. That sounds familiar. Oh, isn't that where—?'

'Yes,' Jake said curtly, cutting her off as he started the car. He didn't want to talk about Bonnie meeting Robyn and Eleanor at Wilbur's Bookstore last Christmas. Bonnie and Robyn had been the last people to speak to Eleanor before she'd arrived at the ski slopes on Christmas Day before the accident.

Faye fell silent. He glanced at her. 'Sorry, that was rude of me.'

'No, please don't apologise. I shouldn't have brought that up.'

'Brought what up?' Natty asked from the back seat.

Jake and Faye exchanged a glance. Faye turned in her seat. 'Natty, why don't you put on your headphones and listen to a story.'

'That's what I'm doing!'

Jake backed out of their parking space and headed out of the car park.

Faye turned to Jake. 'What do you think happened to Robyn?'

Jake shrugged. 'Goodness knows.'

'Imagine all that time, since Christmas Day, when Bonnie had that car accident and lost her memories, thinking she was Robyn Parker – all because by a sheer fluke she'd borrowed Robyn's car to drive Eleanor to the ski slopes.'

'Yeah.' Jake shook his head. 'If only Bonnie had returned to Wilbur's Bookstore,' commented Jake, glancing at Faye. 'Instead, she skipped town in Robyn's car – well, almost.'

'Yes, but that was understandable, though, wasn't it? Fleeing from her abusive boyfriend.'

'Of course – I'm sure anyone given the opportunity would have done the same thing. But look where that got her.'

'Yes, the car accident, and months thinking she was someone else. But it is all very romantic, because she fell in love with David and found a life for herself here in this beautiful place, so all's well that ends well.'

'Not in terms of Robyn.' *Or Eleanor*, thought Jake, although he couldn't blame Bonnie for driving Eleanor to the ski slopes. From what Bonnie had said, Robyn had been packing to leave Wilbur's Bookstore, where she'd been working during the Christmas holidays. Bonnie had done as Robyn had asked and driven Eleanor to the ski slopes while she packed; the favour was going to be returned when Bonnie came back to the bookstore because the plan had been that Robyn would give Bonnie a lift on the way out of town. Jake said as much to Faye.

'I wonder where Robyn could have gone. With no car. On Christmas Day.'

'It's like she disappeared into thin air,' commented Jake.

'Exactly.'

They fell silent for a time. Jake could see Natty in his rear-view mirror with her headphones on, looking out of the car window as she listened to a story.

'I heard that Bonnie wants to find Robyn.'

Jake glanced at Faye. He wasn't surprised. After all, she had stolen Robyn's car. It sounded as though her intention had been to get as far away from Aviemore, and Logan, as she could, and then phone Wilbur's Bookstore and let Robyn know where she could find her car. Of course, that hadn't happened. He wasn't surprised that she wanted to find Robyn and make amends. Even so, he said, 'Where did you hear that?'

'I got chatting to Evie's mum, Annie, who is minding Bonnie's outlet at Mr Gillespie's store while she's … away.'

Jake nodded, even though Bonnie wasn't away. She was still at home in the boathouse.

'Maybe if Judith tells Bonnie and David everything about her stepdaughter, they might glean a clue as to her whereabouts.'

'Perhaps.'

Faye shot Jake a look. 'I don't think you hold out much hope of them tracking her down.'

'It's just all rather odd, if you really think about it. Most of Robyn's possessions were in that car, including her money – that savings book with the money left to her in her late father's will, and all those deposited cheques from Judith that she'd sent to Robyn while she was on her travels. She must have walked out of

Wilbur's Bookstore with not much more than the clothes on her back.'

'People start over.'

Jake knew all about that – he was a poster child for starting over, leaving his job as a corporate lawyer for the Ross Corporation and going into teaching. But he had money behind him to make such a substantial change. By the sound of it, Robyn had not taken her money with her. And she hadn't even told her stepmum what she was up to, although it did sound as though they were estranged.

'What are you thinking?' Faye asked.

Jake didn't really want to voice his thoughts, not after such a perfect day together, and spoil the mood.

'Jake?'

He breathed a sigh. 'I'm thinking something happened to her.' He glanced at Faye, expecting her to ask him what exactly he thought that could be. Of course, he had no clue. But her pensive expression suggested she felt the same way.

A few minutes silence followed, until Faye said, 'I'm not sure I want to visit Wilbur's Bookstore after all.'

'I thought you wanted to buy journals. They're likely to sell them in a bookshop.'

When he didn't get a reply, he glanced at her. She was staring out of the side window. 'What is it?' There was something on her mind, he could tell.

Faye turned from the window. 'This is going to sound really stupid …' She paused.

'Go on, Faye, please. I can't imagine anything you say would be stupid.'

'Yeah, well, I think you'll revise that opinion.' Faye looked over her shoulder at Natty.

'She's still listening to a story, so whatever it is she won't hear it.'

Faye lowered her voice all the same. 'It's just that three people were in Wilbur's Bookstore on Christmas Day, and … well … two of them had accidents, and the other one … well, god knows what happened to Robyn.'

Despite everything, Jake smiled. Faye caught him smiling. 'See, I knew you'd think I was being silly.'

'Seriously, Faye, the bookstore is not jinxed. Remember at the party you met Melissa and Brodie?'

'Melissa and Brodie?'

Jake kept his eye on the road ahead. 'Yeah, Wilbur has retired, and now Brodie, his grandson, runs the bookstore. I heard he is an aspiring writer too. Melissa, his fiancée, has a law degree and is working for a local law firm, working towards qualifying as a solicitor.'

Faye nodded, although she still didn't appear that receptive to changing her mind about the bookshop.

'Look, they live there. They told me they've moved into the flat above the shop. They haven't had an accident – or disappeared.'

He took his eyes off the road a few times, looking her way.

'Well, all right. I did want to buy Natty a couple of reading books, and a novel for myself. I like to read a few pages before I go to sleep.'

'Nothing in Gayle's study take your fancy?' Jake quipped, knowing full well the books were self-help books.

Unsurprisingly, Faye shook her head. 'Thinking of missing people …' ventured Faye.

Jake frowned. He thought they'd moved on from Robyn, and

what may or may not have happened to her.

'If you want to go and visit Martha again, please don't hold off doing that on our account. I'm sure we can figure out how to fill in a couple of hours while you're gone.'

Jake felt terribly guilty that he had all but forgotten the old lady with dementia to whom he'd made a promise he couldn't keep – that he would find her son. He'd guessed she'd given her son up for adoption. He wished he hadn't made the promise. He wished he'd never answered a random phone call and ended up visiting an old lady living in the wing of Cedar Grove – once a stately home, and now a hospice.

But Martha and he were connected in a way. She'd known William Ross and William's wife Grace years ago, through her brother, Ralph Delaney – known to Jake as Aubrey Jones.

'Jake?'

He would rather she hadn't reminded him. He wanted to spend all his time, every second, with the woman he loved. All he wanted to think about was arriving in Aviemore and booking a table at a restaurant for their first date. He said, 'Look, in all honesty, I don't want to see Martha this week. It's not as though I'd have any news to give her regarding her son.'

'That's understandable,' replied Faye. 'You know, you could still approach Aubrey. I know you've been holding off doing that in case he doesn't know that his sister had a baby years ago and that her son would now be in his thirties. But what if he does know, and not only that, but he can also tell you, and Martha, her son's whereabouts? Or at least help in the search. I'm sure Aubrey has …'

Jake had stopped the car at a junction, indicating he was turning left. There were no cars behind him. He paused to look at

Faye when she didn't finish her sentence. 'You were saying …?'

Faye scratched her head. 'I was going to say that I bet Aubrey has ways of finding out things.'

'What do you mean?'

'Oh, I don't know. I'm probably being silly again. I was just thinking back to when I first met him.'

'Oh, right.' Jake would rather not revisit that episode when he'd discovered Marcus had been on a bender. Instead of returning home to his fiancée, Lydia, he'd tried to crash at Jake's house. Except Jake hadn't been in that night. He stayed over on the sofa at Faye's after babysitting. When he'd got a frantic call at work saying Marcus hadn't returned home, Faye had given him a lift home. That was when she'd met Aubrey and discovered he'd been keeping an eye on Jake.

The conversation wasn't doing Jake any good, especially when he knew he'd succumbed to switching off his mobile phone, afraid he'd get another one of those calls from Lydia to say Marcus was missing. What could he do about that scenario when he was hundreds of miles away in Scotland? Even so, as he turned left and continued along the next stretch of road, he still had to ask, 'Silly how?'

'Aubrey. He's a bit of an enigma, isn't he? I get the feeling there's more to him than meets the eye. In fact, it's more than just a feeling. What exactly is his job at the Ross Corporation?'

That was a good question, and one Jake wanted to avoid. 'Why is that relevant?' he said. He could feel himself getting defensive. He had a soft spot for Aubrey, and the feeling was mutual.

Faye sighed. 'I don't know, but I can just imagine he might play it a bit hard and fast when it comes to the law. The fact that he uses a false name …' She trailed off.

'I hope you're not suggesting he's some sort of criminal, because I can tell you now that William Ross would not hire someone like that to work for him in the Ross Corporation.'

Jake expected Faye to remonstrate with him, saying it was not what she was suggesting. She didn't. 'But you said yourself that William and Aubrey go way back.'

'That doesn't mean—'

'And do you know that he carries a gun?'

Jake pursed his lips. Of course he knew. And he knew where Aubrey kept it too – or at least his spare. Jake had borrowed it and taken it with him to confront Patrick after Natty had gone missing. He'd assumed Patrick, who'd been estranged from Faye, had taken Natty, and that it had had something to do with Natty's father, Yousaf. Of course, that hadn't turned out to be the case. Natty had gone AWOL from school. She hadn't been kidnapped, and her going missing had had nothing to do with Patrick or Yousaf.

In hindsight, Jake had no idea what he had been thinking at the time, taking a loaded weapon with him to confront Patrick, apart from the fact that he'd have done anything to get Natty back. But anything could have happened. He didn't know the first thing about guns. It could have gone off and killed somebody. He cringed at the memory that it had gone off accidentally, and thanked his lucky stars that Patrick had not mentioned to Faye the gun that had been in Jake's possession.

'You *do* know – about Aubrey's gun, don't you?'

Guns, plural, thought Jake. But he didn't let on about that. Instead, he asked, 'How do you know he carries one?'

'Because he got one out of his briefcase that time he appeared at your front door after that commotion when we were at your house and discovered Marcus was there. That's when I realised that he must be following you, keeping an eye out for one of his employers.'

And his dear friend, thought Jake. He could feel himself getting defensive again. 'Look, you don't know anything about my past life with the Rosses – and you certainly should not be judging Aubrey.'

'Why don't you fill me in about your past life? You never talk about it.'

'Let's just drop it – can we?'

It was true that Jake never talked about it, and he certainly had no intention of raising the subject this week, of all weeks, when he knew he should be back in London, doing as he'd promised and heading up the Ross Corporation while Marcus checked into rehab. It was the last thing he intended to talk about.

He stared at Faye, thinking, *just tell her what's on your mind.* The he thought, *no.* If he could have folded his arms and stamped his foot like a child, he would have. But he couldn't. Instead, he set his jaw forward and just frowned at the road ahead. He could feel Faye's eyes on him and hoped she realised it was the end of the conversation. They had a little under fifteen minutes to go until they arrived in Aviemore. Jake nudged the accelerator. He couldn't get there fast enough to get out from under Faye's gaze.

'Fine!'

Jake glanced at Faye. 'What do you mean – fine?'

'You don't really want us to stay at The Lake House. I was rather hoping we would, and was a little surprised, not to mention disappointed, when we first arrived in Aviemore and it turned out we weren't staying in your house, but a guesthouse.'

Jake had to tear his eyes away from Faye to keep an eye on the road, but he couldn't help but think *how did this conversation turn to The Lake House and Lark Lodge?*

'Don't get me wrong,' continued Faye. 'I love Lark Lodge, along with the people I've met there, and wouldn't have it any other way. But I don't see how this, *us*, is going to work if we can't talk about your past.' She lowered her voice. 'I'm afraid that you'll walk out any moment, and back to your old life.'

'What are you talking about?' He'd thought the conversation was about Aubrey.

'What do you think I'm talking about? That promise you made to Marcus.'

'It was only going to be temporary, and besides, I'm here, aren't I?'

'That's only because Natty went missing.'

Jake was about to protest when he realised this was an argument he wasn't going to win.

'Is date night off?' Jake asked in a small voice, even though he already knew the answer.

'What do *you* think?'

25

Faye and Natty walked along the high street in Aviemore, looking for Wilbur's Bookstore. Although there were some children's books in Gayle's library at Lark Lodge, most were a bit young for Natty. Faye was distracted for a moment by a window display, the soft furnishings draped with an assortment of colourful throws and cushions. It was the tartan cushions and throws that had caught her attention. The other shop window was displaying the usual items you might expect to find in a grocery store.

'Gillespie's General Store,' she said out loud, stopping to take a closer look.

'No mum, that's not the shop. We're looking for a bookshop,' Natty said, sounding a little exasperated. 'Remember – we went in there to buy ribbons for Olive.'

Of course Faye remembered. It had been the first day of their holiday, and while Jake had been visiting the tourist information and getting them tickets for the steam train, she'd visited Robyn's Interior Design because Natty had dragged her into the shop. She hadn't had a chance to check out the window display. It had certainly caught her attention this time around.

'Look, there's Jake!'

Faye glanced at Natty, who was waving. She saw Jake drive by on his way back to Lark Lodge.

'What time is he picking us up?'

Faye frowned and mumbled, 'I wish we could make our own way back.'

'What was that, Mummy?'

'Oh, nothing.'

Faye pushed the door open and stepped inside the shop, thinking of the last time she and Natty had visited. She'd been so full of the holiday, and all the amazing days out she imagined Jake was in the throes of planning during his visit to the tourist information. Now there they were, just a few days later, and the date night she'd been looking forward to, that she'd already planned, having asking Gayle to babysit, was out of the window. In fact, now the whole holiday was.

Jake should have been booking a table at a restaurant in Aviemore for their meal out together while she and Natty bought their journals. Instead, he was heading back to Lark Lodge. He didn't say why he had to return there straight away and couldn't just hang around the car for them. But she could make a good guess – he was packing to leave early; to head back to London and the Ross Corporation.

Faye was feeling very sorry for herself. She wished she'd never brought up Martha and Aubrey. Then they wouldn't have argued. Then again, it had only brought to the fore her secret fear – that his new life away from his corporate career wasn't a new life at all but a means to an end – some sort of mental breakdown that he had to work through away from the corporation and the Rosses.

Seeing the broken memorial stone to Eleanor in the garden of The Lake House hadn't allayed her fears but had actually compounded them. She'd been trying to ignore such thoughts, especially as the holiday was going so well. But Jake *had* been having some sort of breakdown. And with the help of his teaching post, and her and Natty, he had been working his way towards returning to that life after the pain of losing his wife. She and Natty, they'd been a means to an end, a way through the healing process. That was all they were to him. She was convinced of it.

'Mummy, what are we standing here for?'

Faye snapped out of her unwelcome trip down the rabbit hole she'd been avoiding. When she'd voiced her fears that Jake would return to his old life, he hadn't exactly denied it. She was going over the conversation in her mind. Although he'd said it was only temporary, when she'd questioned why he was really on holiday with them, he hadn't said it was because he wanted to be with her. It was what she'd wanted to hear. But he'd said nothing of the sort.

'I've been such a fool,' she said under her breath.

'What's wrong, Mummy?' Natty took her hand. Faye saw the worried look on her face. She thought of Jake packing to leave, and thought *I've still got our return train tickets. Jake can go back, but I'm going to make the most of the remainder of the holiday.* Faye couldn't remember the last holiday she'd taken with Natty. This was still going to be a holiday to remember for the two of them – she'd make sure of it.

'Come on, let's see if Evie is here. You wanted to tell her about your trip to the castle, didn't you?'

When Faye stepped forward, Natty didn't budge. She was looking through the shop window. 'What is it, sweetheart?'

'I wonder why Jake's gone back to Lark Lodge.' She turned to look up at Faye. 'Do you think he's got a surprise waiting for when we get back?'

Faye could feel the tears welling up. She swallowed. There was going to be a surprise all right; the one Natty least expected – Jake would be leaving. But that wasn't going to be the worst of it. He was going to be leaving them too. This was just why Faye hadn't let a new man into Natty's life since her father left.

Faye was determined not to think about that right now. She wasn't spoiling their one holiday together in years. She'd just have to lie to Natty and say that Jake had been called back to London unexpectedly. Then Faye knew she'd have to drop the bombshell when they returned.

'Come on.' Faye held on to Natty's hand. 'We're going to make this a holiday to remember, you and me. Starting now.'

'All right, Mummy.'

They both stepped forward. Ahead of them in Mr Gillespie's General Store was the sweet aisle.

'Can I have some sweeties, Mummy?'

'Of course you can.'

Natty halted. 'Really? Are you feeling okay, Mummy?'

Faye laughed. She knew why Natty had asked that question. It was a rarity that Faye bought her sweets. Normally it only happened after much cajoling, and even that didn't always work.

'Let's buy Evie some too,' said Faye. She didn't know yet whether Evie was there, and she'd have to check with her mum, Annie, whether Evie could have some sweets too, but she'd just cross that bridge in a minute.

Natty ran ahead, down the sweet aisle. Faye was about to follow when an older man carrying a cardboard box appeared around the corner of the grocery shelves and nearly bumped into Faye.

'Who are you?' he asked gruffly. 'What do you want?'

Faye stared at him. She guessed by the apron and the box of groceries that he was Mr Gillespie. She had the impulse to state the obvious and be very sarcastic by replying, *I am your customer, and I want to buy some sweets for my daughter.* Instead, she said, 'I was admiring your window display and would like to see some more tartan cushions, like the ones you have on display, please.'

She knew it wasn't Mr Gillespie who sold interior design items, but looking through the window a moment ago, it had seemed that there was no one serving in that side of the store. Faye knew that Bonnie wouldn't be in work all week. She'd assumed that Annie was looking after the store. She wondered why she wasn't there.

'Right, well you don't want to speak to me about that,' he said.

Faye had the feeling that he was being unhelpful on purpose. 'So, who do I speak to, then?' Faye couldn't hide her sarcasm. She glanced around the empty shop and thought that it was little wonder there were no customers if he was going to treat people like this. Even so, she added conversationally, 'It's unusual, having an interior design outlet in a grocery store.'

'Is it?'

Faye watched him kneel down to unpack the box of washing-up liquid and put the plastic bottles on the shelf. She could see why Bonnie wasn't returning to work straight away if this was what she had to look forward to – working in a shop with such a grump.

'You're still here,' he said, looking up at her.

Faye really liked the cushions. 'As I said, I'm interested in a couple of tartan cushions like the ones in the window, and possibly a throw.'

'Well, which is it – two cushions and a throw or just two cushions?' Mr Gillespie got off his knees and squashed the small box flat between his hands.

Faye bit her lip before she said something she'd regret. She'd had enough of his short-tempered retorts. She was about to fetch Natty and take her custom elsewhere – there was supermarket on the other side of the street that she imagined had plenty of sweets – when he stopped, looked down the sweet aisle, and bellowed, 'What are doing? I hope you've got the money to pay for those, young lady. If you're shoplifting …'

Natty immediately dropped the sweets in her hand.

'Hey!' Faye strode up to the old man. 'Who do you think you are – accusing my daughter of shoplifting?'

'Ah, I didn't realise she was with someone.'

'Yes – her mother.'

Natty ran passed Mr Gillespie and immediately took her mother's hand. 'I didn't take anything, Mummy. I was just choosing some sweeties.'

'I know, darling.'

Faye hadn't had the pleasure of meeting this grumpy old man the last time she had been in the shop last – although for some reason, he seemed familiar. She just couldn't place where she'd seen him before. But this was the last straw. She held her finger up and pointed at him. 'Nobody accuses my daughter of shoplifting. Come on, sweetheart – let's go. We'll come back when we can speak to Annie, who sold you the ribbon for Olive last time we were here.' Faye glared at the man in front of her. 'Maybe she would like my custom.'

Faye was just storming up to the shop door when Mr Gillespie called out, 'Wait!'

She reluctantly turned around.

'Did you just say Annie sold you some ribbon for Olive?'

Faye shrugged. 'Yeah – what of it?'

Mr Gillespie got out some glasses from the pocket of his apron. He peered at them both. 'Hey, I know you. You were at the party.'

'Party? Bonnie's party?'

'That's right.'

Now Faye knew where she'd seen him before. 'You were there too.'

'Yes, Bonnie is engaged to my son, David.'

'Oh, of course.' It made perfect sense that he'd have been at the party too. There had been so many people, and so much going on that evening that the whole night had gone by in a blur.

'I remember you now. It was the mention of ribbon and Olive. Your daughter and Evie were putting ribbons in Olive's hair.'

Inexplicably, Mr Gillespie suddenly turned and walked down an aisle. He picked up the sweets that Natty had dropped and quickly returned. 'Sorry, but I do have a problem with kids coming in, stealing sweets, after school.'

'Well, that's terrible. Parents should be instilling in their children a moral compass – teaching them right from wrong.'

'I agree.'

Faye followed him to the counter. She continued, 'But in my experience, some parents just have no parenting skills.'

'In your experience …?'

'Oh, I'm a teacher.'

Mr Gillespie stood behind the counter. 'Sad state of affairs, isn't it?'

'I'll say.'

He put the sweets into a small paper bag and secured it with some tape. He handed it to a shy Natty, who was standing beside Faye at the counter.

Faye opened her purse. 'How much do I owe you?'

'It's on the house.'

'Oh, I couldn't …'

'I insist. That was very rude of me to assume …' he trailed off. 'Sometimes I have a problem with out-of-towners too.'

Faye quipped, 'Why does that not surprise me?'

Mr Gillespie looked at her sheepishly. 'You know, most of them are perfectly nice, but some do sweep in here in their posh four-wheel drives, with their second homes, acting like they own the place.'

Faye thought of the Rosses and wondered if that was how they carried on, although somehow, she couldn't imagine it.

'Well, I can assure you, that's not me.' Although she knew she could be guilty by association if that was how the Rosses behaved.

'I'm Duncan, by the way. I'm not surprised we didn't really meet at the party. It all went by in a bit of blur, with what went on … you know.'

Faye smiled. 'Yes, I know.'

Duncan looked again at Natty. 'I am so sorry if I scared you.' His face softened as he broke into a smile. 'And what's your name?'

'I'm Natty. We're on holiday with Jake and staying at Lark Lodge for a whole week. I want to stay longer. I love Scotland. Mummy, can we stay longer – please?'

Faye swallowed. Unfortunately, that was now definitely out of the question.

'Yes, I remember you arrived with Jake Campbell-Ross.'

Faye rolled her eyes at Natty, wishing she hadn't mentioned that. 'Sad state of affairs, what happened to his wife.'

Faye regarded him for a long moment. She looked at Natty. 'Do you want to go and choose some more ribbon for Olive?'

'But there's no one in that side of the shop.'

'It's okay, isn't it?' she asked Duncan.

'Yeah, sure.'

'Bring them back here so I can pay.'

Duncan shook his head. 'It's fine. I'm sorry I behaved like that.'

'Please, Natty, just choose what takes your fancy.'

Faye watched Natty skip across to the other side before she turned to Duncan. 'You were saying … about Jake's wife, Eleanor …'

26

Faye had just finished an illuminating conversation with Duncan about Eleanor Campbell-Ross when Natty ran over with a handful of ribbons.

Faye looked at them. 'Oh, sweetheart! That's a lot of ribbon.' She turned to Duncan. 'I insist I pay for them.'

'Well, how about if you have some spare change, putting it in this instead.' Duncan picked up a charity box and placed it in front of her. The charity was in support of mountain rescue. Apt, thought Faye, considering the conversation they'd just had. She emptied all her spare change into the box. She still felt she should pay for the ribbon, although she expected that Duncan would reimburse Bonnie for the cost.

'What's this?' asked Natty, picking up a leaflet from a stack on the counter.

'Ah, that's the Aviemore ice rink. My son works there now. He coaches the younger children who are members of the junior ice hockey team and want to go on to play in the bigger league games. He also takes some of the ice-skating lessons.'

'I didn't realise Aviemore had its own ice rink.' She picked up one of the leaflets. I've taken Natty ice-skating before at Christmas time in the courtyard of Somerset House in London.'

'Oh, aye. I've heard of that. Don't they do it every year, starting around November?'

'Yes, that's right.'

'But here you can do it all year round.' Duncan pointed at the leaflet. 'Take a look at the photos. It's indoors, in an alpine-themed marquee.'

'What's that?' Natty asked.

Faye looked at Natty. She was pointing at the photos of children skating who were holding on to plastic penguins and polar bears.

Duncan replied, 'Ah, those children are using the penguin and polar bear skating aids.'

Faye heard the shop door opening and the bell above the door signalling more customers.

'I want to go ice-skating, Mummy. Can we?'

'Of course we can. Anything you want, sweetheart.' Faye was so pleased she'd stopped by Mr Gillespie's store. This was just what she needed – something she and Natty could do together.

'Do you think Jake knows how to ice-skate?'

Faye was saved from answering that question by the sound of another child's voice shouting out, 'Natty!'

Faye turned around to see Annie slipping off her coat as she walked towards them.

'You're back already,' remarked Duncan. 'How did Evie's dentist check-up go?'

'Yes, fine. No fillings, thank goodness!'

Natty was showing Evie the ribbons.

'Oh, Annie. Just the person! I wanted to buy a couple of things I saw in the window display.'

'Of course, Faye. What were you after?'

'A couple of tartan cushions and a matching throw.'

She glanced at the leaflet in Faye's hand. 'Oh, if you're interested in ice-skating, and you're after doing something really special, I'd go to the snow disco.'

'The what?'

Duncan overheard them as they walked towards the other side of the shop. 'Oh aye, I forgot about that.'

'Come with us. Joe, myself and Evie are going. Are you around on Saturday night? That's when they hold them.'

'Yes, we leave on Monday.' Faye didn't want to think about Jake leaving already and staying on without him. But she wasn't going to cut her holiday short. Besides, Patrick was collecting them from the train station when they arrived at Paddington. He'd be surprised that Jake wasn't with them, but she wasn't going to think about that right now.

'Great! It's a proper disco with music, disco lights and, of course, snow!'

'Snow – in the summer?'

'Oh, yes. They've got a fantastic snow machine. We all get wet, but that's the fun of it.'

'Oh, it sounds amazing.'

'Hold on. I'll check I can get tickets.' The girls had run ahead to the interior design side of the shop. Annie halted and got out her phone. 'Ah, we're in luck. There are tickets left. Hold on, I'll quickly buy three in case they go. It's ever so popular.'

'Two tickets, Annie. We just need two.'

'Oh, skating not Jake's thing? He could always sit and have a cup of coffee and watch. That's what Joe is going to do. He'll appreciate the company.'

'No, he won't be coming.'

Annie looked at her. 'Everything okay?'

Faye's lip trembled. She swallowed. She couldn't break down and cry now. Not in front of everyone – especially Natty. She'd save that for the evening, when Natty was fast asleep, and have a good cry into her pillow instead.

'No, not really. I think Jake is going home today.'

'Oh, I'm so sorry to hear that.' There followed an awkward silence. Annie soon picked up that Faye wasn't going to elaborate. 'Look, whatever it is, I'm sure things will work out.'

Faye nodded, although she doubted that very much. Right now, she felt such a fool for taking the initiative and organising a date night with Jake.

'I've got them! Two tickets for the snow disco on Saturday evening at six.'

'I don't suppose you could pick me and Natty up?' Faye suddenly realised she didn't have access to a car. Jake would be returning the hire car before he left.

'Of course, no worries.' They were walking over to join the girls when Annie got a text. 'Oh, seriously!'

'Everything all right?' Faye asked.

'Of all the days. My babysitter has let me down. We've booked a meal out this evening in Aviemore. It's our wedding anniversary. Joe is going to be so annoyed when he finds out. I'd normally ask David, and I know he'd come over to babysit, but under the circumstances, spending time with Bonnie this week is his priority, so I don't want to ask.'

Faye glanced at Duncan. 'What about her grandfather?'

'Yeah, I know he'd step in, but we're going to be out really late, and it means he'd have to drive home in the dark in his old van, down the winding lanes from where we live, and I just don't like the thought of that. We haven't got a spare bedroom to put him up, you see.'

Faye watched Annie scroll through her phone and ring a number. 'Hello. Yes, I need to cancel a table reservation this evening, please.' Annie gave her name, waiting, and then said, 'Yeah, we'll book another time. I'll phone you when I've fixed another date.'

Faye suddenly had an idea. 'Does she like sleepovers?'

Annie was about to slip her phone in the back pocket of her jeans. She looked at Faye. 'Huh?'

'What if she could come and stay the night with me and Natty at Lark Lodge? Then you could have a sleep in, and come to collect her tomorrow when you're ready. And you'd be able to have that meal in the restaurant.'

'Really? You'd do that?'

'Of course. Natty will love it.'

'But will it be okay with the other guests, having two giggling little girls, probably up until goodness knows when?'

'Oh, we're up in the attic. I'm sure no one will hear them.'

'But what about you?'

'It'll be fun. At home, she's asked for a friend to come over for a sleepover, but I've never got the time for it. This would be just perfect. I'll just phone Gayle, though, to make sure.'

'Oh, just the person – I was going to ring you,' said Gayle down the phone.

Faye frowned wondering why that was.

'I'm coming to pick you and Natty up.'

Faye's heart lurched. She'd thought Jake might be packing up to leave, although in her heart she really hoped she was overreacting and that wasn't the case. But now she knew. He'd probably left already. And he hadn't even said goodbye.

'Faye – are you still there?'

'Yes, I am.'

'Are you finished shopping for your journals?'

'Oh, the journals.' Faye didn't fancy doing one now.

'Oh, Mummy, I want a journal.'

'Hold on, Natty.' Faye nearly forgot the reason she was calling. 'Look, I wonder if I could ask a huge favour. Annie has been let down by her babysitter, and they wanted to have a meal out this evening – it's their wedding anniversary. They would have called on Joe's brother, David, to fill in but they don't want to ask them to babysit under the circumstances. Is it okay if Evie comes over and stays the night with me and Natty?'

'Hey, the more the merrier. In fact, that'll work out perfectly this evening.'

Faye was sure it would. The interconnecting attic bedroom that Jake had vacated would be free for the girls.

'Are you ready for me to come and collect you now?'

'Hold on just a moment, Gayle. I'm just going to have a word with Annie.' She looked at Annie. 'It's all organised. She can come.' Faye looked at her watch. 'How shall we organise this? Will you bring Evie a little later, or should she come back with us now and have dinner with us?'

'Actually, that is a good idea. She'll need her pyjamas and toothbrush, and a teddy – or two.'

'Oh, of course.'

'I've got an idea. Why don't you choose your cushions and throw? By that time, the store will be closing. We'll all nip back to my house to collect Evie's things for the sleepover, then we'll go to Lark Lodge, and I can drop you all off. Save Gayle a trip into Aviemore.'

Faye nodded. That sounded like a plan, and a perfect way of getting out of the inevitable conversation with Gayle in the car about Jake leaving. She did not want that bombshell dropped on Natty just yet, spoiling what remained of her holiday, before she had a chance to tell Natty herself.

'Gayle, you don't have to come and collect us. Annie will drop us at yours.'

'Okay, great. See you soon-ish.' She turned to Annie after she ended the call to Gayle. 'I suggest you phone the restaurant back and get that table reservation reinstated.'

'Oh, crumbs.' Annie looked at her wide-eyed. 'I'll do that right now.'

Faye chose her cushions and throws while Annie made the call. When she got off the phone, with the table booked again, Faye said, 'I just have to shop for a couple of journals before we leave.'

'Well, there's a bit of time before the shop shuts. Meet you back here at five?'

Faye nodded. 'Natty, come on.'

'No, I don't want to come.'

'But I thought you wanted to choose a journal?'

Natty looked at Evie. 'Can Evie come too?'

'Yes, can I come too?'

'Is that all right, Annie?' Faye asked.

'Of course. If *you* don't mind.'

'Not at all.'

'There's a couple of nice gift shops. I'm sure you'll pick up some journals in there, and you've got a bit of time to kill before I shut up shop here, I can suggest a very nice little coffee shop –

it's not far from here. Evie likes their hot chocolates, and the coffee there is amazing.' Annie tried to give Faye some money for the coffee and hot chocolates.

Faye shook her head. 'No, this is my treat. Anyway, I'm not sure we're going to get as far as stopping for hot chocolate and coffee. I was going to visit Wilbur's Bookstore to buy Natty some story books. I didn't get around to buying some for the holiday.'

'Oh, Evie has got loads. Natty can choose some when she comes round.'

Natty overheard. 'Are we going to Evie's house?'

Faye told her about the sleepover. As she was leaving the shop, the two girls were jumping up and down with excitement. Faye guessed she wouldn't be getting much sleep that night.

Annie ran over before she stepped outside and gave her a hug. 'Thank you so much, Faye.'

'No – thank you, Annie.' Faye realised that of all nights, a sleepover tonight would be a godsend. She would be too busy entertaining the girls and too exhausted to cry into her pillow.

27

'Is this the place?' Faye asked Evie.

'Yes. This is where me and Mummy come for a hot chocolate.'

Faye stepped inside the café. Unfortunately, it was extremely small, with a handful of tables that were already taken.

'Can I help you?' asked a young man, briefly looking up. He was in the middle of cleaning a table right by the door for a couple who had just arrived.

'No, it's okay. We were just leaving.'

'Did you want something to eat or drink?'

'Yes, hot chocolate and coffee.'

'We have a small garden area at the back if you'd like to sit there. It's a beautiful day – you can make the most of the sunshine.'

Evie tugged on Faye's arm. 'That's where me and Mummy sit – in the garden.'

'Oh, okay.' Faye looked at the young man. 'Lead the way.'

'I'll show you,' said Evie.

The young man looked at Evie. 'Hey, Evie. I didn't see you there. How's things?'

'Great. This is Natty, my new friend. We're having a sleepover tonight at Lark Lodge.'

'That sounds amazing. Say hi to Gayle for me.'

'I will.'

Faye's head bobbed from Evie to the young man as she listened to this exchange, although she didn't know why she was acting all surprised. Evie obviously went in there a lot with her mother. Even so, she couldn't get over how friendly people were. She said to the young man, 'You know Gayle?'

'Oh, yeah. Gayle's father was my family's GP for years and years. He was such a lovely man. I remember when I was a child, he'd come and do home visits whatever the weather. We were all so pleased to hear that his old place wasn't being sold and that Gayle had turned into a guesthouse.'

Faye nodded. 'It's a lovely place. I'm staying there this week. I just wish there had been vacancies after then because I might have stayed on.' Faye was a bit surprised she'd come out with that, especially considering that Jake wouldn't be with them. But there was no denying the fact that, just like Natty, she loved it there. She had surprised herself in finding that she wanted to stay on.

'That's okay, Mum,' said Natty. 'We're going to stay at The Lake House.'

The young man immediately stopped cleaning the table. 'The Lake House? But isn't that the Rosses' holiday home?' His eyes went wide. 'Who are you? Are you a Ross?'

The café had gone noticeably quiet all of a sudden. Faye glanced sheepishly around and found that everyone's eyes were on her. She needed to put a stop to the conversation. She opened her mouth to say something, when Natty got there first.

'Jake owns The Lake House.'

'Jake Campbell-Ross?'

Natty nodded. 'My mum and Jake are getting married.'

'Natty!' Faye wanted to the ground to swallow her up. She shook her head. 'Look, ignore her. I don't know where she got that idea from.'

'But it's true. I saw you kissing.'

'Right, come on.' She took Natty's hand. 'Did you say the garden is this way?'

The young man nodded dumbly, staring after her.

Faye could hear the chatter of voices and the mention of Jake's name. Fortunately, the garden seating area was quiet. The garden was compact, with an assortment of different coloured bistro tables and chairs in varying pastel shades. They were colourful and vibrant. Each had a little parasol.

The garden was enclosed by a high brick wall, with colourful clematis creeper and pots of summer flowers, making it feel more like someone's private garden than a café.

Evie took Natty's hand. 'Come on, let's sit in there.'

Faye watched Evie lead Natty over to a small summerhouse in the corner, painted in pastel blue. The double doors were open, and inside Faye could see lots of colourful cushions on a rug, along with a shelf of small toys and books. They quickly made themselves at home, both lying on their stomachs with a book between them.

There were three other small children in there – toddlers playing with toys while their mothers sat with hot drinks. Faye could smell the rich aroma of coffee wafting from their table.

'How lovely,' Faye commented as the waiter returned with a menu. She hoped he didn't mention Jake Campbell-Ross or The Lake House. 'I like the cosy summerhouse filled with books and toys,' she said pointing.

'Yes, it's very popular with our younger visitors. We get a lot of young mothers and toddlers come in when their older children are at school for a catch-up and a natter,' he continued. 'The cosy corner keeps the little ones entertained while the mums have a bit of time to relax and to enjoy their drinks together.'

Faye thought it was a shame that this outside space wasn't open in winter too. She said as much.

'It's open all year round. We have a marquee we put up in the colder months, along with a patio heater and glow lights. Mums often stop by here straight after the school run. It's quite magical. Don't forget, it gets quite dark in this part of the world, so by half-past three, when school's out in the winter, it's already getting dark.'

'Can I have my hot chocolate in here?' Natty asked, looking at the waiter.

'I'm afraid hot drinks aren't allowed in the summerhouse.'

Faye looked at the toddlers sitting with the toy cars and understood why hot drinks weren't allowed in there. 'That's all right, Natty. When the drinks arrive, you can both sit with me and keep me company for a bit.'

'That sounds like a good plan,' said the waiter. Before he left the garden with their order, he paused. 'If you're very good, you might find our resident tiger comes to join you.'

Faye's eyes went wide. 'Did you just say a resident tiger?'

Evie sniggered into her hand.

'Oh, yes.' He winked at Evie, and added, 'But you have to be on your best behaviour, otherwise she might bite.'

'I know,' said Evie.

Faye stared after the waiter and then turned her attention to Evie. He couldn't be serious – surely. But who knew what surprises were in store. Her whole holiday had been one long, lovely surprise – until that day, when she and Jake had rowed.

'What does resident mean?' Natty asked, not at all concerned by the mention of a tiger.

'It means they live here.'

'A tiger lives here?' Natty looked at Evie, so did Faye.

She just sat there smiling and nodding her head. 'You'll see.'

'Evie, is your mum busy working in the shop?' one of the young mothers seated at another table asked.

'Yes. This is my new friend, Natty, and her mum, Faye.'

'Would you like to come and join us?'

Faye looked over at the other table with the four young women seated around it. She glanced around the small garden and realised one of them must have been talking to her. 'I'm sorry – what?'

'Come join us. It's no fun sitting alone.'

Faye didn't mind sitting alone if it meant she wouldn't get the third degree. She was wondering if one of them had been inside when they'd first walked in and had overheard what Natty had said, and whether they were now under the impression that Faye and Jake were getting married. She'd have some explaining to do when they returned to Gayle's house and Jake was nowhere to be seen.

Unfortunately, Faye thought it rude to decline the invitation to join the four young women at the table. Everyone there knew everyone else. She went to join them with a question on her lips. She took her seat and said, 'I have to ask – this is going to sound so silly, but is there a resident tiger?'

All the young women surprised her by nodding their heads. 'She's over there – look.'

There was a hushed silence. Faye could hear purring before she saw a very large ginger cat with vivid, stripy markings. 'Thank goodness it's just a cat,' she said.

'Oh, she isn't just any cat,' said the waiter, depositing two tall glasses of hot chocolate and a cup of coffee on the table. 'That's Tyger.'

Faye watched the cat sit beside the book and paw at it when they tried to turn the page.

Evie said, 'Hello, Tyger,' and gave her a scratch behind the ear.

Natty tentatively stroked the cat.

Evie said, 'It's all right, she doesn't really bite.'

Faye grinned. 'You weren't joking when you said you have a resident tiger.'

'She can put on the charm when she wants to, especially with food around, so we do have to ask for everyone not to be tempted to share any food with her. Tyger is on a diet.'

'Oh, dear.'

'Yeah, she's spoiled rotten. We could just take her home out of harm's way, but everyone loves her, and a lot of people come here and enjoy stroking the cat while they have a cup of coffee or lunch.'

Suddenly, Tyger ran out of the hut and pounced on the table, surprising Faye.

She hadn't surprised anyone else on that table. The waiter said, 'Tyger, I've got nothing to eat on this tray, only drinks.'

Tyger sniffed one of the hot chocolates.

'Oh no you don't.' He lifted her off the table, as he said to Faye, 'That's why we've got the sign …' he pointed.

Faye smiled at the sign: *Don't Feed the Tyger.*

Faye looked around the table. She didn't remember this sort of thing when she had been a young mother in London. There just hadn't been a sense of community. The only time she'd had a sense of that had been through Natty's school or her own school.

But outside of work, it was difficult to make friends or even have time for friends.

What had Jake said about his childhood there?

Faye sat watching Natty lying there on a cushion next to Evie. They were both reading the same book, checking with each other when they were both finished reading and ready to turn the page. He'd referred to his childhood as *slow*. Sitting there, watching Natty with a new friend, she was getting a sense of what Jake meant. There was nothing slow about living in London – at least not for her. It was frenetic – work, home, marking, schoolwork, bedtime, and yet more work. There was little wonder she never relaxed or spent time with Natty, real time together, in the moment, not thinking of the endless list of things she had to do at work. This made such a lovely change, just being present.

She looked at the other women seated around the table as they each introduced themselves. Faye told them she was there on holiday, with her daughter and a family friend. She did not want to specify who that was. Especially as their friendship was no more, and he was probably already on the train back to London.

She didn't want to think about that. Instead, she said, 'I love the sense of community here. It's nothing like where I'm from.'

'I bet you wish you didn't have to go home,' one of them remarked.

'Don't be silly. Of course she wants to go home. She lives in London. Just imagine the theatres and art galleries, and all the museums to visit on those winter days. And the gorgeous public parks in the summer.'

'If you love it so much, why didn't you stay there? Why did you move here with your husband, hundreds of miles away?'

Faye leaned forward in her chair, interested to hear what the woman had to say to that. She'd assumed all the young mothers seated at the table had lived there all their lives.

'Oh, do stop teasing. You know very well why, Milly. I wanted to come home and raise my children in Aviemore. I mean, just look at it. What could beat this?'

Faye glanced at Natty, who was having the time of her life – she was going to have her very first sleepover tonight. Faye decided that she was going to make the next couple of days extra-special. Suddenly, an odd thought occurred to her. She regretted the remark she'd made to Jake when he'd spoken about his father and those wild camping trips they'd been on together. The fact that he remembered them decades later, when he must have been all of four or five when they took place, meant that they must have made a lasting impression. When he'd suggested the three of them went camping, she'd immediately rejected the idea. Now she regretted not being open to new experiences. Even if the thought of a night or two under canvas didn't immediately appeal to her, she'd done other things that didn't – like going on a bike ride – and had found she'd had the time of her life.

Faye breathed a heavy sigh, realising there was no going back on the camping idea now. *I could take her myself one day*, she thought. I could persuade my dad to come instead. She called Natty and Evie over to sit at the table for their drinks.

She turned to the friendly young women who'd asked her to join them. 'I think it's a wonderful place to raise children,' commented Faye. 'If I could get a teaching position here, I'd have no qualms moving.' Faye halted. Her mouth dropped open. *Did I really say that?* She gave Natty a sideways glance. The grin on her face said she'd heard every word. 'Can I go to the same school as Evie?' she asked, as though the arrangements to move were already in the pipeline.

'Oh, Natty, this is just grown-up talk.'

'You mean we're not moving?'

Evie said, 'I go to the primary school in Aviemore. It's fun. Can Natty come too in September?'

'There are places at the school,' one of the mothers told her.

Faye sighed. 'I'm sorry, I shouldn't have said anything. It's not as simple as that.'

Natty said, 'Why not?'

'Because Mummy needs a job,' Faye replied.

One of the young mothers, Milly, said. 'Do you teach secondary school by any chance? My eldest is starting his second year in September, but he's very disappointed because the headteacher is leaving. They're taking applications.'

'Milly, she would need to be a head, not just a secondary school teacher. Not just anyone with a teaching qualification can apply.'

'Actually, I've just finished my training course to become a headteacher, so I can look for positions.'

'Really? What a stroke of good luck. Why don't you apply?'

'Yes, Mummy, why don't you apply?'

Faye hesitated. As much as she loved it there, she couldn't move there – not without the love of her life. All it would do would remind her of him – the man she realised she'd been in love with since she'd first set eyes on him; the new trainee teacher who had walked into her school and into her life. Besides, there were also the practicalities, even if things had worked out with Jake. She would need to give at least a term's notice in her current job if she was leaving to take up another position. And then, of course, Jake would have needed to secure a position too.

As if Natty had read her mind, she said, 'Jake would need a job too.'

Faye's eyebrows shot up. *Oh, god,* she thought. *Why did she have to bring up Jake in front of all these people?*

'Who's Jake?' Milly asked.

'Natty, drink up your hot chocolate.'

Natty didn't do as she was told. 'Jake owns The Lake House.'

'The Lake House?' one of the young mother's said in surprise, nearly choking on her drink. 'But isn't that the Rosses' holiday home?'

'Are you talking about Jake Campbell-Ross?' Milly asked.

Natty nodded. 'My mum and Jake are getting married, and then we're going to live in The Lake House.'

Faye sighed heavily. It was a repeat of what had happened when they'd first walked into the café.

'Didn't he lose his wife here last Christmas?'

Faye would rather not answer that, although this time she *was* going to set the record straight. 'Look, Natty, no one is getting married, and no one is going to live in The Lake House.'

'That's a shame,' one of the mothers commented. 'I heard it's such a lovely house. Such a shame after what happened last Christmas that the place has been abandoned.'

'Yeah, I heard not one member of the family has been there since, and the place is going downhill fast.'

Faye ignored those comments. She did not want to talk about The Lake House.

'But you're going on a date with Jake this evening,' said Natty.

'Does it look like we're going on a date? You're having a sleepover with Evie.'

'But I thought—'

'There is no date.'

'But I saw you kiss.'

'Well, grownups do silly things that don't mean anything. Right now, Jake is on the train back to London. It's over, Natty, whatever I thought was going to happen, whatever you thought was going to happen. Well, it's not. And that's that. So, you better finish up that hot chocolate so we can get going.' Faye sat back in her seat and folded her arms.

Everyone, even the cat, who had been circling the table, stopped dead. The silence up the table was broken by Natty bursting into tears.

She was still crying when they walked back into Mr Gillespie's store.

'Oh, what happened?' said Annie. She had been pulling on her coat and was about to put the *Closed* sign in the window when they'd all trooped in. Mr Gillespie had left already. Annie was about to lock up the shop.

Evie had an arm around Natty's shoulder.

'A dose of reality, I'm afraid. Things didn't work with me and Jake.' She lowered her voice. 'I was going to wait to tell her.'

Annie said, 'I'm so sorry to hear that. But perhaps it's for the best that she knows now, rather than prolong the inevitable.'

'Natty, let's collect your ribbons,' said Evie. 'We can make Olive look pretty. Would you like that?'

Natty wiped her runny nose with the back of her hand, and said, 'Yes.' Faye decided not to tell her off this time for not using a tissue.

As they all walked out of the shop, Annie said, 'What about you? Are you okay?'

'No, not really.'

'Listen, you don't have to do the sleepover after all. I really understand if you want to cancel it.'

'Not at all. I'm really looking forward to it. It couldn't have come at a better time, honestly. It will keep my mind off … things.'

'Yes, I get it. You'll be so exhausted after those two keep you awake, no doubt nattering until the early hours, that you'll fall into a coma until morning, with no time to ruminate.'

'Exactly. It's just what I need.'

As they headed to Annie's car, she said, 'You know, maybe things aren't as bad as you think.'

Yes, they are, thought Faye. Annie didn't understand.

As they got in the car, Natty was chatting happily to Evie. Faye looked at her, surprised. Although she was relieved that her daughter seemed to have bounced back remarkably quickly, she was amazed at the sudden change.

'Are you all right, Natty?' she asked.

'Evie says her mum and dad argue and then they kiss and make up.'

'Evie!'

'Well, it's true.'

Faye grimaced. The problem was that she and Jake weren't in a relationship and certainly weren't married. And Jake had a lot of baggage. And so did she. She was about to tell Natty that this was different, that things were a hell of a lot more complicated, and that they weren't just going to kiss and make up. But the innocent smile on Natty's face stopped her in her tracks. She would let her enjoy the journey back to Gayle's in blissful ignorance that what Evie had told her about her mum and dad was true for Jake and her mum. She would just give her that and wait until they arrived for her to find out the truth.

Faye turned in her seat. She was not looking forward to going through all the tears again with Natty when she found out the truth – for real this time.

28

As soon as Gayle opened the door and greeted them, Natty said, 'Where's Jake?'

'He's gone—'

'See, Natty. What did I tell you?' Faye sighed. 'He's gone back to London without us.'

Natty's bottom lip started to quiver. 'It's not true!' She shoved passed Gayle and ran down the hallway to the kitchen.

'Of course it's not true,' Gayle called after her.

Natty emerged from the kitchen and ran back down the hallway.

Evie said, 'Where are you going?'

Natty suddenly bolted up the stairs, calling out, 'Jake! Jake!'

Faye watched Evie follow Natty up the stairs. Faye didn't have to ask Natty what she was doing. She was going up to Jake's bedroom. A moment later, she heard two pairs of feet running down the stairs.

'He's not in his bedroom!' exclaimed Natty.

Faye sighed again. 'When are you going to get the message that he's not here?'

'But his clothes are still in the wardrobe, and his phone is charging on the bedside table.'

Faye creased her brow. 'Huh?'

Gayle said, 'Isn't anyone listening to me?' She turned to Faye. 'I don't know what you're on about, saying Jake has gone to London. I can assure you he hasn't.'

Faye was still convinced he had, despite Natty saying his clothes and mobile were still there. Perhaps he hadn't been able to get a train that day and had needed to postpone the trip back until the next day.

'There's a little surprise awaiting you,' Gayle said to Natty.

Natty jumped up and down. 'See, Mummy. I told you!'

Faye folded her arms. 'What do you mean – *I told you*?'

'That Jake came back here after he dropped us in Aviemore because he had a surprise for us.'

'It's true,' said Gayle, grinning.

Faye turned to Gayle. 'What do you mean – a surprise?'

'Ah, now that would be telling …'

Faye would much rather she did tell. She was not in the mood for surprises, and certainly not one from Jake.

'Marty!' Gayle called out. 'Can you do the honours?'

'Do what?'

Marty emerged from the lounge. 'Ah, I thought you'd never arrive back. You were *ages*.'

'Evie has come for a sleepover. Annie has just dropped us off, but we had to go to Annie's house first to collect some things for Evie.' Faye was standing there holding Evie's overnight bag. Jake hadn't vacated his room yet, which meant the girls would not be sleeping next door. There were only two single beds in her room. She hoped Gayle had a put-you-up bed. She asked Gayle.

'No need. Now, Marty did you find what I asked for?'

'Will this do?' Marty asked, producing a black tie from behind his back.

'That will do nicely.'

Faye looked at the tie, wondering what on earth was going on. She didn't bother asking. Instead, she said, 'The three of us haven't had dinner, so obviously I hope it's okay to join you this evening.'

Gayle didn't answer. Instead, she walked over to Marty and took the tie. She walked up to Faye. 'Now, let's just put this on.'

Faye looked at her wide-eyed. 'Pardon me?'

'It's part of the surprise.'

'Are you saying I have to wear a tie?'

'Oh, dear me no. Well, not in the normal sense.'

Faye frowned. It had been a long day. 'Look, Gayle. I just want to take Evie's things up to the bedroom.'

Gayle took Evie's bag out of Faye's hand and gave it to Evie. She then knelt and whispered something in Natty's ear.

Natty shouted, 'For real?' She turned on her heel and ran upstairs.

'What on earth …?' said Faye.

'Now, Faye, I want you to put on this blindfold.' She held up the tie.

'What?'

'Just humour me.'

Faye really was too tired for games. But she was too tired to argue either. As Gayle put on the blindfold, she heard Natty thundering back down the stairs.

'Right, we're all set,' said Gayle.

'For what?' Faye asked, feeling foolish standing there with a tie around her head.

'For the surprise,' said Gayle, chuckling.

'It'd better be good,' Faye mumbled under her breath as Gayle led her down the hallway. She suddenly felt a wet nose on her hand. 'Olive, is that you?'

Olive whined.

Well, at least I'm not the only one who thinks this is all really weird, Faye thought. Next she heard the key in the lock and the back door opening.

'Are we going outside?'

A moment later, holding Gayle's hand, she could feel grass underfoot and knew they were in the back garden. It was a warm summer evening. She could hear birds chirping and could smell freshly mowed grass.

Gayle took tentative steps forward.

'Nearly there,' said Gayle reassuringly.

'Nearly where?' Faye said, frowning, wondering what all the song and dance was about. 'Can't you just tell me what the big surprise is?' In that instant the blindfold was off, and Faye stood there, wide-eyed, while the girls did a happy dance in delight.

In front of her were two tents. They weren't just any tents; they were old-fashioned cream-coloured pitched-roofed style canvas tents, the like of which she'd only ever seen in old movies or photos of English men from another era travelling abroad. The flaps were tied back, revealing two camp beds with sleeping bags in each tent.

Natty and Evie ran into one of the tents. Evie had her overnight bag and started to unpack. Natty had a bag too. Now Faye knew what she'd run upstairs all excited about while Faye was being blindfolded.

Faye just stood there, dumbfounded. She didn't know what had surprised her the most – the two old tents, all set up at an angle next to each other, with fairy lights hanging across both, or the small camp table for two outside of one of the tents, complete with two chairs, place mats, knives and forks, and a bottle of wine, already uncorked, with two wine glasses.

But the biggest surprise of all was Jake, who was pulling out a camp chair and motioning for Faye to join him at the table.

'Well, I'll leave you two lovebirds,' said Faye. 'Natty, Evie,' she called. You're coming with me.'

'But we want to play in the tent,' Natty whined.

'And you will. You'll have all night to spend in your tent. But you're hungry, aren't you?'

They both nodded.

'We're going to eat in the kitchen with Marty and Nick.'

Olive came running across the lawn, straight up to the table.

'Oh no you don't.' Gayle grabbed Olive too. 'Right, let's go.'

'Can we go back to the tent after dinner?'

'Of course you can. When Faye and Jake have finished their dinner.'

'All right,' said Natty.

Before they returned to the house, Natty ran up to Jake and threw her arms around him. 'I love you. You're the best.'

Jake put his arms around Natty. 'And I love you too.'

'I knew Mummy was wrong.'

'Wrong about what?'

'That you were leaving us.' Natty wiped tears from her eyes.

Jake knelt and took Natty's shoulders. 'I'd never do that. Not in a million years. Not for anything in the world. You know that – right?'

Faye saw Jake lift his eyes and look straight at her while Natty was nodding. Jake stood. 'Now, off you go.'

Natty looked at the table for two, and grinned. 'Are you and Mummy having a date?'

'I hope so,' said Jake looking sheepishly at Faye as Natty ran off to join Gayle, Evie and Olive.

29

Jake put his hands on the back of the camp chair.

'Is this why you couldn't come and pick us up? You were doing all this?'

'Yeah, sorry about that. I trawled around Aviemore to make a table booking for this evening …'

'You were still going to book a table after we rowed?'

'Yes, and then make a massive, grovelling apology, and hope you accepted said apology, and we could still have our date.'

Faye looked at the camp table. 'What happened to the restaurant meal?'

Jake frowned. 'Fully booked. I couldn't get a table for love nor money. Although there was one restaurant that had had a call to cancel, but then just as I was about to book, would you believe, the customer called back to confirm they could come after all, as they'd managed to sort out babysitting.'

Faye raised her eyebrows and looked towards the house.

'So, when I couldn't get a restaurant booking, I texted you that I was going back to Gayle's. I'd had an idea. I still wanted the date, and to make it extra-special, but honestly, I didn't think it would take that long to put up a couple of tents. Marty and Nick pitched in to help, but these old tents are as fiddly as hell to put up.'

'The tents are your dad's – aren't they? The ones you used to use on your camping trips when you were a child.'

'Yes, but we only took one with us, which we shared. After the fun and games of setting them up, now I know why.' Jake shook his head. They were also heavy to carry, which was another reason they would not have taken both. 'I knew they'd be in the house somewhere. I found them in the basement, along with the camp beds. When I heard Natty was bringing a friend for a sleepover, I set up an extra camp bed, and Nick had two sleeping bags, and Gayle had a couple too. She supplied the fairy lights. The old camp table and the lamps are my dad's. Before I set off back to Gayle's, I went shopping for ingredients for the meal.'

Faye stared again at the table. She didn't know what to say. She couldn't believe he'd done all this for her.

'Oh, god. I knew it. You hate this. I shouldn't have … you told me you didn't want to go camping. I should have listened. Look, please have the meal with me, out here in the garden. But we don't have to sleep in the tents.'

'*Wild* camping. I said I didn't fancy wild camping. I think I'd freak out, us being all alone in the middle of nowhere in a tent. But this …' Faye still couldn't believe he'd done all this. 'After we argued, I thought …' Faye trailed off, avoiding his gaze.

'You thought I'd packed up my stuff and gone back to London.'

Faye nodded.

'Look, about that. I've made a decision. I'm not going back to the Ross Corporation – not now, not ever.'

'But you made a promise to Marcus,' Faye said as she took a seat at the table.

Jake took a seat opposite her. 'Yeah, in the heat of the moment. In hindsight, it was foolish. I haven't worked there in months. Of course, that wouldn't be a problem. I've worked there all my life. But the problem I could foresee was getting sucked back into that life and finding it difficult to leave again.'

That was exactly what Faye had been afraid of. She didn't say anything; she just listened.

'Someone else will just have to step up and mind the shop, so to speak, while Marcus sorts himself out. There are many very capable people who could step into Marcus's shoes for a time.'

'What about Derrick?' Faye asked. Jake had told her about the young employee in whom he'd seen great potential. So much so, that he'd done something quite unprecedented and very controversial within the Ross Corporation. Jake had given the young boy from a rough London council estate his apartment, the one reserved for the likes of Marcus and Jake, who had worked their way up to the top of the corporation, just one step down from William, the CEO.

'Yes, I was thinking of him, but he's got a way to go yet. He's only eighteen.'

'Still at night school, doing his law degree?'

'Yes, that's him. He's in no way ready to head up the corporation. But he will be one day.'

'But he was ready for that apartment.'

'You know why I did that.'

Of course Faye knew. It wasn't just the potential he saw in Derrick, but the fact that one day he might not make it into work. He had no protection on the estate. He stood out because he'd refused to join a gang – a gang, incidentally, that could protect him.

'You know you saved him, and his brothers.'

'I know.'

'How is Derrick's mum settling in?'

'Yeah, she took some persuading to take the apartment.'

Faye knew Derrick's mum was a nurse, and a single parent trying to raise three boys and keep them off the streets. She'd been wary at first. Why wouldn't she be after finding out her son had been given a luxury apartment that he didn't yet deserve? Jake had convinced her that Derrick would earn his place in the corporation soon enough, and Faye remembered he'd mentioned that he had hopes for Derrick's younger brothers too. He was imagining a future in which Derrick and his brothers, much like Marcus and Jake, were heading up the corporation. He hoped that one day Marcus might pass the baton to Derrick. He'd said that in Derrick he felt the future of the business was assured.

'I'll tell you another thing,' said Jake, pouring the wine into the two glasses. 'The more I thought about it, the more I was convinced that I played right into Marcus's hands. He wants me back. Aubrey and William want me back – for good. I know they think this teaching malarkey is just me having a breakdown … but that's just not true. This is me. This is my life, here … with you and Natty. Well, not here, here, anywhere you are. Although it would be rather nice if—' Jake halted.

'If …?' She caught him looking over the hedge in the direction of The Lake House.

'Oh, never mind. I'm just making the point that I'm never going back to my old life. No matter what happens, I am *not* going back.'

Faye stared at him. She knew what he meant when he said, *no matter what happens.* He was talking about Marcus. She bet when Marcus found out, he'd tell Jake he wasn't going to rehab unless he came back. It was emotional blackmail – pure and simple. Faye knew how close they had been – best friends, as close as brothers, before they had fallen out over the accident. But Faye thought Jake was doing the right thing, distancing himself from Marcus and the Ross Corporation – not just for her and Natty's sake, but for his wellbeing too. Jake was right; there would be pressure for him leave his life with them behind and return to the family business for good. But still she worried about the ramifications. About Marcus.

'When are you going to tell Marcus your decision?'

Jake put the bottle down and passed Faye a glass of wine. 'I already have.'

Faye was about to raise the glass to her lips. She put the glass down. 'You've told him already?'

'Of course. I've also told him I'm in Scotland right now, on holiday.'

'How did he take it?' Faye asked nervously.

Jake shrugged. 'Who knows.'

'But what did he say?'

'Nothing.'

'Nothing?'

Jake sighed and got his mobile phone out of the pocket of his jeans. 'Nope, no reply to my text.'

'You didn't speak to him?'

Jake shook his head and looked at her sheepishly. 'Look, Marcus can be very persuasive. I just thought if I spoke to him, I might give in. Believe me, it's better this way. Although I know you like Marcus, and you think I've done the wrong thing not speaking to him.'

Faye thought no such thing. She knew Jake. He always put everyone else first. It was just how he was. He was right when he said he'd probably give in and end up back at the Ross Corporation. This trip, ignoring Marcus's texts and calls so he could come away, was probably the first time he'd ever done that – put himself first. And it was all for her. *He does love me,* thought Faye. She reached across the table and took his hand. 'If he calls – don't answer that phone.'

Jake grinned. 'I won't.'

They stared at each other for a long moment. 'You really thought I was packing up and returning to London without you and Natty?'

Faye dropped her eyes from his gaze, embarrassed. 'Yeah. It was so stupid; I realise that now. But all my fears about you leaving us and returning to your old life just surfaced, and I convinced myself that was the case.' She added in a small voice. 'I even told Natty. I wasn't going to. I was going to lie and say you'd been called away, back to London. But it just came out.' Faye looked up at Jake. 'Oh, she cried, Jake. It was terrible. She was beside herself at the thought that you'd left us.'

Jake was still holding her hand. He squeezed tightly. 'Patrick warned me you wouldn't commit to a long-term relationship. I understood. Yousaf had let you down, you and Natty, and I know you didn't want to let another man into Natty's life who she'd get emotionally attached to and might let her down again if things didn't work out. So, you kept your relationships at a distance.'

It was true. As far as Faye was concerned, she'd been going out having fun, having sex, and she wasn't hurting anybody – least of all Natty. 'Things were working,' she said. *Or I assumed they were*, she thought. 'And then you came along.'

'Yes. I came along and threw a spanner in the works, didn't I?'

'Yes, and do you know what that spanner was?' Faye asked.

Jake squeezed her hand. 'I think I do. At least I hope I do.' He took a deep breath. 'Love. You fell in love, didn't you?'

'It wasn't meant to happen.'

'I guessed that. Not until Natty was eighteen, and gone to university, I'll bet.'

Faye nodded. 'I wanted to protect Natty.'

'And yourself.'

Faye nodded. It was true. By not committing fully to any relationship and not falling in love – Faye realised she was barely with any of the guys she'd dated long enough to get to know them properly, let alone fall in love – she was protecting herself too.

Jake sat there, holding her hand. 'I didn't think I'd fall in love with anybody after Eleanor.'

'Jake, you don't have to—'

'I want, I need to tell you this, so you understand. Eleanor will never be the third person in our relationship, if that's what you think.'

It had crossed Faye's mind that if it wasn't for the accident, Jake would still be happily married to his wife, and they would never have met. She spoke her mind, surprised when Jake vehemently shook his head.

'Here's the thing, Faye. The cracks were starting to appear in our marriage long before Christmas and the accident.'

'How do you mean?'

'If you'd asked me that question before I met you – which sounds ludicrous, I know – but if you had, although I would have had to acknowledge something wasn't right between Eleanor and me, I couldn't really put my finger on what it was. I can now.'

'How come?'

'This is still something I'm coming to terms with. I loved

Eleanor, of course I did. But since meeting you, I realise it was never in the way I thought.'

'What do you mean?'

'I'd known Eleanor practically all my life. I loved her, of course I did. But I was never *in love* with her.'

Faye stared at him.

'I fell in love for the first time in my life when I met you, Faye. And … and I felt so guilty that I just couldn't love Eleanor in the same way. And … and then when I look back on last Christmas, when she found out she was pregnant. I was over the moon at the thought of being a parent, but … but she wasn't – at least not with me. Looking back, I realise that now. And it makes me wonder if she knew I was never in love with her.'

'But how would she have known that? Unless …' Faye trailed off.

'Unless …?'

'Sorry, never mind.'

Jake stared at her. 'Unless she didn't love me either – not in that way.'

Faye pursed her lips. She'd been thinking something else – just like Jake had fallen in love, had Eleanor fallen in love with someone else too? Faye certainly was not going to voice that thought.

'You know, when I was abroad working in Washington for a time, she stayed behind in London, alone. She didn't enjoy following me around being a corporate wife. She wanted a career of her own. She was looking at starting a business. When I returned from Washington, she went up to Scotland for a time – Edinburgh – said she was looking into starting her business.'

'In Edinburgh?'

'No, I don't think so. I presumed she was up there looking for materials and ideas. To be honest, I didn't get involved. Although I remember we did argue about it. I didn't want her to go.'

'But she went anyway.'

He nodded. 'But when she got back, she seemed … different.'

Faye thought that could have been to do with going away, having some independence for a time, although she suspected it was more than that – a lot more.

Faye wanted to change the subject. What good would it do him if he were to find out she had met someone, and she'd had an affair? Although if that *had* happened, she couldn't see how he'd find out about it unless someone came forward.

Faye took his other hand in hers. 'Why don't we let sleeping dogs lie, eh? The accident happened, and Eleanor … well, whatever went on before in your marriage, it's all in the past now.' Faye wanted him to move on. It was very selfish of her, she knew, but then again, if Jake was going to have a life with them, he had to.

'Let sleeping dogs lie …' Jake cast his eyes up to the mountain beyond the house.

Faye followed his gaze, remembering what Duncan had said in the shop when he'd told her some things about the skiing accident at Christmas that Jake hadn't long found out himself.

Jake dropped his gaze. 'I can't. I didn't tell you this before, but there was someone else up there on the mountain with us when the accident happened. Well, two people, actually.'

Jake went on to tell her about the guy who had taken his own life. 'Sorry, not the nicest subject to bring up during our date, is it?'

That was what Duncan had mentioned to her in the shop. In the spring, when the snow had thawed, a body had been discovered, along with an abandoned car in a car park. The poor man on the mountain had shot himself. Duncan had mentioned that the man had paid for a car parking ticket, which he said was rather strange for someone who was about to take their own life. But it was how they had been able to pinpoint his time of death – that and the gunshot people had heard at that time. However, Faye didn't think it was strange at all – getting a parking ticket. The poor guy clearly wasn't in his right mind.

'And there was some other person up there off-piste too,' said Jake. They must have phoned the emergency services. It's how we were found so quickly. The strange thing is that they never came forward to take any credit for saving us.'

'Perhaps they didn't want any recognition and were just content with knowing they'd saved lives that day.'

Jake shrugged. 'I guess. But I'd still like to know who both of them were.'

'Oh, you don't know?'

Jake shook his head. 'I've been meaning to talk to David, or Joe, ask them if they heard who they were. But at the party it didn't seem appropriate.'

Faye stared at Jake. Was it appropriate to tell him the identity of one of them now? She didn't know who the guy was who had saved them, but Duncan had found out who the poor guy was who'd lost his life on the mountain on Christmas Day – it was a former employee of the Ross Corporation. Duncan had found a small newspaper article in a local paper. The man had been fired from the Ross Corporation on Christmas Eve. Faye had no idea why he'd been fired, but losing a well-paid job like that, especially at Christmas, would have been bound to send someone into a spin – or worse; they might even consider doing what he'd done.

'Jake, look about what happened on that mountain …'

'No, let's not talk about it anymore, please Faye.'

'But—'

'I'll get around to seeing David at some point. And I have a feeling Bonnie knows something.'

'How do you mean?'

'She was avoiding me at the party – I just know it.'

'Jake, she wasn't avoiding you. She wasn't really talking to anybody, apart from David. She must have been so embarrassed, feeling as though she'd deceived her friends, even though it wasn't her fault she'd believed she was Robyn. I bet it will take time to get over that.'

'Even so, I still think she knows something about Eleanor that she hasn't revealed for some reason.'

Faye cocked her head to one side. 'I thought you said you didn't want to talk about it anymore?'

'No, you're right. I don't. Not right now. In fact, I'm not sure how we got on to the subject of the accident – do you?'

Faye did. They had been talking about letting sleeping dogs lie. She would be happy to do that. But whatever had really happened up on the mountain, Faye knew Jake couldn't let it go. She didn't know what good it would do, but she'd promised Duncan she'd tell Jake about what he'd discovered. Jake was right, though: this wasn't the time or the place. He'd gone to so much trouble to make their date extra-special. She glanced at the tents. It wasn't just extra-special, it was so unexpected – the al fresco meal and the tents set up like they were on an expedition in some far-flung part of the world, in an age where travel really was a great big adventure. She did not want anything from his past spoiling their first ever date together.

30

'How old are these tents?'

'You know I think they pre-date the Second World War.'

Faye thought so too. 'They're in incredibly good condition.'

'While I was scouting around, I found my dad's old oil lamps, which I thought would add to the atmosphere. Then again, I didn't think they'd be very safe, so Nick lent me a couple of proper modern tenting lamps. My dad was a bit of a collector. You'll find all sorts of weird and wonderful paraphernalia in boxes in the loft of The Lake House.'

'I'd like to see some more of your father's old things.'

'I'll give you the grand tour, then we can finish in the loft. There's a proper flight of stairs up there, so it's easy getting access.'

Faye stared at him. *Did he just invite me over for a tour of* The Lake *House?* she thought.

'I'd like that very much,' said Faye.

'Good. Because I'd very much like to show you the house. Ah, here comes dinner!' Jake exclaimed.

Faye followed his gaze. Five people were crossing the lawn, one behind the other, carrying an assortment of plates and dishes. An excitable Old English Sheepdog brought up the rear, sniffing the air. Tufts of her fur, which were tied with multicoloured ribbon, stood on end.

Evie and Natty arrived first, each carrying a dinner plate.

Faye picked up her serviette. So did Jake. The girls put a dinner plate down in front of each of them.

Olive bounded over. Faye stared at the ribbons.

'Doesn't she look pretty?' said Natty.

Faye reserved judgement. She felt sorry for Olive, although she was such a good sport. 'Will you just make sure to take the ribbons out before bedtime? Otherwise Olive might not be comfortable during the night.'

'We will,' replied Natty. She pointed. 'That's our tent. Gayle said we could come back out when you've finished your romantic dinner.' She puckered her lips.

'All right, you,' said Faye. 'Off you go and play.'

Gayle appeared next, putting a casserole dish with a lid on down on the table. Nick and Marty followed with roast potatoes and roast vegetables, and quickly retreated, taking Olive with them.

Faye heard Nick remark, 'You know, I wouldn't mind spending a night or two in one of those tents.'

'Yeah, looks fun, doesn't it?' Marty replied. 'I'd like to as well. Not sure what Dee would make of it. It would be quite a novelty, wouldn't it? Bit like a little film set.'

'Yes, like something out of a movie.'

'An old movie.'

Their voices grew faint as they approached the back door to the house.

Faye stared at the spread on the table as Jake lifted the lid on the casserole dish. 'It's minty lamb.'

'It smells delicious. Did you do all this too?'

'Yes, all prepared. I just needed to give Gayle some directions as to how to cook the lamb. She's been keeping an eye on the meal while me, Marty and Nick put up the tents.'

As Jake dished up the meal, Faye said, 'This is so great.'

'I'm so relieved to hear it.' He added some lamb to her plate. 'To be honest, I really didn't know what you'd make of all this. It's not really what you do on a first date – or any date, for that matter.'

'And that's what makes it really special.' Faye knew she was going to remember this night, with Jake, under canvas in Gayle's back garden, for the rest of her life. 'It's going to be a date to remember,' said Faye.

'For all the right reasons, I hope,' quipped Jake.

Faye grinned, 'For all the right reasons.' The icing on the cake was that Natty was going to share in their little adventure too. She shared her thoughts.

Jake grinned. 'Those were my sentiments exactly.' He glanced at the tents. 'You know I originally set these up so there was one for you and Natty, and one for myself. But, um, now she's got a friend for a sleepover, looks like you and me will have to share instead. Hope that's okay.'

Faye did a double-take. Was he seriously asking her that question after everything they'd both said? *Ever the gentleman*, she thought. She glanced at the tent. The first thing she was going to do was push those camp beds together, once Natty and Evie were fast asleep and she'd closed the flaps on the tents.

'Faye?'

Faye lifted her glass. 'To our first night together.'

It was Jake's turn to do a double-take. The expression on his face made Faye burst out laughing. 'You look a little worried.' Faye had an idea what it was about. She'd been on numerous dates, had flings, and sex. Jake, on the other hand …

'Eleanor was my first and only …' he trailed off. 'What if …?'

Faye stared at him. There were lots of *what if* scenarios she could think of right now that must be going through his mind. What if he wasn't ready? What if he was a disappointment? What if their night together was a disaster? It hadn't occurred to her that Jake wasn't ready to jump into bed with her tonight, whereas looking across the table at Jake, that was all she wanted to do. Well, that and eat dinner. She was famished.

Jake looked at her sheepishly. 'Can we …?'

'Take things slowly?' Faye guessed that was what he was going to say. She glanced at the tent and thought that she'd move the beds just a little closer instead.

He nodded.

She looked at the tents, and their little camp table, and the fairy lights, and all the effort he'd put into their date. Most guys would have had one thing on their mind – getting her into bed. But Jake wasn't most guys. He was Jake. The love of her life. And they had their whole lives ahead of them to take things slowly and enjoy each moment.

'I get it – you know.'

He looked at her quizzically.

'When you said your childhood here was … slow.' She looked about them. 'I want that … this. For time to slow down and live in the moment. These sorts of moments, like your parents used to do – make the most out of the simple things in life.'

Jake grinned at her. 'You do, you finally understand.'

Faye nodded. 'This is so perfect, Jake. I couldn't have asked for more on our first date.'

Across the small wobbly table, they held hands for a moment

before raising their glasses. Faye said, 'You know, this could catch on.'

Jake creased his brow. 'What could catch on?'

'Well, you know, people enjoy staying in unusual places, like yurts, and such like.'

'Yeah, seems to be all the rage now. But I don't see—'

'I bet some people would really enjoy this, having an old-fashioned camping experience but safely in the back of Gayle's back garden right here at Lark Lodge.'

'You're thinking I should leave them here?'

'The children would have a whale of a time.'

Jake smiled. He'd loved wild camping with his dad. It had been a simpler time, when you could do as you pleased. You still could in Scotland; it was one of the things he loved about the place, compared to England where people might find themselves fined for doing something like that. 'I'll ask Gayle in the morning.'

Faye smiled. 'I would. I bet she'll think it's a brilliant idea.'

'It did take us a hell of a long time, putting them up. Be a shame to take them down.'

'Wouldn't it just?'

'Gayle would be able to accommodate more guests.'

'She would.'

They smiled and toasted their future and the new accommodation at Gayle's guesthouse.

They'd barely finished their meal when Natty and Evie appeared, along with Olive. An apologetic Gayle followed in their wake. 'So sorry, but I couldn't keep them in the house any longer.'

Natty and Evie darted into their tent, followed by Olive. Faye could see Natty and Evie each sitting on a camp bed, unpacking their bags as though they were moving in for a long stay rather than just a night.

Faye and Jake said in unison, 'It's fine, Gayle, honestly.' They exchanged a smile.

'Well, if you're sure.'

They both nodded. 'I'll take those plates while I'm here.'

Jake jumped up. 'Let me help.'

'I wouldn't hear of it. Sit back down.'

Faye caught Jake's expression – he looked like a small child who'd been told off. He sat back down.

Gayle looked at him, satisfied. 'Good. Now I'm going to leave the back door unlocked if any of you need to use the facilities during the night. Or the girls want a midnight snack. I expect those two are going to be awake until late tonight.'

They all turned to look at Evie and Natty, who were bouncing up and down on the springy camp beds. They picked up pillows and started to have a pillow fight, their hysterical laughter making the adults smile.

Faye said, 'Thank you, Gayle, for letting us camp out in your garden.'

'Not at all. I think it's a great idea. The tents look like something out of a film set. I'll be sorry to see them go when you dismantle them tomorrow, Jake.'

'Who said anything about dismantling them?'

Faye and Jake exchanged a smile.

'You're camping in the garden more than one night?'

'I suppose we could.'

Natty ran out of the tent. 'Oh, can we? Please!' She'd overheard them.

Faye said, 'Maybe. Depends how late we get home from the snow disco tomorrow evening, and how wet we are.'

'Snow disco?'

'Yes, Annie got us tickets. It sounds like such fun.'

'It is fun,' said Gayle. 'I haven't actually been, but I've heard they are quite the event, and tickets sell out fast.'

'I think Annie managed to bag us the last two. Sorry, Jake. It will just be Natty and me going.'

'That is not a problem.'

'Bet you're glad you got out of it.'

'Not at all. I just think it's nice for you to spend some time with Natty, just the two of you. I know how busy you are at home with work. I want you to be able to spend some time with Natty this holiday too, not just me.'

Jake had just reminded Faye why she loved him so. She stared at him across the table.

'Ahem. Well, I'll take these dishes in,' said Gayle. She turned on her heel, about to return to the house. 'I'm glad you're not taking the tents down tomorrow, by the way.'

'Actually,' said Jake, 'we were wondering how you'd feel if we didn't take the tents down at all …'

31

Gayle crossed the lawn to the house with a spring in her step, delighted by Jake's suggestion. Natty had overheard every word of the conversation about keeping the tents up in the garden as a permanent fixture, and additional accommodation, albeit a bit quirky. 'That means we can stay here all summer if you book the tents, Mummy.'

Faye rolled her eyes, thinking *nothing gets past my daughter*. 'Why don't you go back into your tent and finish that pillow fight with Evie?'

'But can we, Mummy, stay here?'

'As much as I love …' She looked at the tents festooned with fairy lights that Gayle had switched on. '… glamping—'

Jake butted in. 'Oh, I've tried to make it as comfortable as possible, but I wouldn't go so far as to call it glamping – it's not exactly luxurious.'

Faye said, 'All right, let's christen this *gamping* – garden camping.'

Jake laughed. 'Great! You've just invented a new name. I think Gayle should use that to advertise her new accommodation. Not to be confused with glamping, obviously.'

'Obviously,' said Faye, smiling.

Natty knitted her brow and repeated her question. 'But can we, Mummy, stay in the tents for the summer?'

'Ah, Natty, what I was saying before I invented my new word was that as much as I love gamping, I don't think Mummy and Daddy will want to sleep in a tent for the entire summer – do you?'

'All right. But can we stay in The Lake House then?'

Faye sighed. 'Just go and play.' When she turned to look at Jake, he was staring at her open-mouthed.

Faye looked at Jake. 'What?'

'You just called me her daddy!'

'I did – didn't I? Sorry, I don't know where that came from.'

'I do. At least I hope I do. I hope you see me as father material. Oh, Faye, I so want to be her dad – if you'd let me.'

It was Faye's turn to stare at Jake open-mouthed. It hadn't occurred to her the implications of falling in love with him. Of course she saw him as father material – why wouldn't she? He and Natty had a close relationship – just like father and daughter. She should know; it reminded Faye of her own relationship with her father when she was growing up.

Now she was fast-forwarding their relationship. Would they get married? Oh god, she hoped so. But where did that leave Natty – officially speaking? What if Jake wanted to adopt? Did she want Natty to be a Ross?

Jake leaned across the table and took her hand again. 'Look, I don't want to get ahead of myself. Of course I'd love to adopt her, but I'm happy, ecstatic actually, if she just calls me Dad, unofficially, you know? She does not have to be a Campbell-Ross. In fact, you don't have to be a Campbell-Ross if you don't want to get—'

'Yes! I want to get married to you,' she blurted.

Jake sat back in his chair. 'Did you just propose to me?'

Faye shook her head. 'No, I think you proposed to me.'

Jake grinned. 'Just sit tight and hold that thought!'

Faye watched Jake get up and rush to the tent where Natty and Evie were playing. She craned her neck, wondering what on earth was going on. She heard whispering in the tent.

'What's going on?' Faye called out.

Nobody answered. Although she heard Jake ask, 'What about this one?'

Natty replied, 'Uh-uh, this is her favourite colour.'

'Got it! Thank you, Natty.'

'Can we come and watch?'

'Of course you can.'

'Watch what?' said Faye, as Natty, Evie, Jake and Olive emerged from the tent. She looked at Jake. He had one arm behind his back. 'What's going on?'

He walked over to the table, picked up his glass of wine, downed the remains in one big gulp, and set the glass down.

'Jake, what on earth …?'

From behind his back, he produced a box. Faye looked at it, then looked at him. She recognised the small box. It was one of Natty's travel games. 'Travel connect?'

'Pretend it's just a little box.'

Faye stifled a giggle. 'All right. I'll try.'

He slowly opened the box to reveal a ring-shaped piece of ribbon in her favourite colour, and then slowly lowered himself beside her chair until he was on bended knee.

'Jake – what are you doing?'

Jake got out the ribbon. 'Faye – I know this is our first date, but in the last few months I've learned something – life is short, and it can change in a heartbeat. I don't want to wait.'

Faye looked at Jake, and then at the ribbon. She held out her finger. 'Neither do I.'

'Did you just say yes – for real?'

'For real.'

Natty ran over and put one arm around Jake, and one around her mum. 'This is my best day – ever!'

Faye said, 'And mine!'

'And mine!' Jake added.

'Now you two have to do the smoochy-smoochy.'

Faye rolled her eyes at her daughter. 'You're thinking of the wedding when the groom kisses the bride after the ceremony.' Faye happened to glance at the tent, thinking there'd be plenty of time for that later.

She caught Jake looking at the tent too. They were about to spend their first night together, under canvas, on two camp beds, with two extremely excited, giggly girls in the next tent, who were going to be awake into the wee small hours. It wasn't a recipe for the most romantic night together, but Faye didn't care one jot. There would be plenty of nights for romance. All she wanted tonight was for Jake to hold her in his arms – and finally kiss her.

Jake got off his knees. 'So, I wonder what plans I should make for our day out tomorrow, with my future wife.'

'Well, I think my future husband shouldn't make any plans.'

'Huh?' Jake looked at her quizzically.

'The future Mrs Jake would like to have a slow day with her future husband.' She watched Jake's face light up. 'You mean just wake up and take the day as it comes?'

'Oh, yes. Let's just wake up and do what takes our fancy, no plans, just live in the moment.'

'I like the sound of that.'

'Until teatime, when Annie is going to pick me and Natty up to go to the snow disco.'

Jake laughed. 'Until teatime then.'

'Sorry you can't come. Should I cancel?'

'Of course not! As I said, I want you to spend some time with Natty without me.'

'What will *you* do while we're gone this evening?'

'I'll think up another surprise for when you get back.'

'Well, good luck with that! I don't think you'll better this!' She flung her arms wide, indicating the tents, and then caught sight of the purple ribbon on her finger.

'You'll need a proper ring,' Jake pointed out.

Faye looked at the tents, thinking, *we'll need a proper home too.* Her gaze shifted to the hedge at the bottom of the garden. She was thinking of the house, Jake's house, beyond that hedge.

'What are you thinking?'

Faye would rather not say, although she did comment, 'I'm wondering what your next surprise will be.'

Jake's phone buzzed with a text.

Faye's heart leapt in her mouth, afraid that it was Marcus, or Lydia to tell Jake that Marcus had done something stupid as a result of Jake's text, and he had to return to London straight away.

'Is that a text message?' Faye asked, wide-eyed.

'Ah,' Jake checked his phone. 'It's just a reminder I put in my phone calendar of our return train journey on Monday.'

Faye exhaled in relief.

Jake said, 'I can't believe we've got just two days left here.'

'Me neither. I'm going to be so sad to leave.' She knew who

else was going to be sad to leave. She glanced at Natty, who was lying on her front on the camp bed. Evie was doing the same. They were both reading a book. Lying on the floor between their beds was Olive, head on paws, eyes closed.

'Me too,' Jake said, commiserating. 'Do we have to?'

'Leave?'

'Yes. It's not like I've got to return to London now I've sent that text. I get to spend the whole summer with you and Natty.'

Jake stood up and moved his chair to sit next to Faye. 'How about it?'

'As much as I love this …' Faye cast her eyes around their little camp in the garden. 'I don't think I could spend the rest of the summer living in the tent.'

'I know. First things first. Do we want to stay on? I'll have to change our return train tickets if so.'

Faye turned in her chair to face Jake. 'I can't think of anything I want more.' That wasn't true. Faye leaned forward in her seat and put a gentle hand on Jake's cheek. The studied each other for a long moment before their lips met, and they kissed deeply.

32

It was morning. Jake wandered down the stairs. They'd spent another night gamping after Faye and Natty had returned from the snow disco. Annie had dropped them back after the disco, along with Evie, who had stayed another night too. Faye had pushed her and Jake's camp beds together, but as was the case on their first night in the tent, the thick bars of the camp beds made intimacy impossible – although Jake had managed to squeeze beside Faye in her camp bed for a time so he could hold her in his arms as they chatted late into the night. The old camp bed had creaked and groaned under the weight of the two of them, and eventually he'd had to move back to his own for fear it would collapse.

He'd showered and changed in his bedroom upstairs while Faye and the girls used the bathroom in her bedroom to wash and change. They were meeting in the kitchen for breakfast. Despite talking into the early hours – Evie and Natty, unsurprisingly, had fallen asleep quite late too – they'd all woken up early and crept back to the house to use their bedrooms to get ready. Everyone had tiptoed around, doing their best not to disturb the other guests, who weren't up. Only Gayle was already up and about in the kitchen. Jake smiled as he walked down the stairs. He was looking forward to the surprise he had in store for Faye that day. He'd spent all evening while they were out at the disco getting things prepared. She'd arrived back from the snow disco in anticipation of the surprise he'd promised, but it was late, they were all tired, and he didn't think it was a good time. He wanted to savour what he had in store.

Faye told him she had a surprise for him too. She'd said she hoped he hadn't made any plans for that day because just for a change she'd planned something herself – with a little bit of help from Annie, who'd come up with an idea for their last day in the Cairngorms.

Jake had been intrigued, but no amount of pestering the previous night would make her reveal what they were doing that day. Even Natty, who had obviously been sworn to secrecy, wouldn't tell.

He could hear Faye in the kitchen, already chatting to Gayle, and could smell bacon and sausages sizzling in a pan on the stove. Jake's mouth watered. Gayle was preparing a fry-up. As he stepped off the last stair he heard Faye's voice. 'I'm not sure I've done the right thing.'

Jake halted.

'What do you mean?' Gayle asked.

Jake didn't want to eavesdrop, but he couldn't help himself.

'You know, about my plan for today.'

'You're having second thoughts?'

'Can you blame me?'

Jake frowned, surprised by the conversation. He'd just taken another step towards the kitchen, hoping to catch what was said next about what Faye had planned for that day, when the floorboard beneath his foot creaked loudly. *Damn!*

Jake coughed loudly and walked into the kitchen, acting as though he'd just walked down the stairs and hadn't overheard them while he'd been hovering in the hallway.

'Good morning!' He forced a smile, still concerned about why Faye was having second thoughts about her plans for the day. Whatever it was, he was sure he'd enjoy it. He didn't much care what they were doing, as long as they were spending the day together.

He kissed Faye on the top of the head and wanted to reassure her that whatever she'd planned would be fine by him. Of course, he couldn't do that, otherwise he'd give the game away that he'd been eavesdropping.

'Where're Natty and Evie?' Jake asked, surprised they weren't in the kitchen. He'd thought they'd be at breakfast too, although he bet he knew where they were – back in the tents in the garden.

Faye got up from her seat at the table. 'They're in the dining room.'

Jake frowned. 'What are they doing in there?'

'You're all having breakfast in the dining room this morning,' said Gayle.

'Why? It's nice us all sitting around the kitchen table.' Jake liked the informal family atmosphere of Gayle's guesthouse. Which reminded him that Gayle's guesthouse was fully booked. 'Are the other guests in the dining room too?'

Gayle shook her head. 'Have you seen the time? Breakfast hasn't officially started yet.'

Jake knew it was early. The dawn chorus had woken them all up, and despite trying to go back to sleep when the birds had stopped singing, they'd then heard the girls giggling in the tent next door.

Jake was still wondering why breakfast wasn't in the kitchen. He said as much.

Gayle replied, 'I've been reading some reviews posted by guests, and while some like sitting around the table in the kitchen chatting to other guests, I've had some negative feedback about this arrangement and the lack of tables to accommodate couples who just want to sit together.'

'That's a shame,' commented Jake. He glanced at Faye. 'But I understand.'

'Good. Now, you are my guinea pigs this morning.'

Jake frowned. 'Pardon me?'

'I've been googling how other guesthouses do things. So, take a seat in the dining room and I'll bring out the breakfast menus.'

'Breakfast menus?'

'Yes. Now I want your honest opinion about the new breakfast arrangements this morning before I make the changes permanent.'

Faye took Jake's hand. 'Come on, let's choose a table.'

'But there's just one table in the dining room.'

'Not anymore,' said Gayle.

Jake stepped across the hall and stopped in the doorway to the dining room, surprised to find that the large dining room table was gone and had been replaced by several small, square, light oak tables for two, dotted about the room, with matching chairs.

'When did this happen?'

'Yesterday evening while Natty and I were out at the disco, apparently. She'd ordered them online. You were out too, then, when they were delivered?'

'Clearly.'

'I didn't realise you were out yesterday evening too. You didn't say …'

Jake tapped his nose and smiled. 'Now, that would be telling.'

Faye frowned. 'I was rather hoping I might catch you out and find out what you were up to.'

'You mean find out about the surprise I still have in store for you.' Jake wasn't giving anything away. 'Come on, let's join Natty and Evie.' Jake walked over to the window, where there were two tables pushed together to make a table for four.

Faye said, 'Gayle put two tables together for us. She said she was aware that not all guests would be couples – there might be families, or groups who want to sit together. But she still went with the small tables with a view to doing this – putting them together to accommodate larger parties.'

'Makes sense,' Jake replied, sitting down next to Natty. The two girls were busy with sketch pads.

'What are you two drawing?' asked Jake.

'This is me, Natty, Mummy and Faye at the snow disco.'

'That's a wonderful drawing, Evie.' Jake turned to Natty and looked at the page open in her sketch pad. 'Is that the snow disco too?'

Natty shook her head. 'This is a ski slope, with you, Mummy, and Evie skiing.'

Jake pursed his lips. Of all things, why had she chosen to draw that? All the same, it was a nice drawing. 'That's very good, Natty. Well done.' He glanced at Faye and caught her frowning. She obviously didn't appreciate the drawing either.

Gayle appeared by their table and passed around four menus. 'Now, if you look at the menu, you can see the drinks are at the top – tea, coffee, orange juice. Then there's a choice of cereal, toast, pancakes, muffins – that sort of thing. You can help yourself to those over there.'

Jake looked over at the sideboard against the wall on the other side of the room. Where once there had been family photos, a lamp and a vase of flowers, there were now jugs of orange juice, packets of cereal, baskets of fresh bread, rolls, pancakes, and muffins. There were little pots of jam, marmalade and butter. There was even a platter of ham, and different cheeses, and a large, round dish containing a home-baked cake.

'Wow – that's quite some spread,' commented Jake.

'Yes, that's the continental breakfast. Now the cooked is to order. At the bottom of the menu there's a list of things you can have for the cooked breakfast. You can choose from the list or just order the full Scottish, which will have everything.'

Gayle spotted their drawings. 'That's a very nice drawing, Evie.'

Evie had been busy colouring it in. She looked up at Gayle and smiled. Gayle glanced at Natty's too. 'Oh, that's … um, nice too, Natty.'

Jake caught Gayle looking Faye's way. 'Right, does anyone want tea or coffee?'

Jake said, 'I'd love a cup of coffee.'

'Tea for me, please, Gayle.'

Gayle pointed at the menu. I'll be back in a jiffy with tea and coffee, then I'll take your order.'

Jake nodded. He was missing the informality of breakfast in the kitchen already, and the feeling of being in a family home rather than a guesthouse. He sighed and picked up the menu, which had a picture of Lark Lodge on the front and a picture of a lark perched on a post in the garden. The menus looked very professional. Jake wondered who had designed them. He suspected it might be Bonnie, as her design flare and skills were obvious throughout the guesthouse.

He caught Faye and Natty whispering conspiratorially together and guessed they were talking about the day Faye had planned. Jake put the menu down and folded his arms, eyeing them. 'You can't leave me in suspense any longer. Which of you young ladies is going to tell me what you have planned for our day out together?'

Natty was just going to speak up when Gayle came back, carrying a tea tray laden with tea and coffee. As she passed Jake and Faye their hot drinks, she said, 'I took the liberty of making you both some toast. Now, can I take your order?'

Jake looked at the menu. 'I'll have the full Scottish please.'

'Me too,' said Faye. 'It will keep us going when we—' She stopped abruptly.

'When we …?' teased Jake. 'Come on, you have to tell me some time.' Once again, he caught Faye and Gayle exchange a glance.

Gayle said, 'Natty, Evie, would you like some hot food this morning?'

They both settled on sausages and beans.

As Gayle took the menus, she asked, 'How are things so far, with the new breakfast arrangements?'

Jake looked up and smiled at Gayle. 'Perfect, Gayle. Really … perfect.'

Gayle frowned. 'It's not – is it? What am I doing wrong?'

Faye stepped in, 'Nothing, Gayle. It's just as Jake said, it's perfect – the tables, the menus, the continental spread over there, and the choice of cooked breakfast on the menu. It's just perfect.'

'So, why do I still get the feeling it isn't?'

Jake exchanged a glance with Faye, realising she felt the same way.

'Oh, come on. Out with it. We're friends, aren't we? We can tell each other anything.'

'Well, that's just it, Gayle,' said Jake. 'We are friends. In fact, you've made me, us, feel so welcome, and we've got to know you and Marty and Nick, you all feel like family. And the guesthouse …'

'The guesthouse …' Gayle prompted.

'It doesn't feel like a guesthouse – at least not to us.'

Faye nodded her head in agreement.

Gayle frowned at them. 'Ah, I can see where I've gone wrong.'

'Oh, please don't apologise for making us feel so at home,' said Faye.

'I wasn't going to. You're my friends, more than that, you feel like family – it's true. I'm talking about using you guys as my guinea pigs to assess the new breakfast arrangements.'

Jake pursed his lips. 'Yeah, not the best idea. I'm afraid we're biased.'

'What does that mean?' asked Natty, looking up from her drawing.

Faye explained, 'It means we'd rather have breakfast in the kitchen.'

Natty jumped out of her chair and looked at Evie. 'Us too! Olive isn't allowed in the dining room, and we miss seeing her at breakfast.'

Gayle rolled her eyes and picked up the coffee and tea, placing it back on the tray. As they trooped out of the dining room and crossed the hall, following Gayle carrying their tea and coffee back in the kitchen, Jake spotted some of the new guests walking down the stairs. They'd come down for breakfast early. He thought perhaps they'd forgotten the time that Gayle had told them. One of them said, 'Excuse me, do you know where we go for breakfast?'

Jake smiled. He guessed Gayle had got her guinea pigs after all. 'Of course. It's in the dining room.' He pointed at the door opposite the kitchen. 'Just choose a table and Gayle will be with you shortly.'

'Thank you.'

He heard them talking as they entered the room. 'Oh, how lovely, the room overlooks the garden. Shall we take a seat in the window?'

'That would be grand, dear.'

Jake smiled to himself as he walked into the kitchen and took a seat next to Faye at the table. 'Gayle, you have some guests waiting in the dining room.'

'Oh, crumbs.' She smoothed down her apron, and picked up her notepad and pen, along with some menus. 'Well, here goes …' She paused in the doorway. 'I feel absurdly nervous. How silly.'

'You'll be fine,' Faye said encouragingly.

Jake added, 'I overheard them say it's lovely that the dining room overlooks the garden.'

'Really?'

'Oh, yes.'

'Sounds like you're onto a winner,' said Faye.

'Well, I'm glad someone appreciates the changes.'

'I still prefer the kitchen,' said Natty.

Faye looked at Natty. 'Shush!'

'But I do.'

Faye whispered, 'So do I.'

Jake got up and checked the sausages and bacon sizzling in the pan. He picked up a spatula and turned them over. He said conversationally, 'So, when are you going to let me in on what we're doing today?'

'It was Annie's idea,' said Faye.

Jake glanced at her, wondering why she wasn't taking all the credit for the day she had planned, even if Annie had suggested it. In fact, it sounded like she was blaming Annie, saying it was her idea. How odd.

He turned back to the pan as Natty spoke up, 'Evie's mum said that as we were having such fun ice-skating last night, perhaps we'd like to book a lesson.'

'Ice-skating?' Jake asked conversationally as he turned over another sausage.

'No, not ice-skating. Skiing!'

Jake froze.

'Annie said we'd have to hire the clothes and the skis. Evie has her own snowsuit. It's a whole four-hour lesson. Annie says that includes a pass up to the beginner's slopes. Here – look!'

Natty appeared by Jake's side and thrust a leaflet at him. He took it, staring at the images of skiing lessons. His face drained of colour.

'Afterwards, there's snowboarding.' Natty ran back to sit down next to Evie at the table.

Jake stood at the cooker, his back to them, staring at the leaflet in his hand. *This can't be happening*, he thought. He felt a heavy knot of anxiety tightening in his chest. The memory of the accident on the ski slopes was still raw. The thought of Faye and Natty, the two people he now loved most in the world, stepping onto those same slopes terrified him. He knew they were just beginners, but the fear of history repeating itself consumed him. Every instinct screamed to protect them, to keep them safe, even if it meant asking them not to go. The idea of losing them too was something he couldn't bear.

'Natty, why did you give Jake that leaflet? We're not going skiing now. You can only do that in the winter season.'

'When's that?' Natty asked.

'From December to April – I told you this already.'

'I forgot.'

Jake closed his eyes and breathed the biggest sigh of relief. He'd also forgotten for a moment, so consumed was he by the thought of Faye and Natty going up on that mountain, that it was summer.

'Remember, Natty? Annie suggested all those things we could do instead.'

Jake put the leaflet to one side and continued moving the sausages around in the pan, thinking that when the winter came along, there would be no skiing lesson for Natty – not now, not ever. Jake intended to put his foot down. Obviously, he wouldn't mention that fact now, and cause an argument, especially when, unfortunately, Natty seemed so keen on the idea. Jake had every intention of putting her off when the time came.

He glanced at the leaflet, wondering about the conversation he'd overheard Faye having with Gayle in the kitchen earlier, when Faye had said she wasn't sure she'd done the right thing about the plan for that day. They weren't going skiing, thank god, so whatever she had planned, he didn't see what the big deal was.

'Now, Natty,' said Faye, 'why don't you tell Jake what we've got planned for today rather than months down the road.'

'Okay.'

Jake felt a small knot in his stomach again, wondering why Faye had been having second thoughts.

'Today, we're going up a mountain.'

Jake turned around, eyeing Natty.

Evie said, 'We're going up Cairngorm Mountain.'

Faye said, 'I've made the arrangements, and booked the tickets. We're going with Evie and her parents, Joe and Annie.'

Jake stared at Faye.

'Annie suggested it. They take Evie every summer. They run the funicular railway to Top Station, where there's a visitor experience and viewing terrace. Annie says it's the perfect place to see the breathtaking views of Loch Morlich and the surrounding pine forests. And you can join a guided walk to the summit of the mountain.'

Natty added, 'There's snow up there even in summer, isn't there, Mummy?'

'At the summit, yes, sweetheart.'

'Can you buy me a snowsuit just like Evie's?'

Jake stared at Faye while the spatula in his hand dripped oil over Gayle's flagstone floor.

'Jake – say something.'

Jake suddenly realised he still had the spatula in his hand. He put it down on the counter and walked up to the table. He knew this wasn't her idea, but Annie's, but even so, he couldn't believe she'd agreed to it.

'No way are you going up that mountain! No. Bloody. Way!' He banged his fist on the table, making Natty and Evie jump, and then stormed out of the kitchen.

'What's happened?' Gayle said rushing into the kitchen, looking at Faye, Natty and Evie. 'I thought I heard a bang?'

Faye bit her lower lip, trying to stifle a sob. 'I should never have booked that trip up the mountain.'

'Where's Jake?'

'I don't know.'

'Please don't cry, Mummy,' said Natty putting her arms around her.

'I won't.'

Faye promptly burst into floods of tears.

33

Faye sat in Gayle's kitchen with her hands wrapped around a comforting mug of tea as she confided in Gayle. She'd told the girls to go and play in the tent in the garden for a bit, after reassuring Natty and Evie that everything was fine, she was fine, and it was just grownups having a silly argument that morning.

As soon as they girls were out of earshot, Faye shook her head. 'I've made a terrible mistake,' she said quietly, her voice tinged with guilt. 'What was I thinking?' She of all people should have known how Jake would feel when he found out she intended to take Natty up on that mountain.

'But you're not going skiing. He does know that – doesn't he?'

'Well, yeah – it is the summer.' Faye breathed a heavy sigh. 'But Jake still has nightmares about what happened to Eleanor on that mountain.'

She'd only spent two nights with Jake, but both nights she'd been woken by his cries.

'I don't want to ruin what has been a perfect holiday all because of this, but I can't bear the thought of disappointing Natty. She's so excited about going up in the funicular to the summit, especially as she's going along with Evie.' Faye felt torn. 'I wish I'd never booked it. How could I have been so thoughtless?'

Gayle sat down next to her at the kitchen table and took Faye's hand. She listened, her expression full of understanding, before she replied, 'You couldn't have known, Faye, what Jake's reaction was going to be.'

'Not for sure, but I had some inkling it was not going to go down well, us going up there. I just didn't anticipate that he'd storm out of the room without at least talking about it.'

'He's frightened he'll lose you and Natty like he lost Eleanor.'

'But that's just not possible. It's not like we're going skiing. I know there's still snow up there, but if we do the walk to the top of the mountain, it will be with an experienced guide – nothing is going to happen. And even if we do return in the winter, and book a skiing lesson, we'd be on the nursery slopes the whole time with two skiing instructors who won't let us out of their sight.'

'Listen, Faye. You're right. Nothing is going to happen to you or Natty up there today. I know this may sound … harsh. But it's his problem, not yours. He's got to face those irrational fears sooner or later. Jake can't wrap you both in cotton wool – especially Natty.'

Faye stared at Gayle. 'I want her to spread her wings and fly – eventually. All these new experiences now will build her confidence.'

'I know,' said Gayle. 'I imagine that's what every parent wants.'

Faye stared at Gayle. 'She can't have someone in her life who is going to hold her back out of fear of something that will probably never happen.'

Gayle nodded. 'I understand.'

Faye noticed something had caught Gayle's eye. Gayle lifted Faye's hand. She pointed at the little purple ribbon she was still wearing on her finger. 'Don't give up on him, Faye. He's clearly still got a long road ahead of him, dealing with what happened. But you and Natty – he loves you both very much. What happened, Jake storming out, just proves that. As I said before, he needs to face his own fears. Perhaps now is the time, if he wants to replace that ribbon with a real ring. He's got to let you both go up there. And ideally, he needs to go too.'

Faye studied the ribbon on her finger and smiled at Gayle. 'I bet you've read all those self-help psychology books sitting on your bookshelves from cover to cover.'

'I have.'

'Did anyone ever tell you that you're in the wrong job?'

Gayle raised an eyebrow. 'Yes, now you mention it, I do have a very good friend who has pointed that out to me on numerous occasions – incidentally, when she didn't want my advice!'

Faye knew who that very good friend was – Bonnie.

'I for one am grateful for your advice, Gayle. You've put things in perspective. I will go and offer an apology to Jake but also hope he understands that if he doesn't feel he can come up there with us, I'm still taking her myself. I cannot deny Natty experiences in life because of what happened to Jake, tragic as it was.'

Gayle frowned.

'What is it?' Faye asked.

'Can you smell that?'

They both turned to look at the frying pan. 'Oh no! I've burnt the sausages. What will my new guests think?'

Faye rushed over and put the extractor on before depositing the burnt sausages in the bin. 'Come on, let's rustle up another breakfast. We'll do it together.'

'What about Jake?'

'Let's put on some extra sausages and bacon. Jake and I are going to have breakfast al fresco.'

'On the camp table outside the tent?'

'Yeah, then we're going to have a heart-to-heart talk.'

'What about Evie and Natty?'

'I'll send them in for their sausages and beans in the kitchen, if that's all right. They'll need a good breakfast before we set off for out adventure up on that mountain.'

Faye got out her phone and texted Jake, *Meet me at the tent – we need to talk.*

Gayle glanced at Faye. 'Did you just text Jake?'

'Yes.' Faye took some eggs out of the fridge.

A moment later, she heard someone coming down the stairs. Faye held her breath, hoping it was Jake. She stole a glance at Gayle. 'Tell me if it's him,' she whispered. Faye carried on cooking the fry-ups, her back to the kitchen door.

'Jake,' said Gayle.

'Gayle,' said Jake.

Faye heard the back door, and Gayle exhale in relief. 'That was Jake.'

'I gathered that.'

'He paused in the kitchen doorway, with his mobile phone to hand, throwing you a searching look, probably wondering why you texted him.'

Faye sighed. 'Because I'm a coward and was afraid to go up to his room and find him packing.'

'Packing?' Gayle turned to her.

'Yeah – as in leaving.'

Gayle avoided eye contact and put two slices of bread in the toaster.

Faye stopped cracking the eggs into a bowl and turned to her. 'You're awfully quiet all of a sudden.' Faye stared at her intently. 'You know something – don't you?'

'Me? Not at all.'

Faye put her hands on her hips. 'You are *such* a bad liar.' Faye had a thought. 'Is it something to do with that surprise Jake had in store for me?' Of course, Faye didn't think she'd be getting whatever nice surprise he had for her now, after how insensitive she'd been, listening to Annie and going ahead with booking the trip up the mountain without a second thought for Jake and his past.

Now she wished he'd gone ahead and given her the surprise the previous night instead of changing his mind and delaying it.

When Gayle refused to say anything more, Faye changed tack. 'What was Jake doing yesterday evening while Natty and I were at the snow disco?'

Gayle sighed. 'Look, all know is what Marty told me.'

'Which is …?'

'Marty had been gardening at The Lake House yesterday. He said that Jake was at The Lake House, busy doing something in there, although he had no idea what.' Gayle slapped her hand over her mouth.

Faye smiled when she heard a muffled, 'Oh, I shouldn't have said that.'

'So, Jake was at The Lake House all evening?'

Gayle obviously realised there was no point denying it now, after what she'd said. She nodded. 'Yes, didn't even have time for dinner. God knows what he was up to.' Gayle ignored the toast when it popped up in the toaster. She was too busy staring at Faye when she said, 'You know what he was doing there – don't you?'

Faye smiled. 'Yes, I think so.' Although she couldn't quite believe it. Was he preparing The Lake House for them to move in for the summer?

'What's going on, Faye?'

Faye thought she'd burst into tears a second time if it turned out she'd screwed up this surprise, if it was what she thought it was, all because of what she'd planned for their day out that day. Despite getting on her high horse about Natty having experiences, all Faye could think about right now was her relationship with Jake, and the fact that if he had been doing what she suspected the previous evening, then he really had turned a corner if he felt able to have her and Natty stay with him in that house.

'Faye?'

'I … I think Jake was preparing The Lake House for us to stay in for the summer.'

Gayle looked as surprised as Faye sounded. 'No way! Seriously, you think that's what he was doing?'

Faye nodded. 'We want to stay in the Highlands for the whole summer.'

'Yes, Natty mentioned that.'

'As much as we'd love to stay here, you haven't got vacancies, but I just didn't think he'd even consider us all staying at The Lake House.'

Gayle said, 'Everyone was convinced he would never return there, and he'd end up selling it.' Gayle stared at Faye. 'You know what this means – don't you?'

Faye looked at the ribbon on her finger. 'He's come to terms with what happened to Eleanor, and he's ready to move on with his life.'

'There's just one more thing for him to conquer,' said Gayle, 'for him to truly be free of that awful accident up here.' Gayle pointed to her temple.

'He's got to conquer his fear of that!' Faye pointed out of the window at the snow-capped mountain.

'Yes. He needs to go with you today.'

Faye frowned.

'What is it?'

'I don't think going with us is going to fix things.'

'But seeing the reality of you both up there, surely, will dispel this irrational fear he has of—'

'Yes, I'm hoping it will, and I do intend to still try and persuade him to come with us. But there's more to it than that – a lot more. Until he finds out what really happened up there when he and Eleanor were buried in the snow … that mountain is going to haunt him. He'll never come here and be free of it.'

'What are you talking about?'

'There was someone else up there on that mountain with them, and he says he needs to find them.'

'Really – who?'

'He doesn't know. Somebody dug them out of the snow and called emergency services. It's like the last piece of the puzzle.'

'But that's a good thing – right? If he can find them?'

Faye pursed her lips. 'I'm not so sure.'

'Why are you not so sure?'

'They didn't come forward – did they?'

Gayle regarded her a long moment before she said, 'Look, not everybody wants their five minutes of fame. Whoever it was, he did a good deed, a bloody good deed saving them, but he obviously wants to remain anonymous.'

'That's what I told him.' Faye breathed a heavy sigh.

'So, what's the problem?'

'I just hope that the anonymous person who saved them isn't somehow connected to the dead guy.'

Gayle looked at her wide-eyed. 'What dead guy?'

'They found him in the spring when the snow thawed. Mr Gillespie … Duncan … told me. The man took his own life on that mountain on Christmas Day. When the rifle went off, the sound may have dislodged some snow and started that avalanche that buried them.'

'How do they know that?'

'It's just a theory. I don't know if it did cause the avalanche. That's what Duncan said, anyway.'

'No, I meant how do they know with certainty that he was up there on Christmas Day?'

'He put a parking ticket in his car with the date, and the time.'

'Doesn't sound like someone who wanted to kill themselves.'

'But he had a shotgun. What else would he have been doing up there, off-piste, with a gun?'

Gayle shrugged. 'Who was he anyway?'

'A former employee of the Ross Corporation. He'd been sacked on Christmas Eve. He shot himself in the head.'

'Did he now?'

Faye looked at her.

Gayle narrowed her eyes.

'What are you thinking, Gayle?'

'So, let me get this straight,' said Gayle, scratching her chin as she thought aloud. 'He travelled from London, which is presumably where he worked before he was sacked, all the way to Scotland, where presumably he knew the Rosses had a holiday home, to end his life?'

Gayle and Faye stared at each other. The second round of sausages and bacon, all but forgotten, were charring nicely in the frying pan.

Gayle said, 'Does Jake know about the employee?'

'He knows there were two men up there, but Duncan hadn't found out who the dead man was when he spoke to Jake about it.'

'So, Duncan told you.'

'Yes. Like I said, I was in his shop. I don't think Jake has visited Mr Gillespie's … Duncan's store, since he's been back here with us.'

'So, you haven't told him the identity of the dead man yet – have you?'

Faye shook her head, fingering the ribbon on her finger. 'I don't see what good it would do – do you? It won't change anything. It won't bring her back – not the Eleanor he was married to.'

'I realise that, Faye, but it might bring him some closure.'

'Or it might open up a whole world of hurt that Jake is not prepared for if he finds out it wasn't an accident.'

Gayle said, 'You're thinking that the person who didn't come forward to take the credit for digging them out of the snow and calling mountain rescue might have saved them from more than an avalanche?'

'It's the parking ticket that bothers me,' said Faye.

'You're wondering about the true intentions of the man found dead with a gun.'

Faye nodded. 'What if he followed them with that shotgun?'

They fell silent, staring at one another, until Gayle said, 'You mean he was after revenge for being sacked?'

'Maybe. But the fact is that whatever he set out to do, he didn't do it – did he? He shot himself instead.' Faye shook her head. 'I can't believe I'm having this conversation.'

They were interrupted by Faye's phone buzzing. She looked at the message. *Faye, change of plan. Meet me at The Lake House.*

'What is it?' Gayle asked.

'He wants to meet at The Lake House.'

'You have to tell him, Faye.'

'Why? It won't bring anybody back. Besides, I can't.'

Gayle folded her arms. 'You mean, you won't.'

'Gayle, don't you see? He's finally moving on from what happened last Christmas.'

'But he said that he still wanted to find the anonymous hero who saved them.'

'I'm going to do my best to make him forget he said that.'

'How are you going to do that?'

Faye held up her finger with the purple ribbon. 'By making sure he focuses on the future with me and Natty.'

Gayle mumbled something under her breath.

'Did you say something, Gayle?'

'I said best-laid plans – and all that.'

Faye frowned at her. 'What does *that* mean?'

'It means that when it comes to making plans, something quite unforeseen may come along that stops things from working out as you expected.'

They both turned to look out of the kitchen window, up at the mountains. Gayle turned to Faye. 'Do you want a piece of advice?'

Faye wasn't so sure she did. But she nodded anyway. Gayle was her friend, and she was interested in what she had to say.

'Who knows what's waiting in the wings. Why don't you just

make the most of your summer here?'

Faye agreed she would make the most of the summer, especially if they were moving into Jake's gorgeous house. She just wished Gayle hadn't mentioned *best-laid plans – and all that.* The trouble was that Faye didn't need Gayle to have said that; she already had a sense of foreboding she was trying to quell.

Gayle continued, 'Whatever really happened up there, it will be a step in the right direction if you can persuade Jake to accompany you and see that there is really nothing to be afraid of – not anymore. The worst has happened – he lost his young wife. But now, if you're all going to enjoy The Lake House, you can't spend your summer in the shadow of that mountain.'

'You're not talking literally, are you? Because The Lake House is kind of in the shadow of that mountain.'

'No, I mean figuratively. Every time he looks at that mountain, I bet he's thinking of one thing.'

'I wouldn't be surprised,' said Faye sadly.

'So, he needs to make new memories on that mountain – happy, fun memories.'

Faye frowned. 'It won't erase what happened.'

'Of course not, but something needs to change so that every time he sees that mountain, he isn't thinking of Eleanor.'

'Yes, especially if we move here permanently.'

'Pardon me?' Gayle's mouth dropped open. 'Did you just say you were moving here perma—'

'Oh, I … I was just thinking out loud.'

'You're really thinking of moving here?'

'Yes … no. Oh, I don't know.'

'But it *has* crossed your mind.'

'There are things I love about here ... for me … for Natty, that just don't exist in our lives back in London. I've made more friends in the handful of days I've been here than in all the years I've lived in London. There's a real sense of community that I never realised was missing from my life until I experienced it first-hand. I found out through a group of mums at a café in Aviemore that there's a headship coming up in a local school.'

'You're thinking of applying? Have you told Jake?'

'No. He'd have to be on board too,' said Faye.

'Of course.' Gayle nodded. 'Perhaps spending the summer here will make up both your minds what you want for your future. I'm biased, so you won't get any balanced feedback from me, especially as I'd love to have you both as my neighbours.'

'Oh, you mean us living at The Lake House?'

'Yes – what else?'

'Oh, I'm not sure that would happen.'

'Why not? I bet you didn't think Jake would have you and Natty stay in The Lake House for the summer.'

'What about your warning around best-laid plans?'

'I know I said that when it comes to making plans, something quite unforeseen may come along that stops things from working out as you expected.'

Faye frowned. She really didn't need to be reminded verbatim – she wished she hadn't asked.

'But here's the thing, Faye. Things might not work out as you expect, but I didn't say it would necessarily be in a bad way – did I? Staying in The Lake House is a case in point.'

Faye grinned. 'I suppose it is.' She liked her thinking – very much.

34

Faye remembered the shortcut down the little lane between Gayle's house and the next that led to a wrought-iron gate into the back garden of The Lake House. Fortunately, the gate wasn't locked.

Gayle had offered to drive her down to The Lake House. With its extensive grounds fronting the loch, it would have been quite a walk – down Gayle's street, and then down the first right turning to continue along a winding country lane to a house that stood on its own, on the very fringes of the town.

She stepped into the garden, closing the gate behind her. The last time she'd been there, she'd crawled through a hedge, desperately looking for Natty, that feeling in the pit of her stomach that she'd lost Natty again.

Faye realised it would take an exceedingly long time to get over the horrendous time she'd gone through when Natty had bunked off school and gone missing. She'd only been missing a matter of hours. It was all well and good looking back on that dreadful experience in hindsight, now that she had Natty back with her, safe and well. But at the time she had no idea whether her daughter was alive or dead, or whether she'd ever see her again. Since that experience, she hadn't wanted to let her daughter out of her sight.

It helped tremendously that it had happened on the last day of the summer term. It meant no more school for Natty or work for Faye for six weeks, and she could spend every waking hour with Natty, ensuring she was safe and wouldn't go missing again. Faye knew it was unhealthy; she'd have to let her go again to start school in September.

Spending as much time as possible with Natty had been the plan for the summer anyway, before Jake had shown up and suggested the holiday. The fact that she'd even been able to contemplate leaving Natty to be babysat by Gayle while she went out for an evening meal with Jake wasn't proof that she'd got over what had happened. She hadn't. She probably never would, although she knew it was something she'd come to terms with, given time.

She thought about Aviemore, where she felt Natty was safe in a community of people she trusted. She suddenly had an epiphany. A saying came to mind out of nowhere – *it takes a village to raise a child.* She'd never really understood that saying until she'd spent time there. In London, apart from Jake, and her father, whom she'd stupidly become estranged from, there was no village – no extended support network. But Aviemore was different; she had suddenly found herself with friends, people she could rely on, people Natty could rely on, a place of safety and security born of steadfast friendships that she realised would last a lifetime.

She'd thought she didn't have time to cultivate friendships and create that village because of her hectic life and the demands of her job. But it wasn't that. It was her. She'd kept people at arm's length after Yousaf had let her down, thinking she and Natty would be better off without anyone else permanently in their lives.

But it had been a mistake. Jake had taught her that. They needed people, friends, special friends – they needed a village just like this.

Faye shook her head. No, not just *like* this. They needed *this* one, this group of friends.

Faye stared at The Lake House. 'I don't want Natty growing up in London,' she whispered, surprising herself. She'd seen nothing wrong with where they lived, and the lifestyle they led, until Natty had gone missing. But it wasn't even that. It was being in Aviemore. It was finding her village of people; the ones that Natty could grow up relying on. She'd said to Gayle, that she wanted Natty to have experiences which would enable her to spread her wings and fly. But it wasn't just experiences. Faye realised her daughter needed people in her life – friends like Evie, and Gayle, Nick and Marty, and Annie, Joe, Bonnie, and David. And even grumpy old Duncan, whom she knew would turn out to be another good friend. Natty needed more than the two of them against the world – they both did.

Faye thought of her last conversation with Gayle about how when it came to making plans, something unforeseen might come along which meant that things didn't turn out as expected. Something unforeseen had come along all right. She'd had her life all mapped out – she'd got her headship qualification, which she'd planned to use once the current head of her school retired. It wouldn't be long now. She'd seen herself working there until she retired. She'd seen Natty going to school in London, and to university, and had thought that one day she might, just might, be able to buy a small one-bedroomed flat for herself when Natty eventually left home. That was all she'd be able to afford in London.

And now she'd experienced another life – one she'd only ever seen on television shows and in movies, with friends who were like one big extended family. The sort of family she'd never had. How could she take Natty away from all this? How could she take herself back to a life that she realised now was just existing – getting through each day, week, month, year, the end goal being just to see Natty through school and university and to move up in her career. That wasn't living. Living was sitting around a campfire toasting marshmallows, and sleeping on a camp bed trying to cuddle the man you loved while your daughter was having the time of her life, giggling with her new friend in the tent next door. And cycling in the forest, getting a sore backside, and visiting castles, and picking wildflowers to press to go into a journal. And sitting around big tables in kitchens with Agas. Not that Faye needed a large kitchen with an Aga – she was thinking of Gayle's house; she loved nothing more than a natter about everything and nothing with Gayle. And playing board games in the evening with friends.

Faye stared at The Lake House. Was she looking at her future – with Jake? Would they have friends around and chat long into the evening while the children played? Would Bonnie come over with her baby, and would Natty and Evie coo over the new addition to their friendship group, watching her grow into a toddler, and then a little girl who they could play with, and who would then annoy them when they were teenagers and she was still a little girl who wanted to be grown-up like them and use their makeup? Would Faye have another child of her own?

Faye raised her eyebrows at that thought, which had come out of nowhere. Natty was nine. That was all behind her, that yearning to have more children – wasn't it? Not to mention physically going through all that again, along with the sleepless nights with a newborn. Of course it was behind her, Faye thought, even as she as thinking what wonderful father material Jake was. She wouldn't even have to ask Jake if he wanted a child of his own. Of course he did. But he'd never brought that up when he'd put the ribbon on her finger, and neither had she, because she knew, and so did he, that if it didn't happen, or she didn't want it to, they already had a child. Natty was like a daughter to him.

Faye swallowed as she stared at the house, fast-forwarding in her mind to their future there. 'Oh, god! I want this more than anything.'

She wanted to be Gayle's neighbour, and for Natty to run down the hidden lane and visit her second home – Lark Lodge – whenever she wanted to, and run to Gayle when she was a teenager, after she'd had another big falling-out with her mum, because that's what teenagers did. And for Olive to sneak through the hedge to visit Natty whenever she wanted.

That thought made Faye smile, despite remembering what she'd looked like when she'd followed Olive, on her hands and knees, through the hedge.

This time she was a lot more composed. At least she looked more composed. Her clothes were clean, with no muddy patches on the knees, her hair was devoid of twigs and leaves and didn't look as though it had been backcombed. 'Goodness, I must have looked a sight,' she commented under her breath. But her appearance belied what she was feeling – extremely nervous. Last time, Marty had offered to give her a tour of the house. He had a key and used the kitchen to make cups of coffee and to have a break while he was gardening. Although interested, she'd politely declined for the simple reason that she'd feel she was snooping.

Now, she couldn't have felt more different. She couldn't wait to see the house. As she walked up the garden towards the house she thought, *is this really happening?* She couldn't quite believe they were moving in for the summer. *Could we move in for good?* Her last thought, as she walked around to the front of the house and stood on the doorstep to lift the heavy doorknocker, was *when am I going to tell Jake my plans for our future?*

35

Faye stood on the doorstep, waiting for Jake to answer the door. She slipped her mobile phone out of the back pocket of her jeans and checked for any further texts from Jake in case there had been a change of plan. The last one she'd had said to meet him at The Lake House. Nothing more.

Faye put her phone away. She'd only been in the back garden, never around the front of the house before. She turned to look at the large driveway. She knew Jake was there. His car was parked out front. The lawn in front of the house sloped down to the shores of a small loch, and she wondered if it was man-made and had been created when the house was built. She couldn't imagine the shore, at least this side, was open to the public. The only way to get to it appeared to be up the drive from the house.

She peered down the drive and saw double wrought-iron gates. She was surprised they were open. She glanced at Jake's hire car. He obviously hadn't bothered to close the gates when he drove through.

Faye tried the knocker again, then took several steps back to peer up at the house, wondering if Jake had heard the door this time. Perhaps he was somewhere upstairs in the house. She looked up, eyeing the large Georgian windows, but didn't see anyone.

The front of the house was impressive. It had been built in the arts and crafts tradition – Faye had touched upon this type of architectural style during some teaching lessons she'd prepared earlier on in her career – and she recognised the style of the hip roof, the turrets and gables, and the bay windows on the ground floor. They all made the house interesting and imposing.

Faye was thinking of the surprise Jake had said he had in store. She knew this must be it – he was preparing the house for them to spend the summer there. It was little wonder that he'd thought they were all too tired for his surprise the evening before – it would have meant they'd all have to troop over to The Lake House for a tour late in the evening, after he'd spent the evening getting the house organised and Faye and Natty had been at the snow disco until late. Faye thought this was much better, apart from the fact that Natty wasn't with her. She would have liked Natty to see it too before they moved in the next day. Then again, after the row that morning over her plans to go up the Cairngorm Mountain, Faye knew it was for the best that she came alone.

She frowned when she remembered why she had left Natty behind having sausage and beans with Evie. She cast her gaze up at the mountain, shaking her head, her good mood evaporating. She wasn't looking forward to broaching the subject of their trip out together. She hoped he'd decided to come with them, and not try and put them off.

How would they possibly spend the summer in this house, in the shadow of that mountain, let alone live there, if he couldn't put the past, and what had happened on that mountain, behind him? *He has to come with us, he just has to*, thought Faye, stepping back up to the door. She was wondering why Jake hadn't answered the door, especially when he'd asked her to come. She would have thought he'd have kept an ear out for her arrival.

Faye didn't bother with the knocker again, and instead did something she should have done in the first place – texted Jake to say she'd arrived. After she'd done that, she tried the front door, only to find it was unlocked. Faye sighed. 'Of course it is. How silly of me not to think. He expects me to just walk right in.'

Despite her happy mood quickly disintegrating at the thought of Jake's reaction to their planned trip up the mountain, she did manage a smile when she realised Jake wasn't keeping an ear or eye out for her arrival because he'd expected she'd just walk right in and give him a shout-out that she was there.

Faye did just that. As soon as she'd stepped into the spacious central hallway with an impressive, curved staircase rising to the next floor, she called out, 'Jake – I'm here!'

Jake answered immediately. 'I'm upstairs.'

Faye looked up the stairs. 'I'll come right up, then.'

'Okay.'

Faye smiled. She guessed the tour was starting upstairs, in the bedrooms. Maybe in *their* bedroom. Faye's smile widened. This was a turn-up for the books. What did they say about make-up sex? Faye found herself taking the stairs two at a time while loosening the top button of her blouse and running her fingers through her hair. She wasn't thinking of that argument they'd had at the breakfast table. Jake had obviously texted her to go there so he could show her around the surprise, meaning The Lake House, and could make amends. All she could think right now was that she wished she had a mirror, just to check her appearance. *Oh, never mind that*, she thought. There wouldn't be time for him to notice her appearance before his lips were planted on hers; they'd barely take a breath as shoes were kicked off and clothes hastily removed on their way to their bed. It occurred to her that this wouldn't be make-up sex; they hadn't made love at all yet. Hadn't had the opportunity. Pushing the camp beds together in the tent hadn't worked quite as Faye had intended. But wasn't this the perfect time? They had the whole house to themselves.

She nearly ran into Jake as he suddenly emerged from a room at the top of the stairs. He looked at her. 'Are you alright? You seem a bit … out of breath.'

'Um, I ran up the stairs, just anxious to see you.'

He broke into a grin. 'Oh, thank goodness. I was feeling absurdly nervous, thinking you might not come after the way I acted earlier, like a right idiot, over your plans today.'

Faye grinned too. She'd been absurdly nervous about meeting him too, over that. Now her mind had been put at ease. He'd obviously realised he'd over-reacted. She hoped he'd decided to come with them.

'What's in there?' she asked, as he closed the door.

'Oh, I've finished in that room.'

'Oh, okay.' She imagined he'd finished getting it prepared for their stay. It obviously wasn't their bedroom, otherwise he'd be taking her in his arms, and—

'I've just got a few more rooms to see to,' said Jake striding down the hall.

Faye followed, still grinning, wondering when they were going to get to their bedroom, and who would make the first move. Walking behind him, Faye undid another button on her blouse, revealing her bra strap, thinking, *I don't mind if it's me.*

When Jake opened another door, Faye was right behind him, hoping this was their bedroom. Except it couldn't be because it was full of furniture covered in white sheets – presumably being used as dust sheets to look after the furniture while nobody was there. Faye thought, *but that's what he's here to sort out – removing the dust sheets.*

'Ah, everything seems to be in order here,' commented Jake, suddenly turning around, and taking a step back, clearly surprised to find Faye had followed him in the room and was standing right behind him. He'd nearly walked into her again. He apologised, 'Sorry.'

Faye noticed his eyes drifting down to her blouse. She smiled. 'No need to apologise.'

Jake extended his arm, indicating the door.

'Oh, right.' Faye turned for the door. It was such a large house, she hadn't expected they'd need to use all the rooms – not until they moved in properly.

'So, where's my surprise?' asked Faye, knowing full well what it was. Any minute now Jake was going to open one of these doors and show her their bedroom. Would there be a rose on her pillow? Or lots of candles surrounding their bed?

Faye shook her head thinking that she really was being silly. It was only a short time ago that they'd rowed. Why on earth would Jake think she'd want to make love? Maybe he'd set up the lounge in a romantic way, with candles and flowers for when they moved in the next day. Perhaps that was the surprise.

Along the hall, Jake opened more doors, and Faye caught sight of more white dust sheets. She was beginning to get a knot in her stomach, wondering if she'd got things all wrong, when they reached the end of the hallway, and she spotted another flight of stairs. The house was on three levels. Ahead, Jake had already stepped onto the first stair. He turned around. 'You don't have to follow me up here.'

Was that code for *you don't have to make love to me if you don't want to*? She said, 'But I want to.'

'You do?'

'Oh, yes.'

'But there's nothing much to see, just more of the same – rooms with furniture covered in dust sheets.'

Faye gaped at him.

'Why don't you wait downstairs?'

'All right,' Faye said slowly. Was the plan to spend the summer on the ground floor of the house so Bonnie could continue redecorating while they were there? That wouldn't be ideal. On the other hand, if it meant the house would be ready for them to move in permanently by the time she'd sorted out a new teaching position, and Jake a school locally where he could continue his on-the-job teacher training, then so be it.

Jake stepped off the bottom stair and took her hands in his. 'I'm so glad we broke the ice here, Faye, after that row in Gayle's kitchen. It's kept me busy, checking things over while I waited to see if you'd accept my apology when you turned up. I don't think I could have waited by the tent, drumming my fingers on the table and stewing. I just had too much pent-up energy.'

'Okay.' Once again Faye noticed his eyes dropping to her blouse.

'Wow, your blouse is very … unbuttoned.' He pointed at her blouse. 'Do you mind if I—?'

Faye smiled up at him. 'Not at all.' She could feel his fingers on her bare skin. The next thing she knew was that he'd buttoned up her blouse. 'Oh.' She looked down at her blouse.

'There,' said Jake. 'You're all buttoned up. It can get cold in this place, you know, even in summer. It's a big house. Wouldn't want you catching a chill and it spoiling the rest of our holiday.'

'So, we are staying on for the summer? It's decided?'

'Only if you want to, Faye.' He got out his mobile phone. 'I haven't cancelled the return train tickets tomorrow in case you wanted to go home after what I did.' His eyes dropped to the floor.

'I think I scared Natty and Evie, the way I behaved, banging my fist on the table like that. I don't know what got into me.'

'I do.' Faye gently lifted his chin to look at her. 'I didn't think, Jake, when I went along with Annie's suggestion to spend the day on the mountain. I'm so sorry for being thoughtless,' she said, her eyes filled with regret.

Jake sighed, running a hand through his hair, the weight of his emotions heavy. 'I shouldn't have reacted like that,' he said again, his voice tight. 'But I know why I did. It was the thought of you and Natty up there after losing Eleanor ... it terrifies me. I can't go through that again.'

Faye gently placed her hand on his. 'I understand, Jake, I do. But here's the thing – we can't let what happened stop Natty from having her own experiences in life. She's just a little girl, and I don't want her to grow up afraid of everything.'

They stood in silence for a moment before Jake nodded, his gaze softening. 'You're right. I just ... need to learn how to manage this fear.'

Faye squeezed his hand, and in that quiet moment, they reached an understanding. She knew they would face it together. Faye looked around. She couldn't think of a better place for Jake to face his demons and finally move on. 'Cancel the train ticket for tomorrow, Jake. We're spending the summer in the Highlands.'

36

'Is the surprise downstairs then?' Faye asked, relieved that Jake had agreed to join them and spend the day on the mountain as planned, and happy that they'd decided to spend the entire summer in Scotland.

Jake shook his head and laughed. 'You are hysterical.'

'Am I?' Faye didn't get the joke.

'Sorry, but I thought I would have got round the house by the time you arrived, then we could head off.'

'Head off?'

'Yeah. Look, I'll be with you in a moment. Promise. Just wait downstairs.' He fumbled in his pocket and passed her the car key. 'Better still, why don't you go and wait in the car.'

Faye frowned as she walked down the stairs. Was he messing with her, and the rooms were ready downstairs as she'd thought? Was he just delaying telling her about the redecoration planned on the top two floors because he knew she might be disappointed that they didn't have the whole house to themselves over the summer?

Although Faye didn't want to spoil the surprise, she did intend to have a look round herself and then psyche herself up to look all surprised when he finally showed her their new holiday accommodation right there in The Lake House.

As she walked down the stairs, she thought of the conversation they'd had about his fears over her and Natty going up on to the mountain. Faye had said, 'But you'll come with us today? Please say you'll come.'

He had promised he would. She'd reassured him that they were all going to have the best time, making great memories on that mountain. It made her feel full of hope, the fact that he'd agreed to go, and that she was there in the house with him. Since he'd proposed the day before yesterday, every time she'd looked at the ribbon on her finger, she'd been concerned that he hadn't left the past behind. After all, this wasn't a proper engagement. He was still married. Faye would have loved an engagement party like Bonnie had had, when she'd invited all her new friends from Aviemore to a party at the boathouse.

That gave Faye a lovely thought as she walked down the stairs – when the time was right, they could tell everyone and organise a party just like Bonnie and David's. It would be an engagement and housewarming party in their new home – The Lake House.

The only other person who knew about the proposal was Gayle. She had spotted the ribbon that Faye wouldn't take off her finger, so Faye had told her what had transpired. Gayle understood why they couldn't tell anybody else just yet. Natty had been sworn to secrecy too. When Natty had asked why, Faye had told her the truth. She realised in hindsight she hadn't run the conversation by Jake first, but the question had taken her by surprise, and in that moment she knew honesty was the best policy. Jake was still married to his first wife, and he would need to get a divorce before he and Faye could marry, so technically, although Jake had proposed, they wouldn't be officially engaged to be married until Jake had sorted out his affairs.

It was a rather grown-up conversation, but Natty seemed to take it in her stride. All she wanted to hear was that they would be married. Then Natty had asked her a question she had been expecting – *does that mean Jake is going to be my new daddy*?

Faye thought it was about time she talked about her old daddy, whom she didn't see. Natty didn't ask about him, perhaps because she knew he lived a long way away, and maybe in her mind that was the reason she didn't see him. He lived in some far-flung place. But there had been no contact since she was three. And now she knew why. He'd married, and had another family, and Natty being in his life would just complicate matters. Yousaf's wife knew nothing about his past relationship with Faye and his child. Faye was happy for things to remain that way. Although Natty did have a question that took Faye by surprise. 'Do you have to get a divorce before you can marry Jake?'

Faye sighed as she walked the stairs. Natty had no idea that she and Yousaf had never married. Faye didn't want to get into that. All she'd said was, 'No. I am free to marry Jake,' crossing her fingers and hoping that Natty didn't ask any further questions. Natty would learn the details soon enough, when she got older and no doubt wanted to know more about her father and his background. For now, she knew Natty was focused on making sure her mummy got married to Jake and that nothing stood in their way.

Faye was focused on that too. She was quite shocked at how much she'd changed. She didn't think twice when Jake had asked her to marry him; she'd been more than ready to take on the second biggest commitment of her life. Before, with the other guys she'd had flings with, she hadn't been and had known she never would be. It was what had made them safe, and fun. And yet, with Jake, making that commitment felt so right, even though he'd proposed while he was still a married man.

She was aware that he had a lot to go through, divorcing Eleanor, but the fact that he'd agreed to go up the mountain, and they were in The Lake House together … well, as Gayle had wisely said, things might not always work out as expected, but that was not necessarily bad. She'd said that their staying in The Lake House would be a case in point.

Faye smiled at that thought as she stepped off the bottom stair and randomly opened one of the doors off the hallway, anticipating cosy rooms, set up without a dust sheet in sight, ready for them to move in.

Five minutes later, she'd opened each door and stepped into the kitchen – the only room in the house that wasn't full of dust sheets.

As soon as Jake walked into the kitchen, saying, 'There you are,' Faye replied, 'What's going on, Jake?'

'How do you mean?'

'The house – all the rooms are covered in dust sheets.'

'Oh, that,' he said. 'Gayle had a conversation with Bonnie. She wants to resume work on the house, so I just popped in to check and make sure things were all ready for her to redecorate.'

'She's working on the whole house all at once?'

'Well, I'm not exactly sure where she'll start. I noticed there's some paint pots and wallpaper upstairs, so I'm guessing the bedrooms maybe.' Jake shrugged. 'Anyway, I'm sure you don't want to hear all about that.'

Actually, Faye did. Was it a coincidence and she was reading way too much into things, or did he not want her there? What had he said? That he thought he'd be done there by the time she arrived. The car was waiting outside, ready for him to leave as soon as she arrived. He'd been keen for her to wait downstairs or in the car, which she got the distinct impression he would have preferred.

Faye frowned at him. 'What happened to the tour?' Faye asked, trying hard not to sound sarcastic, although it was difficult.

'Huh?'

'Of the house. I thought you were going to show me round the house?'

'What's there to see? The whole place is covered in dustsheets.'

Faye stared at him. 'But you texted me to meet you here.' Had he changed his mind? Was he using Bonnie, and the redecorating, as an excuse to keep her and Natty away from this house? Had he not moved on as she'd thought? Faye eyed the ribbon on her finger. Worse still – had she been too hasty accepting his marriage proposal when she should have waited? Maybe he should have waited to propose until he had sorted out his unresolved issues.

Unless there was another explanation. 'So, what are your plans once the place has been redecorated?' Faye had a lovely thought: *what if he's having the place done up, hoping we might move to Scotland and live here when we're married?* She had another thought: *Why would he assume that?* As far as he was concerned, her life was in London. He wouldn't know that was what she wanted unless she told him. And would he believe her if she did tell him that's what she'd decided? She'd only been in Scotland for a week. Was that long enough to make up her mind?

If she needed more time, which she was convinced she didn't, there were five more weeks in which they could stay in Scotland before the new school term began and they had to return. But was that what he wanted himself, or was he doing up the house to put it on the market and get rid of it?

She'd seen how happy he had been when talking about his early childhood. Clearly being in Scotland with Natty had brought that all back – memories of his early years spent living in the house with his parents. Happier times, before they were suddenly gone and his life changed forever. But that didn't mean he'd want to move back there and live in the shadow of the past.

All these questions were swirling around her head. She was afraid to ask him, afraid her lovely dream of living there with Jake and Natty would be just that, a dream, when Jake said, 'Now, about that surprise I promised you …'

As they stepped out of the house, and Jake locked the door on what she'd assumed was their future together in Aviemore, Jake turned around and must have caught her expression. 'What is it?'

She looked up at the house. 'I thought …'

'You thought …?'

Faye shook her head. Perhaps this was for the best, even though she'd known, the moment she stepped inside the house, that she'd be happy there. Who wouldn't? It would make a wonderful family home. It had an amazing garden, something that Natty had never had, living in a flat in London. She might even consider getting Natty a dog. There would certainly be the space.

Faye looked again at the ribbon on her finger and thought that maybe it was for the best, not staying there. It would only rub salt in the wound if his plan was to sell the place. Besides, who knew what would happen when they returned to London after the summer? She was thinking of Gayle's best-laid plans.

37

Faye sat in the car and turned to Jake. 'Do I need a blindfold?'

He looked at her quizzically. 'Pardon me?'

'You know, like the last surprise, when Gayle led me out into the back garden blindfolded before you revealed the tents you'd set up.'

'Ah,' he grinned. 'No, not this time.'

'Oh.'

'You sound disappointed. I'm sure I can find something to use as a blindfold if that's what you want.' He threw her a wisp of a smile, clearly making a little joke out of it.

'No, no, I'm fine.'

'Great.'

Faye stared up at the house. As Jake backed the car around, and started down the driveway, she turned in her seat to catch a last glimpse of the beautiful home through the back window, wondering if this would be the last time she saw The Lake House.

She touched the ribbon on her finger and turned to look at Jake. As long as they were together – that was what mattered. She knew that. But even so, she couldn't resist one more glance over her shoulder, one more thought about living in his childhood home. Natty would love it. And so would she. *So, tell him how you feel before he does something stupid – like selling the place.*

Faye turned in her seat to say something, but almost immediately thought better of it. For one thing, it wasn't her decision to make, and she didn't want to put Jake in an impossible position, where he would feel torn – she knew Jake, he'd give her anything she wanted, do anything for them. But that didn't mean he could do this – live in this house, with them. Not yet, anyway. Perhaps when things from his past life with Eleanor had been resolved.

It might still happen. Faye smiled at that thought.

Jake caught her looking at him, and said, 'Are you looking forward to your surprise?'

'Actually, yes.' Now, she realised she really shouldn't make a thing of not staying at his house. They were spending the entire school summer holidays together in the Highlands – that was what mattered. She would have liked it to be at Jake's home, with the house to themselves, like a real family having a summer holiday together. But she realised The Lake House wouldn't have worked if Bonnie was in and out all summer redecorating. Faye wanted to spend the time with just Jake and Natty.

Although Faye loved staying at Gayle's, and would miss her new friends, their time at the guesthouse in separate bedrooms with no privacy or evenings they could spend alone together had run its course. Especially now they were officially a couple. But she would miss her new friends. She resolved to pop in and see Gayle, Marty, Nick and Doris during the summer, as well as spending time with Annie, Joe and Evie that day, going with them up on the mountain. She was sure she'd find some excuse to visit Duncan's store and catch up with them, and no doubt Natty would be after another sleepover with her new best friend.

Faye suddenly had a thought. She wondered why it hadn't crossed her mind before. 'But where are we going to stay for the summer?' she asked.

'Ah, now, that's where the surprise comes in.'

'You've booked something – haven't you?'

'I know it was quite presumptuous of me, to go ahead and do that—'

'But you would have lost the money if we'd returned tomorrow after all.'

'Well, I was going to do my very best to persuade you to stay for the summer.'

She caught him frowning when he added, 'Then I very nearly blew it this morning.'

'There's no need to talk about that now,' Faye said reassuringly. 'Everything is working out perfectly.'

'I hope so. I hope you like the surprise.'

Faye couldn't wait to see what he'd booked for them to stay in for the summer. 'I know I will.'

'It's just that I got the impression you thought we might be spending the summer at The Lake House.'

Faye fell silent.

'Oh. So, it's true.'

'It's just when you sent me that text, yeah I kind of assumed …'

'It wouldn't have been a good idea.'

'No, no – of course not.' Faye turned her head and frowned. So, it was true, what she had suspected. He didn't want her and Natty there. She didn't ask him if he was going to sell. She didn't want to hear it. Faye reminded herself that it shouldn't matter, as long as they were all together. Perhaps letting go of the house was the only way for him to let go of the past.

Faye didn't want to think about it. Instead, she asked, 'Did you find somewhere for us to stay around here?' She halted. 'It is around Aviemore, isn't it?' When he nodded his head, she felt so relieved. Natty would want to see Evie, and Faye loved it in this part of Scotland, and wanted to check in with her new friends too.

Faye still couldn't believe that a week had gone by since they'd arrived in Aviemore by train. The next day, the day they were meant to leave, was Monday. Thinking of leaving Lark Lodge, she did add, 'I thought all the accommodation in and around Aviemore was pretty much fully booked?' She was sure Jake had mentioned that after he'd visited the tourist information office.

'Yes, pretty much,' Jake replied.

Faye's heart sank. That meant only the dregs were left that nobody else wanted. She did think it was odd, checking in on a Monday. Normally holiday accommodation was a Friday or Saturday check-in.

'Yep, two types of property left. The really, really cheap ones which are so basic I just wouldn't want to book them for you and Natty – certainly not after staying at Gayle's amazing guest house.'

Or seeing your amazing home, thought Faye. She kept it to herself.

'So, what's the other type of property?'

'Ah, now, that would be telling. You'll have to wait and see, otherwise I'll be spoiling the surprise.'

Faye fell silent until she glanced at her phone and found a text from Natty. 'Oh, crumbs – Annie and Joe have arrived already to pick us up and take us for our trip up the mountain.'

'We're going with Annie and Joe?'

'Yes, that's the plan.'

'Can you text Natty, let her know we'll be back very soon? It's not far now. Annie and Joe could have a cup of coffee or something while they wait. It's not far now, I promise, then we can head on back to Lark Lodge.'

'All right.' Faye started to text but changed her mind. 'I'll give Natty a call.' Faye rang Natty's number.

'Mummy! Where are you? Gayle said you're with Jake at The Lake House. I went with Olive and Evie to fetch you, but you're not here.'

'Are you there right now?'

'Yes.'

'On your own?' Faye felt the panic rising even though she knew it was irrational, and she had nothing to worry about. She was perfectly safe walking over there from Gayle's house. Faye did glance at Jake. Now she really knew the panic Jake felt at his own fear of that mountain, although it was just as irrational.

'No, I'm not on my own, Mummy. I said I'm with Evie and Olive.'

'I meant is there an adult with you?'

'Yes, Marty was going to do some gardening, so we walked down the lane to the back gate together. Bonnie is there too.'

'Bonnie?'

'Yes, she's just arrived in a van with David. He's helping her unload some things. Bonnie said she's going to transform The Lake House. What does that mean?'

Faye swallowed. 'It means she's going to make the place look amazing.' *And then Jake is going to sell up and another family will live there and enjoy it.* She willed herself not to think about that.

Jake interrupted her. 'Did you say Bonnie is at The Lake House?'

Faye nodded. 'Yes. Natty said she'd just arrived.'

'Ah, I didn't realise she was starting today.'

Faye breathed a sigh. 'Just as well you checked the place over then, ready for her to start.'

'Yes – isn't it?'

'Mummy, where are you?' Faye heard Natty ask again down the phone.

'Jake and I are just going to check out the holiday accommodation Jake has booked for us.' Faye smiled. 'Guess what? We're staying on in Aviemore for the whole summer!' She had to hold the phone away from her ear when Natty screamed with joy, and then quite inexplicably started to cry. 'Natty, what's wrong?'

'I'm just so happy, Mummy.'

'Well, so am I.'

Jake's head darted in Faye's direction. 'Faye, is everything all right?'

'Oh, yes.'

'She's still okay spending the summer here?'

'Very, very happy.'

'Oh, thank god!' Jake remembered to breath. 'I know it was her idea. She'd been badgering us to stay longer. I just hoped she hadn't changed her mind.'

'Nope, not at all.'

Jake grinned as he turned into a driveway.

'Oh, my god. You have got to be joking.'

'No joke,' said Jake.

'Mummy, what's the matter?'

Faye forgot for a moment she was still on the phone to Natty. 'Nothing is the matter, sweetheart. Everything is just perfect.'

'Then why did you say that? You sounded cross.'

'Because Jake has spent far, far too much money on our holiday accommodation.'

Jake grinned. 'And I am not apologising. I did say there were just two choices of holiday rentals left. This was the other type.'

Faye stared at the property in shock, although she should have known that the ones that would be left were the very expensive ones.

'Is it nice?' Natty asked, 'where we're staying?'

Nice didn't quite begin to describe it, but Faye just said, 'Oh yes, it's rather nice. Now look, will you tell Annie and Joe we'll be back very soon? Then we can all head off on our little adventure up the mountain today.'

'All right, I will. Bye bye, Mummy. Love you.'

'And I love you too, sweetheart. See you soon.' Faye lowered her phone and turned in her seat to look at Jake. 'Don't tell me you've booked this for the entire summer?'

'I got a deal.'

'I should hope so,' Faye said flatly, although she was not about to ask how much it had cost. It was not something either of them would be able to afford on their salaries. Being a Ross obviously had its advantages. She looked at him and had no idea how much he was worth. Was he a millionaire? It was possible. She supposed he didn't really need a job, and she wouldn't either when they married. But it wouldn't be like her or Jake to sit around, wafting through their days, doing not much at all – unless they were on holiday. And she knew it wasn't an example either of them would want to set for their daughter – even though Natty would have no money worries in the future because her new daddy was a Ross.

Jake was looking worried. 'I wouldn't have booked something so … so …'

'Lovely?'

'I was going to say outrageously expensive, ostentatious. If it hadn't been so last-minute and there had been other choices …'

'Oh, so you would rather have not treated us to a holiday in this?' Faye kept a straight face. Of course she was kidding, but the surprised look on Jake's face, sent her into a fit of giggles. 'Oh, Jake, I was only kidding.'

'It is a bit much though – isn't it?'

They both turned to look at the property, named *Cabin in the Woods*. However, it was no little cabin of the sort that Faye would have conjured up in her mind, with an all-in-one sitting and dining room and kitchen and a couple of small mezzanine bedrooms in the loft space. Something small and cosy. This was unlike any cabin she'd ever seen in magazines or on TV – or could even imagine. Luxurious was all she could think of. It was obviously a luxury log cabin, with huge windows and doors, a beautiful wooden wraparound veranda, and she imagined vaulted ceilings inside. But because of the sheer scale of it, the sprawling cabin looked more like a small hotel. It was ridiculously big for three people.

As if reading her mind, Jake said, 'It sleeps ten people in six bedrooms, and has as many bathrooms.'

Faye wasn't surprised. She suddenly leaned forward and kissed him. When she drew back, he looked at her wide-eyed. 'What was that for?' He quickly added, 'Not that I'm complaining.' He grinned at her. 'I take it you do like the place?'

Faye said, 'Oh, yes. But that wasn't what the kiss was about. That was for just being you.' She knew he was rich. But his attitude was typical of a Ross. He was worried about appearing ostentatious, flaunting his wealth. She knew that he wouldn't have chosen this if there had been somewhere cheaper that was of the same standard, but smaller, more modest. The Rosses weren't the type of family who flashed their cash – unless they were helping other people. She was thinking of Marty and Derrick.

'It's a lot bigger than I expected. The photos on the website don't quite do it justice.'

'Natty is going to love this place.'

Jake grinned. 'I know. Apparently, the wildlife comes right up to the windows, so you can be sitting in the lounge on the massive sofa in front of the roaring fire, and you'll see foxes and deer, and if she's really lucky some wildcats right here in the garden.'

'No bears, then.'

Jake looked at her for a moment before breaking into a grin. She was having a joke with him again. 'Nope – no grizzly bears like Hercules.'

'Did you say a roaring fire?' Faye asked.

'Yes, we can light one, as the summer evenings in Scotland can be quite cool, and sit on the big rug in front of the fire and play board games.'

Faye liked the sound of that. 'And cuddle up on the sofa when Natty has gone to bed.'

'Ah, we can do one better than that. The location of the cabin is renowned for its dark skies, meaning no light pollution. I was reading about it on the website. We can wrap ourselves up in a blanket and sit together with a hot chocolate on the veranda and just marvel at the bright stars in the velvety black sky.'

'That sounds amazing.'

'Doesn't it?' Jake agreed. 'Shall we go and have a look inside the cabin before we head back?'

'Have you got the keys already?' Faye asked, surprised.

'No, but there's a key box outside the front door. I have the key code.'

'We can't!' exclaimed Faye.

'Why not?'

'Because we're renting the cabin from tomorrow night, remember? We've still got one more night at Gayle's.'

'Yes, of course we have.'

Faye shot him a look. 'You've rented it from today, haven't you.'

Jake was silent for a moment as she studied him. He looked at her sheepishly. 'I know it means we're double-booked, but I just thought if I booked the place from today, then we wouldn't have to wait around on Monday until four pm for check-in. It means we can move in for the rest summer any time tomorrow.'

'Or tonight.'

'Or tonight,' Jake said slowly, raising his eyebrows. 'I didn't think that's something you'd consider, leaving Lark Lodge a day early. I know you'll miss Gayle, Doris, Marty and Nick.'

'And don't forget Olive,' Faye said, smiling. She looked at the cabin. 'But who could resist this?'

'Yes, I feel the same way.'

'I think Natty will love it, it's just …'

Jake said, 'I know what you're going to say. She's going to miss her playmate.'

'Olive can't come with us – can she?'

Jake sat drumming his hands on the steering wheel. 'You know, the guesthouse is fully booked from tomorrow night. Gayle is going to have a house full, and Olive …'

'Olive …' Faye prompted.

'Well, you know what she's like. That dog just loves all the attention.'

'She certainly does,' said Faye, beginning to get an idea of where the conversation was leading. 'She's going to get under everyone's feet, isn't she?'

'She is the sweetest dog,' said Jake, 'but I think a big dog like that … not all the guests are going to appreciate her around. Gayle or Nick will have to keep her shut up in another room in the house away from the guests and the communal areas.'

'But that's most of downstairs,' exclaimed Faye. 'That's not fair on Olive.'

'Nope, but I don't think either Nick or Gayle factored in what would happen with Olive living at the guesthouse during peak season when the house is full and there's not just Nick and Marty there.'

Faye nodded. 'Unless there was somewhere else she could be for the summer.'

Jake nodded. 'Like doggy day care.'

'Gayle said that Olive does go to Duncan's store during the day.'

'Yes, but with her guesthouse full, she'll need doggy night care too,' added Jake.

Faye looked up at the cabin. 'Does this rental accept pets?'

'Yes, one well-behaved dog.'

Faye frowned. 'I wouldn't always call Olive well-behaved. She does beg at the table.'

'Yes, and slobber.'

'That's true.' Faye nodded. 'And she loves stealing shoes. But if we clear up after her …' she trailed off. 'Wouldn't Nick miss his dog?'

'Nick is terribly busy with work. I'm sure he wouldn't mind. He can visit, take her out for runs in the forest at the weekends.'

Faye knew Nick wasn't the only one who would miss his dog. 'We can pop into Lark Lodge for a cuppa and a catch-up with Gayle and Doris and take Olive along.'

'Yes, I thought you might like to do that over the summer, and Natty would like to see Evie. I'm sure she'd love to have her for a sleepover here. That's why I booked a place as close as I could to Aviemore.'

'You're so thoughtful, Jake.'

'Do I deserve another kiss?'

'I think you deserve more than a kiss,' she said suggestively.

Jake looked at her wide-eyed.

They both turned to the cabin. Faye said, 'Perhaps we'd have time to take a peek at our new holiday accommodation after all.'

Jake opened the car door. 'Shall we start upstairs … in the master bedroom?'

Faye laughed. 'You read my mind.'

38

Jake kept looking in Faye's direction, catching her smiling to herself as he drove back to Lark Lodge. He caught her looking his way too, checking, like he was, that they were both okay with what had just happened. There had been no awkward silences or embarrassed looks as they'd stepped out of the cabin, Jake tucking in his shirt, Faye doing up the last button on her blouse. They were a couple in love. What had just happened was the most natural thing in the world.

They exchanged a smile. 'Faye, do you mind if I drop you back at Lark Lodge and just pop round to The Lake House before we go out today?'

Faye raised her eyebrows. 'But you've been to the house already, and checked everything was in order for Bonnie to start work.'

'Yes, but I want to see Bonnie.'

'Can't you see her another day?' Faye glanced at her phone. 'Natty texted again. Everyone's waiting for us.'

'I won't be long, I promise. It's just I need to see her.'

Faye fell silent for a moment. 'It's not really about the redecorating – is it?'

Jake shook his head.

'It's about something you think she's holding back about Eleanor.'

'Yes, I can't get it out of my head, the fact that I'm sure she was avoiding me at the party. There's something she's not telling me.'

'Jake, we've been over this before. Look at what she'd just been through with the hypnotherapy, and finding out who she really is. I think you're reading way too much into things.'

'Well, I don't.' Jake bit his lower lip. 'Sorry, I didn't mean to be rude.'

Faye stared at him. Was this the real reason he wanted to stay on in Scotland – was it still all about Eleanor, and getting to the bottom of what had happened on that mountain?

Don't think like that, she told herself. He proposed. *He's in love with you*. She just had to accept that there were still things that were not yet resolved. She knew that. What if there *was* something Bonnie had been keeping from him?

Faye was about to tell Jake she'd much rather he didn't go to see Bonnie when she realised she was a fine one to talk. She thought of what she was keeping from Jake about the identity of the dead man they'd found on the mountain – a former employee of the Ross Corporation. Faye was afraid of what else he might find out. More than that, she didn't want anything to intrude on their summer. She didn't want him called back to London unexpectedly. Thinking of which, she looked at Jake. 'Have you heard from Marcus?'

'No. Nothing.'

That's worrying, thought Faye.

'He's just sulking because I reneged on my promise. He'll

come round,' Jake said.

Faye really hoped that was all it was and that he didn't get a frantic call from Lydia saying that Marcus had gone missing again.

Her thoughts turned to Bonnie. She was sure that Jake was just being paranoid, and Bonnie knew nothing more about Eleanor than she'd told everyone in the hypnotherapy session. But the thought occurred to her that even if there was something, why would she tell him now, at The Lake House? Perhaps, like the secret Faye was keeping from Jake about that former employee, Bonnie's thinking was that whatever she knew, it would do him no good now. Perhaps, if she did know something, she felt the same way as Faye. Perhaps she was keeping things from him to save him from further heartache.

'All right,' said Faye.

'You mean you're okay with me going round to the house to see her now?'

Faye still wasn't, not really. But if he didn't go now, it would be there hanging over their heads all day, when they had the stress of the mountain trip to deal with, and Faye didn't want that either.

Jake leaned towards her and kissed her. He drew back. 'I promise I won't be long.'

'I'll walk up Gayle's drive if you just want to drop me by the gates to Lark Lodge.'

'Great idea. Then I can turn the car around and go to The Lake House. Look out for me because when I arrive back, you can both just jump in the car, and we'll head off.'

'Okay.' Faye looked at her phone. 'I think Natty wants to go with Evie in her parents' car.'

'Oh, okay. Just you and me then.'

'We'll meet them in the car park.'

Faye thought it was for the best – then they could chat about Jake's meeting with Bonnie. Faye was crossing her fingers that there was nothing of consequence to talk about.

'Will you give her my best wishes? I hope things are working out with Judith staying on at the boathouse. Perhaps they've made some headway with the search for Robyn.'

Jake nodded. 'Perhaps.'

They exchanged a knowing glance, aware that neither of them imagined that Bonnie and Judith were any closer to finding Robyn.

❖

Jake waved and sat watching Faye walk through the gates to Lark Lodge before he turned the car around. He had a knot in his stomach at the thought of meeting Bonnie. Despite Faye's assurance that Bonnie wasn't avoiding him or keeping something from him, he imagined she was thinking he was being paranoid – even if she hadn't actually said it. But Jake was convinced he was not being paranoid.

The problem was that if Bonnie wouldn't tell him at the party, why would she tell him now at The Lake House? That thought had crossed his mind, and so had something else – it had been over a week since the party. She'd be more inclined to talk to him now she'd had time to get over the shock of finding out her true identity during the hypnotherapy session.

As Jake turned down the single-track lane to The Lake House, he pulled over in a passing place as he saw a van approach. He recognised it before it passed – the van belonged to Mr Gillespie. He wasn't surprised. He'd overheard Natty's loud voice down the phone earlier saying that Bonnie had arrived with David in the van, and he was helping her unload some things.

Rather than pass as Jake expected, the van came to a halt beside his car. David wound the window down. 'Jake?'

Jake wound his own window down and waved. 'Hi, David – how's things?' Jake knew that was a bit of a loaded question after what David had discovered.

'Yeah, um … fine.'

He caught David nervously glancing over his shoulder, back in the direction of the house. David turned back in his seat. 'Are you heading to The Lake House?'

Jake nodded, avoiding a sarcastic, *where else would I be going?* There were no other houses along the stretch of road.

'Bonnie didn't mention you were visiting.'

'She doesn't know. I heard she was resuming work on The Lake House today, so I thought I'd pop along and say hi.'

Jake anticipated that David would say, *great, that's handy, as she's going to want to go over the plan for the house,* or some such reply. Instead, David frowned and mumbled, 'I told her not to phone Gayle.'

Jake regarded David for a long moment, wondering why he was getting the impression neither David nor Bonnie would be pleased to see him. Then it dawned on him. It was something he hadn't considered, but should have. He stared at David. *She told you. Whatever she's hiding, you know too.*

David said, 'I've got to go.' He started winding his window up.

'Wait – can we talk?' Perhaps he'd get more out of David than Bonnie. He knew David had heard him because he turned to look at him out of the window. Was that a mobile phone in his hand? As David sped off, Jake caught him speaking into his phone. Jake looked over at the house at the end of the lane. He knew David was calling Bonnie to warn her of his arrival – and why.

'Oh no!' Jake exclaimed. Bonnie would be prepared for his

visit. He had been hoping to arrive unexpectedly and catch her unawares. There was no malicious intent, and he wasn't spying on her to check she was doing her job. As far as that was concerned, he had every faith in her choice of décor, and the furnishings would be spot on. But he did want to see, if he caught her off-guard, whether she'd spill the beans – if there were any to spill.

Jake adjusted his rear-view mirror so he could watch David's van disappear down the road. He shifted his gaze to the road ahead as he pulled out of the layby and continued to his house. He was surprised to find Bonnie standing on the doorstep when he arrived. He thought she'd be inside and would say she was far too busy to stop and talk.

She approached his car, her mobile to hand. As Jake opened the car door she said, 'David just phoned to say you were on your way. I didn't expect you.'

I bet you didn't, Jake thought as he slammed the car door shut and turned around to face her. He was surprised she was smiling. He'd anticipated she'd be a little nervous, meeting him there at his house, especially as she was hiding something. If doubt had been creeping in before, while he was talking to Faye, he was convinced of it now he'd spoken with David. He was hiding something too.

Jake decided not to open with the real reason he was there. He said, 'You look well, Bonnie.' In fact, she looked very well, positively radiant. 'The Highlands agree with you.'

The area agreed with Faye too. In a week, her pale complexion had been replaced with rosy, red cheeks and her fair hair was noticeably glossy. She was taking more exercise and getting more fresh air than she was used to, and eating properly. In her normal working routine in London, there wasn't time for exercise and hearty meals, and time spent outside in the fresh air, having fun.

It made him wonder if the hours working as a head were worth it. She'd no longer need the money once they were married. In fact, neither of them needed such a stressful job. They could retire on the money he had in his bank account, albeit modestly, and live off it for the rest of their lives.

Jake hadn't told her that, and he knew that if he did, she would not even consider it. And truth be told, neither would he. What sort of example would it set for Natty if neither of her parents were in work? Jake wanted to be a good role model for her. But that didn't mean Faye had to take on a more stressful job. She could consider working as an ordinary classroom teacher. In fact, if they moved to Aviemore, they could do a job share, work part-time, and have plenty of time to smell the roses.

Oh, how Jake was enjoying his little fantasy of Faye giving up living in the city, which he knew she loved, and moving to the back of beyond. His brow creased into a frown. When he thought of it like that—

'Yeah, but I think it's not just the Highlands …'

Jake looked at Bonnie. 'Huh?'

'You said this part of Scotland agrees with me, and I was just saying that it's more than that.'

Jake saw her place a gentle hand on her stomach. 'Oh, right! Of course.' He'd clean forgotten about her baby announcement at the party. 'So, how are you doing?'

'We're doing well, thank you.'

'Great.' Jake leaned against the car door, wondering what to say next – how to broach the subject of the hypnotherapy session and Eleanor. 'How's your week been?'

'Great, actually. Judith has really settled into the boathouse with us, so much so that David is getting a little worried she's never going to leave.' Bonnie laughed.

Jake joined in her laughter. 'Oh, dear – living with his mother-in-law. I bet he's getting worried.'

'She won't actually be his mother-in-law.'

'Oh, sorry. How stupid of me. I forgot.'

Bonnie reached out and touched his arm. 'It's all right. I understand. What happened at the party … that was an awful lot to take in for everybody.'

Jake nodded, still feeling embarrassed over his gaffe.

'The thing is, I get on so well with Judith, it's like she actually is my mum.'

'That's great, Bonnie, I'm so happy for you that things are working out,' Jake said, with genuine feeling. Bonnie had had a rough start in life. She deserved better – a whole lot better.

'Do you want to come in and see the paint and wallpaper I'll be using in each room? We could start at the top and work our way down.'

'Are you redecorating this whole house by yourself?' Jake was concerned, what with her business in town as well, that she was taking on too much work – especially given her pregnancy.

Bonnie rolled her eyes. 'Oh, god, not another one!'

'Excuse me?'

'Another man thinking I should be in confinement.'

'Confinement?'

'You know, like years and years ago, when women were meant to confine themselves to doing nothing for the duration of their pregnancy, like they were some sort of invalid. I swear that's what David is after, and Duncan is just as bad, wanting me to take it easy – meaning not work. But I want to work. I need to. I can't sit around all day just doing nothing.'

Jake raised his eyebrows. Eleanor suddenly came to mind. He remembered the previous Christmas, when he'd found out she was pregnant. She hadn't exactly been elated by the news like he had been. All he'd ever wanted was to be a father. All she'd ever wanted was to have her own career, but because she'd married him, she'd slipped into becoming a corporate wife – and having a baby would have trapped her even more into a life she didn't want.

But we could have changed things. Jake had already decided back then to stop travelling and working abroad at the Rosses' different headquarters, and settle in London, so she could start her career. They could have got a nanny. Women could both work and have children. But to his lasting regret, he'd never had the chance to have that conversation. He thought of Faye. When they married, she'd still have her career in teaching – if that was what she wanted.

'I don't want to be a stay-at-home mum either. I've worked hard to build my business. I know they just want me to take it easy, but I just can't.'

Jake said, 'It is a big house, though.'

'Look, don't worry. I've enlisted help. I'm not actually doing the decorating myself. I'm overseeing the work.'

Jake was pleased to hear it. 'So, who will be working on the house?'

'There are students from Inverness University doing art and design. Getting placements isn't easy, so I approached the university, and they'll be coming here.' She glanced at her watch. 'I'm waiting for them to arrive.' Bonnie glanced past Jake down the driveway. 'They should be here any minute.'

'Oh, I see.' Jake turned to look down the driveway.

'They're also going to get some experience working at Duncan's store in my design outlet.'

Jake turned back to look at her. 'You mean Robyn's outlet.'

Bonnie cocked her head to one side.

'It's what it's called – isn't it?' Jake wasn't being rude, but it was a bit confusing. He thought, *why not just rename it?*

'Yes, and I'm not renaming it – if that's what you're thinking, although I know it's a bit confusing now that my name is Bonnie.'

Jake just nodded.

Bonnie sighed. 'I don't know what happened to her, and I can't help thinking if I hadn't taken her car, she'd still be here or somewhere like back at university. I feel so guilty.'

'You think something happened to her?'

'Well, it must have. Nobody disappears off the face of the planet.'

Those were Jake's sentiments exactly. 'I take it you've tried searching for her with no luck?'

'Yes. We've completely drawn a blank.'

'Sorry to hear that.'

'Not as sorry as Judith. David and I asked her to try and think where she might have gone, and the sort of things she enjoyed doing, to see if we might be able to piece together her whereabouts.'

'And …?'

'She liked skiing, apparently – that's why she was here working in Wilbur's Bookstore over the Christmas break, choosing not to join Judith abroad.'

Jake lifted his gaze to the mountain beyond the house. 'Do you think …?' He swallowed, starting to feel the panic rising at the thought of being trapped on the snow up there. It was going to be a massive thing for him to venture back up that mountain, especially as he knew they'd probably be heading up to the snow-capped summit. But Faye was right: he couldn't wrap them both in cotton wool, and he couldn't hold Natty back in life because of his own fears. He had to face them some day – and it may as well be *that* day.

Bonnie followed his gaze. 'We've looked everywhere in Aviemore, and the surrounding towns and villages, with Joe and the local police force's help, but there's been no sighting of her whatsoever.'

'What about if she took a taxi out of town?' suggested Jake.

'We checked all the local taxi companies, and no one booked a taxi on Christmas Day.'

'I guess she could have just hitched a ride from a passing motorist.'

Bonnie nodded. 'We thought of that. But then again, she was packing to leave. She'd already loaded some of her stuff into the car that I took. Why on earth would she just take off without her belongings? It doesn't make sense.'

Jake supposed it didn't. He asked, 'Did the police get a call on Christmas Day to say her car had been stolen?'

'No. At first, I thought that was understandable. She knew I'd taken Eleanor in her car to the ski slopes, and might be some time, dropping her off and making it back. But as the time went on and I didn't return to the bookshop as planned, I would have assumed she'd have thought something had happened.'

'Something happened all right,' Jake said sadly, thinking of Eleanor, but also of poor Bonnie, speeding out of town and colliding with David.

'So, do you want to come in the house and see what I'm up to?'

Jake shook his head. It wasn't what he was there for. 'Look,

Bonnie, the reason I'm here is that at the party I got the impression you were avoiding—'

Jake was interrupted by a loud bark. He turned to see a familiar Old English Sheepdog appear in the doorway from inside the house. She belted across the driveway, making straight for Jake.

'Oh, for goodness' sake, Olive! What mischief have you been getting up to now?' Bonnie said, exasperated.

Olive had left turquoise paint paw prints in her wake. Jake imagined she'd tipped over a paint pot indoors. 'Do you want help clearing her mess up?'

Bonnie shook her head. 'No, I'll sort it out.'

'What's she doing here, anyway?'

'Oh, she was in with Annie at the shop first thing this morning – at least, that was the plan, as she was royally getting under the feet of Gayle and her new guests – but then she was causing trouble at the shop too. She wasn't staying on her cushion like she normally does. She kept going up to customers, and following them around, being a nuisance. She was driving the customers away. She wasn't staying in the design outlet part of the shop either, but running around the shop, annoying Duncan's customers too. So, David decided to bring her in the van with him on his deliveries.' She frowned.

Jake saw her expression and guessed that hadn't exactly worked out either.

Bonnie confirmed what Jake was thinking when she said, 'Unfortunately, that wasn't the best idea because she got in the back of the van and peed on one of the packages.'

'Oh, dear.' Jake stifled a smile.

'Yes, oh dear is right. It was David's first day back at work, and Duncan was not impressed. So, David left Olive with me, thinking she'd just play in the garden. Well, she's not going to play on her own, is she?'

Olive dropped a ball by Jake's feet. Poor Olive. He felt sorry for her. She just wanted some attention and to play, but all her friends – Gayle, Annie, Bonnie, David, Duncan – were just too busy.

Jake picked up the ball. 'I'll take her.'

'Back to Gayle's?'

'Yes, for now, but I'm happy to look after Olive for the summer. That was what I was I going to talk to Nick about. Faye and I are spending the rest of the summer here.'

'Yes, I heard.'

'News travels fast.'

'It does around here,' quipped Bonnie.

Jake was not at all surprised. He smiled and looked at Bonnie, expecting her to say she was pleased to hear it, and that they'd done the right thing deciding to stay on in Scotland for the summer. Instead, she avoided his gaze. Jake guessed why. If she was keeping something from him, she probably wanted him to go back to London the next day as planned. Now he had the whole summer to see her again and find out what that was. Jake looked at Bonnie. She was clearly busy organising the house, ready to start. He realised now wasn't the time to confront her about whatever she was keeping from him about Eleanor.

Bonnie asked, 'So, what are your plans when I've finished doing up your house?'

'It's a surprise.'

Bonnie grinned. 'Oh, okay. I'll look forward to it.'

'Oh, I meant it's a surprise for Faye.'

Bonnie smiled. 'Of course! How silly of me.'

It was to be the biggest surprise of all. Jake had wondered whether, if Faye wanted to stay on for the summer, she would consider staying on for good. It wasn't something he wanted to broach straight away. He was afraid he was just reading too much into things, and she'd say how silly he was being, and that her life was in London. He thought, though, that the renovation of The Lake House might encourage her to stay. Then again, she wouldn't want that – a house with the ghosts from his past. Perhaps it was time to let it go.

He didn't know why, but he suddenly had the urge to tell Bonnie all this.

'You need to tell her what you've just told me.'

'But—'

'Don't be afraid, Jake. You never know, Faye might surprise you.'

She already had – his city girl wanting to stay on for the entire summer in Scotland. Jake raised his eyes to the mountain. Bonnie was right. It was time to face his fears. Not only his fears of what Faye might say, but of making a visit to see Eleanor, and getting the wheels in motion to divorce her on their return.

'I proposed to Faye.'

'Oh, Jake! How wonderful.' Bonnie stepped forward and gave him a hug.

Olive, still by his feet, whined for attention too. Jake bent down, gave her a fuss, and picked up the ball. He tossed it up and down in his hand, staring at the house. Jake had always wanted a dog, and a family, and an ordinary life, far removed from the Rosses' corporate high-flying world.

'You'll have to have an engagement party and invite everyone.'

Jake dropped his eyes to Bonnie. 'Pardon me?'

'An engagement party. We'd all love to come.'

Jake frowned. 'I can't do that just yet.' Now he wished he hadn't mentioned that he'd proposed. He knew what Bonnie was going to say: *how come you can't have a party?* She wouldn't understand that it would be inappropriate to celebrate their engagement yet unless he explained about Eleanor still being alive.

Jake turned around and had just thrown the ball, realising too late he'd thrown it too hard, and it had gone over the hedge into the memorial garden, when Bonnie said, 'Oh, that's right. I suppose it's not appropriate right now, until you've divorced Eleanor.'

Jake had just turned to her, wide-eyed, wondering how she even knew Eleanor was alive – the family had closed ranks and not told anybody anything, leaving the world to surmise that she'd died – when he heard someone shout out, 'Ow! Who the bloody hell threw that ball?'

'Oh, dear,' said Bonnie. 'That's Marty.'

Jake frowned when he heard another noise. A loud thud. He knew Marty was somewhere in the grounds gardening that morning, but what was he doing in the memorial garden? It didn't sound like gardening. There was that sound again, as though he was dropping something heavy into the wheelbarrow.

'What's he doing in there?'

Bonnie pursed her lips.

Jake took off towards the memorial garden, Olive scampering ahead. Bonnie followed.

39

Jake stepped through the gap in the hedge to find Marty standing by a wheelbarrow next to Eleanor's memorial stone. Bonnie followed him through. Most of the broken pieces were now in the wheelbarrow, and Marty was holding the ball, nursing his sore head where it had unfortunately hit him and saying to Olive, 'Who threw this ball?'

'It was me, I'm afraid,' said Jake. 'Sorry.'

'Oh, Jake, I didn't know you were here …' he trailed off. He looked at the wheelbarrow. 'I was just clearing things up.'

Jake looked at the broken memorial stone. The sledgehammer he'd borrowed from Duncan, which he'd used to smash the stone, was still there on the wet ground. He'd have to return it. He dropped his gaze, embarrassed. Marty knew what had happened there. Jake had had some sort of breakdown. He frowned at Marty, guessing he'd told Bonnie the whole sorry story about Eleanor and about what had happened in the garden.

Marty looked at Bonnie and dropped his gaze. 'I'll just go back to the house and make a cup of coffee, if that's all right.' He stole a glance at Jake.

Jake replied, 'Yeah, sure. I hope your head's okay.'

'I'll be fine.' As he walked out of the memorial garden, he did an about-turn. 'I thought you were going on a trip with Faye, Natty, Annie, Joe and Evie up the mountain today?'

Jake heaved a sigh. 'Yes, I am. I was just stopping by to …' he looked at Bonnie, 'I was just stopping by to say hi to Bonnie before we go.'

Marty stared at him for a long moment. Jake wondered what he was thinking, until he caught Marty's gaze shift momentarily to the wheelbarrow. 'Brave man. I'm glad you're going. Everyone thought you'd bottle out. It's the right thing to do, Jake.'

Jake knew who he meant by *everyone* – his friends back at Lark Lodge.

'I need to go up there to move on.'

'I know.'

He watched Marty walk up to the house, Olive following him in the expectation that he'd throw the ball in his hand.

Bonnie was still standing by Jake's side. He felt a gentle hand on his shoulder. 'Jake?'

He turned around. 'Marty told you about that – didn't he?' Jake pointed at the broken memorial stone. It wasn't a question. How else would she have known for sure that Eleanor was still alive? Jake studied her for a long moment, searching her face.

Bonnie dropped her gaze and looked away.

Jake looked at her, wide-eyed. She'd already known! But how was that possible? He frowned. This wasn't the time to bring that up. He had other more pressing things on his mind. He raised his eyes to look up at the mountain, thinking of the day ahead, which he wasn't looking forward to, before he dropped his gaze to what remained of the memorial stone. He had a feeling that Bonnie wouldn't tell him how she knew about Eleanor, even if he asked her. Not just then, there in the memorial garden, at any rate. Bonnie stood beside him, looking at the memorial stones too.

'It's a funny thing,' Jake began.

She turned to look at him.

'Change,' he continued.

'Yes,' she said, turning back to the shattered stone.

'Kind of rears up behind you when you're going about your ordinary, everyday life, minding your own business, and wham, just like that …'

'Your life's changed forever,' Bonnie said, 'and it takes such a long time to …' Bonnie trailed off and this time it was Jake's turn to finish.

'Accept it.'

Bonnie nodded. 'And move on.'

They stood in silence again.

'I wanted to be her, you know,' Bonnie confided.

Jake knew who she was talking about. He remembered the hypnotherapy session when Bonnie had spoken about that. She was deep into the session, reliving Christmas Day, when she'd arrived in Aviemore with her awful boyfriend, Logan, and escaped him to find sanctuary with two women. It was Eleanor she'd spotted first, sitting in the window of Wilbur's Bookstore.

She stole a look at Jake. 'I really wanted to have grown up in a home with happy childhood memories – like you and Eleanor.'

Jake laughed a sad laugh. 'Imagine that,' he said, putting an arm around Bonnie's shoulder. He was aware, after sitting in on that session, that she'd had a difficult childhood.

'I wish we'd had more time,' Bonnie contemplated aloud, 'to get to know one another. I think Eleanor and I would have been good friends – great friends.'

'Best friends,' Jake said, looking down at her, smiling.

Bonnie looked up at him. 'I guess we've both done a little bit of running away from it. From change, I mean.'

They stood in silence together, each in their own thoughts, contemplating their own journeys to this point.

Bonnie said, 'Can you forgive me?'

Jake knitted his brow. 'What for?'

'Driving Eleanor to the ski slopes where she had the accident. If I hadn't agreed to take her …' she trailed off.

Jake thought that maybe he'd got it all wrong. Bonnie wasn't hiding anything from him but this – the guilt she'd been carrying over her part in the events that had taken place last Christmas.

He shook his head, and affectionately squeezed her shoulder, drawing her close. She was the last person to see Eleanor, speak to her, before he'd lost Eleanor forever.

'Honestly, Bonnie, it's not your fault – what happened. If you hadn't driven her there, then Robyn would have taken her. And if she hadn't, knowing Eleanor, she'd have found a way to get there and surprise us. But it wasn't some random taxi driver, or even Robyn – I've never met her and don't know her – it was you, Bonnie. And what brings me great comfort is that I can't think of a nicer person, a better friend with whom she could have spent those last few moments before she stepped on to the ski slopes.'

Bonnie began to cry.

'Oh, goodness, I'm sorry. I didn't mean to make you cry.'

Bonnie got out a tissue. 'It means a lot to me, what you said.' She dabbed her eyes. 'Sorry, but since I got pregnant, I just cry at the drop of a hat.'

She dried her eyes.

Jake heard his phone bleep with a text. 'Look, I'd better get going. They're all waiting for me to go and pick up Faye before we head off – up there.' Jake raised his eyes to the snow-capped peak.

'Jake – before you go. Can I ask you a question?'

Jake wasn't sure he really wanted to talk further about Eleanor right now.

'After your day out, are you coming back to Lark Lodge for dinner?'

'Oh, right.' He hadn't anticipated *that* question.

'Gayle said you've got one more night at her guesthouse before you leave tomorrow. She's has asked me to pop round when David comes to pick me up, to have dinner this evening at the guesthouse. I know she's also asked Annie and Joe too, along with Evie. It will be a bit of a squeeze around the kitchen table, what with Marty, Nick, and Doris there as well. And Duncan.'

'Wow that is going to be a squeeze. You know, I haven't told Gayle this yet, because we've sort of just decided, and I know she might be a bit … upset.' They were good friends, and he knew they'd all be sad to see them leave. 'The thing is, I've taken on the holiday rental from today, so we've decided to collect our things when we return from … up there … and leave the guesthouse to check in to our rental today.'

'Oh, no. That won't do at all. You can't leave!'

'What do you mean?'

'Not before dinner.'

'But you just said with everyone Gayle has invited, it's going to be a house full, so it makes sense if we just go.'

'No, you don't understand. It doesn't make sense at all.'

Jake frowned. 'Bonnie, what's going on?'

'Oh, dear, she's going to be really cross with me when she finds out I've ruined the surprise.'

'Surprise?'

Bonnie heaved a sigh. 'You know everyone is coming, so it's not really going to be a surprise now, is it?'

'I still don't understand …'

'Gayle is throwing you and Faye – and little Natty, of course – a small dinner party with friends on your last evening at the guesthouse. She's cooking up a special evening meal. She mentioned that you're all probably staying on in Scotland for the summer. She knew it wouldn't be in the guesthouse, and that you'll probably book a holiday rental locally. But even so, who knows when or if you'll return to Scotland – that's what she said. So, she wanted to do something special for her new friends before you leave. Although she did slip in that she was hoping that if I worked my magic on The Lake House, you, Faye and Natty would love it so much that you'd move in, and so her new neighbours, and good friends, would never leave.'

Jake stared at her.

'So, are you coming to dinner? Please say you are, because Gayle would be heartbroken if you just packed your bags and left today.'

Jake realised he'd be heartbroken too. 'I've made such good friends here.' He swallowed a lump in his throat at the thought of selling up his childhood home and leaving the place forever.

'I know.'

So, you'll stay for dinner?'

'I wouldn't have it any other way.' Jake imagined they'd stay the night, the dinner party going on so late into the evening that Evie would end up having another sleepover with Natty – this time in the twin attic room Natty had been sharing with her mother, leaving Jake and Faye to share his room with the double bed next door. That way, they could have one more breakfast with Gayle, Doris, Marty and Nick – and Olive of course – before they said their final farewell to Lark Lodge and its occupants and headed off. Of course they'd be back, visiting Gayle and Lark Lodge, during the summer, but it was a lovely thought of Gayle's to throw a dinner party before they left.

Bonnie lowered her voice, touched his arm, and whispered, 'Gayle's made us all promise that we won't talk about …' she raised her eyes. 'The past.'

Jake raised his eyes to the mountain too. He knew why Gayle had made them all promise; after the revelation about Bonnie's real identity, and her connection – albeit briefly – with Robyn and Eleanor, it would be natural to bring up what had happened at Christmas when they all got together again for the evening.

'It's time to focus on the future. That's what Gayle said. I agree – don't you?'

Of course, he agreed with that sentiment. That was why he was elated when Faye had agreed to spend the rest of the summer there. He envisaged they would spend the summer making plans for their future – whether those plans would involve moving there permanently, he had yet to find out.

But in the meantime, they were going to have an amazing summer, once he'd faced one of his biggest fears – going back up the mountain.

Bonnie said, 'Well, I'd better crack on if I want your house ready by the end of the summer.'

'You can take as long as you like, Bonnie. There's no rush.'

She smiled. 'I'm giving myself a deadline for when your holiday rental ends at the end of the summer.'

'Why?'

'So that The Lake House is ready for you to move into in the autumn.'

'That's a rather lovely thought, Bonnie, but I'm afraid we can't just jack in our jobs and never return to London.'

Bonnie sighed. 'You know, life is short, and as we both know, it can change in a heartbeat. Sometimes we have to bite the bullet and just take a leap of faith.'

Jake looked at her. Unfortunately, the word *bullet* reminded him of the guy they'd found on that mountain in the spring when the snow had thawed, along with the mystery of the person who had been up there and saved them. He wouldn't bring it up at the dinner party. But he had every intention of speaking to Duncan at some point during the summer, to find out what further information he may have on the two people who'd been up there with them when tragedy struck. Jake didn't know why, but he had a feeling it was significant somehow.

He looked up at the mountain. As much as he wanted to think about the future – especially his dream of a future there with Faye and Natty – the past kept coming back to haunt him. Until he returned to London and faced his other fear – seeing Eleanor – he knew he'd never truly be free of his past and able to move on in the life he dreamed of.

As Bonnie turned to leave and head back to the house, he caught her hand. 'Bonnie?'

'Yes?'

'I don't think I ever thanked you for paying Marty to look after the gardens of this house when we abandoned the place after …' he trailed off.

She waved it away with the flick of her hand.

He looked past her at the house. 'You're a good friend, Bonnie, you and David and Gayle. I just wished we'd all met under different circumstances.'

'So do I,' Bonnie said. 'Now go on, scoot.' She gently pushed him in the direction of the house. 'And get that car off the lawn – Marty will have kittens!'

Jake turned, 'Sorry about that.' He'd been in such a hurry to see Bonnie, he'd parked haphazardly, skidding to a halt with half the car on the lawn.

'Next time,' Bonnie shouted after him, 'try parking in the drive like everybody else. Do you know how hard Marty works on this place for you?'

'I know.' Jake said softly, his face beaming.

'So, what are you hanging around for? Get going. Everyone is waiting for you.'

He did just that. Looking up at the house as he headed to the car, he decided he'd let Bonnie get on with the work over the summer uninterrupted. He thought of what she'd said about getting the house finished, ready to move into in September. He'd told her why that wouldn't happen, but who knew what the future held? He smiled, thinking about how he'd come away on holiday that week with no idea he'd propose to Faye in Scotland, or that they'd end up spending the summer there.

Jake glanced in his rear-view mirror and spotted Bonnie waving goodbye. He paused at the end of the drive and turned in his seat to wave, but she'd already disappeared into the house.

He suddenly felt at peace when he thought of the two people who were uppermost in his mind. He didn't know when he'd return to The Lake House, if he ever did, but as he turned out of the driveway, heading back to Lark Lodge, all he could think of was the glorious summer ahead in the Scottish Highlands with

Faye and Natty. He was no stranger to best-laid plans, but in that moment, he knew that wherever the future took them, as long as they were together, it was where he belonged.

The Scottish Highlands Series continues in

Coming Home to Aviemore

If you enjoyed *Summer in the Scottish Highlands* I would be grateful if you would leave a review on Amazon.

For further details about the author and her novels please visit the author's website.

www.elisedarcy.com

Also by Elise Darcy

The Sunrise Coast Series

New Beginnings at the Harbour Inn

The Secret of the Summerhouse

The Cottage by the Sea

The Guest House at Shingle Cove

The Houseboat by the Quay

Return to Willow Tree Cottage

The Bookshop of Memories

The Beach House

A Summer to Remember

The Living Apart Together Series

Living Apart Together

It Takes 2 to Tango

Dear John

Love on the Rooftop

Standalone Novels

Lola & The Man

A Mallorcan Affair

We'll Meet Again

The Villa in Sicily

Printed in Dunstable, United Kingdom

66444306R00201